**Jonathan Wylie** is the pseudonym of Mark and Julia Smith, a married couple who live and work in Norfolk. Having met while working for a major London publishing house, they sparked each other into creative life and began writing as a team a few months after setting up home together. For the past five years, they have been writing full-time. *Other Lands* is their twelfth novel.

# *Other Lands*

## Jonathan Wylie

ORBIT

An *Orbit* Book

First published in Great Britain by Orbit in 1995
This edition published by Orbit in 1996

Copyright © Jonathan Wylie 1995

The moral right of the author has been asserted.

A CIP catalogue record for this book
is available from the British Library.

ISBN 1 85723 364 6

Printed and bound in England by Clays Ltd, St Ives plc

Orbit
A Division of
Little, Brown and Company (UK)
Brettenham House
Lancaster Place
London WC2E 7EN

*This book is dedicated to Meg Davis,*
*with much love and many thanks.*

# Acknowledgement

Grateful thanks are due to Greg Forde
for his help and advice.

*Other Lands*

# Prologue

Ghyl could hear the approach of his executioner. The horseman was hidden beyond a ridge, but flight was useless now. The open fields on either side of the rough track gave no hope of cover and, even in the gathering dusk, he knew he could not escape Jevan's sharp eyes. He was in no doubt about the identity of his pursuer.

A haunted look replaced the gleam of anticipation in Ghyl's eyes, and his breath hissed between clenched teeth. He had been walking fast and, while the weather was overcast and windy, it had remained dry and warm for the time of year. Now that he had stopped moving sweat prickled beneath the unfamiliar coarse material of his shirt and leggings. The desolate sound of an owl hooting came from somewhere in the distance.

Ghyl silently cursed fate and his own foolishness and tried in vain to think of a way out of his predicament. He had been so close! Accepting his own downfall was easy enough, but to fail in his work now – his *life's* work – when so many people were depending on him, would be bitter indeed. And doubly so, because he had been warned. Why hadn't he listened to Zenna? Her predictions of betrayal had seemed mere scaremongering, and he had not *wanted* to believe her. Yet she must have been right. Why else would a mounted man – by definition someone of importance – be riding along this remote road?

Angrily pushing aside such pointless speculation, Ghyl listened intently. The rhythmic thud of hooves on the track

1

spoke of only one horse. At least Jevan had chosen to do his own dirty work.

The rider came into view then, cresting the ridge at speed. Even from a distance, his bulky figure and dark features were unmistakable, and his great white charger was equally conspicuous. Ghyl's last faint hope vanished, and he wished angrily that he had ignored his own advice and come armed. That way, although he knew that he would still have died, at least he would have had the satisfaction of putting up a fight. Perhaps, if he got lucky, or if Jevan's protection was not as infallible as rumour had it, he might even have managed to wound or maim his hated overlord. But, dressed as he was, carrying any weapon other than a simple hunting knife or a farmer's tool would have aroused instant suspicion in anyone who saw him. As it had turned out, Ghyl thought ironically, that would hardly have mattered. Some traitorous tongue had done its work, and his simple disguise now only confirmed his guilt rather than affording any protection. And his death was assured.

In a way, such knowledge was some small comfort. Jevan's legendary temper and violent nature meant that he would give no quarter. A cooler head might have decided to capture the renegade and learn more of his plans before killing him. Ghyl was fully determined never to betray any of his schemes or any of his fellow conspirators, but he had no wish to discover whether his overlord's torture chamber deserved its gruesome reputation.

Jevan had slowed his pace as soon as he had seen the other man and was sure of his quarry, but now he was only a short distance away, the great horse walking slowly. Its half mad eyes were wide in the gloom, and it bore the considerable weight of its rider with ease. As befitted a nobleman, Jevan was dressed in fine clothes, his doublet embroidered and quilted, and his lustrous black beard and hair were neatly trimmed. A long sword hung from his finely crafted leather belt, a single dark jewel glinting in its pommel, reflecting the malicious glow in the lord's eyes.

A cold, cruel smile settled upon Jevan's lips.

'Did you think that dressing as a peasant would fool me?' he asked, his blunt features twisting with contempt.

'How could I ever hope to best such a great lord, such a great *intellect*?' Ghyl replied with vicious sarcasm, hoping to goad his enemy into precipitous action. To his surprise, however, Jevan brought his mount to a halt a few paces away and stared at his prey thoughtfully. Ghyl's dread deepened, and the evening's chill seemed to settle over him like a cloak of ice.

'How did you even *hope* to succeed?' his overlord asked with uncharacteristic calm. 'The borders are sealed.'

Ghyl said nothing. He would volunteer no secrets. A few moments passed in silence.

'I have squashed worthier foes than you,' Jevan remarked blithely – and then the composed façade cracked and he glared, his face darkening suddenly. 'I should have stepped on a treacherous louse like you years ago!' he yelled furiously.

Ghyl answered with a brief, obscene suggestion, and had the small satisfaction of seeing his barb strike home. Without another word, the nobleman unsheathed his blade and spurred his mount forward. Both men knew that the outcome of their encounter was inevitable, but Ghyl stood his ground. It was almost dark now.

The sword flashed down but, at the last instant, Ghyl dived away and hit out wildly at the horse's solid flank, hoping to make it rear and spill its rider. The stallion was too well trained for that, however, and Jevan wheeled round for another attack, roaring with anger and in anticipation of his triumph. The unanswerable instinct of self-preservation had finally overtaken Ghyl and he began to run. He knew that there was no hope for him – but he had to *try*, his resolve shattered by unthinking fear. His heart laboured as he flung himself forward; in a few more beats it would all be over.

Behind him he heard the clatter of harness amid the thud of heavy hooves, and sensed the sword raised to deliver the final blow. But it never came.

To the utter consternation of both men, two impossibly bright lights appeared out of nowhere, side by side above the track ahead of them, then rushed towards them as if driven by a fierce wind. The blinding white glare swept past, accompanied by a horrible, unnatural roaring. Jevan's mount reared, whinnying in sudden terror, and causing his already distracted rider to mistime his stroke completely. The blade flashed past its target, but Ghyl stumbled as he whirled round in fear, trying to watch the progress of those strange lights. As he fell, one of the stallion's hooves caught him a terrible blow to the side of his head, and he collapsed to the ground.

For a few moments he lay stunned and helpless, waiting almost without apprehension for his enemy's blade to finish him off – and noting, incongruously, that there was an unpleasant, acrid smell of burning oil and hot metal in the air. Then even that mystery failed to keep his mind afloat and he sank into an impenetrable blackness, darker than any night.

Jevan, disconcerted though he was, had felt and heard the crack of hoof on bone and seen his opponent fall, so after quieting his skittish mount he paid Ghyl no more attention. Instead he watched in awe as the lights sped on their way, following the course of the track and finally disappearing from sight. He had no way of explaining what had happened, but at the same time he had no doubt about who must have been responsible. Even so, he had never seen them do anything like this before. Instinctively, he glanced up at the newly risen moon. It was not even full, showing only three quarters of its face to the light.

Finally he turned back to stare at the unmoving figure sprawled on the ground. There was no sign of life and Jevan grunted, satisfied that – one way or another – his purpose was achieved. He had no wish to linger here now and, sheathing his unstained sword once more, he rode away in the direction he had come, muttering under his breath.

'Damned warlocks! What are they up to now?'

# 1

The brandy glass exploded as it hit the wall. Crystal splinters and drops of liquid flew outwards, glittering in the torchlight. For a few moments Zoe could only stare at the dark stain, at the drips running down towards the carpet. The sudden violence with which Thomas had hurled his drink had shocked even her into stillness, silence. But that was only the beginning of her husband's tirade.

'You think you're so clever, don't you!' he yelled. 'You and your little books.'

His contempt was more intimidating than his fury. Zoe felt sick and cold.

'If it weren't for the fact that you're married to *me*,' he ranted, one thick finger stabbing at his own chest, 'no one would even take you seriously.'

Thomas advanced on her suddenly, a large, threatening presence, and Zoe thought he was going to hit her, such was his rage. Her feet seemed frozen to the ground. She raised her arms instinctively but instead of knocking them aside he grabbed her wrists, crushing them in his powerful hands. He was still shouting, but Zoe had stopped hearing his words, the increasingly venomous obscenities – and yet she could not avoid his overwhelming disdain. Her field of vision was filled with his bulging crimson face, only inches away from her own, enveloping her in the malevolence he reserved only for his wife. To everyone else this ravening monster was invariably suave and charming, every inch the successful publishing executive.

Only Zoe had seen the vile darkness beneath his bright smile.

Her arms hurt intolerably. Thomas's fingers gouged like steel manacles, and he was shaking her as a dog might a rat. Zoe cowered, helpless in the face of such unreason, knowing that she might never find the will to match or even oppose his violent tyranny. She could not escape, she could only wait for release – when and if he chose to relent. Her only recourse was to hide inside the private core of her being, where Thomas could not touch her, and abandon her outer self, her body, to him. And yet all the time a small voice inside her head was protesting. *This is wrong!* Screaming silently in frustration, anger and fear. *This is wrong! You know it is.*

Thomas's mouth was still working furiously, vitriol pouring forth in an apparently endless stream, spittle flying from his swollen lips. Zoe felt herself being drawn into that repulsive maw, and inside her something snapped.

'No!'

She packed all her terror, all her resolve, into that one syllable.

Her own cry woke her. She was lying in bed, curled up, her arms protecting her face. She turned to look at the peaceful face on the pillow next to hers, and breathed a shaky sigh of relief. She knew that everything was all right now. Michael was struggling from his own more restful dream and was not yet fully awake, but his mere presence was more than enough to calm her. The heartfelt relief that flooded through Zoe was almost physical in its intensity. She lay there, happy just to look at him.

Michael opened his eyes and smiled at her, and then, as he saw the remnants of the dream reflected in her hazel eyes, he was instantly concerned, realising what had woken them both.

'I thought the nightmares had stopped,' he said sleepily. 'I'm *here*.'

'I know,' she whispered gratefully, close to tears.

'Thomas?' he asked as he moved across and she snuggled into his arms.

6

'Yes.'

'It's time you got that subconscious of yours under control,' he commented gently. 'You're usually quite sensible when you're awake.'

Zoe smiled, revelling in the touch of his skin on her own. She had always had remarkably vivid dreams. The usually meaningless imagery could be fascinating, but sometimes it was all too real and unpleasant. During their seemingly endless and acrimonious divorce she had dreamt of Thomas often, something that surprised no one, but now – four years after they had separated – she had thought that these horrible trips back into the past had stopped. In one particular dream, a few months ago, she had actually had the sense to tell him to go away. Much to her surprise, he *had* gone, and had not bothered her since. She had no idea what had prompted his return to her nocturnal world, or why it had taken such a nasty form. She could remember no incident like the one in her nightmare, although there had been others just as bad. Zoe wished she could share Michael's ability to forget his dreams from almost the moment of waking, but the night's images would not leave her. Something about the scene was wrong, even beyond the obvious hideousness of the confrontation – something subtle, unseen and disturbing.

'Want to talk about it?' Michael asked.

'No. I'm all right now.' But even while she luxuriated in the warm safety of Michael's arms, her mind kept gnawing away at the problem. Although her dread and fear were slowly fading – they were only shadows and whispers now, still there but insubstantial – the images remained: Thomas's grotesque face, his fingers crushing her wrists, the glass flying apart, the splinters flashing . . . That was it, she realised suddenly. The light. They had been standing in the sitting room of their house in London, but although the furniture, the windows, even the colour of the paint on the wall had been exactly as she remembered, the light had been all wrong. Instead of daylight, or the cool, even light of electricity, the scene had shimmered in the wavering light of naked flames. In her dream, there had been torches burning in brackets on the walls all around

7

them, like a medieval hall. Zoe could not imagine what this might mean, and because she knew what Michael's response would be – that very little of her dreams made any sense – she decided to say nothing. Together they slipped back to sleep.

Two hours later, the watery autumnal sun was well above the horizon but Zoe and Michael were still in bed, sitting up and reading. One of the many advantages of their both being self-employed and working from home was that the hours were theirs to organise as they chose, and they occasionally indulged themselves in such pleasures. Michael was engrossed in a William Gibson novel, while Zoe was struggling through a dog-eared paperback with a lurid cover, entitled *Magic, Mysteries and the Mind*. Although she had happily embraced several 'alternative' ideas – about healing especially – this was not her usual reading matter. She had been prompted by a strange impulse to buy the book from a second-hand bookstall in Norwich market and, to her surprise, had found it fascinating. Belying the appearance of the cover, the writing was quite scholarly and the research was well catalogued. While many of the author's conclusions appeared far-fetched, the evidence for some paranormal phenomena was very convincing. At the end of a chapter on tribal magic, Zoè turned to Michael.

'Do you believe in magic?'

'What?' He looked up blankly, his mind still lost in cyberspace.

'Magic,' she repeated. 'Do you think the human mind has hidden powers?'

Michael merely raised his eyebrows.

'There's so much we don't know about, so much of our brains that we don't even use,' she went on.

'So *that's* why you can't change a plug,' he remarked.

'Pig!' she exclaimed. 'I'm trying to make a serious point here.'

'So am I.' He was still smiling. 'It's what we do with the parts of our brain we *do* use that matters.'

'But doesn't the possibility of something more even interest you?'

8

'Ideas like that are certainly intriguing but I don't think they're really important.' He pulled a face. 'You're not going weird on me are you?'

'All authors are weird.'

'But you're the only author I care about. Just don't come home with a crystal ball, OK?'

'Scrying is a very old and venerable art,' she informed him with all the confidence of recently acquired expertise. 'It's still used in many parts of the world – by psychologists and—'

'Oh, please,' he protested mildly.

'Just because the subject has been given a bad name because of some charlatans, that's no reason to dismiss the whole field out of hand.'

'All right.' Michael sighed, then gave in without rancour. 'Tell me about magic.' He closed his book and set it aside.

Zoe felt hesitant at first, then warmed to her subject.

'I think we all do it,' she began, 'but it's given names like "intuition" or "déjà vu", so we can pretend to understand it.'

'I thought you meant *real* magic – you know, summoning demons, spontaneous combustion, the telekinesis of Stonehenge, that sort of thing,' he commented dryly. 'Not just "Gosh, I think I've been here before".'

'It's all connected,' she replied, ignoring his guileless mockery. 'But it seems that the mind is most capable of magic when in a state of emotional upheaval.'

'Hence the attachment of poltergeists to adolescents,' he put in seriously, surprising her.

'Yes. It needs effort and preparation to produce really powerful results,' she went on. 'Which explains the rituals in so-called primitive tribes – or of the mystics – that involve things like prolonged fasting, dancing, drugs, sexual exhaustion . . .'

'Mmm. That sounds interesting,' Michael said softly. 'I could help you with that last one.' He slid his hand under the duvet and stroked the curve of her hip.

'Get off!' Zoe ordered, laughing, but made no move to push him away.

'I can show you all the magic you need,' he persisted, his fingers tiptoeing over her stomach. 'I don't know why you need to fill your head with all this other nonsense.'

'That's rich, coming from someone who spends half his life fighting dragons and kung fu zombies in worlds that don't even exist!'

'Designing computer games is just the imaginative use of technology,' he muttered defensively. 'They're real, not some occult *idea*.'

'Tell that to the kids you've addicted.' There was no heat in Zoe's accusation. This was an old argument – and besides, she was much more interested in what Michael's hand was doing.

Some time later, when they were snuggled down under the duvet once more, Zoe felt safely cocooned and very happy. After the traumas of recent years her life was making sense at last. She let her thoughts wander aimlessly and, prompted by Michael's frivolous words – *Gosh, I think I've been here before* – she found herself thinking of an earlier chapter in *Magic, Mysteries and the Mind*, one that had covered ground already somewhat familiar to her. She drew back a little so that she could look at Michael's face.

'Have you ever been hypnotised?'

He gazed at her with a wide-eyed, imbecilic expression.

'Only by your wondrous eyes,' he sighed.

'I'm serious,' she said, though she could not help smiling.

'Well, stop being serious,' he instructed her. 'Laughing improves your body's immune systems – that's a scientific fact – so being light-hearted is much better for you. And I want you to live a very long time.'

'Why?' she asked, fishing.

'Because I love you.'

'I'll do my best,' she told him. 'I love you too. But you're avoiding the question.'

'What question?' he asked innocently.

'Have you ever been hypnotised?'

'Don't be daft. You know what I think about that stuff.'

'Owen helped me a lot,' she protested.

10

'Sure,' he admitted quickly, backing down a little. 'Buried memories from your own lifetime can obviously affect your subconscious. But that's not what you're thinking about now, is it. I saw the chapter heading. "Reincarnation and Past Lives".' The way he said it made it quite clear that he had no truck with such theories.

'*Is* it so ridiculous?' she asked. 'Can't you even admit the possibility? Millions of people believe in reincarnation, and some of the stories—'

'And we were obviously lovers in a previous life,' he put in, with only a slight question in his voice. 'Otherwise why did we know so soon?'

'It's a nice thought,' Zoe said.

'Next time round, let's make sure we meet as kids,' Michael went on, but he was still humouring her. Zoe knew this, but chose to accept his comment at face value.

'Yes, let's. I hate to think of all that time we wasted,' she said, meaning every word.

'Perhaps if we'd met as five-year-olds, I'd've pulled your hair and put slugs in your wellies, and you'd've hated me for ever.'

'I'd have loved you anyway – and I'd have got my own back,' she responded confidently.

Michael shuddered theatrically.

'You still haven't answered my question,' she persisted. For some reason, it had become important to complete their discussion, not to be sidetracked. Why, she wondered, did Michael seem so reluctant to talk about this?

'No,' he answered finally. 'I've never been hypnotised, and I don't ever want to be.'

'Why not?'

He shrugged.

'You always remain in control,' Zoe reassured him, speaking from experience. 'You can't go into a trance unless you want to, and you're conscious throughout. It's actually very restful.'

'Some of the memories hidden away aren't so pleasant though,' he countered.

11

'True.' Again she spoke from self-knowledge. 'But letting them out takes away their power.'

'Catharsis,' he said gravely. 'I always thought that was some sort of nasal infection.'

'You,' she informed him affectionately, 'are an idiot.'

'You're trying to convince me about reincarnation and *I'm* the idiot?'

'I'm not trying to convince you,' she replied. 'I'm not even sure if I believe in it, really. I just think you should be a little more open-minded.'

'Open-minded? About half the population having been Napoleon or Cleopatra in an earlier life?' he asked incredulously.

'Most past lives are perfectly mundane.' Zoe had the feeling that Michael was already aware of this and was teasing her – but she was not about to back down now. 'Soldiers, housewives, that sort of thing. And if the memories aren't really from a previous life, then where *do* they come from?'

'They're probably make believe,' he replied. 'Symbolic dramas created either to try and please the hypnotist or to help the subject cope with their real life.'

These were standard arguments – which fitted the known facts very well – but they were not enough for Zoe. She wanted there to be more to it than that. Surely the unused, hidden recesses of the human mind were capable of more than just imagination?

'So how do you explain the incredible detail some people come up with?' she asked. 'Stuff they couldn't possibly know?'

'Cryptomnesia,' he answered promptly.

Zoe was impressed. For all his apparent scepticism, Michael constantly surprised her with strange nuggets of knowledge about all sorts of things. And, in spite of his automatic tendency to be flippant, he always listened to her, even when he disagreed. It was one of the many things she loved about him.

'I didn't realise technobabblers like you knew words like that,' she remarked.

12

Michael immediately went into robotic data retrieval mode, his face blank and his words deliberately lacking inflection.

'Cryp-tom-nes-ia: Re-call under hyp-nosis of sub-consciously held infor-mation. Makes sense though, doesn't it?' he went on, returning to his normal voice. 'If we store away everything we've ever seen or read, but don't normally have access to it, then all you need to have done is read Mary Renault and, hey presto, you're a Greek hoplite.'

'That still doesn't explain the *detail*, things that couldn't possibly come from novels,' she countered. 'Verifiable facts about real but unimportant people who never made it into the history books.'

Michael shrugged again.

'Maybe Jung was right. Perhaps there *is* a collective uncon-scious we all share. Something that exists here, now. I'd find that easier to accept than reincarnation.' He was getting into his stride now. 'What really bugs me is that it's yet another variation on heaven and hell, a religious ploy to keep people in line. Be good in this life and you might not come back as a cockroach.'

'All right.' Zoe conceded defeat – for now. 'Go and play with your computers. I've got a book to finish, and we should have been up hours ago.'

'Why haven't you asked Owen to regress *you*?' Michael asked curiously, making no move.

Zoe was silent for a while.

'I'm afraid to,' she admitted eventually. 'Now that we're together, here, *this* life is too good. I've finally got it right – and I don't want to know about my other attempts.'

Michael grinned.

'My point exactly,' he said. 'Today, now, that's what matters. The past can take care of itself.'

# 2

After a very late breakfast, Zoe left Michael pottering happily in the kitchen and went back upstairs to her study. This occupied the whole of the western end of the cottage's first floor and, in Zoe's opinion, was by far the nicest room in the house. Unusually large windows – which were not original – on three sides meant that although the room could be cold in winter, it was always filled with light, especially so below the wonderful west-facing bay window. It was here that Zoe's vast, old-fashioned, wooden desk stood and where, as she had informed Michael, 'the sun shone on the writer'.

An electric typewriter sat at one end of the desk, neatly protected by its dust cover, and an adjustable reading lamp stood at the other end. The surface of the desk was covered with various note pads, cardboard folders, tubs of pens and pencils and a mound of paper covered with Zoe's handwriting. Her novels were all written in longhand, then revised and edited in that state, so that when they were eventually committed to type, only minor corrections were needed before they were ready to be sent off to her agent. It seemed a haphazard way of working, but it suited Zoe. She had no word processor or any other sophisticated equipment. By her own admission she was still in the Stone Age technologically speaking – and happy to be there.

The walls of the room were whitewashed, with only a few pictures providing decoration – except for the inner wall beside the door, which was covered with bookshelves. The study was a cheerful place and one which rarely failed to lift

14

Zoe's spirits, especially when, as now, the sun was shining in the vast East Anglian sky and the views from her windows reminded her just how lucky she was to be there.

The cottage stood in a lane on the outskirts of the remote north Norfolk village of Thornmere. Its small garden was surrounded by fields, with a copse to the north and, some distance away, a few other houses and modern bungalows. The subtly changing rural scenes always delighted Zoe as she watched from her eyrie. After having lived in London for so many years, the quiet tranquillity of her new home was a constant joy – even if it was occasionally and briefly shattered by farm vehicles or low-flying RAF jets. Even those intrusions were easy to accept. Thornmere – and rural Norfolk in general – were *real* places, where people worked and lived, where people knew their neighbours.

The cottage was called 'Ash Ring', although as far as Zoe could tell there were no ash trees anywhere near. She had wondered about changing the name, but when Michael suggested calling it 'Dunroamin 2: The Sequel', she had decided to drop the subject.

When the purchase of the house had gone through, some six months earlier, they had both known that it would need a lot of work, but the charms of the place had more than overridden its run down state. Fortunately, the bathroom had been renovated by the previous owner. Michael was quite happy to renew wiring – indeed he had already done most of the circuits – but he was no plumber. There was still much to do before everything would be completed to their liking but, in the meantime, it was comfortable enough and suited their needs admirably.

Zoe sat at her desk and shuffled paper, her mind not really on the task in hand. The disturbing dream, her reading and the subsequent conversation with Michael, as well as the remembered mixture of tenderness and passion which characterised their lovemaking, still filled her mind, and she had to force herself to concentrate. She was nearly at the end of her latest novel, and ordinarily she would be working fast and hard as the story's own momentum carried her along.

15

But today a pleasant lethargy enveloped her, and because her delivery deadline was still some weeks away, it did not matter so much if progress was slow. More than once Zoe found herself gazing out of the window at the trees, their own half-tended garden, at the woodsmoke curling gently from the village chimneys. A half-remembered quotation from Goethe came into her head – *There are three human activities that occupy the exact middle ground between nature and art – cooking, gardening and sex* – and she made a note to check the precise wording. It was perfect for what she wanted.

She slipped the reminder under the title page of the typescript. The top page read '"Fields of Plenty" by Zoe March'. She still liked the title, and felt pleased with the appropriateness of the quotation. She told herself with a rueful smile that her morning had not been entirely wasted.

It was some years ago that the type of book Zoe wrote had come into vogue, providing her with a measure of literary recognition and financial success. Her gentle, funny and poignant stories dealt with universal topics – love, families, disappointments and dreams – and were set in the rural landscapes she remembered from her childhood and to which she had now returned. Zoe had originally started writing for her own amusement, to escape from the claustrophobic nature of her life as it had been then into her 'other lands' – which was how she thought of her imaginary realms. Her first husband, Thomas Forbes, had been instrumental in getting her published initially with the company he worked for and, for a long time, Zoe had been plagued with insecurity about her talent. The years with Thomas had undermined her self-confidence so that she had found it easy to believe that her husband's marketing expertise was the only reason her books sold at all. Others, including Zoe's agent, Alexandra Henderson, shared none of these doubts and, when the divorce had come, Zoe had been surprised by how easy it had been to find a new publisher. Alex had been a tower of strength throughout that difficult time, and had made sure that Zoe continued to receive all the royalties due to her on her earlier books – in spite of Thomas's

Machiavellian strategies. At one point, he had even claimed that he was a co-author of some of the novels – a claim he had quickly been forced to withdraw – but his anger and spite had prolonged the whole agonising business as he contested every issue. The nightmarish legal procedures had seemed designed specifically to take as long as possible, and to benefit only the lawyers involved.

It had been meeting Michael Glover that had finally given Zoe the courage to extricate herself from her loveless first marriage. Although they had been in their middle thirties when they first met, she and Michael had both felt like teenagers again when their affair began – that mixture of uncertainty, pleasure and anguish they thought they had left behind long ago.

Ironically, it had been Thomas's decision to buy a second house, near the north Norfolk coast, which had led to Zoe and Michael's meeting. The holiday home had become her refuge, and she was soon making excuses to spend as much time there as possible, in spite of Thomas's complaints. Zoe had been aware of Michael for some time before talking to him one night in a local restaurant and finding – to her astonishment – that the attraction she felt was fully reciprocated. Events had snowballed rapidly, and Zoe's emotions had alternated between almost delirious joy at the intensity of her new-found love, and utter misery when they were apart. She and Michael had very quickly realised what their course of action must be.

Thomas had been outraged by the fact that Zoe had the effrontery to even consider leaving him, and he became more violent and abusive at home, while in public – at work and eventually in court – he gave the impression of sweet reason and injured calm. The four years that had followed had been an emotional roller coaster for Zoe, and she knew that she could never have seen it through without Michael's fierce love and support. Now they spent almost all their time together, content in each other's company, and neither wanting nor needing much outside social life. While the passionate excesses of their original affair had been mellowed a little by time – by the lack of that initial desperation which had made every second together infinitely precious – they still made love a great deal. In bed they revelled in their mutual certainty and in a sense of playfulness neither had experienced before. They were both nearing forty now but, as Michael put it, they were 'not bad for a pair of old fogeys'.

Their physical compatability was matched by the nature of their characters – sufficiently alike to be comfortable, but with enough differences to make the relationship continually interesting. They were never in danger of taking each other for granted.

Zoe glanced up at the enlarged photograph of Michael that hung on her wall. His face grinned back at her, reminding her as always of a young Sam Shepard – although Michael himself had trouble seeing the resemblance. Deep blue eyes, a Roman nose and straight, dark hair – now showing a few touches of grey – complemented his smile. He was tall and thin, with the sturdy legs of a runner and the elegant hands of an artist. Zoe sometimes felt weak-kneed just looking at him, and often wondered what he saw in *her*. On impulse, she got up and fetched a hardback copy of her latest novel, and looked at the photograph inside the back cover. It had been taken two years ago, and only showed her head and shoulders, but that was enough – she hoped – to give an impression of sensitivity and intelligence. Michael thought she was beautiful and told her so frequently, but he was biased and she had difficulty believing him. Looking at the picture now, Zoe had to admit that her decent bone structure lent some grace to her delicate features, and her hazel eyes went well with the short, light brown hair with its slight natural curl, but she still could not think of herself as beautiful. And she worried constantly about the parts of her the picture did not show. She had lost a lot of weight during the traumas of her divorce – infinitely more effective than any diet – but had put much of it back on now that her life was happily settled. There were some consequences of growing older that could not be avoided, however young in heart she felt. Michael told her constantly that she worried about her figure too much, and that the only thing that mattered was to feel comfortable in your own body. Which was all very well for him, Zoe thought ruefully. He weighed the same as he had when he was eighteen.

She replaced the book and, as she turned back to her desk, her eye was caught by another of the items hanging on the wall. She smiled. The necklace was pinned within a wooden frame, and was on display both as a constant reminder of Michael's desire to please her and of the fact that they did not know everything about each other. The jewellery was made of silver-coloured metal, set with iridescent glass beads. Michael had made it himself and Zoe had been entranced by his gift, but she would never wear it. She had an inexplicable aversion to anything – either clothes or jewellery – which was tight around her neck. Her neck was long and sometimes stiff and painful – which her physiotherapist had told her was due to an occasionally displaced vertebra – but there was nothing physically wrong that could account for her fear.

When Michael had presented Zoe with the necklace, she had forced herself to try it on, wanting to please him, but it was designed to sit high, like a choker, and she had soon found herself suffering an unbearable anxiety attack. Feeling wretched and guilty she had taken it off again and tried to explain. Michael had been understandably disappointed, and had offered to modify the necklace, but Zoe had asked instead that he make a frame to display his gift. It remained one of her most precious possessions.

# 3

Zoe finally managed to get some work done, and made it through to the late afternoon fortified only by the occasional cups of coffee or tea that she and Michael made for each other. When hunger and the need to be together drove her downstairs, she found that Michael had already given up on his own work and was sitting on the back doorstep, talking to Stripe, one of their neighbours' cats. The grey tabby often visited their garden. As Zoe sat beside Michael, linking her arm through his, Stripe came to greet her, and allowed her head to be stroked.

'Done for the day?' Michael asked.

'Yes.'

Stripe was purring now and Zoe knew just how the cat felt. She was very contented.

'Do you realise we've been married nine months now?' she said.

'My God!' he exclaimed, pretending to be surprised. 'So long. And no sign of any children yet. Have I been failing in my duties?'

'Oh no. You've been most satisfactory,' she replied, laughing. 'I might even decide to keep you.'

The break-up of Zoe's marriage to Thomas had been hard enough, and it had been a matter of some relief that they had never had children. Now neither she nor Michael wanted any of their own. They were all the family they needed.

'The evenings are getting colder,' Michael remarked after they had sat in silence for a while.

'And I need my dinner,' Zoe added. 'And a drink.'

After eating at the kitchen table, they retired to the sitting room with the last of the wine.

'There's nothing on TV,' Michael said. 'What do you want to do?'

'We could sort out another couple of boxes,' she suggested.

Michael groaned. Zoe had brought very little with her from her first marriage, wanting as few reminders of her earlier life as possible, but his own possessions had been rather more of a problem. All the really important stuff had now found its own space in the cottage, but the small storeroom at the rear was still half full of cardboard crates – just where the removal men had left them. Michael found it difficult to remember what was even in most of them.

'I should have just thrown the whole lot away,' he muttered. 'I'm sure we don't need it.'

'Don't be silly,' she told him. 'It's fun. And I discover new things about you with every box.'

'That's what I'm afraid of.'

'Come on,' she ordered, pulling him to his feet.

They each fetched a crate and carried them back inside. The first appeared to contain nothing but wires and a bewildering variety of plugs and sockets. Michael grunted as he poked through the tangle, then carried the whole box off to his workroom while Zoe opened the other. This one contained several books, technical manuals and a few tools, none of which struck her as very interesting. Then she found a small box of inlaid wood near the bottom and took it out just as Michael returned.

'What's this?'

'A jewellery box. I bought it in Morocco eons ago.'

'It's beautiful,' she said, tipping it so that its surface caught the light. The contents shifted and rattled as she did so, and she gently prised open the lid. 'Treasure trove!' she exclaimed.

The box was full of a variety of small coins which, on closer inspection, proved to be from several different countries in Europe and North Africa as well as the USA.

'My travelling days,' Michael commented. 'When I was young and foolish.'

'I wish I'd known you then,' Zoe told him.

In amongst the coins were a few beautiful shells and a set of flat pebbles with small holes crudely bored through them.

'You see, I was into making jewellery even then.'

The last item was a small felt bag, and Zoe's exploring fingers told her what was inside before she took it out.

'Wow! You didn't make this too, did you?'

Michael appeared dumbstruck, staring at the ring as though he had never seen it before. Zoe went to slip it over her finger but stopped abruptly when he spoke.

'Don't!'

Something in his tone made her feel suddenly nervous. Was there a secret in Michael's past that she would rather not learn about? The ring itself was a work of art. The band was made of interwoven strands of different coloured metals, and was set with a deep red stone that glowed like firelight. She had never seen anything like it, and assumed that the ring was very old, probably an antique.

Michael had not moved or spoken since his single command, and his face was an unreadable mask.

'What is it? What's the matter?' Zoe was getting worried now.

'It's not important,' he lied, trying in vain to make light of his own reaction. 'I'd forgotten it was there.'

Zoe sensed that, in that at least, he was telling the truth.

'Where did you get it? In Morocco?' she asked, trying not to betray her unease.

'No. Someone gave it to me,' he replied. 'A long time ago.'

'Someone?' Zoe probed gently.

'It's a long story,' he said reluctantly, knowing there was no escape.

'Tell me,' she said.

More than twenty years earlier, Michael had taken a temporary job as a salesman in the electrical department of Brands, a large store in Norwich. It was one of several jobs he had

had while making his erratic way through college. He had not enjoyed the effort of making himself presentable each day, but at least he got to deal with all the latest televisions and hi-fi systems – all the technological paraphernalia which even then were the focus of much of his attention. Indeed, it was his knowledge of these complicated bits of machinery that had got him the job in the first place. For much of the time, in fact, he had to curb his enthusiasm or risk taking all day to make a sale, or – even worse – drive a potential buyer away with his bombardment of information. Most customers didn't care what went on *inside* a television set.

One morning, when the store was quiet in the aftermath of the January sales, a disreputable-looking figure with straggly grey hair and a long dirty coat entered the shop. He shuffled along, looking down at his feet and muttering to himself. Michael saw him almost immediately, and was moved by the mixture of pity and revulsion which most people feel when confronted with such human flotsam. The derelict was a sad sight, but he was someone else's problem. The security people would take care of him.

By now the intruder had received several disapproving glances from both the predominantly middle-class customers and members of staff, but he kept moving, apparently unaware of the unease he was causing. Michael reflected disgustedly that it was only in 'uncivilised' places such as India that there was supposed to be an untouchable caste.

The man was making his way towards the electrical section and eventually, much to his embarrassment, Michael realised that, slowly but unerringly, the tramp was heading straight for his own station. A quick look around confirmed that none of the store detectives was in sight. Even the department manager was not on the floor. Michael considered doing as others had done and simply moving away, avoiding the issue, but that seemed cowardly and hypocritical. Perhaps, he thought, the old man would go straight past. Michael stood his ground behind one of the cash desks, and waited. It could not be long before security were alerted. Until then, this was his problem – to be dealt with as tactfully as he could.

The tramp came to a halt at the other side of the desk, and looked up. The eyes in his dirty, unshaven face were old and rheumy, but he seemed pleased to have reached his destination. Michael was about to ask if he could be of any assistance when the visitor spoke.

'I have your wife's ring.' One gnarled hand emerged from the dark recesses of his coat pocket and held up something for Michael to inspect. Old fingers trembled slightly.

Michael stared at the man's face, then at the proffered ring, then back again.

'Pardon me?' he said eventually.

'Your wife's ring,' the derelict repeated with a touch of impatience. His hand was still extended, holding a metal ring set with a dark red stone. Michael could not help noticing the grime under the man's fingernails.

'I'm sorry, sir,' he said hesitantly. 'You must be mistaken.'

'No mistake!' The words were louder now, more aggressive. 'Take it.'

Michael assumed that the derelict was either an alcoholic, addled with drink, or hopelessly mad, though his words were neither slurred nor random. And yet they still made no sense – and the situation was getting more embarrassing by the minute. Where was the detective?

'I'm not married,' Michael said, shaking his head. In fact he was adamantly single at the time, and marriage was the last thing on his mind. 'I think you'd better leave.'

'Here it is.' The old man waved the ring in the air, as if this explained everything. 'You must take it!'

'Don't be ridiculous!' Michael hissed, getting angry now in spite of his good intentions. 'I shall have to call security unless you leave.' His finger hovered over the alarm button beneath the till, but he could not bring himself to press it.

'Take it and I'll go,' the derelict responded fiercely.

The strange altercation was now causing something of a stir, and several people were watching from a distance. Michael saw out of the corner of his eyes that – at last – his department manager and a burly, uniformed security guard were approaching. Yet something about the old man's

desperate tone and the dejected slump of his wretched frame
made Michael want to keep him from any further indignity.
Without really understanding his own motives, he made a
sign to his colleagues – who halted uncertainly – and then
began to circle the counter.

'Take it,' the tramp pleaded insistently. 'You must take it
to her.' He put the ring down beside the till and Michael
stopped again.

'But I told you. I'm not married.'

The old man shrugged as if this was of no importance, then
snarled suddenly.

'Fool!' he snapped. 'It's hers. Take it.'

'All right, all right,' Michael said placatingly. 'I'll take it.'
Anything to put an end to this awkward scene. 'Will you go
now?' He picked up the ring and put it in his pocket.

'When you pay me,' the derelict replied, sounding mollified,
almost smug.

'Pay you?' Michael exclaimed. 'You *are* crazy.' He beckoned
to the guard, although there was no need. He was already
striding towards them, his face grim.

'Just give me something,' the old man begged quickly, a
panic-stricken look in his sad eyes. 'Anything.'

Michael said nothing but took the ring from his pocket and
tried to give it back. The other waved it away.

'Give me something of yours, please!' he wailed piteously.

'Come along, sir,' the guard interjected, drawing near. 'We
don't want to cause a scene, do we?'

'Anything,' the tramp repeated, ignoring the newcomer,
his disturbing gaze still fixed on Michael. 'I haven't got
much time.'

The security man glanced at Michael and nodded. Bewildered, Michael picked the first thing that came to hand,
pulling a ballpoint pen from his shirt pocket and offering
it tentatively. The derelict snatched it with a grateful sigh
and then, to everyone's surprise, turned to go without further
objection, apparently quite satisfied with the transaction. As
he shuffled away, the guard just behind him, he paused only
once to turn back and give Michael one last piece of advice.

What he said was as ridiculous as all that had gone before, but it made the ring's new owner shiver with a sudden chill.

As the unresisting old man was led from the store, the department manager came up to Michael.

'What was all that about? Who was that man?'

'I've no idea.' The ring was back in Michael's pocket and he saw no reason to make things more complicated than they already were. 'I've never seen him before.'

'Brain's been pickled by drink, no doubt,' the manager commented sanctimoniously. 'Poor old sod. Sorry we didn't get to you sooner, but you seemed to handle it admirably. Well done.'

With that he left, obviously putting the unfortunate incident from his mind. Michael could not do the same and, although the day returned to normal, he was unable to relax. In quiet moments he found himself taking out the ring and looking at it – until a friend and fellow salesman saw what he was doing.

'Is that what the old guy gave you?' Robbie asked.

Michael nodded.

'Can I see?'

The ring was handed over, and Robbie examined it speculatively.

'I don't know what the stone is,' he said, 'but the band could be gold. My sister's got a necklace that's three different colours like that.'

'Don't be daft. It must be tin or something. It can't be valuable.'

'Looks old to me,' Robbie persisted. 'You never know. You should get it valued.'

'The stupid old bugger was mad,' Michael objected. 'And so are you if you think this is worth anything. He swapped it for a biro!'

'You've got nothing to lose then,' his friend argued cheerfully. 'Why don't we nip out on our break? There's a jeweller's just round the corner.'

Michael shook his head and the conversation ended as a customer approached. But the idea – ridiculous though it was

26

– stuck in his mind and the next day, without telling anyone, he did as Robbie had suggested.

'Could you give me any idea what this might be worth? I don't think it's valuable, but . . .'

The man behind the counter took the ring and turned it appreciatively, then got out an eyeglass. From his expression he seemed to be taking the examination seriously, and Michael began to wonder whether Robbie had been right after all. The idea did not make him feel any more comfortable. After a time, the jeweller looked up and stared at Michael curiously.

'I've never seen anything quite like this,' he said. 'The metal is gold, though there's no hallmark, with three colours interwoven. That in itself, plus the weight of the gold, would make it worth £50 or so, but the craftsmanship is masterly. I'd guess that this is very old, certainly not this century. Interesting,' he mused, handing the ring back reluctantly. 'I'm afraid I'm not qualified to give you a proper estimate. It could be very valuable indeed. I can give you the name of a good assayer if you like, one who specialises in pieces like this.' He looked at Michael expectantly but the young man was too bemused by the unexpected information to answer immediately. 'Do you mind me asking where you obtained it?' the jeweller enquired.

Michael immediately felt guilty, as though he were being accused of robbing a museum, even though he knew he had done nothing wrong. It felt like walking through the customs hall at an airport, knowing that all your purchases were within the allowances but still being unable to act normally.

'Er . . . someone gave it to me,' he mumbled. 'A present.'

'Unusual present for a man,' the jeweller remarked. 'Too small for you, I'd have thought.'

'It's not for me,' Michael said. 'Thank you.' He turned and fled into the street.

He was preoccupied for the rest of the day. The derelict's actions now seemed all the more insane. In the days that followed, Michael thought of trying to find the man, but had no idea where to start. He had no name, no address – even supposing the tramp had a home – and only his own memory

27

of the man's appearance to guide him. It occurred to Michael that he could turn the ring over to the police as lost, but knew that idea was absurd. In the end he searched those places in the city where the winos and the homeless congregated, but he never saw the derelict again.

Zoe had been fingering the ring, glancing at it occasionally while Michael told his strange tale. The mystery gave the ring an added allure – it was indeed a thing of beauty in its own right – but there had been an undertone of genuine unease in Michael's voice.

'I could never bring myself to sell it, even when I was broke,' he concluded. 'I just hid it away and forgot about it.'

'And now we've found it again,' Zoe put in. 'And I'm your wife.'

'Yes.' His expression betrayed none of his thoughts.

'Don't you want me to have it?'

Michael said nothing, and Zoe steeled herself to ask about the one thing he had all too obviously left out of the story.

'What was the last thing the tramp said to you?'

'I don't remember,' he answered awkwardly.

'Yes, you do. Tell me.' She wondered what could be making him so reluctant.

'It's stupid,' Michael replied, trying to smile but failing miserably.

'Let me decide that,' she told him firmly, smiling herself.

Michael took a deep breath.

'He said, "Keep it safe always. Your wife will have need of it when you leave her."'

# 4

'I'll never leave you, Zoe. I swear.'

He looked so hurt, so wide-eyed and solemn, that she suddenly realised what he must have looked like as a little boy. Her heart went out to him. She had been shocked by the tramp's words, but the idea of Michael leaving her was so ridiculous it was laughable.

'I know you won't,' she said gently, getting up to hug him. 'You needn't look so worried.' He held her so tight it almost hurt, but Zoe did not object. 'You don't think I'm going to let you out of my clutches now, do you?'

After a while he relaxed, but only a little.

'Why now?' he whispered.

'It's just coincidence,' she told him, and then, after a pause, 'Hey, come on. You're the one who doesn't believe in weird stuff. That old man was no more a prophet than you or I. You're taking this far too seriously.'

She guided him back to the sofa. The ring lay on the coffee table, its dark stone winking in the lamplight. Neither of them looked at it.

'I shouldn't have told you,' Michael said heavily.

'You had no choice. I made you – and I'm glad you did.'

'Really?' He looked into her eyes. 'I never could lie to you.'

'And you never will,' she told him with a grin, 'so don't get any ideas.'

'But it was so long ago,' he breathed in disbelief. 'I really had forgotten all about it. Perhaps I'd deliberately blocked it out.'

He was serious again, his eyes haunted, and Zoe wondered how much truth there was in his assertion. Pushing aside her doubts, she sought to reassure him.

'This ring's good enough for me,' she told him, showing her own plain gold band. 'We can forget about that one for *another* twenty years.'

From the way Michael glanced at her, she knew that it would not be that easy for him – or for herself.

'I never even thought back then that I'd ever get married,' he told her.

'You were just waiting for the right girl,' Zoe replied, smiling.

'So the whole episode made no sense,' he went on, 'and I forgot all about it. Why has the ring waited until now to resurface?'

Zoe chose to ignore the fact that he was talking about the ring as if it could act on its own volition.

'Because you haven't had a reason to clear out all the clutter in your life till now,' she answered. 'You know what your old flat was like. I'm surprised you ever found anything.'

Michael nodded, brightening a little.

'But it *was* so weird,' he said, staring into space. 'It makes me feel odd just remembering it.'

'Don't get all nostalgic on me,' she joked. 'You told me this morning that *now* was what mattered. Just because some old eccentric chose you as the audience for his deranged, alcoholic delusions, that's no reason to get your emotional knickers in a twist.'

Michael smiled gratefully.

'I still wonder where on earth he got the ring in the first place,' he remarked.

'Perhaps *he* stole it from a museum,' Zoe suggested, then added brightly, 'I know. It must have belonged to your wife in a previous life, and he was trying to return it to its rightful owner.'

Michael gave her a long-suffering look, but his eyes were smiling again now, and Zoe was relieved.

'I wonder how valuable it really is?' she said mischievously.

'Who knows?'

They both glanced at the ring.

'Enough for me to hire a private detective to bring you back?' she asked. 'Or to buy my own Lear jet to follow you?'

'You won't need them,' he replied. 'The only way I'm leaving you is in a wooden box.'

'Uh-uh.' Zoe shook her head. 'I get to go first. We agreed on that, remember? You have to live a very long time.'

'I'll do my best,' he told her.

That night they lay quietly in each other's arms for a long time before going to sleep. They were both half afraid of what their dreams might bring, but in the morning Michael remembered nothing and Zoe only fragments, which seemed to have nothing to do with either the discovery of the ring or her previous nightmare about Thomas. The only image she could recall with any clarity was that of an unknown man on a white horse, riding away from her – and the feeling of relief and anticipation which accompanied his departure. Even that was soon forgotten as the day began.

By their own lax standards the couple were up early. Zoe's impending deadline and her lack of progress the previous day were weighing on her, and Michael had hit upon a solution to a particular problem while he was still half asleep. Hypnopompic intuition, he called it. He seemed quite excited as he got dressed, but would not tell Zoe anything about the project, promising only to show her when he had finished.

By lunchtime Zoe had completed a detailed set of notes for her next chapter, and was now ready to write the final draft. Feeling pleased with herself, she sat back and found herself thinking of the garnet ring. One part of her, she realised, desperately wanted to try it on, to see if it fitted. But another part – absurdly – was afraid to do anything that might make the derelict's words seem more plausible. The ring had been replaced in its bag inside the box, which was now resting on a space on the bookshelves in their sitting room. And there it would stay, Zoe told herself firmly. At least until Michael decided otherwise.

At that moment, his voice rang up the stairwell.

'If you can tear yourself away from your deathless prose, I've got something to show you.'

Zoe smiled at his youthful enthusiasm. Michael rarely showed her anything to do with his work in progress, unless she specifically asked him to, and anything he made a point of sharing with her was usually worth seeing.

'Coming!' she called.

Michael met her in the hallway and led her into his workroom – which was much smaller and less airy than her own study. It was crammed with equipment spread over tables and stands set around three of the walls. There were several computers, two television sets, a CD player, speakers, printers and disk drives, joysticks and keyboards – plus a vast number of other gadgets whose purpose Zoe could not even begin to imagine. They were all seemingly connected by a veritable maze of wiring, socket boards and multiple plugs. This surfeit of technology always intimidated Zoe, making her feel inadequate and helpless. She envied Michael his easy affinity with micro-voltages, circuit boards and silicon chips, but knew that such a bond was impossible for her. Indeed, to her eyes, there was something almost demonic about his lair. If Hell had a control room, she had decided some time ago, it would look just like this. She was surprised sometimes not to see red smoke and flames seeping up from the floorboards. The one small window provided insufficient light, and the fluorescent glow of the tube lighting on the ceiling was bright but painfully unnatural. And yet Michael was in his element here.

From a very early age he had displayed outstanding technical skills and understanding, almost as though he could 'see' the internal workings and logic of intricate machinery. Incomprehensible equations and diagrams were expressions of obvious fact to him, but his own idiosyncrasies and lack of motivation meant that he had been unable to find any job which suited him for more than a few months. As a result, his career had been a succession of frustrations, temporary enthusiasms and dead ends, until he had found his niche in creative electronics. After working for several design and marketing companies, he was now a successful freelance designer of upmarket computer games, one of which he was undoubtedly going to demonstrate now.

'OK. I won't bore you with any technicalities.'

'Good.'

'It's all set up,' he continued. 'You sit here.' He guided her to one of two mobile office chairs and stood at her shoulder. 'Press Z.'

Obediently, Zoe tapped the key. Immediately, the program sprang into action. A small dot appeared in the centre of the screen and then grew rapidly larger, swirling round in a kaleidoscope of flickering images. At the same time the speakers on either side played 'Funeral' from Philip Glass's opera *Akhnaten*. Belying its title, this was a rousing, energetic piece of music, and one of the limited number of works where both Zoe and Michael's tastes overlapped. She looked at him appreciatively.

'Nice start.'

'Thought you'd like that. I won't be able to use it in the real thing, worse luck,' he replied, then nodded towards the screen.

Zoe looked and saw the title appear in ghostly letters that coalesced before her eyes. *Otherlands*.

'Hey, that's *my* word!' she exclaimed, pretending to be affronted but secretly pleased.

'I know,' he confessed. 'I'm calling it that for now, but they'll probably change it before it goes into production.'

'"Aliens Ate My Babysitter"?' Zoe suggested.

'No. Someone's already used that,' he replied seriously. 'But you're getting the idea.'

'"Dungeon of the Lost Zombies"?' she tried, clearly inspired.

'Enough. Credit me with a little subtlety,' he said in a pained tone.

'I do,' Zoe responded. 'It's the people you have to sell this to I'm not sure about.'

'Press Z again,' he told her, grinning.

As she did so, the music stopped and Michael's voice, mutilated by some metallic filter, came from the speakers.

33

'You have reached the gates of Otherlands. Identify your-self.'

'Now what do I do?'

For answer, Michael opened a drawer and took out a photograph. It was a full length portrait of Zoe, taken on a beach of the Greek island they had visited that summer. She was dressed only in a black bikini, and was pointing at the camera, a threatening expression on her face. Zoe scowled. She hated the picture, although Michael thought she looked wonderful.

'I should have burnt that – and the negative,' she said.

'Not a chance. This is a classic.'

'What's it got to do with the game?'

Michael grinned.

'Feed it into that slot there,' he instructed, giving her the picture and pointing to a box-like machine that looked like a cross between a fax and a photocopier.

'Oh, no. You're not serious?' she said, jumping to con-clusions.

'Just do it.'

Giggling now, she pushed the photograph into place and felt it jerk as it was drawn inside. The machine clicked and hummed briefly.

'Type your name and title on screen,' the speakers intoned. A cursor flashed insistently.

Zoe tapped out the three letters of her first name and then, on impulse, added 'QUEEN OF OTHERLANDS'.

'Welcome Zo-e, Queen of Oth-er-lands,' the computer responded. The writing disappeared from the screen and then, to the accompaniment of some eerie music – more Philip Glass, Zoe suspected – a scene slowly appeared, as if a heavy fog were clearing away. It showed a magnificent fortress upon a hill, surrounded by a rolling plain with a vast forest in the distance. As she watched, the perspective drew in, closer and closer, until the screen was filled with a small door set into the great gates of the gargoyle-infested castle. The door opened slowly and a figure stepped out.

Zoe had been expecting something of the sort, but even so

the effectiveness of the trick made her gasp. The figure was *her*, down to the finest detail of which the graphics were capable. She was dressed in the black bikini and her expression was fierce. The colour and shape of her hair – and even the colour of her eyes – were exactly right. The figure paraded up and down in front of the gates as the real Zoe laughed aloud. Beside her, Michael was grinning happily.

'In this game, the player really gets to be the hero,' he said. 'Neat, huh?'

'It's brilliant,' she replied truthfully. 'But you might have chosen a better photo.'

'You're joking. This one's perfect. You look every inch the tigerish Queen of Otherlands.'

'Hmmm. Talking of inches,' Zoe said, 'my chest is *not* that big.'

'There are a few ... er, enhancements built into the program,' he admitted, unabashed. 'Bigger muscles for the men ...'

'Remembering your market, eh?' she teased. 'Just think of the fun some adolescent could have with this and a copy of *Playboy*.' But she could not be angry. She was fascinated as she watched her image marching up and down.

'Is that all I do?'

'Of course not. There are lots of options and characteristics to determine. You can't get those from a photo. In the finished version it'll move a lot faster. You'd have been facing the first ghosts by now, on the way to collecting your first secret artefact. But this is what I wanted you to see. Shall I show you some of the tricks the Queen can do?'

Zoe moved out of the way, and let Michael run his fingers over the keyboard. In response to each sequence, the figure crouched, jumped, whirled around, picked up a stone and hurled it at the gates where it hit the wood with a dull thud. The miniature Zoe began to breathe heavily and her skin glowed with a sheen of perspiration.

'I hope you gave her a good deodorant,' the real Zoe commented, laughing delightedly.

'Sound and vision only – as yet,' Michael retorted. 'I'm still working on the other three senses. The rat-infested sewers could be interesting . . .'

'God forbid.'

'You'll look even more impressive with a sword in your hands, or a magic talisman,' he told her, as the figure performed a spectacular backflip. 'What do you think?'

'I think you're a genius.'

'I know,' he said modestly. 'You're right.'

'Warped, but a genius nonetheless.'

'Even better.' He grinned, genuinely pleased. 'Of course, it's been possible to digitise stuff from video for ages, but not in game situations, and doing it from an ordinary photo is even better. That used to be possible only on CDs.'

'I don't think I like the idea of being digitised,' Zoe remarked.

'Oh, it won't stop here,' Michael said eagerly. 'Virtual Reality will soon be so advanced we'll be able to transfer our own consciousness into a computer, actually *live* in the games – or anywhere else we care to invent. Then we won't need these cumbersome physical bodies at all.'

'I *like* my physical body,' she objected, 'cumbersome though it may be.'

'I'm quite fond of it too,' he said, moving closer. 'And I meant cumbersome only by comparison with a few billion encoded electron pulses. You're not cumbersome at all.'

'Physical bodies do have their uses,' Zoe mused.

She led him upstairs and proved her point emphatically.

# 5

'I'm going round to the Post Office. Fancy a walk?'

Zoe had been working hard all morning, and the interruption was welcome. She turned and smiled at Michael, who was peering round the door of her study.

'Yes. These people can take care of themselves for a while.' She waved a hand at her manuscript.

After an overcast morning, the cloud was broken now and the sun still held the remnants of the summer's warmth, even though the breeze was cold. It was perfect walking weather.

On the way out Michael picked up a small package, and Zoe glanced at the address label.

'The Terrible Triplets?'

Michael nodded.

'*Otherlands*?' Zoe asked.

'Yes. Minus the photo-input stuff,' he replied. 'They don't have the equipment, and I'd never keep it a secret if they got their hands on the idea. To be honest, I'm not sure that part will ever be commercially viable, even if it is a neat gimmick. The game'll have to work on its own merits.'

The Terrible Triplets were three games-mad teenagers who lived in Norwich and who regularly tested Michael's prototypes. Seeing new developments long before they were generally available gave the trio a sense of self-importance and enabled them to brag to their cronies – on the condition that they returned everything to Michael and never made copies. They knew he would catch them if they tried and leave them out in the cold, but they would probably have remained loyal

37

anyway: honour among hackers, as Michael called it. Their exhaustive testing was invaluable.

'If they find the cheats in this one,' Michael went on, as he and Zoe turned into the lane, 'they're better than I thought. I've put in a few very convoluted wrinkles, just to confuse them.'

'They'll love that.'

'I know,' he said, grinning.

'Why don't you ever invite them here?' Zoe asked. 'Wouldn't it be more convenient?'

'You're joking. They're animals. I'd have no secrets left at all – and they'd probably steal half my equipment.'

'Oh, they can't be that bad,' she protested.

'Want a bet?' he replied. 'They can resist anything but temptation.'

'But you trust them with that?' Zoe indicated the package.

'Yes,' he admitted. 'This way I control what they see and what they don't. Set the guidelines and they're OK. But here? No chance.' He paused and gave her an innocent look. 'Besides, I didn't think you'd want computer junkies in the house. Addicts don't have many social graces, you know.'

Zoe refused to rise to the bait. They strolled into the village, enjoying the fresh air and the smell of woodsmoke, and making for the small Post Office, Thornmere's only shop. Even though there was very little traffic, Michael unthinkingly took Zoe's hand when they crossed the road. His automatic protectiveness was an endearing trait, even if it sometimes made her feel like a small child.

Their business complete, they returned home by a round-about route until the approach of some ominous-looking clouds made them hurry. Zoe went back to work after lunch, leaving Michael at a temporary loose end. He was unable to think of beginning a new project while the jury was out on *Otherlands*. He read for a while, watched some American football – a sport which fascinated him – on videotape, and then decided to go for a run before it got dark. After changing and warming up, he went upstairs to tell Zoe.

'How long will you be?' she wanted to know.

'About an hour.'

'Better take a key. I've run out of corrector ribbons,' she told him, 'and I'll have to go into Fakenham before you get back.'

'OK. Of course, if you had a word processor you wouldn't need those things.'

'Some of us antiquated misfits still feel that words are precious,' she responded, her tone that of a stern schoolmistress. 'I prefer technology I can control, rather than the other way round.'

Michael refrained from arguing and they grinned at each other.

'Drive carefully.'

'Of course. See you later.' She kissed him goodbye.

The Norfolk countryside was crisscrossed with a maze of small, quiet lanes, and Michael had plenty of routes to choose from. He always preferred to take a circular route, to avoid retracing his footsteps as much as possible, but wherever he went, the changing panorama of gently rolling fields was a pleasure he never tired of. He particularly liked the sinuous geometry of newly ploughed land when the sun was low in the sky and dark shadows outlined the furrows. Throughout the year he saw new crops sprouting and others being harvested; poppies, wild roses and blackberries decorated the hedgerows in their season; startled pheasants screamed and flapped away and rabbits bolted when he invaded their territory, their fleetness of foot mocking his own more ponderous tread.

For Michael, running was a way of keeping fit, now that the more strenuous exercises of his youth had been abandoned, but it also provided time for contemplation. He got some of his best ideas while on the move. Thinking of work-related problems, of future or past events and, especially, of Zoe, made the miles pass more quickly and enabled him to forget his aching legs and lungs.

This afternoon he found his thoughts unwillingly returning to the scene in which the derelict had given him the ring – and wondering why he still found the memory disturbing. He was grateful that Zoe had treated the whole thing lightly – but, in a way, her reaction only made him feel even more foolish. Perhaps he should sell the thing or give it to a museum, so that he could forget all about the stupid prediction. Maybe he should stop being so superstitious and let Zoe wear it after all, rather than let her see his own misgivings. Perhaps he should never have told her the story at all – but he knew he could not have done that. The discovery of the ring had taken him by surprise, and he had been unable to hide the truth from her.

Michael's thoughts were disturbed then by the sudden emergence of a barn owl from a dilapidated old shed. In the gathering dusk, the bird looked almost white as it glided along the road, staying ahead of him as though it were acting as a guide or escort. Michael watched delightedly until the bird flew away over a field of sugar beet. From the distance came the sound of its hunting shriek. Immediately, Michael's pleasure at the sight of the beautiful creature fell away and he had the weirdest sensation that he was being followed, hunted almost, as though he were a tiny field mouse cowering at the approach of silent wings.

The clouds were gathering again, making it darker than it would normally have been at that time of day, but although the weather was overcast and windy, it was warm for the time of year and Michael was sweating profusely. Even so, he told his legs to go faster, knowing that he only had two miles to go. He suddenly wanted to get home as quickly as possible.

By the time he crested the last ridge before the village, Michael was breathing hard, and was glad that the route ran gently downhill for the rest of the way. A few moments later, he heard the sound of a horse approaching from behind him, its hooves ringing on the tarmac. He glanced round, knowing that horses could be spooked by a runner, and preparing to move onto the verge. But there was no one in sight and, for some reason, his irrational sense of unease deepened. Turning a corner of the lane, he looked back but again could see nothing, even though he could still hear the approaching hoofbeats, now slowed to a walking pace.

Turning back once more, Michael was suddenly blinded by the twin headlights of a large car, being driven far too fast

40

for the narrow lane. He tried to jump aside but his tired legs stumbled, and a glancing blow from the wing of the car spun him round. A second blow caught him on the side of the head as he fell, and he collapsed at the edge of the road. Lying stunned, he found himself thinking, incongruously, that if the driver was not careful, the car must surely hit the horse and rider. But the vehicle's engine did not slow down as it receded into the distance and the lights vanished over the ridge.

Michael could still hear the horse, even though he could not see it. It had whinnied in fright as the car rushed past, and the rider was now evidently trying to control it. But all of this appeared strangely distant and unimportant now. Michael was not in pain, but his whole body seemed numb, and was refusing to work properly. In fact it felt like staying just where it was. He was aware of a voice muttering somewhere above him, but he could not make out the words. They did not seem important. For a brief moment, a picture of Zoe filled his mind, making him sad, and then even thought disappeared. Michael sank into an impenetrable blackness, darker than any night.

As Zoe walked back to the car park in Fakenham, she experienced a moment's sudden inexplicable terror. It was as though Michael had called to her for help, but the feeling only lasted an instant, like a dream memory, and she told herself not to be silly. Even so, she drove rather faster than normal on her way home. The front door was still locked, and her heart thumped as she fumbled for her keys.

'Michael?'

There was no response. She called again, a small bubble of panic swelling inside her chest. There was still no answer, and she went through all the rooms, worrying that he might have fallen asleep in the bath, but he was nowhere to be found. She glanced at her watch. He had been gone an hour and a quarter now. Perhaps he had decided to do one of his longer routes. That in itself would not be unusual, but he had seemed quite definite about being back in an hour. *There's nothing to worry about*, she told herself. *He'll be back soon.*

Zoe busied herself putting her shopping away and trying to

think about what they might have for dinner, but her anxiety grew worse as the minutes crawled by and still he did not return. She knew that she was a born worrier. Michael had often told her as much, accusing her of constantly expecting to be hit by meteorites, but that was her nature – there was nothing she could do about it.

Michael was rarely out running after dark, and the sun was long gone now. Eventually Zoe could stand it no longer and, feeling a mixture of foolishness and concern, she went out and got into the car again. For the next half hour she drove carefully around as many of Michael's usual routes as she could remember, but saw no one. She returned home, praying that he would be there to tease her about having been so needlessly agitated. But he was not. The house was as quiet and as empty as when she had left it. *Now what do I do?* she wondered tearfully, and looked at the telephone. Who should she call? It was then that she saw that the answering machine indicator showed one, not zero, and she pushed the replay button. As the tape rewound, Zoe's imagination ran riot with all the possibilities, both good and bad, but when an unknown female voice began to speak, her worst fears were confirmed.

'Mrs Glover . . . Er, this is the Norwich Hospital here . . .' There was another awkward pause. The caller had evidently been disconcerted by having to speak to a machine. 'I'm afraid your husband's been in an accident. Doctor Black asked me to call . . . Could you come to the hospital as soon as possible? We're in Alderwick Road . . . Er, thank you.'

By the time the machine sounded the tone that marked the end of the message, Zoe was already on her way out of the front door.

# 6

The doctor was waiting for Zoe at the end of the corridor. The badge on his coat lapel read 'Dr Nicholas Black'.

'Mrs Glover?'

'Yes.' Zoe tried to read his expression. He looked tired and serious, but his eyes were sympathetic. 'Is Michael . . .? Is he . . .?'

'He's alive.'

Zoe let out a long, painful breath. During her frantic drive to the city she had been plagued by the fear that she would come too late, that she would never see him again. That at least had been averted, but . . .

Dr Black was quick to answer her unasked question.

'But he's been in a nasty accident,' he told her gravely. 'Superficially, his injuries are not too severe, but he took a heavy blow to his head, and he's deeply unconscious.'

'Oh.' Something cold and hard was squeezing Zoe's heart, and her throat had contracted so that she was only able to whisper. 'When will he come to?'

'I'm afraid I can't answer that. His condition is stable, and we're doing everything we can, but comas such as this can last anything from a few hours to much longer. It's too soon to tell.'

The word 'coma' made Zoe's senses reel. This was something out of TV movies and horror novels – something that only happened to other people.

'Can I see him?' she asked in a small voice.

'Of course. He doesn't look too good right now,' the doctor

warned, 'but try not to be too upset. He's not suffering. We'll discuss his condition more once you've seen him. OK?'

Zoe nodded dumbly and followed him to one of the rooms along the hallway. Dr Black opened the door and went in ahead of her. The nurse, who was sitting at the bedside, got up and the doctor nodded to her, but Zoe was barely aware of her existence. All she could see was Michael.

He lay in bed, his upper body slightly propped up. His angular face was expressionless, his eyes open but lifeless as they stared at the ceiling. His left cheek was covered with a vast, livid bruise which extended round his eye, and there were cuts on his lip and left ear. Beneath the hair above his ear was a grotesque swelling the size of half an orange. His mouth was open, with a tube disappearing down his throat, and an intravenous drip was connected to his right arm. Beneath the bedclothes there was a bulge over his hips where a cage obviously protected some unseen injury.

He was absolutely still, apart from the slight, slow but regular rise and fall of his chest as he breathed. But it was the lack of any expression in his eyes that had the most profound effect on Zoe. This could not be Michael, *her* Michael. Where was his smile, his laughter, his words of welcome? The man who lay in the bed before her was a precious shell, but a shell nonetheless. *Oh, sweetheart, where have you gone?* she cried silently, fighting back both panic and tears. *Try not to be too upset*, the doctor had said. How was that possible?

She glanced at him now, and he motioned her forward. Feeling as though she were sleepwalking, Zoe went to the bedside and gently took Michael's unresisting hand in her own. She could hear the air as it hissed softly through the tube now, but otherwise he remained motionless.

'Michael? I love you,' she whispered in a choked voice. 'You have to wake up.'

His absolute lack of response made her feel foolish, and she looked up at the nurse and doctor. They regarded her sympathetically. *How can they be so calm?* Zoe wondered. *Why don't they* do *something?* But her gaze soon returned to Michael.

'Oh God, Michael. Don't do this to me,' she breathed softly.

'Mrs Glover?' Dr Black said.

She looked up uncomprehendingly. Was that her name?

'Will you come with me now?'

'No. I want to stay.'

'It's important that we talk,' he told her. 'You can come back in a few minutes.'

Zoe did not move. None of this made sense.

'I'll watch over him till you get back,' the nurse reassured her gently.

Zoe let go of Michael's hand and gazed at his lovely disfigured face for a few moments, then turned and left the room. Once she was in the corridor and the door was closed behind her, she felt herself crumple inside and was suddenly unable to stand up. The next thing she knew she was sitting on the floor with her back against the wall. Dr Black was squatting in front of her, holding her hands. Her face was wet and, as another sob convulsed her, she realised that she was weeping. Wordlessly the doctor offered her a handkerchief and she dabbed at her eyes.

'Are you all right?'

'Yes,' Zoe lied, though her misery was intolerably painful. Her skin felt cold and clammy, and her mouth was dry.

'Let's go to my office.' He helped her to her feet and took her arm, guiding her to a small cluttered room and into a seat. 'I'll get some tea.' He disappeared, returning what seemed like only moments later with two mugs. Zoe took hers and sipped because it seemed to be expected of her. The tea was sweet and milky – which she normally hated – but she did not even taste it. Dr Black sat down beside her – Zoe was glad he was not on the other side of the desk – and began to talk.

Zoe hung on every word. He was going to tell her that everything was all right, that when they went back Michael would be awake and on the road to recovery – but the doctor's first words were about her, not Michael.

'I'm afraid I don't know your first name, Mrs Glover.'

'Zoe. Zoe March usually,' she replied automatically.

'But you are Michael Glover's wife?' he asked.

She nodded.

'Well, Zoe, you're suffering from shock right now, and your first responsibility is to yourself. Drink your tea.'

She sipped obediently, then looked up.

'But Michael . . .' she began. 'He will be all right, won't he?'

'There's every chance he will make a full recovery.'

'But you're not certain?' she asked quietly.

'Medical science doesn't deal in certainties in cases like this,' he replied, 'but in the short time Michael's been here, his condition hasn't worsened – and that's a good sign.'

'Don't some comas last for years?' Zoe frightened herself with the thought.

'In rare cases, yes. But many others last only a few hours, or days at the most. In Michael's case it's obvious that the cause was a blow to the head. It can be a lot more complicated when we don't know *how* it was caused, by disease or drug overdose, for instance. Michael seems to have been pretty fit for his age, so he should be able to fight his way out of it.'

Zoe nodded bleakly, trying to absorb what she was being told, trying to share the doctor's optimism.

'We've already done several tests, just in case,' he went on, 'but can you tell me whether Michael suffered from any long-term illness? Or serious allergy?'

Zoe shook her head. Dr Black asked for the name of Michael's G.P., so that they could check his records, and she told him.

'Was he hit by a car?' she asked, feeling slightly more in control of herself now.

'We presume so. His injuries are certainly consistent with that, but it seems the driver didn't stop. There was no one else around when Michael was found. We've informed the police as a matter of course.'

Zoe could only nod again. A hit-and-run driver. She knew there would be anger later, mixed with her grief – but for now her feelings seemed out of reach. She was numb.

'Who found him?' she asked eventually.

'A couple of cyclists,' he replied. 'Youngsters. Acted very responsibly by all accounts. One of them stayed while the other rode to the nearest house and called an ambulance.'

Zoe was silent again, imagining Michael lying alone in the darkness. What would have happened if the cyclists had not found him when they did? That did not bear thinking about, and her mind shied away, distracted by an inconsequential thought.

'How did you know who he was?' she asked. 'To get in touch with me?' Michael had been wearing only his running kit and was carrying no identification.

'His keyring had a personalised tag on it with an insurance company telephone number,' Dr Black replied. 'We rang them to explain the situation and they agreed to give us his home number. It's a good job they did, or it would have taken us much longer to identify him.'

'John Doe,' Zoe whispered, wondering what she would have done if Michael's disappearance had remained unexplained for hours, even days. 'I think I would've gone mad.'

'You know the worst now, Zoe.'

'Do I? He could die, couldn't he?'

The doctor met her gaze steadfastly.

'It's possible, yes,' he said evenly. 'A coma can lead to irreversible decline, but I think that's most unlikely in Michael's case.'

'Oh, God,' she breathed, close to tears again.

'Perhaps it would help if I explained a little more.' He paused but Zoe did not respond, so he went on calmly. 'Michael's hip is broken, but it's a simple fracture and should heal itself in time. The blow to the side of his head is obviously far more serious. I'll spare you the technicalities, but it's clear he has severe concussion – though the skull is not fractured and there's no sign of internal haemorrhaging, so there aren't too many complications. His breathing has remained stable. The tube you saw is only a precaution, and we should be able to remove it soon.

47

His pulse is steady so we don't have to worry about his heart at the moment. We're monitoring everything very closely. That's what all the machines at his bedside were for.'

Zoe vaguely remembered seeing the devices, the electronic blip marking his heartbeat and other, more mysterious apparatus. They too had seemed like props from a movie.

'But you can't tell when he'll wake up?' she asked, returning to the only question that really mattered.

'No. I'm afraid not. It could be hours, or days.'

'Or longer?'

'Possibly.'

'Can I go back to him now?' Zoe asked after a moment's pause.

'One last thing,' he said. 'When I asked you not to be too upset, it was more than just a doctor's platitude.' He smiled gently. 'It's important. We need you to be brave, Zoe. Michael's conscious mind is asleep, down so deep we can't reach him yet, but his subconscious is still working, allowing his body to keep functioning. And, in some ways we don't understand properly, his subconscious may be aware of what is going on around him. He can't respond yet because his conscious mind is blocking it out, but with everything we do or say in Michael's presence we must act as if he can see and hear us. We don't want to cause his subconscious any distress, if you like. That's one of the reasons we've got him in a private room.'

Zoe nodded, recalling indistinct memories of 'miracle cures' achieved by the devotion of a patient's loved ones. One case in particular had concerned a young boy in a long-term coma, a great fan of the Miami Dolphins. He had eventually been aroused by a tape sent especially by the team's famous quarterback, Dan Marino. Zoe could still hear Michael's voice as he told her about it.

'I'll try,' she said quietly.

'Good.' The doctor got up and walked back to Michael's room with her. 'The nurse'll show you the ropes,' he told her.

'What you can touch and what you can't. She'll be in and out, but the monitors are connected to the nurses' station, and there's a call button if you need anything in a hurry.' They had reached the door. 'Ready?'

'Can I talk to him?'

'Of course. That can only do good – as long as you're positive.'

Zoe tried wanly to return his encouraging smile, and they went inside.

Michael's eyes were closed now, which made it easier to look at him, but Zoe found herself holding her breath until she saw the slight rise and fall of his chest. *He's just asleep*, she told herself. *He'll wake up soon and be my Michael again.*

The nurse filled in some readings on a chart at the foot of the bed, then showed Zoe where everything was.

'He'll be as right as rain soon, Mrs Glover,' the nurse assured her confidently. 'I'll be back in a while'

She and Dr Black went out and, feeling very self-conscious, Zoe sat in the chair provided, moving it closer to the bed. For a long time she remained silent, trying to stay composed, unable to think of anything to say. She felt tongue-tied and very alone, but then a hidden anger fuelled her determination. Fate would *not* take Michael from her. She would be his Dan Marino. She would bring him back.

Zoe began to talk, about happy memories, funny incidents and their plans for the future; she recalled holidays, ridiculous conversations and everyday details of their life together. Once she had started, she found that there was so much to say. They seemed to have packed a whole history into a few short years together.

The nurse, whose name was Claire, made several visits, interrupting the monologue, and the two women talked a little. To Zoe, Claire seemed very young to be charged with such responsibilities, but she seemed capable and did her best to keep Zoe cheerful.

Later, her voice growing hoarse, Zoe sat in silence for a while, pretending that Michael was asleep. She had lost all sense of time, and was surprised when a new nurse appeared. Claire, she discovered, had gone off duty at midnight. An hour later Dr Black returned, looking more tired than ever, though he still greeted her with a smile.

'Are you all right?'

Zoe nodded.

He studied the charts and examined Michael again, taking his pulse and shining a small light into his eyes before closing the lids again. Zoe looked at the doctor, hoping for some sign, but when he spoke he gave nothing away.

'You should think about going home. There's no change in Michael's condition. We're doing all we can for him, and we'll call you the minute there's anything to report.'

'I'd rather stay.'

'Exhausting yourself won't help anyone,' he told her. 'You need your rest.'

At his words, it was as though every one of Zoe's muscles was suddenly filled with lead. Willpower had carried her so far, but the combined effects of shock, worry and simple tiredness had finally taken their toll. In all the hours she had been there, Michael's condition had shown not the slightest change, and the doctor was right. Wearing herself out would do her husband no good. Having admitted as much to herself, Zoe found that she was very close to tears. She did not want to cry there, so she stood up and took her husband's hand again.

'Goodbye for now, Michael. I'll see you again tomorrow. You'll be better then.' She kissed his unresponsive lips and whispered her love in his ear, then followed Dr Black from the room.

'Michael will understand that you need to sleep,' he told her.

Zoe looked at the doctor properly for the first time. He had a kind face, intelligent brown eyes and sandy coloured hair.

'Thank you,' she whispered. 'Thank you for treating him like a real person.' Zoe had only just realised how grateful she was.

50

'That's because he *is*,' the doctor replied. 'Do you need a taxi?' He was obviously concerned about her ability to drive.

'No. I'll be all right.'

He accepted her assurance and escorted her to the entrance hall.

'Will you be here tomorrow?' Zoe asked.

'From 4 p.m. onwards,' he replied. 'I'll see you then.'

Zoe nodded, walked out to her car, unlocked it and sat in the driver's seat without turning on the engine. The tears came then, pouring down her cheeks as all the pent-up emotion of the night overwhelmed her. Alone now, she was relieved of the awesome responsibility of being brave, and she gave in to the clawing grief and a measure of self-pity. But at last her weeping subsided and she dried her face, breathing deeply to try and calm herself before setting the car in motion. She drove home at a deliberate pace on the almost empty roads, concentrating fiercely.

Light spilled from the windows of Ash Ring as the gravel of the drive crunched under the car's tyres. In her haste, Zoe had left several lights on and, in other circumstances, the warm glow would have been welcoming. But now, facing a night alone there for the first time, Zoe felt miserable and cold. Then, as she got out of the car, she sensed something odd about the cottage, something sinister, though she could not say what it was. Frightened now, her unease deepened when she discovered that she had left the front door unlocked. The chances of being burgled in Thornmere had always seemed remote but, these days, anything was possible. Zoe went inside and immediately felt a shiver of fear. There was a presence in the hallway, a male presence, invisible but very real.

'Hello?' she called tentatively.

There was no answer. Nervously, she searched the house. It was empty and quiet. There was nothing missing, nothing disturbed or damaged. Zoe decided that her own emotional state was playing tricks on her, making her imagine things.

51

Yet, as she got ready for bed she could not shake the feeling that – even though he had obviously gone now – someone had been there while she was out.

# 7

Zoe woke to the nightmare of an empty bed. She had turned to Michael, as always, but he was not there, and she was filled with panic and dread as the realisation of where he was came crashing down on her.

To make things worse, fragments of the night's dream still lingered in her mind. She heard again Michael's voice calling to her from an echoing cavern, far below. *Down so deep we can't reach him yet.* Zoe could not hear – or could not recall – what he had been saying, but his desperate need for her had been all too clear. She had been standing in the hospital, looking around helplessly. But the building was all wrong. It was old and dark, with small rooms, and the air was cold and damp. Claire had been there too, but dressed in a ragged cape, not her crisp nurse's uniform. And Michael was lost, beyond Zoe's reach.

Pushing aside the unpleasant imagery, Zoe got up and went downstairs to check the answering machine – just in case she had done the unthinkable and slept through the ringing of the phone. She had been so tired and distressed last night that anything was possible, even though she had had the foresight to leave the bedroom door open. But there was no message. Zoe considered calling the hospital, then decided just to get dressed and go anyway.

At least in daylight Ash Ring held no threatening presence. The eerie sensation of the night before had been dissipated by sleep or sunlight. Now the house just seemed empty.

The journey into Norwich was frustratingly slow this time,

as Zoe got caught up in the morning rush, and when she reached the hospital, she had difficulty finding a parking space. When she finally got inside, she was irritated as well as anxious. However, the calm courtesy of the staff helped her regain her composure before she went to Michael's room. There were two nurses inside now, and Zoe had seen neither of them before. They were bathing their patient, and both looked up enquiringly.

'Can I come in?' Zoe asked. 'I'm Michael's wife.' She was staring at him, hoping to see some welcome sign.

'Of course,' the older nurse replied. 'We've nearly finished here.'

'Has there been any change?'

'Not yet,' the same nurse answered. She was clearly the senior of the two and as she finished drying Michael's arms and face, she nodded to the other. Together they laid him back carefully onto his pillows. 'Can you finish off here, Nurse?'

'Yes, Sister.'

'Please excuse me, Mrs Glover. I have other duties to attend to.'

'Of course,' Zoe replied, feeling a little intimidated.

'Nurse Fairfax will be able to answer any questions you may have,' the sister added, then briskly left the room.

'Call me Amy,' the nurse said, as she held Michael's wrist, taking his pulse. 'I'm not as formal as Sister.' She glanced at Zoe with a friendly smile. 'We'll be seeing a fair bit of each other until Michael wakes up, I expect. What do I call you?'

'Zoe. Are you sure there's been no change at all?'

'Quite sure, but everything is still stable. The consultant saw your husband on his early rounds this morning, and he was quite satisfied.' Amy turned to look at Zoe, having taken Michael's temperature. 'I'm sure he'll be all right. It's just a matter of time. But that doesn't stop you worrying, does it?' she added sympathetically.

'No. It's all been a bit of a shock.' That, Zoe thought, was the understatement of all time. *We need you to be brave.*

The nurse moved away and let Zoe take her place at the bedside, but did not leave the room immediately. Zoe took Michael's hand and drew a deep breath.

'Hello, sweetheart. It's me again. What shall we talk about today?'

That evening Zoe spoke again with Dr Black. He seemed to retain his positive attitude even when they were not in Michael's room, but that did little to alleviate Zoe's despondency after a day in which Michael had made no progress.

'Was I expecting miracles?' she asked. 'Was there ever a chance that he'd wake up today?'

'While his condition remains as it is,' the doctor replied, 'it could happen at any time.'

*Then why didn't it?* Zoe wondered desperately, but said nothing, allowing him to continue. He seemed anxious to reassure her.

'Michael's clinical condition is good, all things considered,' he said. 'The blow that caused his unconsciousness was serious but, as I told you, there's no fracture of the skull. With a coma this deep, you'd normally expect internal damage, a blood clot, but the CT scan was clear. That's good, and since he was admitted there have been none of the signs which might indicate a decline that would necessitate surgery. His breathing and pulse have remained steady. If they'd slowed, it would have been a cause for concern. His blood pressure hasn't gone up and the dilation of his pupils is no greater. So, all in all, there's no sign of an increase in pressure inside his head.'

'And that's good?'

'Yes.'

'Then he will recover?'

'I can't promise you that, but there's an excellent chance that he will.'

'Thank you, Doctor,' Zoe said, wishing he could have given her the answer that would have dulled the ache in her heart.

\*   \*   \*

Over the next few days Michael's condition did not change at all, either for better or worse. Zoe spent almost all her waking hours at the hospital, shuttling between there and Thornmere. She hardly bothered to eat or sleep, grabbing any easily available food when she could, and forcing herself to rest when she was at home. Even then she sometimes found it impossible to relax, always expecting – half in hope and half in dread – that the telephone would ring, and she invented tasks to occupy her mind until sheer fatigue drove her to bed.

When she was with Michael she remained resolutely cheerful and positive, surprising herself with a resilience that allowed her to collapse only when she was alone. Then she was close to despair, a despair that was mixed with undirected anger and misery. In the loneliest hours, she found it hard to accept that, just when she had thought her problems were over at last, new and worse ones had arrived. Her only option was to trust the doctors when they said that there was still every reason to hope for the best – although she could see, as time went on and the days dragged by, that they were becoming slightly more worried. Her only contribution – and one which both doctors and nurses approved of wholeheartedly – was to be there for Michael. She talked to him for hours, hoping in vain for some response, however minute; the twitch of an eyelid or a finger, a small change in the regular pattern of his breathing. And later, when her vocal chords protested at the unaccustomed exercise, she took to bringing in a cassette player with tapes of Michael's favourite pieces of music. When she was restless at home, she even recorded her own voice, reading from books or magazines, and left the tapes in the nurses' charge for him to listen to when she wasn't there. Dr Black encouraged her whenever they met, citing the evidence that, paradoxically, a lot of stimuli seemed to be beneficial to someone in Michael's unresponsive state. *His subconscious is still working.* But all Zoe's efforts went unrewarded. If Michael's subconscious *was* somehow reacting, his responses were undetectable, and she began to sink into periods of bleak depression which made her daily performances harder and harder. She refused to give up hope, however, and found reserves of strength and willpower she had never dreamt she possessed. Privately she was near breaking point, but at the hospital her brave face never faltered.

During those days, Zoe learnt a little of the medical procedures, with the help of Dr Black, Claire and Amy, and gained an enormous respect for their dedication and patience. Her only concern was for Michael; they had a whole hospital full of people who depended on them at all times of the day and night.

Michael's needs were many, because he could do nothing for himself. Many of the medical staff's duties were unpleasant, but they were accepted cheerfully as natural and necessary. Zoe watched the nurses in action, learning from them and eventually offering to help. When she proved competent, they humoured her by letting her take some of the readings – although Zoe noticed that they always checked her results.

There seemed to be so much to do. The tube had long since been removed from Michael's throat but, on every visit, the nurses checked his breathing both visually and by listening to make sure that the passage of air was quiet and unobstructed. Zoe sometimes wondered why they bothered. She had become so attuned to the tiny sounds and movements of her husband's respiration that she would have noticed even the most minuscule variation instantly – even when she was talking or while music was playing quietly.

After the first two days, the intravenous drip was also removed and Michael was fed through an oesophageal tube. Zoe watched both doctors and nurses confirm that its lower end was in his stomach, either by testing samples of gastric juices or by listening for bubbling with a stethoscope while air was injected. The process made her feel quite sick at first, as did the look and consistency of his 'meals', but after a while it became just one more routine aspect of her days. Meticulous records were kept of Michael's fluid intake, his urine and other waste. His skinfold thickness was measured daily, and he was weighed every other day. Dr Black told her that all this was to ensure against both constipation and diarrhoea, as well as maintaining Michael's weight and hydration levels.

His position in the bed was changed, as far as possible, every two hours, to prevent pressure sores and reduce muscle wastage.

'Positioning is important,' Claire explained. 'All the joints have to be put through a full range of passive movement two or three times a day.'

Michael's fractured hip obviously hampered these manoeuvres considerably, but the nurses did as much as they could. Zoe noticed that this was always done before feeding and guessed, correctly, that this was to avoid agitating the digestion process. Eventually a specialist physiotherapist was also called in to work on Michael's chest, to make sure that no fluid built up in his lungs.

In addition the nurses bathed his eyes every few hours.

'Half-strength saline solution,' Amy said, sounding like a training manual. 'There's no corneal reflex, that's why we keep his eyes shut. They'd dry out otherwise. But they still need washing every so often.'

This was the one process Zoe never got used to. The sight of those dead, lost eyes was as unsettling as it had been the first time, and she usually made a point of looking away, in case she betrayed her unease. *We must act as if he can see and hear us.*

Cleanliness was obviously of great importance, and Michael's eyes were not the only part of him to receive regular attention. The nurses gave him a daily, full body sponge bath and washed his hands and face more frequently. They shaved him, attended to his hair and nails when necessary and even brushed his teeth. At first Zoe saw all these procedures as embarrassing, humiliating for a grown man to be so helpless, but she soon came to see them – as the nurses did – as simple necessities, tasks to be completed expertly, with compassion, gentleness and the minimum of fuss. All the nurses, Claire and Amy especially, made a great impression on Zoe. Michael was only one of thousands of patients they had dealt with, yet they gave him all the care she could have wished for. He was obviously not aware of any possible dangers; he had no sensations, could not tell them if something would normally have caused him pain or done some unnoticed damage, so everything was carried out in a protective manner. Zoe's admiration continued to grow, especially when she thought of the long hours they all seemed to work.

One evening, after Michael had been in the hospital for a week, the doctor asked Zoe to come to his office, and she was immediately filled with fear. What was it that he needed to say in private?

'Michael's condition hasn't changed at all,' he began.

'Is that bad?' Zoe interrupted quickly.

'Neither bad nor good,' he replied evenly. 'But it is puzzling. I had hoped to see some improvement by now, but at least there's no sign of him going the other way.' He paused, watching her carefully.

'You're not telling me everything, are you?' Zoe said.

'I'm trying to, but I don't *know* everything.' He appeared genuinely perplexed. 'I'll be honest with you, Zoe. I've never come across a case like this. From the results of all our observations, all our tests, Michael shouldn't even be in a coma now. His injuries don't warrant it. We can't find anything wrong with him that we can fix.'

Zoe remained silent, trying to work out the implications of what she was being told.

'Which leaves us with two possibilities,' Dr Black went on. 'One is that there's something wrong that we haven't found yet, something that's not serious enough to lead to any worsening of his condition but is somehow preventing his recovery. We'll keep looking, but as yet I can't imagine what it might be.'

There was a long pause.

'And the other possibility?' Zoe asked eventually.

'That it's nothing physical at all,' he replied. 'That it's his *mind* that's refusing to wake up.'

'He doesn't *want* to wake up?' she exploded. 'Are you mad?'

'There's a lot we don't understand about the workings of

the human mind,' he told her. 'We'll do everything we can for him, but *you* may be the best chance we have to get through to him.'

'What more can I do?' she wailed.

'Nothing,' he replied promptly. 'You've been magnificent. In a way, that's what worries me the most.'

'What?' Zoe said, not understanding.

'There's still every reason to believe Michael will recover, but it looks as though we may be in for a long haul, Zoe. Are you up to that?'

'Me?' She was surprised.

'You've been here more hours than I have this last week,' he pointed out. 'What you're doing is admirable and I'd be the last one to want you to stop, but you're not doing yourself any good.'

'And I thought I was hiding it so well,' she replied wearily, mocking herself.

'I'm a doctor,' he said, smiling. 'You can't hide things from me. You're overtired physically and emotionally. I think you should be a little easier on yourself. Get more rest. Eat properly.'

'I haven't been sleeping much,' Zoe admitted.

'Why don't you see your own doctor,' he suggested. 'Perhaps he could help.'

'Sleeping pills? No thanks.'

'There are alternatives. What about relaxation techniques? There are therapists—'

'I know,' she cut in. 'I'll be all right.'

'And what about the rest of your life?' he asked.

'Michael is my life.'

'You're a writer,' he went on. 'What about your work?'

Zoe was momentarily taken aback. She had completely forgotten about her book. The impending deadline now seemed totally unimportant – but she supposed she ought at least to let someone know that there would be a delay.

'I do have a book to finish,' she confessed with a shrug, 'but it can wait.' She was more certain of that than ever now.

'Maybe it shouldn't,' he responded. 'It could be just the therapy you need. Take you out of yourself.'

'To the other lands,' Zoe whispered to herself.

'Pardon?'

'It doesn't matter. I don't think I could write now even if I tried, but I'll talk to my agent, put my affairs straight.'

'It's a start,' he conceded with a grin. 'And think about seeing your G.P.'

'Or a psychiatrist?'

'You seem to be in control of your mental faculties, Mrs Glover,' he replied with mock formality, then added seriously, 'but some counselling might help if this goes on much longer.'

'I'll let you know.'

'Do that.'

That evening Zoe went home earlier than usual, forcing herself to leave, and rang Alex to tell her about Michael. Her agent's reaction was immediately sympathetic.

'My God. You poor thing. Do you want me to come up?'

'No. I'm OK.' Zoe was touched by the offer. 'But I'm not doing much work at the moment.'

'Of course not,' Alex exclaimed. 'I'll ring your editor and explain. There's no way they can expect you to stick to the deadline.'

'I was hoping you'd say that.'

'Leave it to me,' her agent stated firmly. 'I just wish there was something more I could do.'

'Don't tell anyone else about this, please,' Zoe went on. 'I'm not up to dealing with mass pity.'

'All right,' Alex agreed. 'But don't shut yourself away. I'm your friend as well as your agent, and there are others like me who'd jump at the chance of helping you if you need it.'

'I'll remember that,' Zoe said gratefully. 'You'd be surprised how much just talking to you has helped already.'

'Call me any time, Zoe. The office'll know where to reach me if I'm out.'

'Thanks, Alex.'

That night, Zoe slept for longer and more deeply than she

had done at any time since the accident, and in the morning she deliberately made herself eat a large healthy breakfast of cereal, toast and fruit while she skimmed through her long-neglected mail. Then she cleared up the debris in the kitchen, put the dishwasher on and went out to the car – with a small, unreasoning hope inside her. *Something is going to happen today*, she told herself optimistically.

As she was fastening her seat belt, Zoe could not remember whether the answering machine was still on. She had been in the habit of leaving it on permanently while she was out so much, but was not sure after the call to Alex the evening before. She got out of the car and went back inside to check. The machine was on – and the indicator showed one. Puzzled, Zoe pushed the replay button. She was sure there had not been any messages last night. Could she really have slept through the telephone ringing?

The tape began to play, and as she listened to the soft, rasping voice, her heart began to turn somersaults.

'Zoe? It's me. Can you hear me?'

That was all, but the sudden rush of joy that flooded through her was intoxicating. It was Michael! He sounded understandably tired and unsure, but it was unmistakably his voice.

Zoe ran out to the car and set off. Every nerve in her body was singing. Every second before she reached him was agony, but she steeled herself to drive safely. Parking crookedly, she ran into the building, her coat flying, and rushed to Michael's room. When she burst in, Amy was at the bedside filling in a chart. The nurse looked startled by the sudden arrival.

'Michael!' Zoe cried.

He did not react, but lay as still as ever.

'Zoe? Are you all right?' Amy asked.

Zoe glanced at her, wild-eyed, her happiness evaporating.

'He can't have had a relapse!' she pleaded. 'He *can't*!'

'No,' the nurse replied, looking bewildered. 'He's still the same.'

'But he phoned me,' Zoe protested desperately. 'He left a message.'

62

The nurse came over and took her hand gently.

'Michael's still in the same coma, Zoe,' she told her softly. 'He hasn't moved at all. There's no way he could have phoned anybody.'

# 8

'Nick, this is Laura. Listen, I know you're not due in till this afternoon, but Mrs Glover's here, and she's very distressed about her husband. I think it would help—'

The doctor's words were cut off as the person on the other end of the telephone line interrupted. A few seconds later she spoke again.

'Yes.' Another pause. 'OK. Thanks.' She put the telephone down and looked at Zoe. 'He'll be here in about fifteen minutes. He lives quite close.'

Zoe nodded, although the words had not really registered. They were sitting in Dr Black's empty office. A cup of tea, the universal panacea, sat untouched on the desk in front of her.

The shaking had stopped now, but she felt almost hysterical, and the desire to scream was still there – even though she had actually been unable to utter a single word. Her thoughts swirled in an endless circle of denial. Even the coaxing of Amy and Dr Ryan – Laura – had not enabled her to explain. Zoe felt cold and sick. What was happening to her? It was impossible. The whole thing was impossible! She had heard him. She had! And yet . . .

'Is there anything else I can get you, Mrs Glover?' Laura asked. 'Until Dr Black arrives?'

Zoe shook her head, still unable to speak. *Did I imagine it? Am I going mad?*

'Mrs Glover?' There was rising concern in the doctor's voice.

Zoe realised that she was still shaking her head, answering

her own internal questions, the repetitive movement un-noticed and obsessive. If she carried on like this they would think she really was cracking up. She deliberately steadied herself, and looked up.

'I'll be all right,' she whispered.

'Good. Dr Black will be here soon,' Laura repeated.

Zoe waited in silence, forcing herself to remain calm. Dr Black arrived after what seemed like only a few moments, and his colleague left after a brief explanation. He knelt in front of Zoe's chair.

'You don't seem to be taking my advice very seriously,' he said gently.

'I did,' Zoe replied feebly. 'I tried, but then . . .'

'Then what?'

She told him about the message and the incredible wave of despair that had swept over her when she reached the hospital. Her words came out in great gulps as she fought to control herself. Dr Black listened gravely, and did not interrupt until it was clear that she had finished.

'I tell you what,' he said then. 'I think I'd like to hear this message. Have you still got the tape?'

'It's in the machine. At home.'

'Let's go then,' he said. 'I'll drive.'

'But . . .' Zoe was surprised. 'Michael . . .'

'He's in good hands,' the doctor told her. 'You wouldn't do him much good in this state anyway. And I've got to be back here by noon, so you'll have the rest of the day to be with him. OK?'

Zoe nodded, grateful that someone was taking charge, telling her what to do. When Dr Black heard the message, they'd all know that she had good reason to be upset. But then he had never heard Michael speak, so how would he recognise his voice? Zoe kept her doubts to herself. During the journey, her companion spoke of inconsequential matters – the weather, the countryside – pausing occasionally to ask directions. At one point he told her that his friends called him Nick, with the clear implication that he would like her to do the same.

Zoe found it odd to be arriving at Ash Ring in a strange car with another man, and then, suddenly, she found herself laughing nervously.

'What is it?' he asked, his smile not entirely hiding the anxiety beneath.

'I was just thinking,' Zoe replied self-consciously, 'that if anyone sees us, there'll be a few rumours flying around Thornmere by the end of the day.'

Dr Black laughed.

'Your reputation is safe with me, madam,' he assured her. 'But I know what village gossip can be like.'

Their mood changed as they entered the cottage. Zoe was suddenly incredibly tense, and Nick grew serious again as he followed her into the sitting room.

The answering machine's indicator showed one, and Zoe's heart sank. That was wrong – it should have reset itself to zero. Had she pressed the 'Save' button? Her pulse racing, she stabbed 'Play'. There was an agonising wait while the tape rewound and then the replay began.

'Hello, Zoe. This is Alex. Just calling to say . . .'

'Oh, no. Oh, God. Oh, *shit*!' Zoe breathed, as the message that had obliterated Michael's brief words went on unheard.

The tape ended, beeped and reset itself. Nick looked at her questioningly.

'It's gone,' she said miserably. 'That message has taped over the top.'

The doctor nodded, his expression grave.

'But it was him!' Zoe exclaimed. 'It *was* Michael.' After a pause, she added, 'You do believe me, don't you?'

'I believe you heard something you thought was Michael,' he began.

'It *was* him!' she shouted. 'It *was*!' She was crying now, from a mixture of unhappiness and sheer frustration.

Nick guided her to the settee and sat beside her.

'You've been under a lot of stress, Zoe,' he began gently. 'That's bound to have taken its toll, especially when you're so tired. Emotions build up—'

'You think I'm mad, don't you?' she interrupted. 'That I

66

made this up?' Abruptly his concern for her seemed to have taken on a sinister aspect.

'No, of course not. But—'

'But what? I'm hysterical, overwrought? What?' Zoe was aware even as she spoke that turning her anger and despair on him was unfair, but she could not help herself.

'Overtired and under strain,' he replied calmly. 'Anyone would be in your situation. I think you need help, Zoe, more than I can give. I know several therapists. I can give you some names and numbers.'

He paused, trying to gauge her response, and suddenly Zoe lost all strength and even the desire to argue. It was easier to just accept his advice, to take the piece of paper he was writing on and give in without further protest. She could not blame him for not believing her story. Without proof, the whole thing sounded absurd. But inside she was sure, she *knew*, that she had not been mistaken. It *had* been Michael's voice on the tape. And yet, what possible explanation could there be?

'Come on,' Dr Black said. 'I'll take you back to the hospital. But you must look after yourself, Zoe. Michael would want that, wouldn't he?'

She nodded and obediently followed him out to his car, remembering to lock the door behind her. They were silent for most of the journey back to Norwich but, as they approached the outskirts of the city, his voice drew Zoe out of her hopelessly introverted thoughts.

'Is Alex your agent?'

'Yes.'

'Do you remember what she said?'

'Not a word,' she admitted. That had been the last thing on her mind.

'The gist of it was that she'd spoken to your editor and it was all fixed,' he told her. 'She said you're not to worry, and she wants you to phone her at home this evening if you have time.'

Zoe nodded absently. It seemed such an inconsequential message to have had such a devastating effect.

'Is she a good friend?'

'Yes.' Zoe wondered where this was leading.

'Would she be able to come and stay with you for a while?' Nick asked. 'Or do you have some family nearby that you could talk to?'

'I can manage on my own,' she said defensively.

'OK,' he said, trying not to push too hard. 'But you must take better care of yourself. Do you want me to have a word with your G.P.?'

At this, something snapped inside her.

'Just shut up, will you!' she cried. 'Michael's the one you should be worrying about. Leave me alone!'

A few moments passed in silence. Zoe was horrified by her outburst, by her unjustifiable harshness.

'I'm sorry,' she said eventually. 'You didn't deserve that. I know you're only trying to help.'

'It doesn't matter,' he replied, a little stiffly.

When they got back to the hospital, Michael's condition was exactly the same. Nothing had changed. Dr Black and the nurses were at first reluctant to leave Zoe alone with her husband, but the necessities of their other duties and her insistence that she was all right eventually persuaded them. Even then, it was a long time before Zoe could bring herself to speak. She leant over his still face, his eyes mercifully closed as usual, and whispered.

'Michael, it's me, Zoe. I *did* hear you. I *did*!'

That evening, much to the doctor's approval, Zoe went home earlier than usual. But it was not because she was concerned with her own welfare. There were things she wanted to do. First she checked the answering machine in case there were any more messages, mysterious or otherwise; then she worked out how to play all of the tape, on both sides, to listen to the old communications that had not been recorded over, but – as she had expected – she heard nothing of interest. After that she rang a few friends in the vain hope that they might have left a message the night before, one which she could have mistaken for Michael, but that bore no fruit either. She even called British Telecom to see whether there might be any faults on the line – there were not – and to ask whether it would be possible to trace the call from the previous night. She was told that incoming calls were impossible to trace without prior notification – and that this was further complicated by the fact that Thornmere was still on one of the old-fashioned exchanges.

By that time, Zoe had run out of ideas, and she called Alex. Her agent's phone rang several times before she answered.

'Hello, Alex. It's Zoe. I didn't wake you up, did I?'

'Of course not. How's Michael?'

'No change.'

'I'm sorry. It'll happen soon, I'm sure. Are *you* OK?'

'Don't you start,' Zoe said wearily, then explained the doctor's concerns.

'He's right,' Alex responded predictably. 'You know that, don't you?'

'I know.'

'Then make sure you take his advice. Did you get my message?'

'Yes,' Zoe answered heavily.

'Diana's fine about the delay,' her agent went on. 'The pub date may have to go back, but we'll cross that bridge when we come to it. And she's promised to be discreet. But you know what this trade is like for gossip.' She paused. 'Even so, there's no reason why Thomas should get to hear of it.'

As usual, Alex's perspicacity was remarkable. Zoe had not even realised herself that she had been worried about this. But she had no time to think about that now.

'Alex?'

'Yes?'

'Oh, nothing. It doesn't matter.' She had been going to tell her about Michael's message, but found that she could not. The whole episode had begun to seem ludicrous even to her.

'Are you sure you're all right?' Alex asked.

'I'm a bit of a mess,' Zoe admitted reluctantly.

'I can be there tomorrow morning,' her agent offered.

'No. You needn't . . .'

'Then why don't you at least go to see that hypnotherapist of yours? What was his name?'

'Owen.'

'That's right. You sang his praises to me a few months back. Couldn't he help you now?'

'Maybe.' Owen Pemberton had helped Zoe a great deal as she struggled through the psychological morass surrounding her divorce, and the idea of going to him now was certainly appealing. The least he could do was help her relax. That was something she needed very badly.

'Ring him now,' Alex persisted. 'As soon as we put the phone down.'

'I can't,' Zoe objected. 'It's too late.'

'All right. Tomorrow then. Promise me.'

'I promise.'

'Good girl. Is there *anything* I can do?'

'Just be there.'

'Always,' Alex replied. 'Give my love to Michael when you see him.'

'I will,' Zoe managed to say as she fought back the tears. 'Bye.'

'Bye.'

Zoe sat quietly for a while after she had put the phone down. The only sounds came from the wuthering of the wind and the small creakings of the house itself. At last she went upstairs, got ready for bed, collected a duvet and a pillow and came downstairs again. Tonight she would sleep – if she managed to sleep at all – on the sofa, next to the telephone. She was determined that if any other messages arrived she would be on hand to intercept them.

In that assumption, as with so many others recently, she was completely wrong.

# 9

The man on the white horse was back. Curiously, even as she felt her fear and revulsion rise, Zoe knew that she was dreaming. The rider was too far away for her to see his face but she knew, with sickening certainty, that he was heading for the cottage. Except that in the dream, the cottage was different – no longer a simple country dwelling but one wing of a vast, sprawling mansion. The room in which she stood was on the second floor, and the leaded bay window looked out over a wide field of grass. In the centre of the pasture stood a small circular copse of trees with light grey bark and straggly, widely spaced branches. The leaves were beginning to fall even though they were still green.

With a lurch the scene shifted. Zoe was in a dark, ground floor room now and the man was there too, his back to her. From outside came the sound of unseen hooves on the stone pavement. The man snapped his fingers and oil lamps flared into life of their own accord, something which surprised neither of them. His heavy riding clothes were speckled with raindrops, iridescent in the new light.

An invisible third person spoke then, startling Zoe.

'He's alive. But he took a heavy blow to his head, and he's deeply unconscious.'

*Shut up!* Zoe urged desperately. *Shut up!* But it was too late. The man with her had heard, and the sudden, angry set of his broad shoulders made her tremble. Then he began to laugh, a cruel, mirthless sound, shaking rainbow drops from his jacket. As he turned round, Zoe was mesmerised, trembling, as she waited to see his face – but then the dream slipped away.

She awoke with only a premonition of those dreadful eyes. Although she had not seen his face, her mind had superimposed Thomas's features. Then the last remnants of the dream vanished and, as usual, her waking thoughts fled to Michael.

Then the pain registered. Zoe had a splitting headache, and her neck was stiff from lying awkwardly on the sofa, so she sat up very gingerly. The day outside was grey as the sun fought its way through thick mist, and she wondered how long she had been asleep. She was still half possessed by the dream's atmosphere of menace, and she groaned aloud. How was it possible to sleep for so long and yet feel she had had so little rest? At least this time she could be sure that the phone had not rung. In her almost feverish state she could not possibly have slept through its strident tone. But, just in case, she glanced at the answering machine – and her heart pounded when she saw that the indicator light showed one.

The steady, impassive glow of the orange light mocked Zoe's efforts to clear her head. *One.* How could that have happened?

Her hand shook as she reached out and, with the exaggerated care of a drunk, pushed the 'Play' button. She held her breath as the tape rewound, not knowing what to expect, or even what to hope for. Hearing Michael's voice again was like a physical blow and she doubled up in pain, fighting to accept the evidence of her own ears, to believe it was real.

'Zoe, where are you? Why don't you come?' He sounded frightened and alone, his whispered words full of a misery that made her heart ache. 'I couldn't see the horse, Zoe. It was too dark. I could hear it but I couldn't . . .' He broke off awkwardly. 'Where are you, Zoe?'

And there, on that forlorn and dejected note, it ended.

Zoe was paralysed, torn between hope and dread. She desperately wanted to believe that the message was genuine, that Michael had woken up and was calling her to him. But after her last shattering disappointment, and with the strangeness of his tone – as well as his odd words about the horse – she could not bring herself to accept anything at face value. And that left only two alternatives. Either someone was playing the most unimaginably cruel trick – or she was going insane.

Zoe picked up the phone and dialled the hospital – a number she knew by heart now. Her fingers trembled so much that she was afraid she would get a wrong number, but the switchboard answered promptly. Zoe explained who she was and asked whether there had been any change in her husband's condition. She suffered the agonising wait in silence, praying for good news, her nerves jangling. Then came a click as the call was transferred and another voice answered.

'Zoe, this is Claire. Michael's exactly the same. There's been no change, I'm afraid.'

'Oh God,' Zoe whispered, closing her eyes.

'Are you all right? Zoe?'

She eventually found the strength to reply.

'I'm OK. I'll be in later. Bye.'

Zoe put the phone down and tried to remember how to breathe. *Now what do I do?* What was happening was impossible – on several counts – and yet she knew she was not deluding herself. It *was* Michael's voice, but how had it got there? He was still in a coma and the phone had not rung. Could the machine be malfunctioning? No, that was ridiculous. She was clutching at straws, and she knew it. Had she truly imagined it all? Were the messages some kind of internal make believe that only seemed real to her because she so wanted Michael to talk to her?

She replayed the message to prove its existence, and in the hope of finding some clue in the rasping words. It was still as agonisingly desolate as before, and it still made no sense – but it *was* there. Zoe hugged that fact to herself. She had hard evidence now, something to share with a witness – and to that end, she went to remove the cassette, to ensure that it would not be recorded over as the other message had been. Then the thought struck her that if further messages were to arrive, there would be nowhere to record them. And if – somehow – they were coming from Michael, she could not take that chance. After a moment's hesitation, Zoe closed the machine again, made sure that it was set up to save the message, and decided to buy a second tape at the earliest opportunity.

All of which left her with her original, insoluble problem. *What do I do now?* One thing was certain; she needed help.

Picking up the phone again, she dialled Dr Black's home number. After four rings, there was a click and the mechanical voice of a recording.

'You are through to Dr Nicholas Black. I'm sorry that I'm not available to take your call at the moment, but if you'd like—'

The message cut off as Zoe slammed the phone down, not knowing whether to laugh or cry.

For a long time, she sat staring at the phone, shivering and fighting back tears. She could remember every word, each inflection and hesitation with agonising clarity, but she made herself play the message over again several times, torturing herself. *I couldn't see the horse.* The macabre parallel with her own dream was obvious, but that could be no more than coincidence. *It was too dark.* The phrase haunted her. Where was Michael now if not in some foreign darkness? But it was the direct appeals to her – *Zoe, where are you? Why don't you come?* – that really tore at her heart.

*I've been by your side as much as I can,* she defended herself silently. *What more am I supposed to do?*

That thought finally brought her out of her stupor and made her pull herself together. Self-pity would get her nowhere. She knew she would have to go to the hospital to check on Michael for herself but, before she set off, there was one last possibility that she could explore. She dialled Owen's number nervously, imploring him to be in. She could not bear to be faced with the disappointment of no reply or, worse still, another answering machine. Much to her relief, the call was answered almost immediately.

'Owen Pemberton.'

'Hello, Owen. It's Zoe March.'

'Hello, Zoe.' The immediate warmth in his voice made her feel a little better. 'How are you?'

'I'm not too good at the moment,' she told him. 'Can I see you?'

'Of course. What's the matter?'

Briefly, Zoe explained about Michael's injury and her own deteriorating physical and mental state, though she did not tell him about the mysterious telephone messages. Somehow she could not bring herself to speak of those until they were face to face. Even so, Owen's concern over and sympathy for her predicament was clear. She had no need to stress the urgency of her request.

'Do you want me to come to the cottage?'

'Yes, please.'

'When?'

'Today?' she suggested hopefully.

'I can't, Zoe, I'm sorry. I've got consultations all day. You were lucky to catch me. And I'm giving a lecture in Cambridge this evening. I'd cancel if I could, but—'

'Tomorrow?'

'Yes, but it'll have to be early.'

'The earlier the better,' she said gratefully.

'Does nine a.m. suit you?'

'Fine. Do you remember the way?'

'To Ash Ring? Yes, no problem.'

'See you tomorrow then.'

'Look after yourself, Zoe. Bye.'

'Bye.' She just managed to replace the receiver before she started crying. At least now she had one ally in this nightmare.

After a while she calmed down, making herself breathe deeply and deliberately, and went upstairs to get dressed. Then, after double-checking the answering machine again and taking some aspirin, she set out for Norwich. Her sore neck made driving difficult at times, but the discomfort actually helped her concentration, making sure her mind did not wander.

Michael was exactly the same, just as Claire had said, and the sight of his expressionless face made Zoe want to cry again, but she steeled herself, and spoke cheerfully.

'Hello, Michael, it's Zoe. I'm here. I've come.' She held his lifeless hand and smiled as best she could. 'I'm *here*, sweetheart. You understand that, don't you? Can you hear me? There's so much I wish I could tell you.'

Later, when Claire came in, Zoe asked her about the previous night, whether there could have been anything odd, even the slightest alteration in her husband's patterns of existence. The nurse was puzzled by her insistence and obviously curious, but humoured Zoe without prying. After examining all the available records, they could find absolutely nothing out of the ordinary – or what passed for ordinary for Michael now.

'Are there any phones near here?' Zoe asked, without thinking.

'There are payphones in the reception area,' Claire replied.

'Any others? Closer?' Zoe went on, ignoring the odd look the nurse was giving her.

'Quite a few . . . in the offices. A lot of the private rooms have them too. There's a socket for one in here. Do you need one installed?' Claire looked worried.

'No. It doesn't matter.'

Around noon, when Zoe had become too exhausted and confused to talk or even think, she sat quietly at the bedside while a music tape played softly. The door opened and Dr Laura Ryan came in.

'Hello, Mrs Glover.'

'Hello, Doctor,' Zoe said wearily.

After a routine examination of the patient, Laura turned to Zoe.

'How are you today?'

Zoe groaned inwardly at the prospect of an interrogation – however kindly – and did her best to answer brightly.

'I'm fine. All I want is for Michael to wake up.'

'That's what we all want.' There was an awkward pause before the doctor continued. 'Claire tells me you were asking about telephones . . .' She left the sentence hanging in the air, and eventually Zoe felt forced to respond.

'I was just wondering . . .' she began hesitantly, looking down at the floor.

'About the message from Michael?' Laura prompted gently. 'Nick, Dr Black, told me you weren't able to find it.'

Zoe nodded bleakly.

'I must have been mistaken,' she said, too tired to argue. 'Will Dr Black be here later?'

'Not today, or tomorrow. He's at a conference in London.'

'Oh.' Was that one ally less? Zoe was not sure.

'Can I do anything for you?' Dr Ryan asked.

'No. Thank you.'

When Zoe was alone again, she turned to Michael and whispered intently.

'I didn't mean it. I *did* hear you. But they might not understand. Not yet.'

When Zoe got home, after a wearying journey made worse by patches of fog, Ash Ring seemed to be sunk in a well of darkness. None of the distant street lamps, still less the moonlight or the stars, could penetrate the enveloping gloom. Zoe left the car lights on so that she could see to reach the front door and find the lock but, as soon as she entered the house, the air struck her as even blacker and more chill than the night outside. The unnerving male presence had returned, its insubstantial invasion made even more baleful by her vulnerable loneliness.

Switching lights on as she went, Zoe moved through the whole house. She checked the answering machine straight away, but it still stood at one – the earlier message that she had made sure of saving. Each room was exactly as she had left it, empty and quiet. Finally she came to her study and, as she opened the door, the air felt cool, making her think she must have left a window open. But when she snapped on the light, although it was clear that the windows were shut, all thought of them flew from her mind.

Her manuscript was strewn all over the room, flung in

riotous confusion over the desk and floor. And, as she stared in stupefied horror, another page flipped up into the air of its own accord and floated gently down to land on the carpet.

# 10

Zoe stood rooted to the spot. The last page settled and the air became perfectly still. Outside, in the darkness, the wind began to moan and whisper, but inside all was quiet. For the first time in her life, Zoe understood how the phrase to have one's skin crawl originated. She felt as though her hair was standing on end, just as Stripe's did when she sensed another cat in her territory. And, surprisingly, it was this incongruous image that triggered Zoe's eventual response. When she had first seen the horrifying shambles to which her work had been reduced, her fear had been instinctive. There was no logical explanation for what had happened and that, combined with her unease engendered by the unknown presence, was enough to temporarily paralyse her thoughts. Yet the two must surely be connected and, as the shock subsided, a second emotion welled up in Zoe. Her fear did not vanish but was overridden by a surge of something even more powerful; anger.

'Get out,' she whispered vehemently. Then, surprising herself with the force of her rage, she screamed, 'Get out!' She put every ounce of resentment and outrage into those two words. Her home had been invaded, her sanctuary defiled and, although she had no idea how or why or by whom, she would not stand for it.

Stepping forward into the room, Zoe looked around but there was nothing, no one to see. It was only then that she realised she had won; the malevolent presence had disappeared entirely. Zoe was now the sole occupant –

79

corporeal or otherwise – of the house. A wave of relief flooded through her and she felt suddenly weak.

Moving round the room slowly, she gathered up the scattered sheets of paper and set them in a neat pile on her desk. She did not bother trying to sort them into any order – that could wait for another day – but she could not bear to leave them strewn about.

Then she ran herself a hot bath and lay soaking in it for a while, trying to relax. She was very quiet, alone with her thoughts and listening for the slightest noise, until she suddenly laughed aloud. She had just remembered a similar scene in the film *Poltergeist*, when a calm, idyllic moment was stretched until it became almost unbearable because the viewer *knew* that something indescribably awful was about to happen – and could do so at any moment. However, if Ash Ring was built on an ancient burial site, the dead continued to sleep soundly as Zoe made herself ready for bed.

After a protracted internal debate, she decided to sleep on the settee once more – in spite of the discomfort – because she could not face the thought of missing any possible message. In the event, her night was disturbed by no more than meaningless, fragmentary dreams, and she woke at daybreak. The answering machine still showed one, and Zoe replayed the message for the umpteenth time, just to convince herself that it was still there.

Further sleep was clearly impossible now, so she got dressed slowly and took a mug of coffee upstairs. There was still some time before Owen was due, and she decided to distract herself by re-collating her typescript. Her study was its usual airy self and, although the atmosphere was not helped by the dull light of a leaden sky, there was no suggestion of the malicious visitation of the previous night.

Zoe concentrated on the mechanical task, trying not to think too much and wishing that Owen would come. His visit had assumed great importance, not because she believed he could explain all the terrible events that were surrounding her, but because he would understand – or so she hoped – what she was going through, and would be able to help her cope. She desperately needed one reliable ally.

Zoe was also not used to anything delaying her daily trip to the hospital. Her longing for Michael was as strong as ever and, even though her rational mind knew that someone would have phoned had there been any change, she could not help but hope – as always – that she would arrive to find him awake. Several times she almost went downstairs to call the hospital, but resolutely stuck to what she was doing. Lost in her task, she jumped when, at last, the door-bell rang.

Owen Pemberton was just as she remembered him. He always gave the impression of being dapper, in spite of his habitually casual dress, and the ready smile on his boyish features made him look younger than his thirty-something years. He had neatly trimmed brown hair and intense dark eyes.

'Hi.'

'Hi. Come on in. Thanks for seeing me at such short notice.'

'It's a pleasure. How's Michael?'

'No change.' She led him into the sitting room, where she automatically checked the answering machine. It still showed one.

'I'm sorry,' Owen said. 'I'll do whatever I can to help.'

'Thank you. I know how good you are at helping me relax – and I need that very much at the moment.' Zoe hesitated.

'But?' he prompted.

'There's more to this than Michael's accident. Either I'm going mad, or . . .' Zoe took a deep breath and then told him about the messages. 'I've lost the first one, but the second is still here on the tape,' she concluded.

Owen had been listening intently, his expression serious.

'Can I hear it?' he asked.

Zoe nodded and set the machine going. She held her breath for a few seconds, until Michael's sad voice sounded again. Zoe had half convinced herself that Owen would not be able to hear it, that it really *was* just a figment of her imagination, repetitively triggered by the movement of the tape – but

81

the hypnotist was paying close attention. When the message ended, he looked at her.

'You're certain that's Michael?' Owen had only met her husband twice, and then only briefly.

For the first time Zoe experienced a moment's doubt – what exactly did Michael's voice sound like? – but the instant of panic soon passed.

'It's him,' she stated. 'Somehow . . .'

'And the phone didn't ring?'

'I'd swear it didn't.'

Owen raised his eyebrows and let out a long, slow breath.

'So you think his subconscious might be trying to contact you?' he said.

'Yes!' Zoe answered eagerly. She had been hoping for such a reaction, for such a lack of scepticism. 'I'd rather not think about the alternatives!'

'You're the only other person who could logically have created the message,' he told her earnestly. 'Your subconscious is just as powerful as Michael's – and in some ways, just as mysterious, even to you. And you are closer at hand.'

'I know,' she conceded. 'But if *I'm* inventing the messages, wouldn't I make them rather more positive? These aren't exactly designed to cheer me up.'

'Perhaps that's not what they're for.'

Zoe did not know how to respond to that.

'What do you make of the reference to the horse?' Owen asked.

'I've no idea, except . . .' She hesitated, feeling rather foolish, then ploughed on. 'I dreamt that night about a man on a horse.'

Owen eyed her speculatively.

'Both messages appeared at night, while you were asleep?' Zoe nodded.

'Well, we'd better get to the bottom of this,' he said calmly. 'Let's see what your subconscious has to say. Are you ready?'

'That's not all,' Zoe told him apologetically.

The hypnotherapist smiled ruefully.

'You don't like to make things too easy, do you?' he remarked.

'Last night, when I got back from the hospital . . . something happened,' she began, and then told him about her manuscript. 'All the doors and windows were locked, there was no sign of a break-in anywhere and yet someone, or something, was here. I felt the male presence stronger than ever.'

'This is hardly my field,' Owen admitted, 'though I've seen a few strange things in my time. Some of my clients have developed previously hidden psychic talents – healing especially – but I'm certainly no expert on the paranormal.'

Zoe was encouraged by his calm acceptance of her story.

'Poltergeists are supposed to be linked with extreme emotional stages,' she said, 'though they're usually connected to teenagers – and I'm hardly that!'

There was a long, thoughtful pause.

'Sorry,' Owen said eventually. 'That was my cue to say something gallant, wasn't it? Missed my opportunity again.'

'Don't be silly,' Zoe told him, nonetheless pleased by his attempt at humour. 'I *could* be responsible for what happened – even at my advanced age – but I don't believe it.'

'We're getting way ahead of ourselves,' Owen said, shaking his head as if to clear it. 'Did anything strange like this ever happen before Michael's accident?'

'No. And no one in the village has ever given us the slightest indication that the cottage might be haunted.'

'So the telephone messages and this poltergeist – if that's what it is – must surely be connected,' he reasoned.

'It's too much of a coincidence otherwise,' Zoe agreed, 'unless you believe in a cosmic joker.'

'Are you sure the male presence isn't Michael?' Owen asked.

'Absolutely sure.' There was not the smallest doubt in Zoe's mind. 'Michael could never make me feel like that.'

'Can you think of anyone who could?' he asked, watching her closely.

Taken aback by the question, Zoe did not respond for some time.

'Thomas,' she replied at last.

Owen nodded, as if he had expected her answer. He was familiar with the story of Zoe's first, disastrous marriage from their earlier sessions. Indeed, he had been influential in helping her come to terms with the separation and divorce, and to understand her emotions surrounding those traumatic events.

'Have you had any contact with him recently?'

'None.'

'In dreams?' One of Owen's successes had been to enable Zoe to stop reliving her marital degradations while she slept.

'Not for months,' she replied, 'although there was a nightmare just before Michael's accident. And then, two nights ago, I thought Thomas was the horseman – though the feeling was very vague.'

'But it does start to fit into a sort of pattern,' he commented.

'You think I'm responsible for it all?' she asked quietly.

'I don't know,' he said. 'But you might be. That's what I'm here for, isn't it?' He stood up, took an upright chair and put it in the centre of the room. Zoe was only too happy to place herself in Owen's capable hands, in spite of her nervousness about what she might discover. She sat in the chair and made herself comfortable, her hands resting in her lap.

'You're already familiar with this process, so I won't waste any time. Relax completely, and let all your muscles go limp. Breathe deeply and evenly.' Owen was speaking very fast now, but clearly, and in a matter of fact, reassuringly businesslike tone. 'Imagine your body getting heavier and heavier, sinking down. Now take a deep breath and let it out slowly.' He moved round so that he stood in front of her. 'Now I'm going to hold up my finger, and I want you to focus on it,' he said, matching his actions to his words. His forefinger was held about a yard away from Zoe, just above her head height. 'Keep watching as I bring it towards you. As I get closer, you'll begin to feel even more relaxed, your eyes will grow heavier and eventually they will close. Keep watching my finger. Your eyes are feeling heavier, and heavier.'

On their first meeting, Zoe had been amazed by how good a hypnotic subject she was, how everything Owen told her became fact an instant later, but now she took it for granted. She expected to be hypnotised, and trusted the therapist's skill. She felt her eyelids flicker and then close. Owen's voice went on, telling her calmly that she was growing ever more relaxed, warm and comfortable.

'Now I'm going to pick up your right hand and when I drop it into your lap on the count of three, you will feel five times more relaxed. Let me take all the weight of your arm. Don't help me.'

Zoe felt her hand being lifted firmly but gently, as Owen repeated his commentary and then counted. When he let her hand fall, she drifted further from the outside world. He repeated the process with her left hand, again keeping up his running commentary, and this time, as her hand flopped into her lap, Zoe felt a wave of pleasant lethargy – so strong that it was almost a physical sensation – run from her head to her toes. She felt heavy and as if she were floating all at the same time, without any sense of contradiction.

'You are now deeply relaxed,' Owen continued evenly. 'Your internal systems are slowing down, your heartbeat, your breathing.'

His voice was part of another world now. Zoe was still quite aware of it, and of other incidental noises – birds singing in the garden, the wind whistling softly around the house – but they were distant and remote.

'I'm holding my finger in front of your forehead now,' he went on. 'You may want to roll your eyes up and look at it through your forehead. In a moment I'm going to ask you to open your eyes and look at my finger. Then I'm going to move closer and touch you between the eyes. At that point you won't be able to keep your eyes open any more and you'll be five times more relaxed again.' After repeating these instructions, he said, 'Now open your eyes and look at my finger.'

Zoe did as she was told, but only with considerable effort. At first her eyelids did not want to open at all, but she eventually persuaded them. His finger was already quite close and it came as a pleasurable relief when he touched the bridge of her nose lightly. Her eyes snapped shut, and she sank even deeper into her trance. She had absolutely no desire now to expend any energy. Moving would have been an impossibility.

'Now I'm going to show you how to relax your mind even more,' Owen said, and led her through a process of imagining numbers of diminishing size and brightness until they vanished from her mind's eye. With each decrease he told her that she would be twice as relaxed, even more comfortable and, at the end of the sequence, he informed her quietly that her subconscious mind was ready now. She was in working state hypnosis.

'Are you ready to go to work, Zoe?'

'Yes.' Her voice seemed faraway, deeper than normal.

The whole process had taken only a few minutes, and some remote part of Zoe's brain marvelled at the effectiveness of his technique, remembering Owen telling her on a previous occasion that the quality of hypnosis was more important than the depth. She was not sure exactly what that meant, but now she felt ready for anything.

'Do you remember when we last had a session like this?' Owen asked.

'Yes.' The details were all very clear.

'We were talking about your parents.'

'I was angry with them.'

'Are you angry with them now?'

'No.'

Zoe's parents had died in a car crash when she was seventeen. Her grief had been coloured by guilt because she had not had a chance to say goodbye, and her emotions had then turned to anger at their abandonment of her. This was something Zoe had only discovered under hypnosis. At the time she had been old enough to be thought capable of looking after herself but young enough to still be very vulnerable. In retrospect, it had been easy to see how her state of mind had contributed directly to her decision to marry Thomas some time later. She had fallen for his strong, self-assured façade, which promised – or so she had believed – the protection and the avoidance of responsibility she so craved.

'Are you angry with Michael?'

Zoe knew that she ought to be surprised by Owen's question, but she was not. Although the connection with her parents had never occurred to her before, it seemed obvious now.

'Yes. A little,' she replied. 'He promised he'd never leave me. And I'm afraid he might never come back.'

'Your feelings are yours, Zoe,' he told her. 'You know that, don't you? Yours to discard or keep as you choose. Do you want to be angry with Michael?'

'No.'

'Then discard your anger. This is for your own good, so your subconscious will accept your decision. Discard your anger. Michael is not out of reach like your parents were. He's alive, and you can help him recover. It's important that you believe that. You can help him.'

'I will. I am,' Zoe promised, feeling a new determination build within her.

'And has Michael responded?' Owen asked. 'Has he tried to talk to you?'

'Yes.' She had no doubts. 'He talked to me on the phone.'

'How did he do that?'

'I don't know.'

'Can you go back to the time when you were asleep and the last message arrived? The one you played me?'

'I was dreaming,' Zoe replied. 'But I don't know when the message came. The phone didn't ring.' Her face was working now, and she sounded distressed. Owen spent a little time reassuring her. When she was calm again, he went on.

'Did you have anything to do with putting the message on the tape?'

'No.'

'Your dream could have been the source of Michael's voice,' he suggested mildly.

'No,' Zoe told him emphatically. 'It's him, not me. I had

87

'nothing to do with it.' She seemed annoyed by his apparent doubts.

'All right,' Owen said placatingly. 'Now come forward to when you arrived home last night. You are quite safe, so nothing can hurt you. What did you see and feel when you got home?'

'It was very dark, so I left the car lights on. Once I was inside, I became afraid. It was as if there was someone here, though I couldn't see anyone.'

'What did you do then?'

'I went into each room, putting the lights on.'

'And when you got to your study?'

'My manuscript had been scattered all over the place. He picked up another page and threw it down as I watched.'

'Who is he?'

'I don't know.'

'What did he look like?'

'He was invisible.'

'What happened then?'

'I told him to get out. And he went.'

'How did he go?'

'He just wasn't there any more.'

'Were any of the windows open?'

'No.'

'So there were no draughts in the room?'

'No. It was very still.'

'Were you afraid?'

'Yes. Then I got angry at him for coming into my house.'

'So you sent him away?'

'Yes.'

'Did you invite him in in the first place?'

'No.' Zoe was indignant.

'But he obeyed you when you told him to get out?' Owen persisted.

'Yes.'

'Then you know you can control him,' he told her. 'Remember that. He can do you no harm.'

Owen continued to question Zoe about the poltergeist-like

phenomenon, and then returned to the telephone messages, but her answers were always consistent and he learnt nothing new. After that he spent a long time reinforcing Zoe's own self-belief, repeating his statements several times and assuring her that the newly formed responses to her present situation would mean that she could remain calm, strong and free from stress. Finally he suggested that, on the count of three, she would open her eyes and be alert but relaxed, happy and invigorated – and would remember what they had discussed.

'One, two, three.'

Zoe opened her eyes, and gazed at the hypnotherapist.

'I was right, wasn't I?' she said quietly after a few moments.

'Well, you're not responsible for either the messages or whatever scattered your manuscript,' he replied, 'but we're no nearer finding an explanation for them.'

'But I'm not going mad,' she said, her eyes shining. 'That was all I needed to know.' She was fired with a new confidence, and could not wait to get to the hospital to see Michael.

'Which means that there's *something* here, in this house,' Owen said, with a meaningful glance. 'Have you considered going to a hotel for a while, somewhere nearer the hospital perhaps?'

'No. I need to be here. This is where Michael will contact me – and you said yourself the other one can't harm me.'

When Owen left, he promised to send her a tape with the appropriate relaxation exercises by the first possible post, and agreed to come to see her again at the same time four days later. As his car pulled out of the drive, Zoe was already collecting her things ready to set off for Norwich. The need to talk to Michael was overwhelming.

But when she turned the key in the car's ignition, there was nothing but a dull click. She tried again several times with the same frustrating result, and then remembered a phrase from her session with Owen. *It was very dark so I left the car lights on.* The battery was dead.

Swearing loudly and fighting to retain her recently improved composure, Zoe went back inside to phone the AA – who promised to be there within the hour. She tried her best not to fret, and eventually made use of the time by reading a short story onto a cassette to leave at the hospital. After that, with still no sign of the AA, she wondered about ringing the hospital. She went over to the phone and automatically glanced down at the answering machine. The indicator showed that there were three messages waiting for her.

# 11

Michael's last message had ended in a cheerless question. *Where are you, Zoe?* The next began with another question, one that made her feel a little more hopeful – but only for a moment. What followed plunged her back into despair.

'Was that you, Zoe? For a moment you seemed so close . . . but it's so dark. I'm not sure I even know what you look like any more.'

The inhuman tone that marked the interval between messages sounded loud and harsh.

*Oh, Michael. What's happening to you?* Zoe wondered, fighting back tears. *To us?*

But then the second new message began.

'There are no machines here.' He sounded rather surprised, but his voice was firm, with none of the pain and hoarseness that had marked his earlier words. This gave Zoe another instantly vanquished moment of optimism, even if what he said made little sense. The rest of the recording was so faint that she could barely hear it, even with the volume turned right up. As far as she could make out – absurd though it seemed – it appeared to be a quotation, almost lost in the crackle of static hiss.

'The chanters' music wraps me round, and stops my ears from mortal sound.'

There might have been more – the tape ran on for a few seconds before the final beep – but if so, Michael's voice, now no more than a wretched whisper, had sunk until it was completely inaudible.

While the personal nature of the first message had been heartwrenchingly painful – *I'm not sure I even know what you look like any more* – the second was in some ways even worse. It could surely only be the product of a delirious or deranged mind, and if Michael *was* trying to communicate something to her, as had seemed likely earlier, then Zoe did not have the faintest idea what it could be.

Feeling utterly dejected, and cursing the fact that Owen was not still there, Zoe played both messages through again – and then felt a new determination fill her. Moping would do neither Michael nor herself any good. She even smiled at the thought of her own recently educated subconscious acting as a combination of nursemaid and nag. Whatever its source, her new-found confidence and calm were doubly welcome.

Once again the phone had not rung, but this time she had been in the house and awake the whole time. That must prove something, but for the moment Zoe was unable to think what it was. In the meantime, there were things that needed doing. Setting the machine to save all three existing messages, she picked up the telephone and rang the hospital. As expected, there had been no change in Michael's condition, but Zoe could not help but feel a twinge of disappointment. What did all this mean if it was having no effect on him? She could not escape the thought that some response was required of her, but could not imagine what this should be.

Zoe's next call was to Alex. After their initial exchange of greetings and a brief report on Michael, Zoe asked her agent if she would ring her back.

'I want to make sure the phone and answering machine are working properly. I'll pick up as soon as you start to leave a message.'

'All right. Have you been having problems with the line?'

'I'm not sure,' Zoe replied. 'That's why I want to test it.'

A few seconds after she put the telephone down, it rang – loud and shrill. It was inconceivable that she would have failed to hear it while she was in the study. After four rings the answering machine switched itself on, intoning Zoe's own message and then winding the tape forward.

'Hello, Zoe. This is Alex . . . er, testing, one, two . . .'

On 'three' Zoe picked up.

'Thanks.'

'Sorry I couldn't think of anything more original,' Alex said. 'It seemed to work OK.'

'Yes, it did.' The indicator was now showing four.

'Have you seen your hypnotherapist yet?'

'Yes. He was here this morning.'

'Good. Did he help?'

'Yes, a lot. I'm seeing him again on Friday.' At that moment, there was the welcome sound of car tyres on gravel. 'I've got to go now, Alex. The AA man's arrived.'

'Car trouble?'

'Yes. It's a long story. Talk to you soon.'

'Bye. Look after yourself.'

It took the mechanic only a few minutes to get Zoe's car going. She was grateful but anxious to be off and, as soon as he was satisfied, she drove away. The AA van followed for a mile or so, checking that there would be no further problems, then went his own way.

At the hospital, in Dr Black's continued absence, Zoe decided not to tell anyone about what had happened. Her reasons were not entirely clear, even to herself, but she knew she must not jeopardise the privilege of being able to spend as much time as she liked with Michael. If the hospital staff got the impression that she was too overwrought and might possibly prove a danger to their patient, the consequences were unthinkable. So she made herself play the role of calm and dependable wife – and found it surprisingly easy. It was only when she was alone with Michael that she allowed any of her real concerns to show. She talked to him earnestly, assuring him that she had heard his messages, repeating them in the hope of provoking some response and asking him to make their meanings plain. She told him again and again that she was listening, would be there as often as she could, and reaffirmed her love.

'I know you're trying to tell me something, sweetheart. And I'm doing all I can to understand. But you have to help me.'

93

The afternoon and evening passed quickly. In spite of Michael's total lack of involvement, Zoe found that she filled the time easily, with the routine visits of the hospital staff, her own one-sided conversations, and the usual complement of taped music and stories. She described all the things they would do when – not if – he woke up. And just being with Michael gave her a strange kind of comfort. Yet in the back of her mind was the now constant speculation about what she would find when she got home. Would there be any more messages? Any more clues to this as yet unfathomable puzzle?

In the end it was fatigue that made her decide to return home. It was only when she got back to the cottage and found – half disappointed, half relieved – that there were no new messages, that she realised she had eaten nothing and had drunk only a few cups of coffee all day. Feeling guilty, she went upstairs to weigh herself on the bathroom scales. She had lost half a stone in the ten days since the accident. *The T-Plan Diet*, she thought blackly. *T for Trauma. Dr Black would not approve.* Even though she was not hungry, she made herself eat supper, then prepared to spend the night on the sofa once more. She felt, perversely, that even though it was unlikely to awaken her, she would still rather be close to the telephone – her only link to Michael.

That night Zoe slept soundly but woke once in the middle of the night with a vivid recollection of the dream she had just left. She had been part of a group of people gathered on a wide platform high above the ground, on the top of some unseen building. The wooden floor was surrounded by ornately carved but sturdy railings, and yet she was still afraid to go too close to the edge and the vertiginous drop. It was nighttime, with faint starlight providing the only illumination. Zoe could not see the faces of any of her companions, nor what they were wearing, but there was laughter and happy – though unintelligible – conversation all around. She alone seemed unable to share in the joyous mood. There was a glass in her hand and the aromas of wine, spice and honey were rich in the cool air. Most of the others were

94

drunk, she realised, then noticed that they were all looking expectantly towards the eastern horizon. There, dark orange at first but rapidly lightening to an almost fierce white glow, rose the full moon. Its progress was followed rapturously by the assembled throng. Glasses were raised in apparent toasts, and the euphoric mood intensified. Even Zoe felt the touch of the Great Midwife's silver magic. The dance began.

She woke to find the duvet twisted round her awkwardly. Disentangling herself, she got up and went to the window, feeling dizzy – as if she too were drunk, like the ghostly revellers of her dream. There was a pale glow in the sky, but thick cloud prevented her from seeing whether the moon was full or not. Shivering, Zoe went back to her makeshift bed.

In the morning, out of curiosity, she checked in her diary and found that it had indeed been a full moon last night.

There had been no further messages, but Zoe played through the existing ones again and, for the first time, was able to listen with a degree of objectivity, trying to make sense of Michael's more obscure utterances. She had repeated the 'quotation' in her head so often that it had begun to sound familiar, but she couldn't find anything similar in any of her books. The couplet conjured up uncomfortable images of funerals and embalming – but it still made no sense, especially in conjunction with his remark about the lack of machines. On impulse, Zoe rang Alex and repeated the lines to her.

'Doesn't ring any bells,' her agent said. 'Is it important?'

'I don't know. It might be.'

'Are you going to tell me what this is all about?' Alex asked.

'It's just something Michael said once.'

'You mustn't brood, Zoe.' Her concern was obvious.

'I'm not brooding, honestly,' Zoe replied. 'I feel better this morning than I've done for ages.' She was surprised to find that this was actually true.

'God, that must have sounded awful,' Alex said. 'I'm sorry, Zoe. I wasn't nagging – I just wish there was something I could *do*.'

'You could find out where that quotation comes from,' Zoe suggested.

'If I can,' her agent promised. 'Are you going to the hospital today?'

'Yes. After breakfast.' She suddenly felt ravenously hungry.

'I'll phone this evening then. Chin up, Zoe. Bye.'

As she was preparing breakfast, Zoe's thoughts returned to the other phrase that had haunted her more than anything else. *I'm not sure I even know what you look like any more.* Well, she could make sure he remembered as soon as he woke up, whether she was actually there in the room with him or not. The choice of photograph was easy, but it was some time before she could remember where it was. When Zoe went into Michael's workroom and retrieved her 'Queen of Otherlands' picture from the machine, she realised that she had hardly been in there since the accident. Michael had only been absent for ten days or so, but his paraphernalia already seemed dusty and neglected. The screens were all blank, and none of the red power lights were glowing. Michael had evidently switched everything off. *Almost as if he'd known . . .* Zoe pushed that thought aside and went back to the kitchen.

The day at the hospital passed uneventfully, apart from a slightly awkward conversation with Dr Black. He came to Michael's room and, after his examination, apologised for not having told Zoe that he was going to be away. Then his eye was caught by the photograph of Zoe which now stood on the bedside cabinet in a plastic frame.

'It's one of Michael's favourite photos,' she explained hurriedly, feeling acutely embarrassed. 'I think it's awful.'

'Then in that case, I think Michael shows better taste than you do,' the doctor remarked, increasing her discomfort.

'Careful,' Zoe advised, surprising herself. 'He'll get jealous.'

Nick dutifully averted his gaze.

'How are you bearing up?' he asked, smiling.

'Fine. I saw a therapist yesterday.'

'Come to my office and tell me about it.'

Once they were installed in the cluttered room, Zoe told him about Owen's efforts to keep her calm and reduce the stress of her situation. She did not mention any of the revelations that had emerged from the hypnosis, and the doctor did not ask her about the original telephone message, apparently content to forget the incident. Zoe instinctively kept the later developments to herself. Nick seemed to approve of the hypnotherapy, and explaining anything more would have been just too complicated.

'I'm glad you're looking after yourself,' he concluded. 'You may need your stamina, because I'm afraid Michael's got us all baffled.' He paused, watching her.

'Me too,' Zoe said before she could stop herself.

Nick looked a little surprised, but went on when she did not elaborate.

'His medical condition has not changed one iota since he's been in here – as you know. His external wound is healing nicely and the leg will be fine in time, but the depth of his coma and the associated symptoms are exactly the same. We've done another scan, but it still shows clear. That's not consistent with the level of the coma, but it's not the *only* inconsistency. Someone in that situation shouldn't be able to breathe on his own, yet he does, without any difficulty at all. We can find no reason for his not waking up. Overall, it doesn't make much sense.'

'So what do we do?' Zoe asked after a pause.

'We could do an exploratory operation, to see whether we can find anything the scans have missed, but I don't want to recommend that while he's still stable. Otherwise, all we can do is care for him . . . and wait.'

*And pray?* Zoe wondered silently.

# 12

As Zoe opened the front door and reached for the hall light switch, a tiny flash of red caught the corner of her eye. She swung round to look through the open door of Michael's workroom and saw that one of the power lights below a computer screen was glowing. Although this unnerved her for a moment, Zoe had no sense of the alien presence; she realised that she must have knocked the switch when she'd gone to retrieve her photograph. She went in and turned the computer off, then checked the answering machine.

All the way home in the car, she had been convinced that there would be another message – and she was right. Nevertheless, she gave a small gasp when she saw the number five on the indicator. *Calm down*, she told herself. *Four of them were there already.* She had not yet learnt how to skip earlier messages, so when she pressed 'Play' she was forced to listen through all three of Michael's previous communications. *Next it's Alex*, she thought, fast-forwarding mentally.

'Hello, Zoe,' the agent's voice said. 'This—'

There was a resounding crack, followed by a loud hissing noise which had obliterated the rest of the short message. Zoe thought at first that the machine must have broken down, but then Michael's voice sounded again, stronger than ever before – and angry.

'What use is this? I have your image. The witches showed it to me. But I have need of *you*.' Although there was a long pause then, the tape kept turning until, at last, he spoke again. This time his voice sounded weak, hoarse and afraid once more.

'Am I dreaming?' he asked softly. 'Am I dreaming, Zoe?'

And there it ended, leaving Zoe paralysed by a whole host of conflicting emotions. Every time Michael spoke to her, his words only seemed to pose even more questions. How could he be aware of her photograph and not her actual presence? Who were the witches? And why the change of tone for his question about dreaming? The list went on and on. Had he been responsible for the deletion of part of Alex's message? And if so, why? Was it her intervention on the tape that had made him angry?

'This is crazy,' Zoe said out loud to the empty room.

Just for a moment she wanted to hurl the answering machine across the room, to smash her inanimate torturer into small pieces. But her frustration soon faded.

'Calm and strong,' she reminded herself.

The main point, surely, was that Michael *had* responded to some external stimulus – the arrival of her photographic image. That *had* to be encouraging. She was just about to play the tape through again when the telephone rang, making her jump violently. Even so, she picked the receiver up quickly, making sure the answering machine did not start up.

'Hi, Zoe,' Alex said. 'How are you?'

'Confused,' she replied truthfully.

'Why? What about?'

Zoe pushed aside all thoughts of recent, inexplicable events, and gave her agent a faltering account of the conversation with Dr Black. Alex was sympathetic.

'Listen, I'm free this weekend,' she offered. 'Why don't I come up? It sounds as though you could do with a bit of company, even if it's just to cook and open a wine bottle or two.'

Zoe hesitated. She was tempted, but some instinct told her that the visit would not be a good idea.

'I couldn't ask you to—' she began.

'Nonsense,' Alex interrupted. 'I wouldn't offer if I didn't mean it.'

'No, Alex. I appreciate it, but really, I'd rather be alone at the moment.'

There was silence for a few moments, and Zoe hoped her friend was not offended.

'OK. Let me know if you change your mind though,' Alex said eventually, then changed the subject. 'You really started something with that quotation of yours. Everyone in the office has been checking through every reference they could think of. It became a sort of challenge. A couple of them even rang me from home earlier this evening, but we've all drawn a blank. Michael must have some very obscure sources.'

'Thanks for trying,' Zoe said, thinking wryly, *About as obscure as it gets!* One more unsolved mystery.

They chatted for a few minutes more and then hung up. Zoe stared at the answering machine for a while, then got up and fetched a bottle of wine, a glass and a corkscrew from the kitchen. Since Michael's accident she had not had a single drink – it had not even occurred to her – but Alex's offer had suddenly made the idea of getting drunk very attractive.

An hour later the wine was all gone and Zoe could hardly keep her eyes open.

'I'm sorry, Michael,' she said, addressing the answering machine, 'but I need a proper bed tonight.' Her neck ached at the thought of another cramped night on the sofa.

Zoe dragged herself upstairs, and more or less collapsed into bed. Just as she was about to fall asleep, a female voice she did not recognise spoke very clearly.

'Come with me.'

The invitation sounded urgent but friendly, and Zoe did not have the strength to open her eyes. She knew there could be no one in the room.

She fell into the dream almost immediately. It felt like a guided tour of a strange world, but although Zoe had no idea why she was being shown these scenes, her invisible director evidently had some purpose in mind – for, as soon as she had taken in the details of one vision, she was whisked off to the next. She stood at first in a village square that was surrounded by crude wooden dwellings. Peasant women were lined up, carrying jars, buckets and pans, waiting in turn to receive water from a well. The water was being drawn up by a patiently trudging horse turning a pulley, and two hawk-eyed men, armed with swords, stood to either side of the well, regarding the women suspiciously. To the far side sat a man in a dark cloak; after filling their containers, each woman went to him and seemed to ask his blessing. He responded by bringing forth a succession of small, curiously shaped pieces of metal from within the dark folds of his cloak and dropping them into each measure of water. Zoe knew, somehow, that this was a way of ensuring that the water was kept pure.

Then, without warning, she was transported to open heathland beneath a wide, clear blue sky. An old man was crouched before her, studying the laborious progress of a stag beetle on the bare earth. A gnarled finger stretched out and flipped the ungainly insect over onto its back. In that instant, lightning blazed overhead, the thunderclap following almost immediately. Then, from a cloudless sky, a cold and heavy rain began to fall.

Time and place changed again. A campfire burned brightly in the night. Although darkness rendered most of the hushed onlookers invisible, Zoe knew that all eyes were fixed on the young man who was holding the long bone of some animal in the flames. After a little while he withdrew the bone and studied it carefully, tracing all the cracks and blackened spots with a fingernail. Then he looked up, smiling, and the tense atmosphere became one of rejoicing – but Zoe never found out why because she was now walking on a long shingle strand – which reminded her of the sea wall at Cley – with the grey waters of the sea rushing and rattling over the stones.

There had evidently been a storm recently, because there were numerous articles by the high tide mark, obviously thrown up by the waves. But there was none of the plastic detritus of modern society that Zoe would have expected, only a collection of variously shaped pieces of driftwood, clumps of seaweed, dead fish and crabs and, most curious of all, huge numbers of brightly coloured, twelve-pointed starfish. Influenced by some unexplained urgency, Zoe looked up and

101

out to sea. A grey-sailed, three-masted vessel was riding proudly before the wind. The pennant at the top of the tallest mast was black except for a slim curve of white, representing the crescent moon. *The moon and stars,* Zoe thought, and in that instant found herself awake. To her astonishment, it was already morning. She had a splitting headache, and her mouth felt as though it were full of cotton wool. Perhaps the wine had not been such a good idea after all.

She got up to clean her teeth, and as she glanced at her own reflection in the bathroom mirror, a thought occurred to her. *Am I dreaming?*

'Am I dreaming?' she asked aloud.

Then Zoe went downstairs and checked the answering machine. It still showed five but, to prove to herself that she *was* awake, she played all the messages again. They still made no sense.

She felt much better after forcing herself to eat breakfast. Now that she could think straight she expected the dream to fade, but the memories remained crystal clear. *Come with me.* The scenes she had witnessed had felt like real experiences, not the ephemeral images of a dream. Had it all been meant to tell her something?

The rest of the day passed quite uneventfully, and brought no answers to any of her questions. In the evening, when she got home from the hospital, Zoe found that Owen's promised tape had been delivered. She listened to it in bed, taking comfort from the strength and warmth of her therapist's voice, as well as from his message. She slept peacefully that night, and when she set off in the morning to renew her one-sided conversation with Michael, the answering machine still registered five.

The hospital and its routines had become very familiar to her now. Painful though it was, walking into Michael's room seemed almost like returning home.

'Hello, my love,' she said, leaning over to kiss him. 'I'm here in person now. You don't have to make do with a photo.' She went on talking, referring to his messages, asking questions and sharing all her thoughts – however absurd – in the

102

hope that he would find some way to respond. Although Michael remained as always perfectly still, expressionless and impassive, Zoe knew that somewhere deep down he *was* aware, searching for a way out of the darkness, a way back to her. And she was determined to do all she could to encourage and help him.

However, her efforts were not without their cost. By mid-afternoon, she found herself dozing in her chair and when Claire and another nurse came in, she woke with a start.

'You can't burn the candle at both ends indefinitely, you know,' Claire told her with a kindly smile. 'Why don't you call it a day. Go home and get some rest.'

'No. I want to stay. But I could do with some fresh air.'

'We've got quite a bit to do here,' the nurse said. 'Go and have half an hour's walk.'

Zoe nodded, told Michael that she would be back soon and went out. It was sunny but bitterly cold in the east wind, and she returned feeling refreshed and wide awake. And she became even more alert when she saw a man she didn't recognise hurry into Michael's room. Her heart pounding suddenly, she ran after him and in through the open door. The room was full of people. Dr Black was at the bedside, taking Michael's pulse, Claire was watching, her face pale, while the other nurse and the man were talking quietly, studying the heart monitor.

'What is it?' Zoe gasped. 'What's happened?' Although Michael looked no different, hope and fear were warring painfully inside her.

'It's all right,' the doctor said quickly. 'Nothing's happened to Michael. We just had a slight technical problem with one of the machines. That's all.'

'We got a flat line on the monitor just as I—' Claire began, then broke off at a warning glance from Dr Black.

'Michael's heart never stopped beating,' he assured Zoe. 'In fact his pulse hasn't changed at all. It was just a technical glitch. I'm sorry if it worried you.'

'It seems to be working fine now,' the man said. 'But I'll check it out as soon as we get a replacement wired up.'

'Thanks, Don,' the doctor said. 'Are you OK, Zoe?'

'I suppose so,' she replied. 'You're sure there was no change at all?'

'None.'

Later, when she was alone with Claire, Zoe took the chance to ask the nurse what she had been prevented from saying.

'It was obviously just a coincidence,' Claire said eventually, obviously embarrassed. 'But it came as a bit of a shock at the time. We'd just finished remaking the bed and I picked up the photo of you, to have a better look at it – I hope you don't mind – and the machine suddenly went wrong. It was so unexpected, I panicked a bit and dropped the photo. I don't think I damaged it.'

'It's not important,' Zoe reassured her. But her thoughts were very different. *I have your image.* Could Michael really have been reacting to the removal of her photo? And if he could affect a telephone answering machine, why not a heart monitor? *The witches showed it to me.* Zoe looked at the nurse, and smiled inwardly. *You don't look much like a witch to me,* she thought.

There were no more crises that day, but on the way back to Thornmere Zoe was filled with a sort of dreadful anticipation, sure that something awaited her. However, when she got home, the answering machine still showed five and she was forced to dismiss her premonition. She tried to settle down to her evening meal, but her appetite was gone and she was restless. Going back to the sitting room, she put some music on quietly, closed her eyes and tried to relax.

A small click brought her out of her reverie. The tape in the machine was revolving.

Spellbound, she watched it turn but the only other sound was the softly playing music, which she quickly turned off. The telephone had not rung, her own message had not played and she could hear no incoming voice but, as she watched, the indicator jumped from five to six. Impulsively, Zoe picked up the receiver and held it to her ear, hardly daring to breathe. The line seemed dead. There was no dialling tone, just a faint, faraway rustling sound as the tape continued to turn.

'Michael? Michael, is that you?' she whispered. 'Can you hear me? Talk to me.'

But there was nothing except the constant sibilance.

'Michael?' she said loudly. 'Please!'

Still the tape ran on. The number changed to seven, then almost immediately to eight.

'Why can't I hear you?' Zoe cried, close to tears now. 'Michael?'.

There was another click and, as the tape began to rewind, Zoe heard the dialling tone in her ear.

'Oh, God,' she breathed helplessly, then put the phone down and rummaged in the drawer for the instruction booklet. She was determined now. She had been right to expect something to happen. There must be a way of going to a new message without having to listen to all the rest. She found the information quickly enough, just as the tape finished resetting itself. Pressing the 'Memo' button, she held it down until the indicator reached five, then released it.

'Am I dreaming, Zoe?' Michael said. Then there was a beep and she held her breath as the sixth message began to play.

'The crescent moon will return.' He sounded troubled. 'They set sail within ten days. Will it all be for nothing?'

His tone changed again for the seventh message, but Zoe was too astonished by his apparent reference to her own vividly remembered dream to notice at first.

'The swords are real here, Zoe. The magic is real. Why don't you come to me, let me hear your voice? Where are you, Zoe?'

On that forlorn repetition of his earlier question, the message ended, and the final one was so short – a single sentence – that it was over almost before Zoe had taken in the one before.

'It's almost as though I'm in another life,' Michael said.

While the tape rewound, and for a long time afterwards, Zoe sat perfectly still and silent. Each word was burned into her memory and, as she went through all the messages, fitting the pieces together, a strange, fragile excitement began to grow within her.

Now, at last, she knew how to contact Michael.

# 13

'Let me get this straight,' Owen said. 'You think Michael's coma has somehow acted like a hypnotic regression, that his messages originated in a past life?'

'Yes.'

Owen was clearly sceptical, but because he was at a loss to explain the apparently crazy mixture of words on the tape, he was prepared to at least listen to Zoe's bizarre theory.

'Aren't the messages strange enough in themselves without assuming they're from the past?' he asked mildly.

'Of course they're strange,' she conceded, 'but that doesn't make them any less real. And you only have to listen to them carefully to see what I'm getting at.'

'Go on,' the hypnotherapist said. He already had a good idea what she meant, but he wanted to hear it from her.

'Well, the historical references for a start,' Zoe said. 'Horses, witches, swords, setting sail.'

'We have horses today,' Owen pointed out, 'and "setting sail" can apply to all craft, not just sailing ships.'

'True enough,' she admitted. 'But Michael never had anything to do with horses. He doesn't even like them. And the ship with the crescent moon was in my dream.'

'*Your* dream?' he said, bewildered.

Zoe explained, describing the curious scenes she had witnessed and how the memory of them had lingered.

'I felt then as if I was in the past,' she went on. 'The sailing ship was one of the things I was taken to see, and I dreamt about men with swords. It's too much of a coincidence that

I remember it all so well, and that it happened at the same time as the messages. There *has* to be a link.'

'The cosmic joker strikes again,' Owen remarked.

'And do you remember Michael said, "There are no machines here"?' Zoe continued eagerly. 'Well, where are there no machines? In the past, of course. And then there's the last thing he said.'

'"It's almost as though I'm in another life",' Owen quoted.

'That's the clincher,' Zoe concluded and gazed at him expectantly.

After a long pause, the hypnotherapist shrugged.

'All right,' he said slowly. 'Let's assume what you say is true – even though we can't be sure it actually is Michael talking . . .'

'*I'm* sure,' she cut in. 'I don't know *how* he's doing it, but it is him. He reacted to my photo and—'

Owen held up his hands in surrender.

'OK. So what's the next step?'

'I want you to regress me.'

'I had a feeling you were going to say that.'

'Michael and I often said we must have been lovers in a previous life,' Zoe added seriously. 'I know we always treated it as something of a joke – but now I'm not so sure. Just before the accident, Michael told me that the past could take care of itself. Well, maybe it can't!'

'The past is still the past, Zoe. You can't change it, only the way you perceive it. And what makes you think being regressed will put you in touch with Michael? That's what you're hoping for, isn't it?'

It was a good question, but Zoe had an answer ready.

'Do you remember what Michael said after my first hypnosis session? "Was that you, Zoe? For a moment you seemed so close . . ." And that was while I was still in this life. If I go back to the one *he's* in . . .'

'That's a big if,' Owen commented. 'How will you know where – or rather when – to find him?'

'I'll find him,' she replied confidently. 'If it achieves nothing else, at least it'll set my mind at rest. Perhaps I need therapy in past lives as well as this one,' she added with a smile. 'In any case, it can't hurt to try, can it?'

'All right. We'll give it a go,' he said. 'We might learn something. But Zoe, it's dangerous to expect too much. It's important you understand that.'

'I'll take my chances,' she said. 'I've got to do *something*.'

For a few moments, Owen looked as if he were going to say something more, but then he evidently thought better of it and began the procedure of inducing hypnosis. Zoe's sense of excitement was such that the induction took longer than before, but she eventually felt her entire body relaxing, her trance deepening so that she was detached and serene. The only constant in this dark and peaceful world was Owen's voice.

'How old are you, Zoe?'

'Thirty-eight.'

'Tell me about your last birthday. Recall it in detail, but remember, if there's anything it would be inappropriate for me to know, you don't have to tell me. But see it all for yourself.'

Zoe smiled inwardly, reliving all the wonderful indulgences she and Michael allowed themselves on their respective birthdays, and described them happily.

'Now go further back,' Owen told her. 'To your birthday six years ago. Tell me about that.'

Details of that far less joyful occasion flooded Zoe's mind. She had still been with Thomas then, and the party he had arranged for her had been full of people she did not really know or like, most of them business acquaintances rather than friends. She remembered all the wasteful, extravagant food, and the music that had been playing in the background. Then came the inevitable drunken argument with her husband after everyone else had gone.

Then Owen moved Zoe on quickly to earlier times – until, after a few more jumps, she reached her fifth birthday, the cake and jelly, balloons and paper hats of a more innocent age. Thereafter, the process speeded up even more, skimming backwards through the first years of her life until she was one year old, then six months, then three, one, and through a few moments of the disorientating experience of birth back into the calm warmth of her mother's womb. But she did not remain in that blood-dark haven for long; Owen's persuasive voice urged her further back, further and further into the unknown.

'Now find your own way to a time that is important for you.'

Zoe had no choice about what happened next. The time and place were dictated to her by forces she could not comprehend, and their sudden pull was so strong that she felt almost dizzy.

The room in which she found herself was wood panelled and dark. The air was cold and a single heavily leaded window looked out onto a dismal scene – rain falling from a leaden sky onto a wide grass field. There were ash trees in the distance and, beyond that, sheep were grazing. It all seemed strangely familiar.

However, Zoe's immediate concern was not where she was but who she was. Her body was unlike her own; it was taller but fuller, more rounded, stronger though somehow less experienced. Her hair was long, tied back and secured by some sort of net or cap. She could feel the weight of it on the back of her neck.

*This is me, but* . . . Zoe felt very odd. Her mind was filled with new and distracting images. There were memories and knowledge that were not her own – an unfamiliar language – and also vague and unsettling intimations of sadness, desperation, even anger. But somehow it would not all come into focus. It made no sense. She, Zoe, was still there – inside this person, this stranger – but observing through her eyes like an outsider.

*I expected you to come*, an unknown voice said within her head, *but not inside me!*

The shock and bewilderment felt by this new person were obvious, and Zoe was equally astonished. What was going on? Who was speaking – or thinking – if it wasn't her?

Owen's clear voice cut through the mental fog.

'Where are you now?'

Zoe sensed the other presence grow quiet and a little afraid at this second intrusion, and her own confusion intensified. Nevertheless, she responded as best she could.

'I'm in an old, wood panelled room,' she began, and went on to describe the scene, including the view from the window, in more detail.

'Who are you?' Owen asked, when she had finished.

'I . . .' She stopped, no longer knowing how to answer that question.

*Is he a spirit?* the silent voice asked.

*Who?*

*The one who asks us questions.*

Zoe's unknown partner evidently saw nothing strange in the idea of communicating with spirits.

*I suppose so.* How else was she to explain Owen?

*Does he want me to answer?*

*Yes*, Zoe told her.

'Do you know your name?' The therapist still sounded calm and relaxed, in spite of the delay. 'Or can you tell me what you do?'

The other memory supplied all the answers; Zoe took a mental step back, left the stage to her companion and translated her responses into words Owen could understand.

'My name is Emmony. I am wife to Quarterman Jevan. I am mistress of this house.'

Zoe sensed strong feelings associated with the formal words – especially about her husband. Was it through this Jevan that Michael would speak to her?

'What year is it?' Owen asked.

'This is the seventh year after the Messenger,' Emmony replied, 'in the . . .'

Here there was a word, an idea, Zoe could not translate. It meant a long but definite period of time. In the end she gave the nearest equivalent, even though she knew it was not accurate.

'. . . in the century of the Winged Helmet.'

'Who is the messenger?' Owen went on, wondering what

111

strange culture Zoe had landed in. The past life was going to be difficult to get a handle on.

'The one in the sky,' Emmony answered, 'who travels backwards in the wheel.'

This excursion into obscure cosmology was clearly going to get them nowhere, so Owen changed tack.

'Who is the ruler of your land?'

'Prince Chandos.'

Zoe sensed a growing unease at the line of questioning.

'And what is his territory called?'

'The Eastern Dominions.'

'Where is Prince Chandos's court, his capital city?'

'At the Marshland Pyramid, a day's ride east of here.' Emmony's consternation deepened. *A spirit should know such things,* her attitude implied.

'How are you dressed?' Owen asked, trying yet another approach.

'Fairly. In linen and fine wool.'

Zoe could have added more. Her clothes were indeed fair, heavy and warm without being cumbersome. The embroidery and other decorations, as well as their good fit, made it obvious that Emmony was a woman of some standing in her community.

'What do you look like?'

'See for yourself,' Emmony replied and turned to look at a portrait hanging on one of the inner walls. Even in the dim light Zoe could see the pale face, dark hair and exquisite clothes of the stately pose. But, even as she stared, she felt Emmony click her fingers – her own fingers – and an oil lamp flared into life, casting its yellow glow on the picture. She was so astonished by this sorcery that for a moment their internal communication broke down, and Zoe found herself remembering Michael's words. *The magic is real.*

*Do I offend you?* Emmony enquired anxiously.

*No,* Zoe replied, but had no time to explain her surprise or ask any questions as Owen spoke again.

'I can't see with your eyes,' he said gently. 'You must tell me.'

112

'She's beautiful,' Zoe told him quietly, realising that Emmony was either too modest or too proud to say more about her own appearance.

'Who is she?' Owen asked quickly.

'Emmony.'

'But you are Emmony.'

Zoe hesitated before going on.

'Yes.'

'Are you looking in a mirror?' Owen guessed.

'No. At a portrait . . . my portrait. Eyes the colour of amber, dark brown hair, white skin, oval face. A long, brocaded dress, and gold jewellery.' Zoe felt distinctly uncomfortable as she stared at the painting.

'What is your age?'

Without prompting, Emmony took up the conversation again.

'I have seen thirty-eight summers, half an . . .'

Here she used the unknown word again, but this time 'century' was clearly an absurd translation, so Zoe settled for something more vague.

'. . . half an era.'

'Go back now to the time when you were twenty-eight,' Owen instructed her.

'You mean remember?' Emmony responded.

'No. Return to that time.'

'I can't remember much that far back,' she persisted, obviously perplexed.

There was a long, thoughtful pause.

'Then let's go forward,' Owen suggested eventually. 'To when you are forty, two years from now.'

'I could wish I had the skill of prophecy,' Emmony replied, 'but I do not. I must rely upon others for that. Shall I call my scryer?'

Zoe sensed that Owen's consternation was turning to something approaching alarm.

'Go back then . . . to anything you can remember.'

Images flooded into Zoe's mind, but they were only memories, no more substantial than a dream. Yet with them came

113

undeniably strong emotions – dominated by unhappiness and fear.

'Ghyl!' Emmony cried suddenly. 'I know where he is now, but I didn't for so long. It was agony. I need to see him so much, and yet I can't go to him. He's hurt, but they won't tell me what's wrong. That's why you've come, isn't it?' She was obviously in great distress now. 'You came to help me find him again.'

Owen's voice, calm but urgent, cut in.

'Zoe, relax. Come forward now, back to your present life, to the sitting room in your house in Thornmere. You feel warm and relaxed. Come back to the present now. You are comfortable, and will remember everything you've experienced during your regression.'

The parting was a wrench, though Zoe could not help but obey. Emmony vanished as Owen repeated his instructions.

'I'm going to count to three now; when I reach three you will open your eyes and come out of hypnosis. You will be alert, aware, relaxed and happy. I'm going to count to three now. One, two, three.'

Zoe opened her eyes and returned to her own home. She and Owen stared at each other, their eyes full of questions.

# 14

'That was incredible,' Zoe whispered, feeling buoyant and optimistic in spite of her confusion. 'Why did you bring me back?'

'You were becoming very distressed—'

'*Emmony* was distressed, not me.'

Owen stared at her.

'And there were too many oddities,' he went on, with heavy emphasis. 'I wasn't sure how best to deal with it. You were Emmony, weren't you?'

'Yes and no.' Zoe was eager to explain, but found that she had to struggle to put her experience into words. 'It was as though we were a dual personality. I was *inside* Emmony – it was her body – but I was still there . . . at the same time as she was. And the first thing she said to me was really weird.'

'Said to *you*?'

'Yes. We could communicate without talking . . . like telepathy I suppose . . . but inside one head.'

'What did she say?'

'"I expected you to come – but not inside me!"' Zoe quoted. A tremor ran through her at the memory of the strange encounter.

'So your arrival had been foreseen?' Owen remarked.

'Yes, though she seemed very vague about it.'

'Prophecy usually is pretty vague,' he said dryly. 'How did Emmony react when *I* spoke?'

'She thought you were a spirit.'

'*She* did, but you didn't?'

115

'No. I knew it was you.'

'That's quite a common form of rationalisation of the hypnotist's questions,' Owen told her, 'provided the society of the past believes in spirit voices.'

'Emmony certainly had no problem with that,' Zoe confirmed. 'She asked me if she should do the answering, and I said yes.'

'So Emmony was doing the talking?'

'Most of the time, yes. I just had to act as translator.'

'She didn't speak English then?'

Zoe frowned.

'No. I'm sure she didn't . . . but I've no idea what language it was.' All knowledge of the alien tongue had vanished from her mind.

'All right,' Owen went on. 'Let's see what else we learnt.'

'It was the seventh year after the Messenger,' Zoe responded, 'in the . . . era of the Winged Helmet.'

'You said "century" before.'

'I know, but that was wrong. It was the closest I could get. If what she said later is accurate, then their "era" is a period of seventy-six years.'

'Twice her own age, thirty-eight summers,' Owen agreed.

'The same as me,' Zoe noted quietly.

'It doesn't resemble any calendar I've ever come across,' the hypnotherapist said. 'It almost sounds as if it comes from Norse mythology – winged helmets and so on.'

'But the Messenger is "in the sky" and "travels backwards in the wheel",' Zoe quoted.

'None of which helps us tie it down to an exact date,' Owen commented. 'I'll check what I can, but . . .' He shrugged. 'Well, if we can't say when, how about where?'

'The Eastern Dominions,' Zoe said. The name meant nothing to either of them.

'And the Marshland Pyramid!' Owen added. 'Who builds pyramids on marshland?'

'Well, I certainly wasn't in Egypt,' she told him. 'It looked cold and wet outside, and there were green fields. Where else could there be pyramids?'

'The Aztecs and Mayans built them in South America, and there were Assyrian shrines that were that shape, but it doesn't sound as if you were there either.' Owen paused. 'Perhaps she didn't mean what we think of as a pyramid,' he added, before moving on. 'Your – I mean Emmony's – appearance was definitely Caucasian, not Asian, Arabic or African?'

'Absolutely. She was very pale.'

'The names are very unusual – Emmony, Chandos, Jevan.'

'Quarterman Jevan,' Zoe reminded him, although the title meant as little to her as it evidently did to Owen.

'And, from the description of your clothes, they could have belonged to almost any period from medieval times onward.'

'Doesn't give us much to go on, does it?'

Owen shook his head. He looked puzzled and far from content.

'There's something else,' Zoe ventured nervously. Owen merely raised his eyebrows and waited for her to continue. 'Emmony . . . I . . . lit a lamp just by clicking her fingers.' Zoe matched actions to her words, but Owen remained silent. 'It was just like Michael said,' she went on. *The magic is real*. It all ties in. And the same thing happened in my dream.' Her companion still did not comment, and she stumbled on. 'And Emmony said *she* didn't have the gift of prophecy, but she implied that others did.'

'Scrying has been common enough throughout history,' Owen said. 'Which doesn't mean that it works.'

'And then there was Ghyl – whoever *he* is.' Zoe was not about to be put off now. 'She's longing to see him, but he's been hurt. I think she was talking to me at the end, not you, when she said we'd come to help.' The parallel with her own situation was too obvious for her to have to spell it out.

'Past lives often mirror the present,' Owen said. 'That's why they can be so useful in helping solve present problems.'

'So—' she began.

'*But*,' he interrupted firmly, 'it's not as simple as that. So much of your experience was peculiar, just didn't fit

117

the pattern of any past life regression I've ever seen.' He began ticking points off on his fingers. 'Past lives are usually visualised in either the first or the third person. This one was neither – or both. Dual personalities shouldn't be possible. Either you were Emmony, or you weren't. Then there's all the apparently nonsensical evidence – without even considering the supposed magic. Nothing corresponds to any time or place we know about.' Forestalling Zoe's objections, he quickly added, 'It may be that it was some obscure culture not recorded in most of the history books – and we can investigate that – but it still all seems rather far-fetched to me. But the oddest thing of all was that we couldn't move back and forth in the past life. That doesn't make any sense. How did you get there in the first place? And *why* couldn't you move within it? What's the significance of that particular time? It's worrying, because one of my responsibilities is to keep you from any situation of undue stress. If I can't move you away from a particular time, that makes my job much more difficult. Lastly,' he went on, determined to say his piece, 'in PLRs you *witness* events, you don't control them, but it seemed you could. Turning to look at the portrait, for example.'

'Emmony could,' Zoe said, somewhat subdued by Owen's arguments. 'It's her life.'

'But it's already happened,' he replied. 'Your arrival, as a witness, should have made absolutely no difference to what happened. You have to face it, Zoe. It's quite possible that what you experienced was not a past life at all.'

'Then what was it?'

Owen did not reply, and the implication of his words slowly sank in.

'You think it was all a figment of my imagination, don't you?' she said quietly.

'You're a writer,' he replied. 'You imagine for a *living*. Who knows what role your subconscious plays in that process?'

'No! It's real . . . or . . . or as real as any past life can be.' Zoe's certainty was absolute. 'And it *is* linked to Michael's messages. It *has* to be.' She was more convinced of that than ever now.

'That I won't dispute,' Owen conceded.

They sat in silence for a while, each thinking about the other's words.

'Well, there are some things we can follow up,' Owen said eventually, 'though what we've got is probably too little and too vague to track anything down for certain.'

'Perhaps next time we should tape the session, so we have a permanent record to refer back to,' Zoe suggested.

'Next time?' he asked. 'Are you sure?'

'Yes! You can't possibly believe I'll leave it at that. This is important, the most important thing I can do right now. It's how I'm going to get through to Michael. I'd go mad if I didn't keep trying.' She laughed. 'That is if I'm not mad already.' Then she grew serious again as doubts entered her mind. 'You will help me, won't you?'

If Owen still had any misgivings, he was prepared to set them aside – at least for the time being. However confused he might be, he had to admit that he was also intrigued – and Zoe's eagerness to continue gave him a measure of confidence.

'I'm free this evening,' he said quietly. 'If you like—'

'Yes!' Zoe almost shouted. 'Please. What time?'

'About eight. I want to solve this mystery too.'

'Thank you.'

As Owen stood up, something occurred to him.

'Have you got a tape recorder with a microphone?'

'Yes, a cassette player.'

'Then I suggest you play back Michael's messages, and transfer them to another tape. That way you won't be in danger of filling up the tape in the answering machine, and you'll still have a complete record.'

'Good idea,' Zoe said, wondering why she had not thought of that earlier. She still had not bought the second miniature tape she had promised herself.

'See you tonight then,' Owen said.

After seeing him out, Zoe transferred the messages, checked the new cassette, and reset the answering machine.

119

'There you are, Michael,' she said aloud when she had finished and the indicator showed zero once more. 'All the tape you need. Now tell me what to do next!'

# 15

For the first time since Michael's accident, Zoe left the hospital for some hours in the middle of the day. She had reluctantly decided that, on this occasion at least, her time would be better spent elsewhere. After all, Michael had never communicated with her while she had been at the hospital; there had not been the slightest flicker of response during all the hours she had spent there. Although she had no intention of abandoning her bedside vigil – her talks with him were too important for that – she could not begrudge some time away now, especially as it was to be spent pursuing other possible avenues of help.

She drove into Norwich city centre, and parked by the main library. The staff in the reference section were very helpful, showing her where the encyclopedias, dictionaries and works of historical biography were kept, and also tutoring her in the use of a computer terminal. Even so, her search for some clue as to where or when Emmony had lived proved fruitless. There was just too little to go on. She could find none of the names of people or places, either in any of the reference books or on the data base.

'Emony', spelt with only one 'm', was the equivalent of anemone, and 'Ghyll', with two 'l's, meant a ravine or stream, but that in itself meant nothing – especially when the difference in languages was taken into account. 'The Messenger' was a phrase sometimes used to describe the prophet Mohammed, the founder of Islam, but that made little sense in the context in which it had been used. Zoe could find no connection between Mohammed and the sky. The United States had once been known as 'The Old Dominions', and both Canada and New Zealand had also once been considered dominions, but none of these could sensibly be regarded as 'eastern'. For a few moments Zoe wondered whether Emmony might have lived in the eastern part of the USA – New England, say – but they certainly had no princes there, and she would surely have recognised the language.

Her final discovery – and one which proved equally unhelpful – was to find that 'Chandos' was the name of a British classical record label. Zoe was pretty sure that Michael had several of their CDs at home. The record company had evidently taken their name from that of a series of anthems by Handel, and Zoe discovered that the famous composer had named them for his patron. James Brydges, the first Duke of Chandos, had lived from 1673 to 1744 and for a few years had lined his pockets as Paymaster-General to Marlborough's armies. The Duke's main residence was in Edgware, then some nine or ten miles from London, and his life style had been so conspicuously sumptuous that he had been commonly known as 'Princely Chandos'. That gave Zoe a moment of bright optimism, but her hopes were soon dashed. The title was certainly not real, at least not in the way Emmony had used it. And so many other things – the language and the religion – could not possibly fit.

And then it became impossible for Zoe to investigate further. Her computer screen went blank, then flickered on again, scrolling up lines of gibberish. Pressing any of the keyboard letters had no effect. When Zoe pointed this out to the harrassed looking staff, she was told that the central computer had gone down, all the terminals were in the same state, and they did not know when the system would be available again.

'I sometimes think we were better off when all we had was drawers and drawers of cards,' one of them said. '*They* couldn't go off line! Did you get what you wanted?'

'Yes, just about,' Zoe replied. She had come to the conclusion that progress would be impossible unless the search could be narrowed down. 'Thanks for your help.'

As she was leaving, Zoe glanced at the terminal she had been using. The screen was now showing a list of books about astronomy and she grinned, wondering where the computer's brainstorm would take it next. On the way back to the hospital, she racked her brains about what other approaches her research could take, and wondered whether Owen had had better luck.

Back in Michael's room, she told him what she had been doing, and of her lack of success – she had already described the past life regression – but as usual there was no response.

'I feel that I'm getting closer, though,' she assured him earnestly. 'Owen's coming again tonight. Will you help me to reach you? I need your help, Michael.'

Some hours later, Zoe said goodbye to her husband, leaving herself plenty of time to get home by eight o'clock. As she passed the main reception desk, she heard one of the duty nurses talking on the telephone, sounding rather aggrieved.

'I'm sorry, Doctor. I *know* it should, but the entire phone system here broke down for nearly an hour this lunchtime and we're still trying to catch up with all the messages.'

Without waiting to ask for details, Zoe ran to her car, certain now that there would be more messages waiting for her at home. But when she reached Ash Ring in the darkness of another cold autumn night, she found more than she had bargained for.

As soon as she opened the front door, she became aware of both noise and light emanating from the sitting room. The sound was a faint, crackling hiss, while the light was a colourless, unnatural flickering. At the same time she felt her skin crawl, and knew that the malevolent presence was back. She had no choice now but to face it, and she moved cautiously into the room. The television was on, its screen filled with shimmering white dots that seemed to be flowing upwards. The lights of the VCR were on too, indicating that it was playing.

Caught between terror and fury, Zoe's mind took refuge in anger, and she snapped on the lights.

'Leave me alone!' she yelled, shivering. 'Whoever you are,

123

go away! Get out!' Owen's words came back to her. *He can do you no harm.* She wished that the hypnotist was there to help her, but it was still only half past seven. 'You belong elsewhere!' she shouted, not caring whether she made any sense. 'I don't want you here.' Zoe was crying now. 'Go away!'

Impulsively, she picked up the TV's remote control, and stabbed at the 'Standby' button. The screen went dead. She repeated the process for the VCR. Although the underlying nature of her tormentor did not change, remaining coldly malignant, Zoe sensed a moment of surprise from the alien presence.

'What do you want from me?'

The silence roared in her ears.

'Get out,' she whispered venomously. 'Get out!'

Her reward was a physical buffeting from invisible hands which shoved her backwards so that she stumbled and fell, landing awkwardly between a chair and the sofa. Shocked beyond measure, she could only stare up at the empty space above her. And then, to her enormous relief, the presence left. It just seemed to fade away, leaving the air clear. Yet the parting itself struck a new chill in Zoe's heart. Although she had seen nothing, she could have sworn that the entity had been *smiling*.

She picked herself up slowly and painfully, trembling still and rubbing her bruised elbow. Only then did she look at the answering machine, and could hardly believe what she saw. The indicator was set at nine, and was flashing to show that more than nine messages had actually been received.

Unable to think straight, Zoe just pushed the 'Play' button and sat down to wait. *Oh, Michael*, she pleaded silently. *Please help me.*

But as the tape began to play, she was faced with yet another shock, another mystery. From beginning to end, all the tape contained was a sibilant hiss that rose and fell like distant waves, but which contained no words, no information, *no Michael*.

Zoe had stopped crying and was attempting to calm herself

when Owen arrived. She jumped at the sound of the doorbell and then, when she saw his reassuringly solid presence on the doorstep, it was all she could do to keep from falling into his arms. She held herself back, but could not hide the fact that she was desperately upset.

'What's the matter?' he asked. 'What's happened?'

Zoe led him inside and told him everything. He took it all calmly in his stride, and listened dutifully to the tape.

'It's all like that,' Zoe said after a minute or two.

'It has a pattern to it,' he commented thoughtfully.

'Like waves,' she agreed. 'But was it like that because Michael couldn't get through to me, or because this . . . other person prevented him.'

'The presence? How could he have done that?' Owen asked.

'How do I know?' Zoe exclaimed. 'How could he switch the TV and video on?'

'I'm sorry,' he said, clearly bewildered. 'This is all a bit beyond my scope. I don't know what to suggest.'

'Well, I could certainly do with some therapy,' she replied, with a wry half smile. 'And I suspect Emmony could too.'

'Are you sure you want to do another regression now? We could just—'

'Of course I do,' she said determinedly. 'It's more important than ever now.'

'But we haven't sorted out what happened in the first one yet,' he objected. He had not had the time to do any research. 'Don't you think we need to make more sense of that before we continue?'

'The only way to make sense of it is to get more information,' she told him. 'I have to go back.'

'Your logic is impeccable,' he said, then smiled reluctantly.

'I wish Michael were here to hear you say that,' Zoe told him ruefully, then forced herself to smile by an act of will. 'Just get on with it, will you?'

This time the process was quicker and easier. Zoe's own life slipped behind her and then – it seemed almost at once – she found herself with Emmony, on horseback! She was riding fast along a track between tall trees. The only light came from the moon above, which silvered the air and leaves and turned the deep shadows into impenetrable voids.

Emmony's initial reaction was one of relief.

*I thought you might never come back. I'm glad you're here now.*

The muffled thud of the horse's hooves spoke of soft ground underfoot, but even so Emmony's pace seemed reckless. She was riding confidently, however; strong legs gripped the mount's flanks and her hands were firm but relaxed on the reins. The cold night air rushed over her face and Zoe felt the traces of tears on Emmony's cheeks.

'Where are you now?' Owen's voice broke into her consciousness, and she described the scene.

'Are you called Emmony?'

'Yes. She's here.'

*The spirit is with you again. Can he help us?*

'Yes. I hope so,' Zoe answered. 'But it will be easier if we speak aloud so he can hear. Will you do that?'

'It . . . feels strange,' Emmony commented, 'but yes, if you wish.'

Owen remained silent then, allowing Zoe to become Emmony's examiner.

'Where are we going?' The trail seemed familiar, somehow, but . . .

'To Blue Tiles, the Sanctuary. We're almost there.' There was excitement in her tone, but also an undercurrent of dread.

'Who lives there?' Zoe asked, but found she knew the answer even before Emmony replied.

'The witches. They've been looking after Ghyl.'

'He's hurt?'

'Yes, but I don't know how badly. Zenna wouldn't say.'

'Is Zenna a witch?'

'Of course. And a prophetess.'

The track left the woods now, and ran between low hedges over gently rolling fields. Again Zoe felt an indistinct sensation of *déjà vu*. She could see a light in the distance.

'There it is,' Emmony said. 'Not far now.'

Zoe was glad when her companion drew their mount to

a halt, dismounted in one easy, flowing movement – which took no account of her own aches and pains – and tossed the reins to the boy who had come out to meet them. She felt sick with anticipation.

Blue Tiles was a large, stone-built farmhouse, but it was dark, and Zoe could not see very much. She stored up what details she could to tell Owen later, but for now she was too intent on what was happening.

Emmony strode to the door, which opened as they approached, and entered the lamplit interior. A young woman with a pale face, wearing a long, dark cape, was there to meet them.

'Where is he, Zenna?'

'In the outer chamber,' the woman replied. 'Is the spirit visitor with you?'

'Yes. She joined me on the ride here.'

'Can you hear me, honoured guest?' Zenna asked. 'What may we call you?'

Zoe answered hesitantly, feeling for the first time that she was, in some way, usurping Emmony's body.

'I can hear you. My name is Zoe.' She knew that Owen could not hear Zenna, but also knew that progress would be impossible if she had to pause and relay everything to him. So she spoke again, hoping to reassure him and forestall any interruptions. 'And the spirit who helps me is called Owen. I will remember all that you tell me and discuss it with him later.'

Zenna bowed, apparently satisfied. If she saw anything strange in this arrangement she gave no sign of it.

'I must see Ghyl,' Emmony burst out. 'Is he well?'

'We cannot tell,' the witch replied. 'He has gone from us.'

'Gone? But you said—'

'You will see for yourself. Come.' Zenna led them through a narrow corridor and round several corners. The Sanctuary was evidently even bigger than it had seemed from outside. Eventually, she opened a door and Emmony rushed in ahead of her.

Another woman stood at the side of a bed, on which a man lay quite still. There was an ugly wound on the side of his head, his eyes were closed and he barely seemed to be breathing. A locket, secured by a chain around his neck, lay on the bedclothes over his chest. Emmony flung herself down on her knees and took his hand in her own.

'Ghyl!' she cried. 'What have they done to you?'

The man did not respond with so much as a flicker of his eyelids. Zoe was helpless, staring at him in absolute horror. Although the face was thicker and more fully fleshed and his hair was the wrong colour, she knew beyond a shadow of a doubt that this shell of a man was more than he seemed. Just as Zoe, for some reason she was as yet unable to comprehend, was sharing an existence with Emmony, he too had a dual identity. Ghyl was Michael. And they were both in a coma.

The enormity of this discovery – which proved in the most hideous way that her every intuition had been right – left her speechless. But not so Emmony.

'What's happened to him?' she asked, turning to Zenna.

'The blow to the head has robbed him of his senses,' the witch replied. 'We don't know how it happened.'

*I do*, Zoe thought dismally. *Or do I?*

'When will he wake up?' Emmony wanted to know.

'We cannot tell. None of our remedies has had any effect,' Zenna replied. 'And even I cannot see ahead for him. His future path is misty, and it would take a greater fire than mine to burn such fog away.'

'But—' Emmony turned back to stare at the unconscious man. 'Ghyl, you must wake up. I love you. I can't live without you.'

This was almost too much for Zoe to bear. Their history was obviously repeating itself in her own lifetime, but she still had no idea how this situation resolved itself, nor what she was supposed to do.

'My lady,' Zenna began, 'we will care for him as best we can, but it is dangerous for you to be here.'

'I don't care,' Emmony sobbed defiantly.

'You must – for all our sakes, as well as Ghyl's. You should return home.'

Zoe did not want to leave any more than Emmony did, but the urgency in the prophetess's tone was unmistakable, and she knew that in her own world Owen would be getting worried.

*Can't* you *help him, Zoe?* Emmony asked unexpectedly.

'If I knew how . . .' she began. Then a thought struck her. Perhaps *she* could burn away the fog and see the future. 'I'll see if my spirit friend can help.'

'I'm here,' Owen said immediately, sounding both relieved and puzzled.

'We need to see the future,' Zoe said pointedly. 'To see when Ghyl emerges from his coma.'

'Then move forward in time,' Owen instructed calmly, 'to where the outcome is known.'

'How can I?' Emmony shot back, angry now. 'If Zenna can't see so far, how may I?'

'Zoe?' Owen queried.

'This isn't going to work,' she told him, filled with an angry disappointment. She was being opposed at every turn – but by whom?

'Then I think—' the hypnotherapist began.

'No. Let me stay, a while longer at least.'

At this point, another man came rushing into the room, out of breath.

'Well, Iven?' Zenna asked, as they all looked at him.

'I've seen the Quarterman's Third Company riding this way,' he told them hurriedly. 'If they find my lady here . . .' He glanced at Emmony.

'You must go,' Zenna decided. 'Now.'

'No!' Emmony wailed.

'*Yes,*' the witch returned in a tone that brooked no argument. 'Iven's long-sight is never wrong, and if you give Jevan fact to confirm rumour, there will be no hope for any of us. Our lives will all be forfeit, to no purpose. You *must* go.'

With one last despairing glance at Ghyl, Emmony stood up and allowed herself to be led out via a back door, where her horse was waiting for her. Zoe went too, having no choice in the matter.

*Be strong, Emmony*, she urged silently. *Calm and strong. We can get through this together.* Even as she spoke, she was aware that some of her own misgivings must be leaking through to the woman whose body she shared, just as some of Emmony's misery was affecting her. But she had to try to be resolute, for both their sakes.

The ride back was even wilder than the last, using a different route. As time passed and Zoe got used to the rhythmic jolting, she sought to reassure her guide.

'Owen?'

'I'm here,' he said promptly. 'Just tell me when.'

'Don't go,' Emmony pleaded. 'Don't take her away. I need a friend.' She was close to tears again.

'Leave me here a while,' Zoe said. 'Until we get home at least. I'm OK.'

They rode on in silence until, in the distance, the lights of a huge house came into view. Many torches lit the way as they entered the stone-paved yard. A groom came forward and took the reins, bowing as Emmony dismounted stiffly. It was then that Zoe saw another horse and recognised it immediately. Emmony, of course, had seen it at the same time and an unmistakable wave of fear swept through her.

'My lord is back?' she asked the servant, but he did not have the chance to reply.

From the massive front doors of the house, a dark, heavily built man emerged. A sword hung from his belt. He made his way towards Emmony and smiled, though there was no warmth in the expression.

'Well, my pretty wife, this is a poor reception,' he said. 'Aren't you glad to see your husband back so soon?'

Emmony's fear and dismay were so great that she was unable to speak – and in that she was not alone. Zoe stared helplessly at Quarterman Jevan. Although the man who confronted her looked quite different from her own first husband, she knew that it was him, just as surely as if he had

130

worn his own sophisticated features. Jevan was Thomas – and, in this life, they were still married.

Her nightmare had become real.

# 16

Owen's competent voice, sounding gentle but firm, had brought Zoe back to her own life, her own room. While she had still been in a hypnotic state, he had tried to reinforce her calm, to distance her from the stress she had obviously experienced. The outward signs of anguish had been enough to prompt his action and Zoe was grateful, although she felt guilty at her abandonment of Emmony. When she admitted this, Owen's reaction was both prompt and forthright.

'You abandoned no one, Zoe. All this is happening inside your head.'

She stared at him for a few seconds, trying to come to terms with this idea.

'That's so hard to believe,' she said eventually. 'It seemed so real.'

'Maybe it was real, once,' he replied. 'But Emmony is only alive now in your mind.'

Zoe chose to ignore the doubt implied by that 'maybe'. She *knew* Emmony was real and, even though she had died long ago, her life still held meaning in the here and now.

'We forgot to tape the session,' she observed. Her idea had been lost in all the traumatic events of the day.

'It wouldn't have made much sense anyway,' Owen remarked. 'Most of the time it seemed as though I was only getting one side of the conversations, and my interrupting wouldn't have been productive. So I didn't get the chance to ask you to describe what was going on.'

'You didn't mind, did you?' Zoe asked. 'It would have made things so much more complicated.'

'We can do without that!' he commented dryly. 'So, tell me what happened.'

After taking a moment to gather her thoughts, Zoe began, hesitantly at first but soon growing more confident. She found that she had total recall of all her experiences, the sights, sounds and even the smells of the past. She described what had happened, the people and places in detail, and even quoted verbatim all that had been said. As she spoke, the various parallels between her own life and Emmony's became clearer – and so many aspects of her recent dreams and even some parts of Michael's messages all seemed to fit into place. But for every answer there were more questions, frustrating Zoe and making it difficult for her to think logically. Owen did his best to keep her calm, and helped her make her way slowly through the maze. Although he was already familiar with Michael's messages, some of the dream images were new to him and so he had a lot to assimilate. But he was able to provide the structural basis Zoe needed and which, more importantly, allowed them to go forward and make plans. That they were doing so implied that there would be more sessions – a fact which did not escape Zoe's notice – but neither commented on that until later.

'So the most important things we've discovered,' Owen said, summing up, 'are that Jevan is almost certainly the man with the white horse in your dreams, that he's the equivalent to Thomas, your first husband—'

'Yes, but in the other life we're still married,' Zoe put in. 'Just like my earlier dreams. It's awful!'

'And Ghyl is Michael?'

Zoe nodded. 'And they're both in comas that aren't responding to treatment.'

'You, Emmony, are in love with Ghyl?'

'Yes.'

'So this could relate to an earlier part of your own life, equivalent to the time before your divorce?'

'Yes, but then why is Ghyl in a coma? That should still

133

be in the future . . . unless, in Emmony's time, divorce was impossible and . . .' Her words faltered as she was unable to complete the appalling thought.

'Come on, back to what we *know*,' Owen said evenly. 'Magic of various kinds seems to be a thread that runs through everything.'

'What they call magic might be different from our ideas of it,' she responded. 'We have so many names for it – the occult, the paranormal, psychic powers, unexplained phenomena. It all seems so much simpler to them, utterly taken for granted. Witches were obviously an accepted part of society then.'

'That was true here until the thirteenth century,' Owen told her. 'Hundreds of thousands of women were put to death all over Europe after that, but there's no doubt that some covens were still welcomed in more remote regions.'

Zoe decided to read again the section on witchcraft in *Magic, Mysteries and the Mind*, but did not mention the book to Owen.

'Whatever's been happening around *here* recently has hardly been normal,' she remarked, indicating the answering machine and the television with a sweep of her hand.

'All right then—' Owen began.

'Some people think poltergeists are spirits,' Zoe cut in as a new thought struck her. 'Do you think the one here could be Jevan's ghost? It would explain why he makes me feel so bad.'

'I'd feel pretty bad if some invisible presence pushed me over,' he responded, 'whoever it was.'

'That's not what I meant . . .'

'I know, but there are other theories about poltergeists, don't forget,' he pointed out. When Zoe did not reply, Owen went on. 'It seems that the only thing we *can* be sure of is that the past life mirrors your present one closely, but with some significant differences. If we're going to take this any further we need answers to a lot of questions. Firstly to tie up the links between the past life, your dreams and Michael's messages, and secondly, to give us a few pointers about what we should do next.'

'I've already been thinking about that,' Zoe agreed. She went and got paper and pen, and together they made a list of questions which would at least meet Owen's first requirement. The second proved far more difficult.

They had already discussed what they had learnt today about the past life, but it was little enough. The names – Zenna, the Sanctuary, Blue Tiles – told them nothing. As Zoe pointed out, she knew of at least two places locally called 'Blue Tile Farm'. The fields and forest she had seen could have existed anywhere with a moderate climate, and the vague mentions of witchcraft and soldiery were equally uninformative.

'We can go on probing, if you like,' Owen said, 'trying to tie down the time and place, but it won't be easy. And I think now that it's important to find out what happens next.'

'Yes,' Zoe agreed wholeheartedly.

'And, professionally speaking, I'd like to know why we can't move in time within the past life. I've never come across that before.' The hypnotherapist was watching her closely, although his expression was still sympathetic.

Knowing that something was expected of her, Zoe tried to hazard an explanation.

'Could it be because I'm not fully . . . integrated, that I'm there *with* Emmony?'

'Why should that make any difference?'

'I don't know. I'm just clutching at straws.'

'Perhaps we could try to direct you to a different time in Emmony's life from the offset,' Owen suggested. 'Start earlier or later?'

'We *could*, but it felt very strongly as if I was meant to go to that particular time. Michael was there then! That's where the answers are.'

'What exactly are you hoping to achieve, Zoe? What do you want to get out of all this?'

'To speak to Michael, of course,' she answered promptly. Surely that was obvious?

'Have you thought that all this might just be an elaborate fantasy, created by you – and you alone?'

She stared at him for a moment, trying not to let her feelings show on her face. 'Do *you* think it is?' she asked quietly.

'I don't know,' Owen replied simply, then smiled. 'But even if it *is*, we should still be able to use it to help you, and perhaps even Michael as well. Your subconscious may find the answers you're looking for, so I'm willing to carry on if you are – not that you seemed to need my help all that much!'

'Oh, I do. And we must carry on!' Zoe exclaimed, horrified that he should even consider giving up.

'So when—?'

'Now?'

Owen laughed.

'No. I'm sorry, Zoe. Have you seen what time it is?' It was nearly midnight. 'And my wife will be wondering where I've got to.'

'Oh God, I'm sorry.' All of a sudden, Zoe felt deflated, as if all the energy had been drained from her. 'I need a drink. How about you?'

'No thanks, but I'd like a coffee. Keep me awake on the way home.'

Zoe went into the kitchen and put the kettle on.

'Mind if I have a look in Michael's study?' Owen called after her. 'My colleagues keep telling me I should get a PC.'

'Go ahead,' she called back. 'How do you like your coffee?'

'Black, no sugar.'

Zoe made the coffee and poured herself a vodka and tonic, then joined Owen in the study.'

'Who's into astronomy?' he asked. 'You or Michael?'

'Neither of us. Why?'

For answer, Owen pointed to one of the computer screens. '*The Nebular Hypothesis and Modern Cosmogony*,' he read. '*Astronomy – Globes, Orreries and other models, Halley's Comet and*—'

Zoe practically shoved him aside as she leant over to look more closely at the display. She stared, mystified.

'That's—' she began, then jumped as the screen gave a flash of light and then went blank. 'Did you touch anything?'

'I don't think so,' Owen replied. 'The screen was on when I came in.'

'But they've all been switched off since before Michael's accident! Except . . .' She recalled the night when she had had to turn one of the machines off.

'So where did all that come from?'

'I've no idea, but I think . . . it might have been the page I saw on the screen in Norwich library, when their computer went wrong.'

'Computer shall talk unto computer,' Owen intoned.

'Yes, but why?' Zoe wanted to know. 'And who made the link?'

'More tricks from your poltergeist, or . . .'

'A message from Michael?' she completed for him.

'If it was, you might ask him to be a little less obscure next time,' he commented.

'You think I haven't?' she replied with a rueful smile.

'No bad feelings associated with this?'

'No. It's just another mystery.'

'Zoe, are you sure you want to stay here?' Owen asked. 'If it's reached the point of physical violence, don't you think you'd be better off in a hotel?'

'No.' She was resolute. 'That would be running away. And anyway, what makes you think he wouldn't find me in a hotel? Think of the bills I'd have to pay if he stole the towels or threw the TV out of the window.'

'This is serious,' he told her, although he was glad she was able to make fun of the situation. 'Aren't you frightened?'

'I'm too busy to think about being frightened,' she replied. 'He just makes me angry. Finding out what happens next to Ghyl – and to Michael – is much more important.' She took a gulp of her drink. 'So when's our next session?'

'I'm really booked up for the next few days,' he told her apologetically, digging out a battered diary and leafing through it.

'Don't say that,' Zoe begged.

'Weekends are often my busiest times,' he explained. 'There are enough enlightened NHS doctors now to keep me in work, and there are always smokers trying to quit and ladies wanting to lose weight. Good grief, this is hopeless,' he added, staring accusingly at his schedule. 'Hang on. Are you going to the hospital tomorrow?'

'Of course.'

'Could you meet me in Norwich at lunchtime?'

'Oh, yes.' Zoe's relief was palpable. 'When and where?'

'The Gooseberry Bush. It's a pub, round the back of—'

'I know it.'

'Twelve thirty?'

'I'll be there, but . . .'

'It'll be a bit of a rush, I'm afraid, because I'll be between sessions. But a friend of mine, a doctor, has consulting rooms near the pub, and I'm sure he'll have a space for us.' Owen smiled. 'And we'll try to get some of the answers we need from Emmony!'

# 17

After Owen had gone, Zoe returned to Michael's workroom and switched various machines on, but nothing unusual happened. The array of technology still unnerved her but, just in case Michael was using the computer as he had the answering machine, she left on the one that had listed the astronomical books.

'God, what a day,' she breathed aloud, then drank the last of her vodka. She wondered, though only for a moment, whether she was prepared to go on like this, but knew she had no choice.

She decided that there was no point in keeping a whole tape of nothing more than a distant hiss, and after setting the answering machine back to zero Zoe went to bed, waking the next morning with no memory of any dreams. Neither the computer nor the answering machine displayed anything new, and she set off for the hospital, eager to see Michael again and tell him what had happened – but more eager still for the meeting with Owen.

By 12.15 she was sitting in The Gooseberry Bush, drinking tomato juice. The hypnotherapist arrived a few minutes later, his dark eyes shining with excitement.

'I'm glad you're here early,' he told her. 'I may have made a little progress.'

'What?' Adrenaline surged through the eager Zoe.

'I think I know what the messenger in the sky is. Halley's Comet.'

'So the computer *was* giving me a message!'

'The comet was the only thing on the screen that meant anything to me, so I looked it up this morning on the off chance. And guess what I found! Although its orbit is not completely constant, it is visible from Earth approximately every seventy-six years.'

'Emmony's "era".'

'Exactly. And it orbits the sun in the opposite direction to the planets.'

'"Travelling backwards in the wheel".'

'So we went into Emmony's life seven years after the latest fly-past,' Owen concluded.

'But we don't know which one,' Zoe pointed out. 'When was the comet first discovered?'

Owen took out a piece of paper on which he had scribbled some notes.

'Halley noted it in 1682, and predicted its return in 1758. He never lived to see it, but it arrived on Christmas night, just as he'd said. There'd been lots of sightings before then, of course – there's even a Chinese record dating back to 1059 BC – but no one seems to have picked up on its regular return until Halley himself.'

'Weren't comets usually associated with ill omens?' Zoe asked.

'Yes. Mr Shakespeare reminded us of that.'

'"When beggars die, there are no comets seen",' Zoe quoted. '"The heavens themselves blaze forth the death of princes".'

'Julius Caesar,' Owen confirmed, then looked at his notes again. 'It caused so much panic in 1456 that Pope Calixtus III even preached against it as an agent of the Devil, and there were other notable sightings in 12 BC, 837 AD – when its tail stretched halfway across the sky – and 1066.'

'That was certainly an interesting year,' Zoe commented. 'And all that.'

Owen grinned, then went on.

'So we know Emmony's society is not only interested in and knowledgeable about astronomy, but it's so important that it governs their calendar. If I'm right, that is.'

'I'm sure you are,' Zoe told him. 'I dreamt about a

celebration that was apparently timed to coincide with the full moon. The heavens must really mean a lot to them. But where does that leave *us*?'

'Not much further forward,' Owen admitted. 'I'm no scholar of astronomical history, but at least it gives us another line of research. In the meantime, are you ready to go and see if we can make any more progress?'

He led her to a modern building, which seemed to be composed mostly of tinted glass. They took the lift to the third floor, where Owen greeted the receptionist and then took Zoe into a small bright room that contained an examination couch, a small desk, two chairs and some metal cabinets. Medical information posters and eyesight charts were the only decorations on the white painted walls.

'Not exactly the perfect ambience,' the hypnotherapist remarked with a grin, 'but we'll do what we can to make you feel at home.'

Zoe was struck by a curious thought. *This is like having an affair*, she decided, remembering her own beginnings with Michael. *The only concern is to be together in private. And then the surroundings don't matter at all*. She smiled, a little uneasily. In a way, hypnosis was as intimate as sex. But it did not even come close as a substitute.

'What's the joke?' Owen asked, grinning.

'Oh, nothing important. Just something that crossed my mind.'

Without prompting, Zoe sat on one of the chairs and relaxed as best she could. Owen's rapid, business-like voice and the now familiar techniques soon calmed her, and the room ceased to exist as she sank into a trance state. As the hypnotherapist took her back through and out of her own lifetime, he varied his instructions slightly.

'I want you to go further back now, to your life as Emmony, but I want you to go to a different time from the last visit – at least a month later. Go there now.'

Zoe felt the pull as time fled past, then found herself sitting in an opulently furnished room that contained a large four-poster bed, canopies and drapes, a dressing table and several chairs. Pale sunlight was pouring through two leaded windows. It was obviously the chamber of a rich and important woman – but it was equally obvious to Zoe that it was also a prison cell.

'Are you with Emmony?' Owen asked. They had agreed beforehand that if Zoe was able to converse with her 'other half', as before, then he would leave her to do the talking, only interrupting if absolutely necessary – or if Zoe forgot any of the questions that needed asking.

'Yes, I am,' Zoe replied, sensing that her arrival had lifted the gloom that filled her hostess.

'Do we need to speak aloud as before?' Emmony asked softly.

'It would be best, yes.'

'Then we must speak quietly. I am forbidden visitors, and there are guards nearby. If they hear us, they'll think someone has come in.'

'I need to talk to you,' Zoe began in a low voice.

'You are the only one I *can* talk to,' Emmony replied miserably. 'My long-hearing is weak, and anyway, my lord's warlocks may have sealed the chamber.'

'Long-hearing is like telepathy?' Zoe guessed.

Two minds in one head compared notes and found the comparison apt.

'Even if I could speak to Ghyl, he could not hear me,' Emmony said despondently.

'How long ago was it that we visited him?'

'Just last night.' Her surprise was evident. 'Surely you remember?'

'I remember, but my time system is . . . different from yours.' The attempt had not worked. They were no further on than Zoe was in her own life. 'Are you and Ghyl lovers?'

Emmony took her time answering, clearly torn by violent emotions.

'We love, yes – oh, the sky knows how much! – but I sense . . .' She hesitated. '. . . that your question means more. We have never lain together.' A sob was stifled with difficulty. '"Fact to confirm rumour",' she quoted bitterly. 'If Jevan could prove that, he would have us both executed. Would that we had dared regardless! Now such joy may be denied us forever.'

Zoe was now having to fight back her own impulse to weep, although she could not be sure from whose eyes the tears would flow.

'Was what happened to Mi—, to Ghyl, an accident?'

'No one knows,' Emmony replied, regaining a measure of composure. 'The world is a treacherous place, and I am kept ignorant for good purpose.' Her bitterness was tinged with regret now.

'Why treacherous?' Zoe asked. She was drifting far from the list of prepared questions, but could not resist this line of enquiry.

'All the lands intrigue,' her companion answered. 'Chandos is no better or worse than the other princes, but there are other powers involved now.'

'What are the other lands called?' Zoe said, feeling an uneasy tremor at her own choice of words.

'There are so many. The Red Peninsula, the Dark West, the wild provinces of the hill country . . .'

'And the names of their princes?'

'What are they to me?' Emmony demanded angrily. 'How can they save Ghyl, or cure a broken heart?'

'What matters to Emmony is what matters to you,' Zoe was reminded by Owen's disembodied voice, his intervention coming like a bolt from the blue. 'Ask her the personal questions we discussed.'

'Your spirit is wise,' Emmony commented. 'He knows you are here to help Ghyl.'

Zoe took a moment to collect her thoughts.

'I've been having vivid dreams recently,' she began.

'So have I.' Emmony seemed eager all of a sudden. 'Dreams of the five shades. It was there that I saw your coming.'

'The five shades?' Zoe was intrigued enough to be side-tracked again.

'You don't know them?'

'No. What are they?'

143

'The shadow symbols which the wise must interpret,' Emmony recited. 'The oracular vision that foretells the future; the message that comes from the sky; the phantasm that brings pain even when awake; and the insomnium which means nothing.'

This made no sense at all to Zoe, and rather than demand a lengthy explanation, she decided to go on with her questions.

'Some of my dreams seemed to be connected to you and your time. Could you interpret them for me?'

Emmony was thoughtful for a moment. 'I am not one of the wise, but I will try.'

Zoe had the feeling that 'wise' was an insufficient translation, but it would have to do for now.

'Does Jevan always ride a white horse?'

'Always. He has three. No one else can stay on them.' There was a note of grudging respect in Emmony's tone.

'I saw a ship flying a pennant that showed the crescent moon. Was it from the Eastern Dominions?'

Her companion evidently felt uneasy about answering this, but did so eventually, speaking even more softly.

'The crescent moon is the sign of Prince Oroc, who rules the lands west of here, on the far side of the flatlands. It is said there will be war soon between Oroc and Chandos, but I do not believe it. They both have too much to lose.'

'Would Ghyl have had any dealings with Oroc or his men?'

'No! He is no traitor, and those that say so' – she was angry now – 'are just rumour-mongers with flapping tongues.'

'All right. I believe you. Does this mean anything to you?' Zoe asked, then began to recite the quotation. '"The chanters' music wraps me round—"'

'"And stops my ears from mortal sound,"' Emmony completed for her.

'You know it!' Zoe exclaimed, delighted to have her theory confirmed.

'Everyone knows it. It's part of the Dead Month Ritual.'

'What's that?'

'Every three years our calendar has an extra month, so that the sun can catch up with the moon and begin the wheel again. We welcome the Dead Month with praise and offerings.'

This led Zoe naturally to her next question.

'The sky is very important to you, isn't it?'

'Everything is written there,' Emmony replied simply.

'I dreamt of a gathering on a high platform,' Zoe went on, 'where all the people were drinking and celebrating as they watched the full moon rise.'

'I was there, on the roof.' Emmony pointed at the ceiling. 'But I was sad. I should not have been sad on the night of the Great Midwife, but I was. I had not heard from Ghyl for ten days. But I would prefer that unhappy ignorance now that I know the truth.'

'Who were the other people there? Your family?'

'I have no family,' Emmony responded grimly, then reluctantly corrected herself. 'Except my husband. My parents are dead long since, and I was their only child. The others on the platform were guests of our house.'

Her distaste for these guests was plain, but Zoe had been struck by yet another similarity between Emmony's life and her own; an only child, orphaned when still young. Had Jevan seemed the perfect protector to the lonely young woman, as Thomas had seemed to her? Pushing this speculation aside, she continued.

'Another dream took me to many different places.'

'The purification of the well water . . .' Emmony put in.

'The stag beetle . . .'

'The bone map . . .'

'The starfish on the beach . . .'

'The ship,' Emmony finished. 'I shared your dream that night. All these scenes are from my past . . . or my future. I was your guide.'

*I was right*, Zoe thought. *It was a guided tour!* She moved on.

'In my time,' she said, 'there is much in your world that would be considered magic. You speak of witchcraft, prophecy, long-seeing and long-hearing as if they were normal. And you light the fires of lamps without touching them.'

145

'Such things are not normal for you?' Emmony was surprised.

Zoe thought about this.

'We can do some of them . . .' she began, but found herself at a loss. How could she explain electric light switches, telephones or any of the other technology which was the nearest equivalent she could think of? '. . . but we use other methods.'

'Spirit messages?' Emmony suggested helpfully.

'Not exactly. Do you know what machines are?'

Zoe's attempted translation clearly meant nothing to Emmony.

'Is magic bad?' she asked unexpectedly.

'No. Just different. We don't really understand it.'

'I could do much more if I had the talisman,' Emmony volunteered, 'but it has been taken from me.'

'What talisman?'

The answer sounded very strange, and the nearest translation Zoe could find was 'the hollow feather'.

'I might be able to get out of here if I had it,' Emmony added.

'Jevan is the one holding you here?' Zoe asked.

'Who else? He has his suspicions, but he can prove nothing. No one here knows where I went yesterday, except you.' She paused, then voiced her sudden, doubt-filled thought. 'You're not his spy, are you?'

'No,' Zoe replied emphatically. 'I want to help you . . . and Ghyl, if I can.'

'I wish I could see how,' her companion said wearily.

Owen's voice broke into their conversation then, like an alien trespasser.

'Zoe, I'm sorry. I've no more time. I've already left it later than I should.'

'I have to go now, Emmony.'

'Yes.' She sounded resigned, as if she had expected this.

'But I'll come back as soon as I can,' Zoe promised.

'I will pray that you do,' Emmony answered. 'It may be that talking to "myself" will be the only thing that keeps me from going insane – in spite of how it might appear to an observer!'

146

The glimmer of humour in her words gladdened Zoe's heart: Emmony had not quite lost hope yet. Then Owen's voice drew her away. In the faint echoes of the widening gulf between the two women, Zoe heard her companion's parting words – but like so much that had gone before they made little sense.

'You brought light into my dark room,' Emmony whispered. 'I sense the pyramid about you. Have you . . .?'

The rest of the question was lost, and presently, with her composure and self-esteem reinforced by Owen's words, Zoe surfaced in the bright, soulless room in the centre of Norwich. She and Owen looked at each other.

'Now tell me it's not all linked!' she challenged.

Owen gave her a mock bow of submission.

'It's all connected,' he conceded. 'Almost too well.'

'*Too* well?'

'It fits so much of your own life that it's getting suspicious,' he said. 'Subjects often recognise people they know in *this* life as other characters in the past, but the relationships are rarely the same. Or as consistently the same.' He held up a hand to forestall any comment. 'Listen, Zoe. I've got to go now, but please think about it. The dreams come from your subconscious, and so do these past life memories, however bizarre. Isn't it just possible that the messages on the answering machine came from there too?'

'But I denied that under hypnosis!' she objected. 'I couldn't have been lying then . . . could I?'

'No. At least I don't know how,' Owen admitted.

'And am I also responsible for the poltergeist?' she persisted.

He threw his hands wide, confessing his inability to find an explanation.

'I really must go,' he said apologetically.

'When can I see you again?'

'The earliest gap I have is Wednesday morning.'

'Wednesday!' It seemed like a lifetime away.

'I'm sorry.' He appeared genuinely upset. 'I'll ring you if I get the chance of anything earlier.'

'But . . .' Zoe began, then saw how unfair she was being. The man had a life of his own. 'OK. What time?'

'Eleven o'clock. I can come to Ash Ring if you like.'

'Yes, please.' Then she was struck by an appalling thought. 'I haven't paid you for any of our sessions,' she said, aghast. 'What do I owe you?'

Owen had already put on his coat and was opening the door.

'We'll talk about that on Wednesday,' he said as he ushered her out. 'I may decide to treat you free of charge. It certainly beats convincing people not to poison their own bodies with tobacco smoke. And when it's all been sorted out, I may be dining out on this story for years – with your permission, of course.'

Zoe nodded, silently blessing him for having said '*when* it's all been sorted out' and not '*if*'.

Owen waved to the receptionist and allowed Zoe to precede him into the lift. Out on the street they went their separate ways.

# 18

Zoe returned to the hospital that afternoon filled with a mixture of excitement and frustration. For all Owen's doubts, and despite the apparent anomalies, she was convinced that her past life as Emmony was real – and that the correspondence between her own life with Michael was clear. This made their lack of progress hard to bear, and the idea of waiting until Wednesday for another session was difficult to cope with. But Owen's therapy *had* made her stronger, and the fact that so many of her theories had proved correct gave her some hope. Although she could not yet go back to Emmony and Ghyl, she was determined to do all she could in her *own* time.

It was not until Zoe entered Michael's room that she recalled what had perhaps been the most significant discovery of the morning. Michael's earlier messages had helped her establish links to Emmony's life, although his words in themselves had meant little. But his producing the computer book listing – and Zoe was convinced that it had been his doing – had proved to her that he was actively trying to help, reacting to her need for knowledge. Zoe was not sure why Michael had chosen so obscure a method – why could he not just have told her on the answering machine? – but it was a start, a vindication of all her efforts to try and reach him. Sitting down at the bedside after greeting him with a kiss, Zoe began yet another one-sided conversation.

'Thank you for telling me about the comet, my love. I'm sure you'd tell me so much more if you could only find the way – and if I knew what questions to ask, and how. But in

149

a sense I know where you *are* now. We were lovers before, just like I told you this morning, and when I find out how Emmony saved Ghyl, I'll know what to do to help you. At least I don't have to worry about *my* first husband – I've already got rid of him!'

That thought prompted a tremor of pity for Emmony, for her earlier self, yet she refused to contemplate the idea that in the earlier life she might have failed, and that Emmony and Ghyl may never have been reunited. That would be unbearably sad – and would make all her efforts, all the investigations, seem pointless. It *had* to be relevant to the present. Why else was all this happening?

Zoe spent some time telling Michael all about her latest regression, relating her conversation with Emmony word for word and describing her surroundings in detail. She was no longer surprised by her effortless total recall of the experience. In some ways the episodes she had shared with her earlier incarnation were more real than her own life. Certainly she was able to remember them with greater clarity. She even wondered aloud whether it was possible to live all one's life as intensely as those brief moments from the past. Perhaps her subconscious really had retained the knowledge of everything that had ever happened to her, and only needed the right stimuli to retrieve all the information.

'Living life to the full,' she mused. 'I'm not sure we're designed to do that literally. It would be so intense we'd go mad. But then why have we evolved with brains far larger than we can ever use?' It was not the first time Zoe had found herself debating such philosophical matters with her unresponsive partner but, as usual, her unaided efforts raised more questions than answers. 'I mean, how do people with photographic memories cope? Do they have to make a conscious effort to remember the things they want, or do they just have better access to their internal filing systems than the rest of us?'

'Personally, I have to write myself notes,' Dr Black remarked. He had come in so quietly that Zoe had not even noticed. She was glad he had not arrived earlier; she would not

150

have wanted him to overhear some of her more bizarre statements.

'Hello, Zoe,' the doctor said, seeing her expression. 'I didn't mean to startle you.'

'Hello, Nick. It's OK. I forget where I am sometimes.'

'How are you keeping?' he asked as she moved aside, automatically allowing him to make his routine checks on Michael's condition.

'I'm fine. The therapy seems to be helping.'

'Owen Pemberton, isn't it?'

'Yes. Do you know him?'

'Not personally, but I hear good things. I'd like to meet him sometime.'

Zoe had no intention of introducing the two men just yet. She was convinced that if they put their heads together they would decide she really was barking mad.

'I just wish Michael would wake up,' she said. 'That would be the best therapy of all.'

'He will,' Nick replied, positive as always in the patient's presence.

'Yes, he will,' Zoe responded dutifully, adding privately, *When I solve all the riddles.* The notion that Michael's recovery was somehow dependent on her efforts had taken a firm hold now. The idea that he might revive or – God forbid – grow worse regardless of her progress no longer seemed possible.

'No change yet though,' the doctor stated evenly, completing his checks and glancing at the monitors.

'Have there been any more problems with the machines?'

'No. We still can't figure out what happened. But Michael was never in any danger,' he replied, mistaking the reason for her enquiry. 'The nurses acted very quickly and . . .'

'I know,' Zoe said. 'We owe you all such a lot.'

'It's our job,' he answered simply, with a smile.

'Well, I'm very grateful anyway,' she added sincerely, then coughed.

'All this talking must be rough on your throat,' the doctor observed.

'Rougher on him.' Zoe smiled and nodded at her husband. 'He has to listen, and can't argue with anything I say. Besides, I don't talk *all* the time. I play tapes to him,' she added, indicating the radio/cassette player. 'Music and stuff.'

'Ever thought of bringing some work in with you?' he asked. 'It'd do you good, and if you've got a laptop computer . . .'

'Good grief, no!' she exclaimed. 'I write in longhand. Most technology seems designed on purpose to intimidate me. I'd be using a quill pen if you could still get them.'

'Even easier then. All you need is pen, paper and a flat surface. It would be as good as therapy, Zoe. And we'd like to see an author at work.'

'I'll think about it,' she promised.

As she drove home that evening, Zoe found herself thinking – for the first time in almost three weeks – about the characters she had abandoned, imagining the scenes they were still to play out in the novel. Nick's suggestion began to make sense. Concentrating hard on her work would surely help the time pass more quickly until her next session with Owen.

There were no surprises waiting for her at the cottage. The answering machine read zero, and the computer screen was blank. Zoe made herself some toast and coffee and took the tray up to her study, where she spent a couple of hours rereading her last chapters and making notes for the next few. She became engrossed, and finally had to force herself to go to bed.

A restless night was capped by an incredibly detailed dream that left her floundering. At the beginning she knew Michael had been injured, but when she rang the hospital she was told that he had been moved to an intensive care unit in another medical centre, but they weren't sure which one or where it was. Zoe was frantic, shouting angrily down the phone and eventually gleaning some clue as to where he might be. Just then there was a knock at the door and, when she opened it, Woody Allen was standing on the step. Without speaking he ushered her into his car, an absurd, enormous, American machine with wings, and drove her towards the hospital. The journey through the rainswept suburban streets seemed endless, and many of the short cuts were too narrow for the giant car. Zoe became more and more fretful, not helped by the occasional remarks of her famous companion.

'You only live once, but once is enough if you can play it right,' he commented helpfully. And he informed her that, 'I'm not afraid to die. I just don't want to be there when it happens.'

Eventually Zoe could stand the delay no longer and got out of the car so that she could run to the hospital. Swerving and dodging through the traffic, she pelted along, at one point darting onto a bus and out of a door on the opposite side. The passengers all looked at her with wide eyes and the conductor, a stooped man with glasses, a ridiculous false moustache and a huge cigar, said, 'Either he's dead or my watch has stopped.'

Finally Zoe reached the hospital – a strange, small place, more like an extended chemist's shop. Michael was on the fourth floor, *not* in intensive care, but in a ward where everyone lay in narrow beds pushed so close together that they were almost touching. The patients, who were all male, took great interest in Zoe and Michael's obvious relief and joy at their reunion.

'Sex is like death,' Woody remarked, having just arrived, out of breath. 'Only after death you don't feel like a pizza.'

'I feel like a pizza, but I don't suppose I look like one,' Zoe said between kisses, then wondered why everyone laughed. She didn't care. She was in Michael's arms now and he was laughing too, his eyes alive and his embrace passionate.

Everyone else tactfully got out of their beds and left the lovers on their own. Even Woody vanished, and things were just becoming really interesting when the doorbell rang – or Zoe thought it did – and she woke up.

She realised miserably that she was still alone. Her joy at Michael's recovery had been cruelly ephemeral.

She lay in bed, feeling hot and drowsy. The distant sound of church bells reminded her that it was Sunday, and a glance at the clock told her that, astonishingly, it was after ten. She had not slept so late in ages. The dream was already fading, unlike her earlier ones. What could Woody Allen possibly have to do with her life? He was Michael's favourite filmmaker, but there was nothing in this dream that could conceivably be connected with Emmony's life – and the director's well-known obsession with death was not something on which Zoe wished to dwell, however funny he could be on the subject.

In a way, though, it was almost a relief to have had a 'normal' dream, one which she did not have to sift through for clues to the past, and one which had given her a much needed, if cruelly fleeting, reminder of how wonderful it would be when Michael woke up.

Before she left the house that morning, Zoe remembered Dr Black's suggestion and collected her notes and some writing materials from her study. She had not worked on her novel for some time now, and if she managed to make even a little progress it would make her feel better. In the past, whenever she had been stuck on a particular passage, she had read the draft aloud to Michael. Sometimes his comments solved her problems; on other occasions the mere act had been enough to clarify matters in her own head. She would do the same now and, even though Michael could not respond, it would still be comforting – and perhaps provide another stimulus for his subconscious mind.

However, once Zoe reached the hospital, the manuscript was forgotten until she ran out of things to talk about. It was Claire, in fact, who brought it back to her attention.

'Is this your new book?' the nurse asked.

Zoe nodded.

'What's it called?'

'*Fields of Plenty*.'

'I've read several of your others,' Claire admitted self-consciously. 'I don't know how you think up all those ideas.'

'That's the easy bit,' Zoe told her, feeling embarrassed

154

and thinking how strange it was to be having this familiar conversation in a hospital room next to her comatose husband. 'It's fitting the ideas into a proper story and getting it all down on paper that's the hard work.'

'When will it come out?'

'Not for eighteen months at least. I'm a bit behind schedule at the moment.'

Claire nodded sympathetically and got on with her duties. When she left, Zoe switched the radio on and, as the music played softly, she began writing. Then she hesitated, looked up at the unmoving figure in the bed and turned the radio off.

'Tell me what you think of this,' she said. 'It's a conversation between Chrissie, the artist's daughter, and David, the actor who's been divorced twice. They're at the gallery's opening party. I'm not sure if it's right.' Her brief introduction completed, Zoe began reading, changing her voice as best she could to represent the different characters.

'"Do you come to things like this to meet new women?"

'"I come because I'm invited," David replied indulgently.

'"You're not paying much attention to the paintings," Chrissie pointed out. "And there *are* unattached women here. Me, for instance."

'"And why should that concern me?" he asked, wondering if he'd ever been so obvious, even as a teenager.

'"Have you forgotten how then?" she enquired archly.

'"No," he said, smiling. "But I must be three times your age. How old are you? Fifteen?"

'"I'm seventeen." She bristled with indignation, and her short cropped hair seemed even spikier.

'"My humblest apologies. I am merely two and a half times your age. In any case, old enough to be your father . . ."

'"You're not going to say old enough to put me over your knee, are you?" Chrissie asked with a mixture of disdain and disbelief.

'"Delightful though that prospect might appear," he answered smoothly, eyeing the long legs whose shapeliness was not

155

wholly disguised by the black leggings and Doc Martens, "I will force myself to resist."

'"Dirty old men are getting younger these days," she commented provocatively.

'"Anyway," David continued, his expression deadly serious, "I rather suspect you'd beat the crap out of me if I tried."'

Zoe looked up.

'Well, what do you think?'

There was no response from Michael, of course, but just reading it aloud had given Zoe a better appreciation of the scene. She went back and made a few amendments, then continued writing, occasionally referring to her notes. After a while she reached over and turned the radio on again. Classical music ebbed and flowed, vaguely familiar and reminding her of the sea. A few minutes later Dr Black came in.

'Claire told me you'd brought some work in. How's it going?'

'Better than I expected.'

The music ended in a dramatic surge of sound, and was followed by the cultured voice of the radio announcer.

'That was the orchestral tone-poem, *Tintagel*, by Sir—'

Zoe jumped as a loud burst of static, like that on a two-way radio, interrupted the broadcast. Then a quite different voice took over.

'I just met a wonderful new man – he's fictional, but you can't have everything.'

Zoe and Nick both laughed, though with an edge of nervousness. The voice on the radio sounded odd, like a man imitating a woman.

'Strange interference,' Nick commented.

Zoe was looking at the radio, wondering whether it needed retuning, when the original announcer returned.

'. . . conducted by Bryden Thomson. Our next piece in this afternoon's programme—'

Again static cut off his words, and the other voice spoke again, this time sounding more natural.

'You're a sweet girl, you deserve an actual human.' After another burst of static, he added exasperatedly, 'You can't learn to be real. It's like learning to be a midget. It's not a thing you can learn.'

Moments later normal service was resumed, and the announcer completed his introduction to Brahm's Fourth Symphony. As the lush, romantic music began, Nick frowned.

'Perhaps it was taxi drivers messing about,' he guessed. 'I hope they're using the right frequencies. Our ambulances need their radio contacts clear, especially near the hospital. I've never heard anything like that before, though.'

For a time Zoe could not think of anything to say. She had not recognised the strange quotations, but they were somehow familiar and, although the voice had been disguised, that too had been familiar. Could this be yet another of Michael's attempts to contact her? If so, what on earth was he trying to say? There seemed to be a vague connection with the passage she had read from her book. David was a fictional man, after all. And it had sounded as though one voice had been talking as two people, just as she had done.

'Zoe? Are you OK?'

'Oh.' She realised she was staring into space. 'I'm fine. Perhaps I should get a new radio.' She tried to smile, but the attempt was not very successful. She would have bet almost anything that there would be nothing wrong with her radio – just as there had been nothing wrong with her answering machine, or the heart monitor, or . . .

'When are you going to talk to me again, Michael?' she whispered. 'When are you going to be able to use your own voice?' She was staring at her husband now. 'This is a nightmare.'

The doctor was beside her instantly, a consoling hand on her shoulder.

'He'll come through, Zoe. This is rough on you I know, but we'll beat it. Come and get some coffee.'

She recognised his concern about displaying negative

emotions in front of Michael, and obediently followed him outside. A small voice inside her was repeating, *Calm and strong, calm and strong*. But it was getting harder and harder to listen.

# 19

That evening, Zoe felt utterly drained physically but was mentally wound up tighter than a watch spring. She tried working again once she got home, but that only made her feel even more restless. She just could not concentrate. After mixing herself a large vodka and tonic, she threw it away and made a mug of herbal tea. She tried to watch a detective story on television, but got up so often to check on the answering machine and Michael's computer that she lost the thread of the mystery. She turned the TV off.

Even the thought of going to sleep offered no prospect of respite. Who knew what her dreams might bring? And then she remembered Owen's tape. Surely that would relax her if anything would.

Zoe got ready for bed, found the cassette, then dug out Michael's old Walkman and fitted new batteries. Tucked beneath the duvet, her head resting on the pillow and with Owen's confident, soothing voice playing softly in the headphones, Zoe began to feel the tension drift out of her. Her muscles relaxed, and she drifted in peaceful darkness. Deeper and deeper she sank into the weightless night until Owen's words ended by telling her that she was free to wake or sleep as she chose – except that now there was another voice calling to her, faint and faraway but urgent in its need for a response.

*Emmony?*

In that instant Zoe found herself back in Emmony's bed-chamber, wide awake and sharing the other woman's body.

The air was chill and she was dressed only in a light shift, but her companion did not seem to heed the cold. The bed was still made and Emmony clearly had no intention of sleeping, even though the night sky outside was pitch black.

'I'm glad you came.'

Zoe did not answer, still half afraid, half in awe of her own achievement. Had the tape really been enough to trigger a regression to her past life? The thought was both wonderful and terrifying. If it was true, then the possibilities were endless.

Emmony was looking out of one of the windows. Outside, the courtyard was illuminated by a few lamps, but the only person to be seen was a ragged youth, whose hair and clothes blew in the wind and whose limbs moved awkwardly, as if they were not fully under his control.

'Who's that?'

'Mason. No one takes any notice of him.' There was a mixture of excitement and satisfaction in Emmony's tone.

'Is he a friend?'

'Almost the only one I have in the house now.'

'He looks like a scarecrow . . .' Zoe faltered. *She* knew what she meant, but the two constituent parts of the word made no sense when put together in Emmony's language.

'Scare-crow?'

'Something made to frighten birds away,' Zoe explained awkwardly. 'To stop them eating the seed before it has a chance to grow.'

'Why should we want to scare them?' Emmony asked, genuinely puzzled. 'It's easier to ask them to take only their due.'

'You can do that? Talk to birds?'

'Some of us have that talent.' Emmony sounded surprised. 'Though it's not true speech, of course. But we can get our meaning across.'

Zoe was left wondering about yet another remarkable aspect of the world Emmony – *she* – had once lived in. Mason had left the lighted area now, disappearing into the darkness beyond.

'He'll bring me word, if he can.'

'Of Ghyl?'

'Yes. I pray he is still alive.'

'He's alive.'

Emmony's sudden elation made Zoe feel quite dizzy.

'You know this? You're certain?'

Zoe hesitated. How *did* she know? Just because Michael's condition had not changed, why should the same be true of Ghyl? And yet the certainty remained.

'Nothing's changed,' she said. 'He's sleeping still.'

Emmony's joy lessened at this news.

'Did your spirit see him?' she asked solemnly.

'No . . . It's hard to explain.'

Emmony accepted her guest's evasion without rancour. Good news about her lover's fate was welcome, whatever the source.

'Well, there's nothing more to do now, except wait,' she said. 'It's hard.'

*I know the feeling*, Zoe thought privately, then asked, 'Are you still a prisoner?'

Emmony laughed bitterly.

'In all but name. To outsiders my husband proclaims me ill, with a contagion that makes men mad. No wonder few have tried to visit me. The seals are still in place, but fear makes a better gaoler.'

'Seals?'

Emmony explained that among Jevan's warlocks were those whose talents extended to curses which could isolate a specific place – in this case her room – from those with the talent of communication. And, if they were strong enough, the curses could physically prevent entry or exit. Zoe listened, half in disbelief, half in growing claustrophobia.

'Then how could you get Mason to run the errand for you?' she asked eventually.

'I am still given my meals,' her companion replied. 'Jevan would not see me starve, in case my ghost returned to feast on him, so they send the food in with the most harmless servants. Mason is thought of as simple, disregarded by

161

all but those who see beyond his fractured shape, but he has sense enough – for those who are kind and whom he trusts.' Emmony left the window and began to pace the room, her bare feet soundless on the rugs that covered the floorboards.

'Tell me, can these seals be broken?' Zoe asked.

'Yes, but only by those who are stronger than the one who made them.' Emmony stopped in her tracks as she was struck by a sudden thought. 'Can you do it? Is that within your talent?'

'I don't have any talents.' To Zoe, the word was the equivalent of 'magic'.

'Everyone has talents,' Emmony replied, matter of fact. 'If you think hard enough you will know yours.'

'My only talent is for writing.'

'Writing!' Emmony exclaimed. 'You have such power?'

'Books are a very diffuse form of power at best,' Zoe said, feeling even more confused.

'You write books?' Emmony's astonishment grew. 'Whole books?'

'Yes.'

'Are you a sky-priest? A ritual master of rune lore?'

'Neither. I just tell stories.'

Emmony seemed momentarily deflated by this, but her amazement was still plain.

'You *write* down stories?'

'Yes.'

'Why?'

Unbidden, another Woody Allen quotation popped into Zoe's head. *My artistic ambition? To forge in the smithy of my soul the uncreated conscience of my race. And then see if I can get them mass-produced in plastic.* Angrily, she pushed the thought aside. Why was the filmmaker so much in her thoughts at the moment?

'It's what I do,' she replied simply. 'It's how I earn my living.'

'Such talent is formidable.' Emmony was obviously impressed, and went on to explain that in her world,

162

stories were passed on by word of mouth. Books were almost solely the preserve of priest-scribes, who guarded their secrets jealously. 'I wish it were not so,' she concluded. 'Even outside ritual, books have the capacity for good, for knowledge . . .'

'Do *you* have any books?' Zoe asked abruptly. Here perhaps was a chance to learn more of Emmony's time, in a way she could readily understand.

'I only have one of my own, though there are many more in Jevan's study. I am forbidden to touch them, though I have disobeyed a few times – when occasion permits.'

'Is your book here?' Zoe said, making a mental note to try to get into Jevan's library if at all possible.

For answer, Emmony went to a section of wood panelling next to her bed and pushed a sequence of points among the intricately carved whorls. An inner panel sprang open, revealing a small cupboard from which she took a leather-bound volume. The craftsmanship and patterned embossing were beautiful. She shut the panel again and climbed into bed.

'We can read safely here, if you want, but if anyone comes in we must hide the book beneath the covers. You won't betray me in this, will you?'

Zoe was about to reply that she was incapable of betraying her, that it was Emmony's body, but then the doubt implied by the question made her wonder. Could she possibly control this unfamiliar frame? After all, she was able to move tongue and lips to talk – why not the rest? She refrained from experimenting, however. It would have seemed like treachery, a denial of a privileged trust.

'Of course not,' she said firmly, and let Emmony open the book.

It had no title. Inside the sturdy covers, the pages were thick and stiff. Emmony was obviously very familiar with the contents, and turned the pages more quickly than Zoe would have liked at first, but certain aspects were nonetheless immediately clear. Each leaf was hand-lettered on one side only with neat black script. The text was set out like verse rather than prose, the lines of unequal length, and the number of lines on any page varied from as few as four to perhaps eight times that number. The letters themselves were a mixture of the familiar alphabet, Greek or Russian characters, and some symbols Zoe did not recognise at all. However, the most remarkable and most obvious aspect of each page was the illuminated letter which began each section. These were exquisite works of art in their own right, sometimes filling almost half the page, but instead of the Celtic geometry, heraldic creatures and floral intricacies that Zoe vaguely recalled from medieval calligraphy, these had looked further afield for their inspiration. Various stellar constellations were picked out in silver, blue and gold; fiery comets blazed yellow and red; the sun and moon shone brightly, surrounded by multicoloured auras; an eclipse was illustrated by sequential pictures. And overlaid upon this stellar backcloth were various symbols representing natural forces – wind and rain, waves and currents – as well as man-made implements such as swords, hooks and other curious tools whose use Zoe could not fathom.

When Emmony eventually stopped at a particular page, giving Zoe the time to study what was written there, she was surprised to find how crude the alphabet was, especially when compared to the way in which it had been used. Zoe could read it well enough, thanks to Emmony's familiarity, but the words did not match their lovely setting. They required considerable interpretation from the reader in order to make sense of them, and even more to derive any satisfaction from the sentiments expressed. Zoe was taken aback because, in all her conversations with Emmony and others of her time, translation had been easy – automatic, in fact – and idiomatic in all but a few instances.

'This is my favourite,' Emmony said wistfully.

Zoe reread the few sparse lines. Translated literally it was little more than a collection of seemingly random words, linked only by a general theme of sadness, love and regret. But through some obscure sensibility – which must have been leaking through from Emmony – Zoe knew it to be a message of tenderness and hope from a dying man to the woman he had loved, chastely but passionately, for many years. The central message was that the malign forces which had kept them apart would be finally defeated by death, and that he would wait for her in the next life.

'It's beautiful,' Zoe whispered, deeply moved.

'It is rare for a scribe to see beauty in worldly things,' Emmony said, then paused before adding, 'Beauty and truth. If Ghyl dies, then so will I. The sky-gods themselves would not dare keep us apart again.'

'No. They will not,' Zoe replied with the certainty of knowledge. Emmony's belief in reincarnation was fully justified. She and Ghyl *were* to be reunited in a later life – Zoe's own. But her problems did not end there. And her obvious contemplation of suicide was doubly unnerving.

'But you must not think such things,' Zoe went on. 'We will find a way to save Ghyl. You and he will be together yet, in *this* life.' That, she knew, was vitally important to them both.

Their conversation came to an abrupt halt then, as the sound of approaching footsteps came from outside the chamber. Emmony closed the book and slid it beneath the bedclothes. Zoe felt her disquiet, shared her fearful anticipation as well as her stubborn determination.

They heard the sound of a muffled conversation outside, and then there was an indefinable but unmistakable change in the atmosphere, a relaxation of the air.

'We must be quiet now,' Emmony whispered. 'Will your spirit understand?'

'Yes.' Zoe realised that she and Emmony had been talking aloud unnecessarily. Owen was not even there! *Our thoughts are enough*, she added silently, feeling foolish.

The door opened and Jevan came in, his bulky presence immediately dominating the room. Zoe saw the spirit of Thomas reflected in his dark, rapacious eyes and fought hard to suppress a shudder.

'Not asleep, my love?' he asked in mock surprise. 'You must rest if you are to recover from this fever.' His smile was cruelly false.

'I have no fever,' Emmony replied contemptuously.

'I am glad you've recovered,' he answered blithely, ignoring her defiance. 'We have important guests arriving tomorrow, and I shall want you to be at my side.'

*He means he would lose face if I was still locked away*, Emmony explained to her internal companion. *That means whoever is coming must be able to sense the screens.*

*Someone powerful, then?* Zoe speculated. *Could he help us?*

*Jevan will already have thought of that – and will have taken steps to prevent it*, Emmony replied with disgust. Aloud she said, 'I will perform my wifely duties, as I always have.'

If her husband sensed any of the anger and defiance beneath the meek words, he gave no sign of it.

'Of that, I never had any doubt,' he stated with arrogant confidence, 'but to do so, you must be well rested. This will help you sleep.' He drew out a small phial from his pocket and held it up between a thick forefinger and thumb.

Emmony stiffened, and Zoe knew that it was not just with fear that her book might be discovered.

'There is no need . . .' she began.

'Ah, but I think there is,' he said mildly, still smiling. 'Sleep tonight – and tomorrow, a little pliancy. What could be better?'

'No!'

The smile snapped out of existence.

'Do not put me to the trouble of forcing you to drink,' he warned coldly. Picking up a goblet, he half filled it with water from a jug, then carefully added three drops from the phial and swirled it round as he approached the bed. Emmony shrank back but with his left hand Jevan grabbed her arm, which had been raised in feeble self-defence, and held it in a vice-like grip.

'Drink. Or it will be the worse for you.'

Zoe's terror was now almost equal to Emmony's, and for a moment she thought of trying to exercise her theoretical powers and dash the goblet aside with her free hand. Who could tell what would happen if Emmony took the drugged potion while Zoe was still with her? But she could only look

166

on in paralysed helplessness as Emmony reached out slowly, took the cup and brought it to her lips. The liquid tasted sour, but not as bitter as the feeling of defeat as Jevan watched her swallow.

'Good.' Although his satisfaction was evident, there was no hint of a smile on his face now. Putting the goblet back on the table, Jevan left the room without another word.

*What's happening?* Zoe cried silently, but already knew the answer. Her vision was blurring, and all her senses were becoming numb. Emmony did not reply, sunk deep in her own despair.

*Owen, get me out of this!* But from somewhere came the knowledge that Owen was not there to help her. *This isn't supposed to affect me too*, she protested feebly, half expecting to wake up in her own bed. *I want to go back to my own life. I want to wake up!* Nonetheless the downward spiral into enforced unconsciousness continued inexorably. *Not me too!* Zoe wailed, then lost even the capacity for thought. Oblivion engulfed her.

# 20

Emmony and Zoe struggled out of the darkness together, and pain mixed with panic as they fought to open their eyes. There was broad daylight outside, but inside the chamber everything was the same. The book still lay, undiscovered, beneath the covers.

'My head,' Emmony groaned. The potion's legacy was a severe headache and a listlessness that made her limbs feel intolerably heavy. Willpower seemed an unattainable illusion, a malicious joke.

*And tomorrow . . .* Zoe remembered, *a little pliancy*. The idea made her shudder. She had to get out. The vulnerability of her position had been made horribly clear, and her only intention now was to end this regression, to escape back to her own life. The realisation on her return to consciousness that she was still in the past had been dreadful, and all consideration of what her departure would mean to Emmony had fled from her mind. She had to get out! But how was this necessary abandonment to be achieved? There was no Owen waiting to recall her to the present, no signal for her to obey. She could not touch anything in her own world. Hysteria began to edge its way into her thoughts.

Far away, a bell began to ring.

'The visitors are arriving,' Emmony said heavily.

But Zoe heard the sound differently. This was not a toll of welcome but both a warning and an invitation, more strident and repetitive than anything in Emmony's world. Zoe yearned towards it, not understanding yet but clutching at the straw it offered. Gradually the sound drew closer, became clearer, until she recognised the sound of her telephone and stumbled back into her own life.

As she absorbed the details of her bedroom with an almost stupefying sense of relief, she heard the answering machine click on and begin to relay its message to the caller. Hurriedly, still feeling dizzy and with her headache pulsing angrily, she staggered out of bed, pulled on a dressing gown and groped her way downstairs. As she entered the sitting room, Alex's voice was already coming from the monitor.

'. . . just thought I'd call to see how you were, but obviously you're already out. There's also a bit of news about work. I know you don't want to be bothered at the moment, but—'

Zoe picked up the receiver.

'Hello, Alex.'

'Oh, hi, Zoe. You *are* there.'

'Been asleep.' She was still trying to clear her thoughts.

'I'm sorry. I didn't mean to wake you.'

'I'm glad you did,' Zoe said with feeling.

'How are you?'

'OK, I guess.'

'And Michael?'

'No change,' Zoe replied wearily, and there was a pause as her agent sensed her reluctance to talk. Alex decided to try a lighter topic in the hope of diverting her friend.

'Ever find out about that quote of yours?'

For a few moments Zoe wondered what Alex was talking about, then eventually remembered. *The Dead Month* ritual.

'Not really,' she said.

'It's got us stumped too.'

'What was the work news?' Zoe asked, changing the subject herself this time.

'I don't suppose you've remembered, with everything you've got on your mind,' her agent replied briskly, 'but the paperback of *Autumn Leaves* comes out in a couple of months. A journalist from the *Independent* wants to do a piece to coincide with publication. An interview.'

'Oh, God,' Zoe groaned. Ordinarily she would have been

immensely flattered and very keen to receive such publicity, but now . . . 'I'm not sure I can remember that far back.'

'The old Dr Who syndrome, I know,' Alex responded sympathetically. 'But it might do you good.'

Zoe had a theory, which she had often expounded to her agent, that being a writer was occasionally like being a time-traveller. *Autumn Leaves* had been finished over two years ago, and Zoe had written another complete novel and most of *Fields of Plenty* since then. Talking about the earlier story would therefore be like stepping back into the past – and an imaginary past at that – something that required a certain kind of mental agility.

'I'm an expert at going back in time,' Zoe found herself saying, and grimaced at the unexpected irony, 'but I'm not sure I can cope with it at the moment.'

'OK,' Alex agreed without complaint. 'I'll put her on hold, but let me know if you change your mind. She can come up to Norfolk or do it over the phone, so it wouldn't take up much time.'

'I'll let you know,' Zoe promised. 'Thanks for bearing with me.'

'Least I can do.'

'I've started to do a bit of work on *Fields*.' She wanted to make up for some of her reluctance about the interview.

'Great!' Alex said with enthusiasm. 'It'll do you good. Take you out of yourself for a bit.'

Zoe grimaced again. 'Thanks for phoning, Alex,' she said.

'Chin up, Zoe. I'll be in touch again soon. Bye.'

'Bye.'

Zoe put the phone down and collapsed into an armchair, her head reeling. Why was she hiding things from Alex, someone who patently had only her good interests at heart? What was she afraid of? Scorn disguised as pity? Being thought insane?

'I'm not mad,' she said aloud. 'These things are real.'

Perhaps the task of explaining it all was just too daunting. It was too complicated. She knew that wasn't the only reason – her decision had been too instinctive for that

– but it was the most comforting one she could come up with.

And now, finally, she had the chance to think back, to consider the advantages – and the pitfalls – of what she had been able to do. It was daylight outside, rain falling from a dull canopy of cloud, so – like Emmony – she had lost the entire night. She felt very tired, in spite of her enforced rest, and her whole body ached. But those physical discomforts paled into insignificance beside the terror she had felt when she'd thought she might not be able to return to her own time, that she might be forced to live out Emmony's life. *And Emmony's death?* What if Emmony had carried out her implied threat to commit suicide while Zoe was still a part of her? Would she be as susceptible to fatal poison as she had obviously been to Jevan's sleeping potion? No, that was absurd. Emmony had died a long time ago. Zoe was here, now. Hypnotised subjects frequently experienced past life deaths with little or no trauma, let alone any physical consequences. Even so, she could not shake off her disquiet.

What was more, the dream-regression, as she had christened it in her mind, had seemed very reluctant to let go. Zoe could only assume that she had been released by the sound of the telephone, and decided that if she should ever try self-regression again – and she had every intention of doing just that – she would make sure that she implanted some definite, externally signalled instruction which would bring the hypnosis to an end.

Having decided that, Zoe's excitement grew. Now she would not have to wait out the eternity until Wednesday and Owen's next visit. Who knew what she might discover in the meantime?

For now, however, the necessities of her own life took precedence. Refreshed by a bath and some breakfast, she set off for the hospital with renewed vigour, taking her manuscript with her. As she drove, she went over recent events as methodically as she could. One obvious extra clue given to her by the dream was Emmony's book. She could look up that type of lettering, and perhaps the strange

171

alphabet. Then there had been the odd messages on the radio the day before. They had stuck in her mind, still vaguely familiar, but she could not place them. That was another possible line of research. She decided on a quick trip to Norwich Library at lunchtime. She longed to know whether Mason's mission had succeeded, and how Emmony had survived the visit of Jevan's 'important guests', but there was nothing she could do about that – yet.

At the hospital, nothing had changed. This was only what Zoe expected, but she still always arrived with a tiny fragment of hope. To have it dashed was as dispiriting as ever, but she quickly overcame her disappointment and went on. She told Michael all about the latest developments and asked for his help, all the time watching his unmoving face – the face that filled her with love and stirred her whole body with impotent longings.

'Oh, Michael, when you're better, you won't need to go running. You'll get all the exercise you need in bed.' She glanced round at the door, blushing at the thought that someone might have overheard, but she was alone.

Zoe said goodbye to her husband in the early afternoon, and drove into the city centre. She had no luck tracing the quotations, but was almost overwhelmed by information on the history of the alphabet. That section in the encyclopedia was incredibly complex, with several tables and pages of text devoted to the development of written language. She struggled through the maze of facts concerning the Brahmin letters of ancient India, hieroglyphs, the Moabite stone symbols, runes and Semitic writings. These led onto a bewildering assortment of alphabets – Cyrillic, Glagolitic, various forms of Greek and Latin – and then to modern European systems. Zoe's head spun, and she soon gave up trying to master the myriad complexities and just skimmed through the diagrams. After nearly an hour, she came reluctantly but resignedly to the conclusion that none of them exactly matched the letters in Emmony's book. Some were the same, some were from supposedly inappropriate combinations, and some did not appear anywhere. She was still unable to pinpoint her location in the past.

Zoe reported her lack of progress to Michael on her return to his quiet room, and then she switched on the cassette player and began to do a little work.

All afternoon the feeling grew in her that she could be achieving more elsewhere and, after explaining her agitation and hoping Michael would understand, Zoe left earlier than normal. There were no surprises awaiting her at Ash Ring, and so she took a deep breath and began to prepare herself to return to Emmony's world.

First she found an old alarm clock – one with a truly barbaric ring – and checked that it still worked. Then she set up Owen's tape in the stereo and recorded her own postscript at the end, instructing herself clearly and firmly that when she heard the alarm she would come forward to her own life and open her eyes, feeling refreshed and remembering all she had experienced. She placed an upright chair in the centre of the room, turned the telephone and answering machine volumes down to zero – so that messages would still be accepted but her regression would not be ended prematurely – set the alarm clock to go off in one hour, and then sat down with the remote control for the hi-fi in her lap.

When she was ready and as relaxed as she could realistically hope to be, Zoe closed her eyes, pushed the 'Play' button and heard the cassette deck click into action. Owen's resonant voice filled the room, and soon that was all her world.

*I'm coming, Emmony,* Zoe said, and felt herself spinning outwards, drawing closer to her other self.

# 21

Everything felt wrong.

Emmony was dressed in her finest clothes – the material soft and dark and glittering with ornamentation – but they were uncomfortable, twisted and constricting as if she had not known how to put them on correctly. She sat on a sort of chaise longue, her hands folded demurely in her lap and her eyes downcast, with hardly a thought in her head. Even Zoe's arrival was greeted with no more than a moment's indifferent stillness. At first Zoe thought this was to make sure she did not betray her to the others in the lamplit room, but then wondered fearfully if Emmony was capable of no more. *A little pliancy.* And yet Zoe did not share in her companion's malaise. She felt alert, with none of the aftereffects of the potion that still seemed to be affecting Emmony. Unless, of course, something else had been done to her during Zoe's absence.

*Emmony?*

There was no direct response, but her body seemed to grow more tense – matching the atmosphere in the room. As Zoe gradually became more aware of her surroundings, she realised that she must be in Jevan's study. The furnishings were dark, sturdy and aggressively masculine. Hunting trophies were fixed to one wall, and there were weapons hung above the large stone fireplace where logs blazed and crackled. That was the only sound in the room, and it made the silence of the three men who sprawled in large padded chairs seem even more awkward. On the surface, each of

174

them appeared content, occasionally drinking from the metal goblets in their hands, but even a moment's observation made it obvious that, within, they were anything but relaxed.

Jevan abruptly raised his cup and drained it, then glanced at his wife.

'More wine,' he snapped. For an instant, Zoe cringed mentally, expecting him to follow up his command with criticism or abuse, but none came.

Emmony rose slowly, without volition, as if she were sleepwalking, and crossed to a table on which stood a tall jug. Carefully and deliberately, as though she were mortally afraid of spilling a single drop, Emmony refilled her husband's goblet and prepared to move on. Her subservient manner made Zoe's blood boil and she had to stop herself from speaking out, perhaps even attempting to throw the wine in Jevan's arrogant face. But the consequences of such actions were too appalling to contemplate and instead she determined to learn all she could through her own senses – and from her companion, if she could be roused from her stupor. Retribution could wait.

The second man was a smaller, meaner version of Jevan, the same dark features compressed into a rat-like face. Even in repose he seemed coiled and ready for sudden movement.

*Who is he?* Zoe asked firmly as the jug was tipped towards the cup he held out.

The only response was a sudden stiffening that made the wine shiver and slop within the jug. The man grinned nastily at her awkwardness.

*Who is he, Emmony?*

Emmony recovered her poise and poured cautiously before answering.

*Killian, Jevan's twin brother. The Grey Wolf.*

Zoe gave a mental sigh of relief at the 'sound' of her companion's voice. Emmony was not lost to her completely. She was not sure whether the last part of the answer was Killian's title or his nickname, but it seemed to suit him very well. He had the eyes of a predator and even though his hair and beard were black, he was clad entirely in grey; even his belt buckle and buttons were forged from dull iron and his well-worn boots were made of dusty leather the colour of winter clouds.

By now, Emmony had moved on to the last member of the party. He was older, his clean-shaven face pale and lined, his thin limbs draped in loose, silky material that seemed to flow over him like a waterfall. He did not move his goblet from where he held it, resting on the wide arm of his chair, and Zoe wondered first whether he actually had the strength to lift it, then – because that was obviously absurd – whether he had taken offence at being served last. Something about him gave the impression that he was used to being deferred to, his every whim indulged.

*This is Lissac, the Pyramid Builder*, Emmony volunteered before Zoe had a chance to ask. *One of Chandos's foremost court sorcerers.*

Zoe began to form a question, but Lissac spoke then and she thought better of it, preferring to concentrate on what was being said.

'Your wife is dutiful as well as decorative.' He was watching her as she put the jug back on the table and returned to her seat. Zoe felt the pressure of his gaze – a *sorcerer's* gaze – even when she could not see him.

Jevan merely grunted in response, not sure of the degree of sarcasm in his guest's words, and there was another edgy pause.

'Well, Lissac,' Killian said eventually. 'You didn't drag me all the way out here for nothing. Suppose you tell us—'

'Hold your tongue, brother!' Jevan interrupted harshly. 'Lissac will choose his own time to speak. You are only a guest here. Do not forget it.'

'In this house?' Killian replied bitterly. 'How could I?'

Zoe understood immediately that there was no love or trust between these two, or even liking, for all that they were twins. And their joint antagonism towards Lissac was equally obvious. The sorcerer's attitude towards the brothers was more difficult to read. Zoe had also begun to wonder why the old man was there, and looked at him curiously. The fact

176

that Emmony's body obeyed her impulse unquestioningly did not even register with her.

It was then that she witnessed something so extraordinary that it emphasised just how unlike her own world Emmony's was. As she watched, Lissac's goblet floated free of his hand and raised itself slowly but smoothly for him to drink. It should have been absurd, comical, with overtones of a baby having to be fed, but it was not. The action was so smooth, so naturally timed and controlled that it was not in the least bit funny. It was a casual display of power, calculated and gratuitous – and everyone there knew it.

Zoe alone was awestruck. Until then the title 'sorcerer' had meant little, just one more mysterious term whose meaning could easily be confused. Now she had seen Lissac's talent at first hand. This was no trick, no cartoon-like make believe; this was true telekinesis, practised and sophisticated, but used for a deliberately trivial purpose. How much more, she wondered, was Lissac capable of? What had Emmony called him? *The Pyramid Builder*.

The goblet returned to its place on the arm of the chair, settling gently into Lissac's fingers again as he swallowed and sighed, deliberately ignoring the silence all about him.

'Excellent,' he commented, then, as if it followed on as a natural consequence of his appreciation of the wine, he said, 'There is a new sport in the Marshland.'

Neither of the other men rose to his bait, and Lissac continued unperturbed.

'It is called Favourites.'

Killian snorted derisively.

'Since when have courtiers done anything other than curry favour?'

'True enough,' the sorcerer agreed amiably, 'but the rules have been changed.' He was clearly enjoying this slow torment, but appeared to relent and came to the point, his pale face and quiet voice serious. 'There is one who now has Chandos's ear and, if not checked, his influence could bode ill for all of us.'

'Who?' Jevan demanded.

'Urbani of Troye.'

'That oily tin-merchant?' Killian exclaimed in disbelief. 'Chandos pays heed to a *foreigner*?'

'The colour of a man's skin is no bar to cunning,' Lissac told him sharply. 'He has taken accurate stock of the Prince's character, and has presented him with a gift beyond price.'

'What gift?' Jevan asked.

'A treatise on princely survival and success,' the sorcerer replied, pausing dramatically before adding, 'Written down.'

'Written down?' Killian exploded. 'That's blasphemy!'

'Not so,' Lissac responded calmly. 'The Sky-Priest's coterie have sanctioned his work.'

'What is the nature of this advice?' Jevan was calmer than his brother – and somehow more frightening because of it.

'I can quote the main points word for word,' the old man replied. 'They're on everyone's lips at present. There is much justification besides, but—'

'Just tell us,' Killian growled.

'A Prince must be miserly, not liberal,' Lissac began, ticking off the items on skeletal fingers. 'He must be feared, not loved – but avoiding hatred; cunning, not honest – while seeming honest; resolute, not fickle and well-regarded by his people, never despised. A Prince must be enterprising, a patron of merit and a provider of festivals and celebrations. He must be impetuous rather than cautious and thinking of war even in times of peace.'

'Such utter shit has been thought worthy to be recorded in script?' Killian's contempt made him shrill. 'What is Chandos thinking of?'

'Is he shrewd or mad?' Jevan wondered softly.

'Urbani's arguments are cogent, and enshrining them in ink was a clever move,' Lissac commented. 'Chandos is charmed, and dislodging this *foreigner* . . .' He smiled as he emphasised the word. '. . . will be a delicate and dangerous undertaking. I think you have been away from the Pyramid for too long, Jevan.'

'I will ride with you tomorrow,' their host declared, decisive now.

Lissac nodded with satisfaction and rose slowly to his feet.

'Then I will bid you goodnight.'

The other two men, then Emmony, got up and remained standing until the old man had left the room. When the door had closed, Killian strode over to the table and poured himself more wine. Emmony moved far too late, ineffectually trying to help. Killian shoved her aside roughly and swore obscenely, giving her such an ugly glare that Zoe shrivelled helplessly in the face of that mixture of hatred and undisguised lust. Emmony raised her hands defensively, but he made no move to strike her and even laughed contemptuously.

'You pathetic cow.'

'Leave her alone,' Jevan grated.

Killian swung round to face his brother.

'You pompous, hypocritical . . . You half poison her and then wonder why she's so stupid . . . Why defend her now? She can't even give you an heir.'

'That's enough,' Jevan whispered in icy rage.

'It's no wonder you seek consolation elsewhere,' Killian continued, equally angry now and encouraged by the effectiveness of his barbs. 'But don't think your bastards will inherit anything. I'm the heir. I *will* be the next Quarterman.'

'Are you threatening me, brother?' Jevan said, so quietly that Killian belatedly recognised the danger he was in and backed down.

'I meant no offence,' he said in a tight voice. 'That old fool and his tales have burnt my beard.'

'For all his mannerisms, Lissac is no fool,' Jevan told him. Emmony had obviously been dismissed from their thoughts now. 'Will you ride with us tomorrow?'

'Yes,' Killian replied grudgingly.

His brother nodded.

'Then leave me. I have preparations to make.'

Without further words, Killian turned to leave. As he

passed Emmony, he leant close to give her a cynical peck on the cheek. She dared not shrink away, although his nearness revolted her. He made the ordeal infinitely worse by whispering in her ear, so that only she could hear.

'I'd wager you'd give *me* a child. Come to my chamber and put it to the test!'

Once again Zoe had to fight to restrain her natural burning resentment and her desire to act. She had felt Emmony's humiliation keenly, and was sick with disgust. Even the revelation that Jevan was unfaithful – although this came as no surprise – had been a cause of shame.

And yet, in another way, eavesdropping on the conversation had been fascinating. She had witnessed magic, and had been given an insight – albeit confusing – into the treacherous politics of the Eastern Dominions. In addition – and best of all – she was now certain that Jevan, and Killian, would be gone for some time from the next morning. Surely then Emmony would be able to help Ghyl.

After Killian had left, Jevan sat down again and held up his cup. Emmony hurried to fill it and watched as her husband drank deeply.

'Leave me,' he ordered shortly then, as Emmony turned to go, added, 'Wait. Bring me the 'chanters stone first.'

Obediently, she went over to a bureau, opened it and picked up a black sphere about the size of an orange. She handled it gingerly and Zoe had to force her to look into its dark, glassy depths. Emmony allowed her to examine it briefly but would clearly rather have averted her eyes, and did so as soon as Zoe relented. Their gaze fell momentarily upon a long, thin satin bag and, before Zoe knew what was happening, Emmony had reached out and slid it into her sleeve. Her heart was thumping as she went back to Jevan, but he had evidently noticed nothing untoward. He accepted the sphere in his cupped hand and waved her away. Emmony went gladly, hiding her trophy, but the music began before she left the room.

At first Zoe could not believe her ears. She could not help but glance back, and saw Jevan, his eyes closed, cradling the 'chanters stone, and knew that the impossible sounds were coming from there. The music was rhythmic, full of phantom percussion and choirs of ethereal voices – and it was somehow demonic, building in intensity and volume as other invisible instruments added their strident or mellifluous voices. The whole thing reminded Zoe of Carl Orff's *Carmina Burana*, with its devils and driving tempos, but this was somehow much more ominous, more potent, and she was filled with unease. And yet it was almost hypnotically enthralling.

*We must go*, Emmony said wearily.

She went outside and shut the door.

*What is he doing?*

*The 'chanters enhance his talents, make him stronger. There are many perils in the Marshland.*

*Tell me . . .* Zoe began, but got no further. Amid the still rising volume of the strange music was a single, continuous, jarring note.

Surely the hour could not be up so soon?

But it was. Zoe found herself back in her own sitting room, listening to the clamour of the alarm bell.

# 22

Zoe immediately wanted to go straight back and find answers to the new questions raised by her latest experience. But she soon put that idea aside. It was late, she was very tired and her self-hypnosis had worked perfectly. There was no reason why she should not go back to Emmony at any time she wished, knowing, with the altered tape, that she would return safely. And tomorrow, with Jevan gone, she would be much more likely to learn what she needed without hindrance.

'Hang on a minute,' she said aloud to the empty room.

She had caught herself in a simple but fallible assumption. Why, just because it would be the next day for her, would it necessarily be the same for Emmony? That implied that Zoe's entry into her past life was predicated by the present, which made no sense. But then, according to Owen, not being able to move within the time span of that past life made no sense either. Was it possible that her lives, both present and past, were somehow moving at the same pace? Looking back, Zoe realised that she had been assuming just that, ever since Emmony had told her she had been to see Ghyl 'last night'. And her most recent 'visit' had obviously taken place the day after Jevan had drugged Emmony. But could this be true? As far as she could remember, daylight in her own time had corresponded to daylight in the past life, and night to night, but surely this was just coincidence. Resolving to try to confirm or refute her theory on future visits, Zoe set aside speculation and went over what she had learnt that evening.

In some ways the most curious fact was that Jevan had a twin. Thomas, his equivalent in her own time, was an only child, with no brothers at all, let alone a twin. This was the first anomaly in the perhaps too perfect match between her two lives – and Zoe had no idea what that implied. Then there had been the discussion about their convoluted politics, and the agitation caused by this Urbani of Troye. *Troy?* Surely it could not be the same one, the Troy of Homer and the wooden horse? But then again why not? Curiosity drove Zoe to look up the ancient city in her one-volume encyclopedia, which told her, among other things, that Troy – one of nine cities buried at that site – was on a tin trade route. *That oily tin-merchant?* Killian had exclaimed, and the memory of his words made Zoe shiver. Urbani was obviously an unpleasant character if his cynical advice to Chandos was anything to go by.

On top of that there had been Lissac's casual magic and Jevan's music – and the unknown object Emmony had snatched up from the bureau. What had that been? Then Zoe remembered something Emmony had said on a previous encounter. *I could do much more if I had the talisman, but it has been taken from me.* Could she have reclaimed it secretly now, the strange object she had described as 'the hollow feather'? Zoe hoped so, without really knowing why.

That night she dreamt she was alone in a bright, modern room. It reminded her of an operating theatre, except that there were large screens all around the walls, like giant televisions or computer consoles. At first these were all blank, but then one flickered on and Michael's face stared out at her. He was speaking urgently, but there was no sound. Zoe searched frantically for the volume control and eventually found it, although it looked more like a dark, spherical paperweight than a remote unit. Immediately, music filled her ears. Michael was shown full length on the screen, almost life-size. He was still talking but his face was shifting, blurring until he became someone she only half recognised. A voice could be heard over the surging music.

'Well, look at it this way. How many times is a man

so taken with a woman that he walks off the screen to get her?'

With that the man who was not quite Michael stepped out of the TV and into the room, holding his arms wide, and as she ran into his embrace Zoe woke up with a rush of adrenaline that made her wrists tingle. Although it was not yet six o'clock and it was still dark outside, she flung off the duvet and ran downstairs, tugging on a dressing gown against the early morning chill. She knew now where the quotations on the radio and from her dream had come from, and why Woody Allen had been in her mind so much recently.

In the sitting room, she ran a finger along Michael's collection of films and pulled out a videotape marked *The Purple Rose of Cairo*. Switching on the television and setting the VCR in motion, Zoe sat back and waited to see why Michael was so anxious for her to play this movie – as she was convinced he was.

*The Purple Rose of Cairo* was a film she both loved – for its ingenuity, inventiveness and blurring of the line between fantasy and reality – and hated – for the heartbreaking sadness of its cynically tragic denouement. Michael had always teased her about her need for happy endings, even though they both knew he shared it to a large degree. But quite why she was now sitting, shivering in the pre-dawn cold, watching the story of a character drawn by love to step down from the movie screen and into the audience, Zoe could not say. What hidden relevance could it have to her situation?

For some minutes she watched, waiting for a revelation, as Cecilia, played by Mia Farrow, found escape from the drudgery of her Depression era life at the cinema. But none came, and Zoe was beginning to wonder whether she could possibly have been mistaken. Then, just as the character Tom Baxter, played by Jeff Daniels, looked out at the cinema audience and, impossibly, started to speak directly to Cecilia, there was a bright flash and a hiss of static. Zoe jumped violently, her eyes transfixed on the blurred pattern now on the screen. What was happening? Was someone going to step out of *this* screen?

184

*Get a grip*, she told herself sternly. This *must* be what she was waiting for.

The hissing faded, and became a general background hum of human activity; voices – though no words were audible – footsteps, other unidentifiable noises. And then the pattern of jumping dots resolved itself, becoming a peculiar, distorted view of what appeared to be the inside of a large shop. The point of view seemed to be fixed near the ceiling, recording events below randomly, as customers and assistants went about their business, oblivious to the fact that they were being watched. Peering closer, Zoe saw that it was a store selling electrical apparatus – televisions, video recorders, computers, and so on – and her view of it must surely be from a security camera. But she couldn't make out much more than that – and certainly couldn't see why such a scene should concern her.

And then, as abruptly as it had come, it was gone and *Purple Rose* resumed.

'Oh, Michael. What was that all about?' she wailed.

Zoe stopped the tape, rewound it and watched it through again. The interruption came again, in the same place. Again, it lasted little more than thirty seconds, but however closely she studied it, she could make no sense of it. In desperation she played through the rest of the film in fast forward but, as she had guessed, there were no more interruptions. Those thirty seconds were all she had. Repeated inspection made her even more frustrated, and yet she persevered. Michael had gone to a lot of trouble to make her see this, so there *must* be something there. Something important.

But as day broke, Zoe had made no progress and now had a splitting headache. Eventually she gave up, took some aspirin, made a cup of tea and went back to bed to try to warm up. She felt thoroughly sorry for herself. What had she done to deserve this? Had she really been so bad – in this life or others – to warrant such punishment? Michael would have scolded her for thinking this way, but depression was difficult to avoid when everything seemed designed to tease and torture her. Soon she would not need to worry about other people's opinions of her sanity – she *would* be mad, driven to it by the incomprehensible events that now filled her life.

Then, whether because of Owen's therapy or because her own natural resilience reasserted itself, Zoe got up and prepared to go on with life. As a result it was still early morning when she arrived at the hospital. It was some time before she could talk to Michael, however, as the staff were in and out as they went about the routine work necessary for his care. But eventually she was able to tell him about her latest regression and the clues that had led her to *The Purple Rose of Cairo*.

'I found it, Michael, the bit of tape you wanted me to see, but I don't understand what it means, or how you put it there. It's just a picture of a big store, selling TVs and so on – like the place you used to work in.' Zoe stopped in her tracks, struck by a sudden thought. 'God, Michael. That's it! It's Brands, isn't it?'

Now she thought about it, she knew it *was* – not the old store, but the modern version that she had been in herself many times. The lay out, distorted though it had been by the wide-angle lens of the security camera, was exactly as she remembered it.

'Am I supposed to go there? Why?' Zoe wondered, then fell silent again as she suddenly realised what it meant. Now that she had the answer it was perfectly obvious, and yet she was still not sure where this was all leading. The idea of the past coming back to haunt her in yet another way made her tremble, but at least her next step was clear enough.

'Goodbye for now, Michael. You know where I'm going. I'll be back as soon as I can.'

The drive back to Thornmere seemed endless but at last she was home, heading straight for the sitting room shelves. The Moroccan jewellery box sat where it had been put what seemed like a lifetime ago, and Zoe lifted it down carefully. Sitting on the sofa, because her legs suddenly felt incapable of supporting her, she opened the lid and stared at the small felt bag. The ring, that's what it had all been leading to. The videotape had evidently been Michael's only way of reminding her of it, by showing her the place where he had met the vagabond all those years ago. The vagrant's parting words echoed again in the silent room. *Keep it safe always. Your wife will have need of it when you leave her.*

Well, in one very real sense, Michael *had* left her – though in a way neither of them could ever have envisaged. And Zoe was glad of all the help she could get – whatever the source.

She gently opened the bag and took out the ring. The blood red stone glistened with secrets. Instinctively, Zoe did the only logical thing to do with a ring. She slipped it onto her finger. It fitted perfectly, just above her wedding band, though it felt heavy and awkward. Zoe did not know what she was expecting – some sudden insight or revelation perhaps – but nothing happened. She sat there for a few minutes, her heart beating fast, feeling rather silly.

Then she remembered another small bag, albeit of a quite different shape, and wondered whether Emmony still had her trophy – and whether it was indeed her prized talisman. Could it be that the ring was *her* talisman, something that would enable her to perform magic?

'Tolkien has a lot to answer for,' she said aloud, trying to keep some sense of proportion, but the idea stuck. There was no way she could ignore it now. And the only way to test her theory was to go back to the one place where magic might reasonably be expected to be of use – Emmony's time.

Everything was still in place from the night before. All she had to do was rewind Owen's tape and reset the alarm clock. Once that was done, Zoe sat in the chair and began. The ring was still on her left hand, her right hand resting on top, touching the stone.

The induction of hypnosis and her passage back in time was so swift that it felt as though she were almost being *dragged* there, by outside forces rather than by her own subconscious. The scene exploded into her sight, long before Owen's unheeded words had played out.

'Well, where is it?' Jevan demanded angrily. 'I know you took it, you deceiving slut. Where is it?' He was approaching her slowly but steadily, and there was murder in his eyes.

Zoe shrank back, waiting for Emmony to answer, but her companion did not speak. Something was different, wrong. Feeling frightened and bewildered, Zoe looked at Emmony's raised hands – but this time she *was* Emmony, the transition whole and complete, body and mind. Emmony was not there at all.

This time, she was on her own.

# 23

'I don't know what you're talking about,' Zoe said truthfully, backing away from the enraged Jevan. She stumbled over a chair she had not realised was behind her.

'Do you take me for an idiot?' Jevan snarled, but he had stopped moving and was watching her closely.

*Does he know?* Zoe wondered, horrified by the thought. *How could he?* She steadied herself, feeling very strange in her new body. Her previous visits had all been as a guest, and had not prepared her to take control completely. She wondered desperately what had happened to Emmony.

'Your eyes look different,' Jevan observed, his voice quieter now, but still accusing. 'What have you been doing?'

'Nothing.'

'Can it be that you are afraid?' he asked, mocking her.

Zoe did not answer. She did not yet trust her new voice, and had no need to feign fear. The situation was horribly familiar, and she saw a reflection of Thomas in Jevan's face, heard her ex-husband's voice in the Quarterman's coldly gentle words.

'You have every reason to be,' he assured her. 'The punishments you have endured in the past for disobeying me are nothing compared to what I *could* do. You are of no consequence, an insect I can crush beneath my heel whenever I wish. You do understand that, don't you?' He paused, but in her half stunned condition, Zoe did not realise that he was waiting for an answer. 'Don't you?' he roared suddenly, and she jumped in terror.

'Yes,' she whispered.

'Then tell me where the talisman is.'

'I don't know,' Zoe replied – and then realised that she did. As she spoke, an unbidden memory – which was not her own – had flashed into her mind, the memory of a small, thin bag being hidden away in Emmony's secret cupboard. The talisman, whatever it was, now lay in darkness beside her precious book. Zoe struggled not to let this knowledge show on her face. She could not betray Emmony – or herself – in such a way.

'You're lying,' Jevan remarked calmly. 'What can you possibly hope to achieve? Your puny talents are no match for mine, still less that of the warlocks at my command. If I had more time now, you would find yourself in a very . . . uncomfortable . . . situation. And I *will* get the talisman back eventually. You know this.' He was trying to sound reasonable – and the effort was obviously trying his patience. But Zoe found her resolve strengthening. His words – *if I had more time* – had given her hope. If she could just hold out a little longer . . .

'Where is the talisman?' he repeated. 'This is your last chance.'

'I don't know,' she answered, then added with a spurt of defiance, 'Why don't you ask Lissac?'

Jevan's face froze. Too late, Zoe recognised her mistake and cursed herself for it.

'You would disgrace me as well, would you!' he yelled, lunging forward. 'You ignorant slut. I'll . . .'

He struck out, aiming for her head, but Zoe had raised her arms to protect herself and took the blow on her left forearm. Even so, the force of it knocked her sideways. She staggered and fell heavily. Black shapes swirled within her head, and she thought she would faint. She did not, but lay still on the hard floor, aware that Jevan stood over her, and praying for release, for some unlikely rescue.

'Get up,' he snarled contemptuously. 'I haven't started yet.'

Instinctively Zoe kept quite still, curled up in a foetal

position. She almost wished she *had* fainted, and hoped that Jevan would believe it.

Then there was a sudden loud knocking at the door.

'What is it?' Jevan shouted angrily.

'The party stays for you, my Lord Quarterman,' a nervous voice replied. 'Lissac grows impatient,' was added more quietly.

Jevan made a small noise deep in his throat, and Zoe held her breath in sudden hope. Had her improbable rescuer arrived?

'I have to go, my love,' Jevan remarked sarcastically. 'We will continue our discussion when I return.' His resentment at being thwarted and at having to obey the unspoken summons of the sorcerer was clear in his voice.

'I'm coming!' he called, adding more quietly, 'Fare you well, wife.'

Relief was just beginning to surge through Zoe for her – and Emmony's – temporary reprieve when she was suddenly overwhelmed by an agonising pain. She gave a stifled scream, then fought to breathe in short, tearing gasps. Jevan's heavy boot had slammed into her lower ribcage, simultaneously hurting her terribly, shattering her nerves and knocking all the wind out of her lungs. As she struggled desperately to breathe and to control her agony, she heard Jevan laugh and – thankfully – make his way to the door and leave.

With her eyes tight shut, Zoe lay curled around the hot core of anguish, all her efforts mindlessly concentrated on getting her tormented lungs to work properly. Blackness threatened again, but she fought against it as she listened to the welcome sound of receding footsteps. That at least was some comfort and, at last, her breathing returned to some semblance of normality. Zoe had no idea how long she lay there; the soreness gradually lessened to a dull, throbbing ache, but the pain was still enough to stop her trying to move. But at least she was now able to control her thoughts a little better. The sudden violence had taken her by surprise, in spite of what she knew of Jevan. She realised – and chided herself for having been so stupid – that she had been equating this

191

confrontation to her own with Thomas. Her first husband's veneer of civilization had meant that his cruelties were rarely of a physical nature, but his earlier counterpart was obviously not so constrained.

Zoe wondered fearfully whether any of her ribs were broken. The slight movement involved in breathing did not seem to make anything worse, which had to be a good sign, but she was too frightened to try any further motion in case the dreadful searing pain returned. Eventually, however, she realised that she had to try, and slowly began to move. Inch by inch, she levered herself up into a sitting position and leant gently back against the chair. She survived the process with only a mild increase in discomfort, and felt better for having made a start.

*What do I do now?* As she asked herself this, warning bells began ringing in her head. Did she have any choice in the matter? Was she merely playing out history – re-enacting Emmony's life – or did she indeed have the capacity to act of her own volition, which is certainly what it *felt* like? But that meant she might be *changing* history, which was surely impossible. Every writer of time travel stories had been confronted with the paradoxes and conundrums implied by such ideas. And if she *did* change the past, would that affect the present – her present? The possible significance of such considerations was quite beyond her.

*Emmony, please. Why won't you talk to me?*

There was no answer, at least not in the sense that Zoe had received them before, but her plea prompted the memory of how she had *known* where Emmony had hidden the talisman. Emmony's knowledge was somehow available to her. They had become integrated in a way Zoe could not understand, but perhaps she *could* test her abilities. If Emmony's memories were indeed inside her own mind – and why should they not? It was her body, her brain, after all – then retrieving them should simply be a matter of specific instructions. In effect, she would have to ask herself questions! But what was she to ask? Where should she begin? All Zoe knew of Emmony's life came from the times she had shared with her.

Searching for inspiration, she began to look round at her surroundings for the first time. The long room was sparsely furnished. Carved wooden seats lined the walls at the end where she sat in the midst of what little furniture there was. The lower part of the hall was completely empty, bare stone walls set with high windows with iron brackets in the spaces between. *For the torches,* Zoe thought, *when Jevan gives a formal audience or delivers verdicts in disputes.* This was not something she had known, but just wondering about the room had dislodged the information from Emmony's mind. Zoe's own consciousness might have taken over from Emmony's, but it was as if her hostess's *subconscious* was still there, waiting to be called upon. The possibilities of that were endless, and the idea of such unlimited scope almost brought Zoe's thoughts to a complete halt. This situation would take some time to get used to.

But the recollection of burning torches triggered yet another memory, and this time Zoe already knew more than she wished about it. Emmony and Jevan had had an argument in this room, the Quarterman's Hall, and had provided Zoe with her first unknowing and distorted glimpse into their world. Her dream of a brandy glass exploding as Thomas hurled it at the wall had been a confused mirror image of the scene here. Jevan had flung his own bulbous glass aside, where it had shattered, leaving a dark stain on the stone beneath one of the torches. Zoe could see it now from where she sat, and Emmony's memory supplied the details.

He had yelled at her, his words hurtful and belittling as always.

'You are nothing, *less* than nothing! You can't even give me a son. Your talent is worthless. If it weren't for the fact that you're married to me . . .' he had raged, pointing at his own broad chest, just as Thomas had done, '. . . no one would even notice you.'

His contempt for his wife had been truly terrifying. When he had lunged towards her and grabbed her arms with the unnatural strength of his fury, she had had no will to resist and had all but collapsed, forced to wait until he relented

– *if* he relented. His face was suffused with blood now as he bellowed obscenities. Then, in a moment of swift, overpowering violence, he had thrown her to the floor, his own body crushing her, holding her down, his hand tearing at her dress.

'No!' Emmony had cried as she fell.

In the dream, that cry had been enough to bring Zoe back to wakefulness, but for Emmony there had been no escape. Zoe tried to close her mind to the scene that had followed, but it could not be forgotten so easily.

'Oh, Emmony,' she whispered aloud, aghast, tears running down her cheeks.

She wanted to kill Jevan then, with an intensity she scarcely believed possible, but from her instinctive reaction – which could only have come from the part of Emmony that remained with her – she knew it was not as simple as that. There were other considerations, other people, forcing her to stay her hand. A brief memory of Ghyl's face, laughing and alive, flashed into her mind, accompanied by a wave of love and longing. But she was given no opportunity to luxuriate in this happier thought because the door behind her opened and someone entered the room.

Zoe looked round fearfully, knowing she was in no condition to face Jevan again, but the man who entered was not known to her. Unprompted, her mind supplied the information that this was Lanier, Jevan's chamberlain, who was entrusted with the running of the house whenever his master was away. He displayed no surprise at finding his mistress on the floor, and made no attempt to assist her. Instead he simply looked at her dispassionately, as though she were an object. Zoe did not need Emmony's knowledge of him as Jevan's lackey, and therefore someone not to be trusted. His manner and the barely concealed disdain on his face confirmed her own first impression. Lanier reminded her of a divorce lawyer.

'You would be well advised to tell me where the talisman is,' he remarked, as if this were a matter of only passing concern. 'My Lord Quarterman bade me recover it, if I could, but I got the distinct impression that he was rather looking forward to extracting the information from you himself when he returns. So I shall not be blamed if I fail.' He waited nonchalantly, picking at his nails, and only went on when it became clear that Zoe was not going to reply. 'So be it. The warlocks could trace it soon enough, no doubt, but they won't dare act with Jevan away.' His low opinion of their timidity was obvious. 'If you choose not to tell me, you bring your misfortune upon yourself. Jevan will not be as polite as I. His methods, as you know, are . . . less subtle.'

Inside, Zoe quailed at the thought of these methods, but tried desperately not to appear afraid. It was all she could do to hide her pain, let alone her fear.

'I don't know where it is,' she breathed eventually. 'Leave me alone.'

Lanier looked askance, as if she had surprised him a little.

'I'm afraid I cannot, yet,' he said, amusement showing in his blue eyes. 'Jevan instructed me to escort you back to your chambers. There you will be guarded, kept safe until his return.'

Zoe experienced a moment's hope then. The talisman was in her bedchamber, with the promise of the powers it might bestow. But she knew – or Emmony did – that it could not be as simple as this, and realised that she had no idea what this prized object might enable her to do. And this time there was no knowledge within Emmony's subconscious to help her. All she knew was that it was important.

'Shall we go?' Lanier asked with sarcastic courtesy.

'Help me up then.'

Again he glanced at her in mild surprise, but he came closer and offered her his hand. She reached up gingerly and took it, half expecting to be roughly jerked upright and tensing herself against the shock and pain. As it was, he drew her up steadily – he was stronger than he looked – but, even so, the shooting pains in her chest made her gasp. She stood still, doubled over, for a few seconds before recovering her poise. Lanier made no comment and waited with no sign of impatience. But when Zoe straightened up and looked him in the eye, she saw a fleeting moment of uncertainty in his face before his normal insolence reasserted its hold.

'Are you ready?' he asked with a slight smile. 'Or shall I call servants to carry you?'

'I'm ready,' she grated.

Quite how Zoe managed to make her way along the gloomy corridors and to climb two long flights of stairs she would never know, but at last she reached her own quarters. Two armed guards stood beside the door and a small man, dressed – or so Zoe thought – like a clown, but who she knew to be a warlock, sat in a nearby alcove. He was muttering something over a small metal brazier, and did not look up. This then was the source of the mysterious magical shield which was to enclose Emmony's chambers. It looked ridiculous, but Zoe knew it was not.

At Lanier's signal, one of the guards opened the door and she walked into the familiar bedroom. A young woman rose from her seat beside the dressing table and regarded the newcomers serenely.

'Ellissa will be keeping you company,' the chamberlain informed Zoe in conversational tones. 'She will be able to tend to your needs, and summon me should you find you have something to tell me after all.' He nodded to the maid, who gave a small curtsey in response.

Zoe thought dismally that even here she was not to be alone, that she was to be spied upon, but such things meant little now. All she could think of was that, surely, her hour was nearly up now and soon – *please, make it soon!* – she would be able to escape this torment and return to her own body, her own home, her own life. In the meantime, all she could do was lie down and try to ease the pain as best she could.

As she edged her way across the room, Ellissa came to her side but hovered there, not sure whether her assistance was required. Lanier left without another word, closing the door behind him, and Zoe heard the chamberlain say something to the men outside. As she carefully lowered herself onto the bed, she knew that Ellissa was not to be trusted; the maid would be incapable of defying Lanier, let alone Jevan. If she did, her life would surely be forfeit.

As soon as her charge was settled, Ellissa returned to her chair, picked up her needlework and went on sewing, glancing across at the unmoving figure on the bed every few moments.

Zoe kept quite still, trying to breathe as slowly and as shallowly as possible, and waited for the waves of pain to subside. She had never known such physical discomfort; it made even thinking difficult.

At long last, after what seemed like an age, Zoe heard the unreal, faraway ringing of a distant bell. As the bed-chamber dissolved into blackness, the relief was indescribable. Moments later, she opened her eyes in her own sitting room, with the clock blaring away on the mantelpiece.

She got up and reached out to turn it off, only to catch her breath with pain as the agony in her chest returned, as strong as before. *No! That's not possible!* she wailed silently. Then, moving much more cautiously, she stopped the alarm ringing and looked down at herself. Slowly, in mounting terror, she unbuttoned her blouse and pulled it open. There, exactly where Jevan had kicked her, was a red mark and the beginnings of a large, ugly, purple-black bruise beneath her right breast. Zoe stared at her body in horror, and found herself shivering uncontrollably.

It was only then that she noticed how unnaturally cold the room was, that the atmosphere was all wrong. The malevolent presence was back – or rather had been back. It was gone now, but the chill of its departure still held the room in thrall.

And that was not all. There was a strange smell too; the acrid, sharp, ugly scent of burning. Instinctively, Zoe turned to look at its source and went slowly towards the answering machine. The indicator showed E for 'error', and as Zoe opened the lid a tiny silver spiral of smoke escaped. For an instant, the stench was overpowering. Inside, the tiny cassette lay in place as usual, but it was black and charred now. When Zoe eventually managed to prise it out, one glance was enough to tell her that the entire tape had been fused into a single lump of scorched plastic.

## 24

'Well, the good news is that nothing's broken,' Dr Black said, showing Zoe the X-rays clipped to the illuminated wall panels. 'And there's no sign of any internal injuries. But you're badly bruised, and there's some ligament damage. You're going to be sore for a while.' His expression was one of professional concern. 'How did it happen?'

Zoe had been ready for this question ever since she had booked herself into the hospital's casualty department, but until now no one had seemed interested. The busy staff had simply been concerned with assessing and treating her injury as quickly as possible.

'I fell and caught myself on the corner of the table. Tripped over my own feet . . .' She did not like lying, and had decided to keep her explanations to a minimum. The truth was too outrageous. Zoe was still not sure she believed or understood it herself.

'Accidents happen,' Nick commented, although he did not look convinced. Zoe wondered whether he knew that the injury had really come from a kick. He must have seen the results of fights many times. But if the doctor harboured any suspicions, he kept them to himself.

'You have to look after yourself,' he told her earnestly. 'Take it easy for a while. Apart from anything else, you've had a nasty shock.'

*More than you know*, Zoe thought, but all she said was, 'Thank you . . . for seeing me yourself.'

'All part of the service,' he replied with a smile that faded as he added, 'I only wish all my patients were as easy to treat.'

They looked at each other, both thinking of Michael, who still lay unmoving and unresponsive in his inexplicably stubborn coma.

'I'm afraid there's no dressing that'll help,' Nick said, returning to Zoe's injury. 'The only way we could immobilise your rib cage would be to prevent you from breathing, which is not recommended medical practice. The tablets should help if you find it hard to sleep.' He glanced at his watch. 'I'd better get on. Are you going in to Michael now?'

Zoe nodded.

'Don't stay too long,' he advised. 'You need rest.'

Zoe did indeed cut short her afternoon stay, but it was not because she needed to rest. The excuse she gave herself was that she had to get to the British Telecom shop before it closed, but the truth was that, for the first time in weeks, she was finding it too hard to accept Michael's condition or to find the words to express her feelings. It was bad enough knowing that he was trying to contact her – by whatever obscure means – but far worse to tell him that his efforts were bringing her into danger, and that she was scared. Although her injuries were trivial compared to his, the pain was still very real – and she knew she had no alternative but to go back to Emmony's life, to try and solve all the mysteries that now surrounded her.

'Goodbye, my love. I'll be in late tomorrow – Owen's coming to see me in the morning. Perhaps he can help me sort all this out.' She kissed him lightly and left.

Zoe drove into the centre of Norwich, wincing every time she had to change gear, and parked outside the library. She bought two spare cassettes for the answering machine from the BT shop, then returned to the car and took her place in the rush hour traffic leaving the city. For once the slow progress did not bother her. When at last she got home, it was dark and very cold, a clear sky threatening a hard frost, but there was no unnatural chill inside the cottage. Even so, Zoe turned up the heating before fitting one of the new tapes into the machine. As far as she could tell, only the tape had been damaged; the rest of the equipment seemed to be in working order. She recorded a new outgoing message, and then rang Alex and asked her to phone back to test it. Much to her relief, all seemed to work satisfactorily and she picked up the receiver to continue the conversation with her agent.

'Still having problems?'

'Yes. I've just had to put a new tape in. And you know what I'm like with machines!'

'How are you?'

'Hurting,' Zoe replied, and went on to tell Alex about her bruised ribs, using the same story she had given Dr Black. Then she gave the latest report on Michael – such as it was.

'Poor you.'

'I've felt better,' Zoe admitted.

'Done any more writing?'

'Spoken like a true agent,' she said, then immediately felt guilty. She hadn't meant to accuse her friend of a lack of sympathy.

'I only thought—' Alex began.

'I'm sorry,' Zoe said quickly. 'You've been more understanding than I deserve.'

'Nonsense.'

'To tell the truth, I've hardly thought about work since we last spoke.'

'Don't worry about it,' her agent told her. 'Remember that journalist I mentioned? I told her what you'd said, but she's still very keen. Even suggested we might do it by post, and sent me a list of questions.'

'What sort of questions?'

'The usual stuff, but she knows what she's talking about. Do you want me to send it to you, in case you feel up to it?'

'OK. But I'm not making any promises.'

'Fine. I won't even tell her I've sent the list. You know, if you had a fax it could be there in a couple of minutes.'

'I have enough trouble with the phone,' Zoe said with

201

feeling. 'Fax machines always go wrong, and without Michael . . .' She broke off, unable to complete the sentence.

'It'll be in the post tomorrow,' Alex assured her quickly.

'Michael always said that if you've got a modem – whatever that is – you don't need a fax,' Zoe went on, recovering as best she could.

'Well, we don't all have access to such sophisticated computers,' her agent replied. 'Look after yourself, Zoe.'

'I'll try,' she said quietly.

After putting the phone down, Zoe found herself staring at the ring on her finger. She had no doubts about its importance – but could it really have been the reason for her complete transference into Emmony's life? There was only one way to find out, she realised, but she was not prepared for that yet. She thought about what had happened, and the dangers involved in her new identity. But surely there must be advantages too. Why else would Michael have gone to such lengths to remind her of the ring's existence? How could it help her? Unless having complete control of Emmony's body, and access to her subconscious knowledge, allowed Zoe to act, to achieve something which was not possible otherwise. Something, moreover, that Emmony could not achieve on her own. Did that make sense? All Zoe had managed to do so far was to get herself hurt. The reality of her damaged ribs frightened her more than she could express, even to herself. What would have happened if Jevan had not been called away? Would any number of other, easily imagined atrocities have been visited upon Zoe's body as well as Emmony's? What if, in his fury, Jevan had actually killed his wife, while Zoe had been there in her place?

She closed her eyes for a moment, feeling sick. This was impossible. She had not believed that her situation could get any more implausible, but it had, and in a way which left her terrified not only for Michael but for herself.

And yet she must go on. Zoe knew that. She had to make sense of it all somehow.

'But not tonight,' she told herself aloud.

Later, as she lay in bed, feeling very tired but unable to

sleep – even that once simple act now seemed fraught with peril – Zoe took comfort from the fact that Owen would be with her the next time she returned to her past life. He would make sure she came to no harm. And, it suddenly occurred to her, if her identification with Emmony was once again complete, then perhaps this time it would be like a *normal* regression, with Owen able to move her about in time. Then she would see how the problems had been resolved, how she had managed to save Ghyl. That was a hopeful thought, but it contradicted her earlier theory that she was going back to *do* something. If everything was predetermined, why was she there at all? Perhaps, in a sense, she had already done something, altered the past – she just didn't know how yet. She took a deep breath, frustrated by the fact that she was still going round in circles, unable to come up with any explanation that fitted all the facts.

Zoe had already taken off the ring. It lay on her bedside table, next to a glass of water and the pills Dr Black had given her. Reluctantly, knowing that she must sleep sometime whatever her dreams might bring, Zoe swallowed a tablet and settled back, hoping for instant oblivion. Even then, she stayed awake for some time, though she felt more relaxed, but when she did eventually fall asleep her night was peaceful and in the morning she could recall no dreams of any kind. Her ribs had stiffened and were very painful, and her mouth and throat were dry and tasted foul, but even so she felt a small, unreasoning rush of happiness. She had come through the night unscathed, Owen would be there soon and, for once, the sun was shining. Maybe this was to be the day when all the mysteries would be solved, when her purpose became clear. She had no idea where this feeling of optimism had originated, but she was not about to question it.

It was not until she had washed, dressed and eaten an unusually leisurely breakfast that Zoe ventured into the sitting room – and saw that the answering machine's indicator showed that a message had been received.

Her heart seemed to skip a beat as the possibilities flashed through her mind. Was it Alex's test message? No, she remembered resetting the machine. Could the phone have rung overnight without her hearing it? In her drugged state, this might have been possible. And then, of course . . .

*Let it be him*, she pleaded silently as she pressed the 'Play' button and watched the tape rewind. It seemed to take for ever. The message was evidently a long one, far longer than anything Michael had ever left before, and Zoe's hopes fell a little. But then, at last, the tape began to play and her husband's longed-for voice rang out, sounding alert and positive.

'Zoe? It's me. Can you hear me?' he began, exactly echoing his very first message, but in a much more confident tone. 'You will, sooner or later,' he went on, 'however hard they try to stop us. They can't maintain the seals for ever, especially now that you're so close. The witches can find the gaps, so why not me?'

There was a short pause then, but the tape ran on as Zoe held her breath, trying to remain calm.

'I know things, see things, that I don't recognise or understand,' Michael continued in a slightly awed tone, 'but I *remember* them. Does that make any sense?' He was almost laughing, and Zoe suddenly knew for certain where her unwarranted cheerfulness had originated. She smiled, but her husband's next words were more serious.

'I know you're trying to help me, but you have to help *him*. The other one. The one whose thoughts I think. He . . . I . . . want you to use the talisman. You know how, you have the talent. We're relying on you.'

There was a second, longer pause. Zoe waited impatiently. 'The other one' could only mean Ghyl, she was sure. But how was she supposed to help him? And how was she supposed to use the ring – if that was what Michael meant.

'This is all so strange,' he said now, his voice sounding full of wonder. 'But I feel so much better now I know you're here too. I love you, Zoe.'

'I love you too, Michael,' she whispered as the cassette began to rewind. 'I love you too.'

## 25

Zoe let the tears come. The realisation of just how much she had wanted – had *needed* to hear Michael's voice again overwhelmed her, and her reaction was one of both joy and sadness; joy at his re-emergence, especially because he had sounded so positive, and sadness because she knew it was still not really him. She rang the hospital, just in case, but was not surprised to hear that there was no change in her husband's condition.

What Michael had said to her strengthened Zoe's resolve beyond measure. The link between his fate and those of Emmony and Ghyl was now forged in steel. 'The one whose thoughts I think' could only be Ghyl, but the phrase could also be used to sum up Zoe's relationship with Emmony. Michael's instruction to help Ghyl was unequivocal, reinforcing Zoe's own instincts, and the only way she could obey him was to go back to her earlier life – with whatever dangers that entailed.

She took heart from the fact that, apparently, the witches and now Michael had been able to break through the seals placed around them. If *they* could find the gaps, why shouldn't she, in Emmony's stead? But to do so obviously involved using her talisman. Michael had implied that this meant more than simply putting the ring on, but Zoe still did not know what she was supposed to do. Unless, of course, the talisman he was referring to was the unknown object secreted in Emmony's cupboard. And what was the 'talent' Zoe was supposed to have? There did not seem to be anything she could use against *them*, the disturbingly powerful enemies that she assumed were Jevan, his henchmen and warlocks. Once again, she knew, there was only one way to find out.

Zoe glanced at her watch, and realised that Owen would be with her in less than half an hour. There would be so much to tell him, but she was not sure that she would be able to curb her impatience to return to Emmony and continue her mission. She made her way upstairs, slowing down as her ribs protested and made her wince with pain. The all too obvious reminder of the inexplicable pitfalls of her chosen course was timely, and she knew that she would have to be very careful.

The ring still lay on her bedside table, and the mid-morning sunlight caught the red stone, making it glow like a dragon's eye. *Now where did that analogy come from?* Zoe wondered, as she picked it up, studied the intricate goldwork and stared into the gem's fiery depths. Then, her decision made, she slipped it onto her finger. If indeed this was the talisman, and it had been responsible for her complete identification with Emmony, then she would not tell Owen about it until after her next regression.

With a sense of anticipation growing inside her, Zoe went downstairs again and began to prepare for the session. First she transferred the recording of Michael's voice to the tape which held his earlier messages, then set up another cassette, ready to record the results of Owen's promptings. Although she could already repeat every word of Michael's latest message from memory, the bittersweet pleasure of hearing him had not diminished. Especially the parts that referred directly to her: *now that you're so close . . . I feel so much better now I know you're here too . . . I love you, Zoe.* The words meant a great deal to her, for all their enigmatic origin.

Her preparations complete, Zoe went to the kitchen to get some coffee ready. When the doorbell rang, she hurried, as best she could, to let Owen in. As soon as she saw him, she felt suddenly overwhelmed by the enormity of the task ahead of them.

'How long can you stay?' she demanded anxiously.

'I don't have to be in King's Lynn till three, so there's plenty of time,' he replied, smiling. 'I take it you've got something to tell me.'

'That's an understatement! I don't know where to begin.' All of a sudden, it just seemed too hopelessly complicated. There was so much that needed explaining, that she needed to discuss with Owen, but Zoe did not want to delay the return to her past life any longer than necessary. Every second seemed precious.

'I smell coffee,' Owen hinted. 'Let's talk for a while.'

He followed her into the kitchen, accepted a mug and listened patiently while Zoe tried to put everything – or almost everything – that had happened since their last meeting into some sort of perspective. He betrayed no great surprise when she told him of her self-induced regressions, although she emphasised that the first had been more like a vivid dream to begin with, glossing over the more deliberate nature of her later efforts.

In describing what she had witnessed, Zoe tried to concentrate on those elements she had been able to follow up later – the strange alphabet in Emmony's book, for example – and other details which might possibly mean something to Owen, such as the foreigner's advice to Prince Chandos. She told him of the unpleasant effects of the drug administered to Emmony, and of Jevan's anger at her surreptitious reclaiming of the mysterious talisman. But she did not tell him of the violence done to her – nor of its repercussions in her own time. Nor did she mention the supposed role of the ring, *her* talisman, in completing her journey into the past. Her latest exploit, as expected, was the one which intrigued Owen the most.

'So your identification with Emmony was complete?'

'Yes. It was just me. All that was left of Emmony was her subconscious, her memories.'

'Which you could call on?'

'If I knew what I wanted, yes.'

'But you were still aware of being yourself?'

'Yes.'

207

'Interesting.'

'Do you think,' Zoe asked hopefully, 'if it's the same today, that you'll be able to make me go back and forth in time?'

'It's possible.' He was keen to get on now. 'We'll see. Perhaps I can help direct your efforts more effectively.'

'I hope so,' she said. 'Every time I think I'm getting somewhere, I just seem to end up with more questions!'

'Well, we may have the answers to one or two, at least,' Owen reassured her. 'Do you remember Emmony telling you about the five-part system for identifying dreams? In our last session together?'

'Yes.'

'The classifications are very like those of Macrobius.'

'Macrobius? Who's he?'

'A Latin grammarian and philosopher of the fourth century AD. I knew I'd heard something like it before, so I looked it up. And,' he went on before Zoe had a chance to protest, 'the princely advice this Urbani chap is supposed to have given Chandos sounds rather like that of Machiavelli. So it's possible in both cases—'

'That I've read about them somewhere and adapted them for my own ends,' Zoe completed for him. 'Is that what you think?'

'It's a possibility,' he told her calmly.

'But I've never even *heard* of Macrobius,' she objected.

'You don't *remember* him. But there's a mass of information stored away in your subconscious that you don't consciously remember. It's obvious from the way you make your living that you have an active imagination, Zoe. Can you honestly believe there was ever a time when sorcerers drank from floating glasses and music came from a stone?'

'Yes!' she answered stubbornly. 'I'm not making this up. I'm not. Do you think it's all a waste of time?'

'No, I don't,' he replied. 'Whatever the source, it's clearly relevant to your present situation.'

'I have to rescue Ghyl in order to help Michael.'

Owen said nothing, and just watched her thoughtfully.

'There's something else,' Zoe went on. 'I've had another message from Michael. Come and listen.'

The therapist finished his coffee and stood up. Zoe waved him ahead and walked behind him as slowly as she dared, not wanting to give any hint of her injury. That, she realised instinctively, would be the last straw for the therapist – as it had nearly been for her – and she desperately wanted his continuing help. At the door of the sitting room he glanced back at her.

'Are you all right?'

'Just very tired,' she said, with a weak smile.

Owen listened to the tape in silence, not looking at Zoe. When it finished he met her gaze.

'I can see why you're so set on helping Ghyl. The identification with Michael is even stronger now. And he sounded much more positive than before.' Owen himself appeared pleased, raising a new suspicion in Zoe's mind.

'It *is* Michael,' she insisted. 'Not just a reflection of my state of mind.'

'Did I say anything of the sort?' he protested innocently.

'No, but you thought it,' she told him, faintly accusing. She wanted to tell him more – about the fused tape, the video of Brands, the radio interruptions – but that would only make the situation even more complicated, so she just smiled and said, 'Can we begin now?'

'The seals Michael talked about,' Owen went on, obviously not finished with the tape yet, 'they're magic too?'

'Yes. I saw the warlock who made them,' Zoe answered. She was aware that she sounded faintly ridiculous, but was determined not to back down.

'And Emmony's talisman? Do you know how to use it?'

'I don't even know what it *is* yet.'

'She called it a "hollow feather" in our earlier session.'

'Which doesn't help much,' Zoe remarked pointedly. 'I've set up the recorder so we can tape today's session.'

'Good.'

'Just press these two buttons, OK?'

Owen nodded, and Zoe lowered herself cautiously into the

chair. The fact that she was holding herself stiffly was not lost on the therapist, and he spent some time encouraging her to relax physically before he switched on the cassette recorder and began the induction. The process seemed almost automatic by now and, after what seemed like only a few fleeting moments, Zoe found herself in Emmony's body, lying in her bed. The pain in her side was still there, worse than in her own time, but she strove to keep that from showing on her face.

On the far side of the chamber, Ellissa sat in the same chair. She had surely not been there the whole time. It was more likely that they were taking it in turns to watch over her, to spy on her. Resentment burned in Emmony's blood, but her conscious mind was absent. Zoe was alone. At least now there seemed to be no trace of the drug left. She was simply in bed to rest and recover from her injury, and her bedchamber made as good a prison as any.

'Where are you now?' Owen asked.

'In my bedchamber,' she replied, then saw the maid look up sharply and realised that she had spoken aloud there as well as to Owen.

He clearly noted her discomfort and was quick to diagnose its source.

'If you would rather,' he said, 'you can speak so that only I can hear. There is no need to disturb anyone who is with you. Are you in bed?'

'Yes,' Zoe answered, finding that he was right. It was simply a matter of control. After a few moments Ellissa stopped watching her and went back to her sewing.

'Is your name Emmony?'

'Yes, but I'm Zoe too.'

'Are Emmony's memories available to you?'

'I think so. If I need to know something specific.'

'Is it nighttime?'

'No. There's daylight outside,' she said, wondering why that mattered.

There was a short pause before Owen spoke again.

'Zoe, I'm going to try something now. I'm going to

hypnotise you again, as Emmony. If it works, we may be able to talk to her subconscious and reveal her history and her future. Is that all right with you?'

'Will it work?' She trusted Owen implicitly, but what would happen to *her*? Would Zoe no longer exist at all? It was a frightening thought.

'I don't know, but it shouldn't frighten her,' Owen replied, mistaking the reason for her unease. 'Hypnosis was a familiar technique in the ancient world. It's quite possible that it was known in her society as well.'

'It is,' Zoe confirmed, having just learnt as much from the hidden parts of Emmony's mind. Even so, she was still nervous.

'Close your eyes now, and relax.'

Zoe closed Emmony's eyes and did her best. Owen repeated the familiar routine, varying it only to take account of the fact that he was working on someone who was not actually there.

Zoe heard the maid get up and come closer to look at her, then retreat, open the door and speak to someone outside.

'She's asleep again. Tell Oliva to come and take over for a bit, will you? I'm bored.'

That was the last thing Zoe heard. As Owen's soothing, insistent words took effect, she felt herself drifting into a neutral, colourless void. It was one of the strangest things she had ever experienced, a feeling of insubstantiality, of irrelevance to her own life, and utter detachment. Whatever happened now was someone else's concern.

There was a conversation going on somewhere, she knew, but she had no idea who was speaking or where they were.

# 26

'You don't remember anything after that?' Owen was clearly puzzled.

'Nothing,' Zoe confirmed. 'Did it work? Did you talk to Emmony?'

'Yes.' He was still frowning.

'Was she able to go back and forth in time?' she asked eagerly.

'Yes. At least . . .' Owen hesitated. 'I think you'd better listen to the tape.' He turned the cassette on, adjusted the volume and skipped the early part of the hypnosis procedure, then came and sat beside Zoe on the sofa. As the voices came over the speakers, both listened intently.

For Zoe, of all the unusual things she had experienced in recent weeks, hearing the recording was in some ways the strangest of all. This was not because it was frightening or inexplicable, but because Emmony's voice – and it was Emmony's, not her own – prompted so many echoes in her own mind, vestigial memories and the aftershocks of emotional upheavals. And yet for all its familiarity, the story that emerged was somehow out of place in the comfortable setting of her own home. It was disturbing and fascinating at the same time.

'Emmony, I want you to go back to when you were a young child,' Owen's voice said, 'to a time which was important to you. Go there now.' After a pause, he added, 'Are you there now?'

'Yes.'

'How old are you?'

'Five.'

'Where are you?'

'At the seaside, watching the Shakers.' There was an unmistakable note of excitement in the child's voice.

'Who are the Shakers?'

'The giants who build the walls that stop the water coming in and drowning the villages.'

'How big are these giants?'

'Taller than ten oak trees. Taller than *anything*,' Emmony exclaimed, pride and awe mixed in her voice.

'Aren't you scared of them?'

'Oh no. That would be silly. The Shakers only do what the sorcerers tell them to. They'd never hurt me. I *like* them.'

'What do the Shakers look like?'

'Like Harrell the farmer, but much bigger,' Emmony replied, giggling. 'With hands as big as our house. But Daddy says everyone sees the Shakers differently. He says that's because we all see magic differently.'

'Is your Daddy with you now?'

'Yes, and Mummy. They're holding my hands.'

Zoe could almost see the contented smile on the little girl's face, and felt a pang of the sorrow to come.

'Do they know you're talking to me?' Owen's voice went on.

'No. It's our secret,' she replied conspiratorially. 'But I think they'd be pleased. They've always wanted me to tell them what my talent is. Maybe this is it.'

'Talent?'

'Magic,' Emmony answered, as though this should be obvious.

Zoe was frustrated. Although she would have liked to pursue this subject, Owen had moved on then. And besides, she realised, a five-year-old child was perhaps not the best source from whom to learn about such things.

'I want you to move forward now, to a time when you're older, another time that's significant for you. Go there now.'

'The Pyramid!' Emmony exclaimed, without further prompting. 'It's so beautiful!'

'Can you describe it to me?'

'It's blue, and it sparkles. The Prince lives inside.' Her voice was less childlike now, but it still conveyed a youthful enthusiasm at seeing something so marvellous for the first time.

'Prince Chandos?'

'No, silly. Prince Farrar. Chandos is his son – and he's younger than I am.'

'And Farrar lives inside the Pyramid?'

'They all do. All the court, and his servants. We're going there to visit.'

'Are you with your parents?'

'With my father.' She was obviously proud that her father was such an important person, and that he had chosen to take her with him to the royal residence.

'Do you know who built the Pyramid, Emmony?'

'Lissac and the other sorcerers, of course,' she replied promptly, sounding rather surprised.

'Can you go forward in time and tell me what it's like inside the Pyramid?'

'It's just like an ordinary town.' Her disappointment was plain. 'It's pretty, but . . .' She had obviously expected something more spectacular. 'You can't see the Pyramid itself from the inside. It just looks like the sky. But it doesn't rain here,' she added, brightening a little. 'And there's a tower.'

'Are you going to climb the tower?'

'Yes.'

'Go to the top now and tell me what you see.'

'I've never been up so high before,' Emmony stated breathlessly.

'But you're still inside the Pyramid?'

'Yes. Of course.'

'What can you see?'

'The town spread out below us, the river like a silver snake, lots of trees, and the marshland beyond.'

'Can you see the sea?'

There was a pause before she answered.

'No. It's too far away. There are some sheep in that field over there,' she added as if by way of compensation.

'Emmony, I want you to move forward in time again now—'

'To the Tests?' she asked unexpectedly.

'What tests are those?'

'You take the Tests when you're twelve,' she explained. 'Everyone does. Unless you already know what your talent is.'

'And you don't?'

'Not yet. I'm only nine, but Father says most people know by then.' She sounded a little ashamed of her failing.

'All right. Go to your tests. Go there now.' Owen paused, then asked, 'Where are you now?'

'In the Hall of Stones, within the Pyramid.' She was evidently no longer in awe of the place.

'Is anyone with you?'

'Goganious the sorcerer is my Testmaster. And there are several warlocks here too.'

'Tell me what you're doing.'

What followed was a long, complex and occasionally confused description of a series of trials, apparently designed to test Emmony's aptitude for a variety of paranormal skills. It was made more complicated by the problems of inexact translation, and Owen had to interrupt several times to clarify something Emmony had said. She got annoyed by this after a while, so he kept his interventions to a minimum. He and Zoe listened to this section of the tape twice, both making notes and comparing their interpretations. Guided by their earlier knowledge of so-called 'talents' in Emmony's time, they concluded that she had been tested for her abilities in telepathy, psychokinesis, prophecy and dowsing, the reading of auras – for both humans and animals – and her affinity with trees and plants and the properties of herbs and roots. She was also tested for other obscure skills which seemed to have something to do with creativity, illusions and sensitivity to colours. She had been given various objects to hold, to

215

see whether she could 'read' their history, and was asked to find others blindfold. And finally she had been asked to interpret various symbols and samples of writing. Her only real successes were in her instinctive understanding of animals – a small bird flew to her and rested, unafraid, on her palm, and a cat and a hound both slept at her command – and with her reading in the final test. This last, Emmony reported ruefully, caused some consternation among her examiners.

'Why is that?' Owen asked.

'Rune lore is only permitted for the sky-priests and their scribes. Certainly not for women. They wanted to know how I learnt to read, but it's just a feeling, something I've always wanted. One day I'll have a book of my own.'

Hearing the longing and the determination in the girl's prophetic words, Zoe and Owen exchanged a glance. Zoe was not surprised to discover that the therapist had moved on from there quickly. The session had already lasted almost half an hour, and there was still a lot of ground to cover. He took Emmony forward to a time soon after her parents had died, and gently drew the details from her. They had been drowned, she informed him, in a sudden storm which had swept their vessel onto a sandbank and then torn it apart. Their bodies had been recovered several days later, washed up on the shore of the north coast. Emmony had been eighteen at the time, a year older than Zoe when she had lost *her* parents, and it had been a bitter time for the young woman. Like her present day counterpart, she had experienced much sadness and insecurity, as well as a great deal of suppressed anger and resentment.

Predictably, it had been shortly after that that she had met Jevan, an apparently strong, confident and protective man, who had the same effect on her as Thomas had had on the grieving Zoe. It was clear from the way Emmony spoke that she had not loved Jevan, but had craved the stability and safety that marriage to him would represent. Her inheritance was respectable though not enormous, and she was beautiful enough to make her relatively modest talents acceptable to a man who had just succeeded his father as Quarterman, and who was urgently seeking a wife. Emmony evidently went into the marriage with her eyes open, but at the time had seen no drawbacks to the arrangement other than an uneasy relationship with Jevan's twin brother, Killian. Her description, from a later memory, of the wedding ceremony itself was so striking that Owen had let her speak at some length, using up a fair bit of tape.

'It was a beautiful night,' Emmony said wistfully.

'You married at night?'

'Of course. With the new moon, to symbolise our beginning. The sky was clear, all the stars giving their blessing. I didn't feel the cold. We walked together down the avenue, between the torches, and as we passed each pair of braziers the flames went out, meaning that there would be no turning back into darkness. Then at last we reached the ancient stone circle where the sky-priests were gathered. Only their candles still burnt. I felt all the onlookers watching from beyond the circle, but I could not see them. In that star-eyed place of silence, we made our vows and drank the ritual wine. We gave offerings and danced. I was contented then. I felt safe. But that was five years ago – and my life has changed.'

'You are unhappy?'

'How can I not be? What do I have to be happy about? The Midwife has granted me no children, Jevan has grown cold and angry, and I hardly see him any more. My talents, such as they are, are denied.'

'Why denied?'

'Working with animals is menial work,' she replied bitterly, 'beneath the dignity of a Quarterman's wife, and books are forbidden to all my sex. I have little skill for anything else. The days drag by.' Her words were made heavy by the weight of her boredom and unhappiness.

'I want you to move forward again now, Emmony, to the day you first met Ghyl.'

'He is one of Adhaf's entourage, a mere captain, but he intrigues me. The way he looks at me . . .' Embarrassment was mixed with pleasure in her tone. 'I wonder if it might

217

be possible to talk to him alone – and then I feel guilty at such treacherous boldness.'

'And did you succeed?' Owen prompted. 'Go forward to that meeting.'

'It's so wonderful! I can't explain it.' Emmony sounded breathless with bewildered joy and excitement. 'He talks to me as an equal, about adult things – and yet I feel like a child again, happy and exhilarated. I hardly know what is happening to me.'

*Oh, I do*, Zoe thought, finding her own nerves tingling as she listened, her whole body remembering those first terrifying assaults of love.

But Owen allowed neither woman to linger in such emotional turmoil – and Zoe felt momentarily disappointed by his haste to move on.

'Go forward three months now, and tell me how your relationship with Ghyl has progressed,' he instructed.

'I have hardly seen him – and yet I think of him constantly.' The excitement had left her voice, and had been replaced by a heartrending misery and helpless yearning. 'I am trapped here.'

On the tape, Emmony was convulsed with a racking sob and, as she fought to control her breathing, Zoe felt a sympathetic tightening in her own chest. Without thinking she reached across and took Owen's hand. When he did not respond, Zoe suddenly realised what she was doing and quickly withdrew. Emmony's voice sounded once again from the speakers.

'Is it so terrible to love? Can the stars condemn me for that?'

'Does Ghyl know of your feelings for him?' Owen asked. 'Does he love you?'

'We have not declared ourselves but . . . yes . . . I know he cares for me. Oh, how I wish there was another world, far away, where we could go, where even the stars could not see us. Nor Jevan ride in pursuit.'

'Does Jevan know of your love?'

'No! He would murder Ghyl – perhaps me too – if he knew

218

the truth. But he senses my distraction. He grows more cruel, more violent when he is here – but mostly he just ignores me.' Emmony sounded thankful for that small mercy.

'There is no possibility of divorce?'

'I don't know what you mean.'

Owen had not pursued that line of questioning, realising, as Zoe did, that it would prove fruitless. Instead, he instructed Emmony to move forward again, to the next significant time in her life.

Zoe expected this to be another episode with Ghyl, and was surprised by Emmony's next words.

'Zenna has called me to see her,' Emmony said. 'She explained that the talisman has some hidden power, but she is not the one to utilise it – and my own talent is much too weak.'

'Where did you find the talisman?'

'Mason gave it to me. I believe he got it from his father, but everything Mason says is . . . He has his own way of talking.'

Owen had then tried to get a clearer idea of exactly what the talisman was, but Emmony's answers were vague and confused. He managed to establish that it was small, thinner but longer than a finger, and made of an unknown substance, but he could get no indication of its purpose. Emmony and Zenna clearly regarded it as both alien and possibly dangerous in nature. There was only one point on which Emmony was perfectly clear.

'Zenna says others will want to take the talisman for themselves, but I must keep it safe. It has a part to play in my road.'

'Your future?'

'My road ahead, yes.'

'But she cannot see what?'

'Not yet.'

'Move forward in time now to when I began to talk to you, when you are in your bed. Can you do that?'

Zoe heard the sharply indrawn breath, and knew the reality of Emmony's sudden return to pain.

219

'Do you still have the talisman?'

'Yes, in my secret place.'

'Do you know how to use it yet?'

'No. I have not the talent. The other woman, Zoe, the one Zenna said would come, *she* is the one to use the talisman. You guide her, do you not?'

'In a way, yes.'

'She is the only one who can help us now. Will she come again?'

There was a pause on the tape. Owen had chosen not to answer, or was still deciding what his response should be, when Emmony spoke again.

'Ghyl is lost to the world and I am trapped here, guarded like a criminal. What is my crime? That I love too well? That my heart cries out for a man who lies near death? And what do men of influence care for such things when intrigue and war rule their thoughts? My life is a wasteland, a sick and evil mockery.'

Her passionate outburst ended in another stifled gasp of pain and instinctively Zoe held herself still, concealing her own injury. The tape ran on.

'Are you ill . . . or hurt?' Owen asked.

Emmony gave a quickly cut off laugh of savage bitterness.

'My mind is infected, why should my body matter?'

'Go forward again now, to a time when you are no longer in pain,' Owen told her quickly.

Zoe held her breath – surely now she would be shown the way forward. But Emmony's next words dashed her hopes.

'I cannot!' she snapped angrily. 'You know I have no talent for prophecy. And even if I had, there is nothing to see. Even Zenna's eyes are blind. She sees only darkness on my road ahead.'

# 27

Owen got up and switched off the tape, then turned back to look at Zoe, who sat quite still on the sofa.

'I'm sorry, Zoe. You can listen to the rest of it later if you want, but all that's left is me bringing you back to your own life and reinforcing your sense of calm. There was nothing more I could get out of Emmony.'

Zoe was surprised to find that she did indeed feel quite calm, though she was still too dumbfounded to speak. Having her hopes dashed yet again had been a cruel blow.

'I know I said we had plenty of time,' Owen went on, 'but this has taken longer than I thought. I'll have to go in about half an hour – and we need to talk.'

'Yes,' Zoe whispered. 'We do.'

'I don't need to tell you that what you have been experiencing is not a normal past life regression,' the therapist continued, his tone a mixture of concern and business-like determination. 'It wasn't right from the beginning, and what happened today has only reinforced that.'

'But we made some progress,' Zoe insisted quietly, the ramifications of what she had heard still echoing in her mind.

'Yes, but not enough,' he responded. 'In a way, what happened is logical enough, *if* you accept the original premise that you and Emmony are somehow coexisting. If it *was* Emmony I hypnotised the second time, then naturally we would be able to explore her past, but not her future. A future which is nevertheless in *your past*. As such it should be available to us, but something is clearly preventing that. Have you any idea what that something might be?'

'Me? How would I know . . .' Zoe paused as his implication became clear. 'You think I'm hiding it deliberately? Why would I do that?'

'I don't know, Zoe. You may not be doing it deliberately. But you *are* the only one with all the answers.'

'Doesn't feel like it,' she commented resentfully.

Owen stared at her for a moment, trying to gauge what her reaction would be to his next words.

'Don't take this the wrong way,' he said eventually, 'but do you think these regressions are actually helping you?'

'Of course . . .' she began, full of indignation, then faltered.

They looked at each other in silence for a while.

'Have you ever considered that they might be doing you harm?' Owen asked finally.

Zoe fought to remain calm. Was her one real ally preparing to desert her?

'I have to be sure,' he explained. 'I'm a therapist. It's my job to help people heal themselves, not to present them with insoluble or even damaging problems. I'm only interested in past lives in so far as they relate to – and can help with – the present.'

'But this *does*!' she exclaimed. 'Isn't that obvious?'

'All too obvious,' he replied heavily.

'You still think I'm making it up?'

Owen did not answer directly, but it was clear where his thoughts were taking him.

'Let's look at the evidence, shall we? Wherever and *when*ever Emmony lived, magic was part of everyday life, taken for granted, even to the extent that everyone was tested, as if a *lack* of talent was abnormal. Most of these abilities, telepathy and so on, are known to us, but they're very rare. Not so in Emmony's time. Even allowing for some childish exaggeration, do you honestly believe there was ever a time in all human history when magical giants built sea-walls? Where sorcerers constructed enormous sparkling pyramids

222

which kept off the rain but were invisible from the inside, where astrology and stone circles, witches and warlocks, were part of *everyday* life for *everyone*?'

Zoe remained stubbornly silent.

'We already know that there's some doubt as to whether this is a genuine past life,' Owen went on doggedly. 'And the nature of the memories makes it hard to believe that it could correspond with a known historical period. Isn't it possible that your own subconscious is playing tricks on you, Zoe? That you're fantasising yourself into a world where anything is possible, where you can use a magic talisman to bring Michael back – in the shape of Ghyl?'

'Even if I am,' Zoe said, finding her voice at last, 'is that necessarily wrong? What if it *works*?'

'Magic won't bring Michael back,' he told her gently. 'Not in the real world.'

'I know that,' she replied desperately. 'But what if the past life is a way to find out how to save Michael in *this* one? Everything points to that. Surely the parallels are too exact to ignore. And you heard what Emmony said, what Michael said on the answering machine. And Zenna. They're all telling me to help Ghyl, to use the talisman.' For an instant she thought of telling him about the ring, but something kept her quiet.

'The parallels *are* precise,' Owen agreed calmly. 'No one could deny that. But if you were designing all this yourself, telling a story in a way, then they *would* be. And it would explain why you don't know the ending yet.'

'Oh, this is hopeless!' Zoe cried. 'You can argue round in circles like that, shoot down everything I say, but it doesn't matter to *me*. Are you going to help me or not?' Her own determination to continue had been reinforced by everything she had heard. She would go on, whatever Owen believed, whatever the cost. *We're relying on you.*

'I'll help you all I can,' he replied. 'I just have to be sure you know what you're doing. I don't think we should do any more regressions for the time being.'

'No,' Zoe exclaimed, aghast. 'We have to . . .'

'Hear me out,' he persisted. 'Hypnotherapy can still help you. The stress reduction alone—'

'I don't want to reduce my stress!' she wailed. 'I want to find out what happened!'

Taken aback by Zoe's vehemence, Owen merely looked at her, his doubts clear in his dark eyes.

'Yes, I'm obsessed.' Zoe was half shouting now, making her injured ribs throb painfully. 'What do you expect? It's your help that's made me strong enough to get this far. You can't abandon me now. Please.'

Several heartbeats passed in silence.

'I won't abandon you, Zoe,' he said eventually. 'We'll try again next time.'

'Thank you,' she replied with profound relief. 'When?'

Owen smiled at her persistence.

'I'll get my diary. It's in the car. And then I really must be going.'

As he turned towards the door, Zoe tried to stand, but a sharp stab of pain left her gasping and she fell back onto the settee. Owen looked back, instantly concerned.

'Are you all right?'

'Yes . . . I'm fine,' she breathed in blatant contradiction of the truth. Her face was white, drained of blood.

Owen came back and knelt down beside her.

'No, you're not. What's the matter?'

The pain was lessening now, but Zoe still could not meet his gaze. She kept her breathing shallow.

'I had a fall,' she mumbled. 'Bruised my ribs. It's nothing.' She was furious with herself and just wanted him to fix another time, then go, and leave her to recover alone.

'Let me see.'

'No. It wouldn't be decent,' she replied, with a feeble smile. 'I've already seen a doctor. Get your diary.'

'How did it happen?' he asked, not moving.

'Does it matter?' Zoe was suddenly unbearably weary. Lying to him took too much effort.

'If it was the poltergeist again, then it most certainly does,' he told her sternly.

'No, not him.' She almost laughed at the idea, then began to wonder. Weren't Jevan and the ghost the same thing? Her sudden abstraction was not lost on Owen.

'You're not telling me everything, are you? Let me see,' he repeated.

Too tired to argue any more, Zoe unbuttoned her blouse and carefully pulled it open. Underneath she was wearing only a bra. Owen gasped when he saw the huge, ugly bruise.

'God Almighty, Zoe!' he breathed. 'How *did* this happen?'

'Jevan kicked me,' she whispered helplessly.

'What?'

'Jevan kicked me. Yesterday morning, when I was Emmony. When I got back it still hurt.'

For a long time he just gazed at her in shocked disbelief. He finally managed to persuade himself that she was serious and, with a visible effort, made himself speak.

'Christ, Zoe. You weren't going to tell me?'

'I'm sorry,' she mumbled, feeling the tears rolling down her cheeks. She was filled with a mixture of shame, relief and fear.

'It's impossible. Impossible!' he burst out. 'Whatever you did wasn't a mere regression. You're into the realms of stigmata and self-mutilation.'

'It happened,' Zoe said, sniffing.

'But you don't leave the room!' he exclaimed helplessly. 'In regression you *can't* be physically harmed. It all takes place inside your head.'

'It happened!' she repeated, growing angry now. 'Jevan kicked me – even if it *is* impossible. Why – how – would I do this to myself?'

'I don't know,' he admitted, shaking his head in bewilderment, 'but don't you see, this just proves my point. The whole process has become dangerous to you. While I could shield you from the worst distress, it was OK – but this . . . This is way out of my league. I can't be party to you hurting yourself. You must give it up, Zoe.'

'I can't.' Suddenly, she realised that this confrontation had

225

been inevitable. Sooner or later the truth would have come out. But even now she could not help fighting, hoping that he could be persuaded. 'I need your help, Owen.'

'No. This is madness,' he replied firmly. 'I'll help you with therapy, but you must give up this so-called past life.'

'Even if it's the only thing that matters to me?' Zoe was crying again. 'Even if it's the only way to save Michael?' *You have to help him!*

'That's only a delusion.' He surprised her by taking her hands in his own. 'I care about you, Zoe. Not just as a client, as a charming and attractive woman who has already suffered too much, but I hope as a friend. But I can't condone this. Look at yourself.'

Zoe quickly withdrew her hands and pulled her blouse together.

'I know I can't stop you initiating your own self-hypnosis,' he went on earnestly. 'But please, listen to me. You *must* stop it. Don't put yourself at risk. You don't know what's going on here, any more than I do.' He took out a handkerchief and offered it to her. Zoe wiped her eyes and blew her nose before looking up. The mixture of apology and defiance in her glowing eyes made the therapist uneasy, but her next words reassured him.

'All right,' she conceded wearily. 'No more regressions.'

'Promise me.'

'I promise. But you will come and see me again, won't you?'

'For therapy, yes.' He did his best to smile. 'I'll get my diary.'

By the time he got back, Zoe had buttoned her blouse and composed herself as best she could.

'Is Friday at four o'clock OK?'

'Yes,' Zoe replied dully. It no longer really mattered very much.

'Here?'

'Yes.'

'Are you all right? Really?'

Zoe nodded.

'I'll be OK,' she said, trying to sound confident. 'You're going to be late for your next appointment.

Owen glanced at his watch.

'I am. Can I use your phone?'

As Owen called his next client and explained that he had been delayed, the strain was evident in his normally calm voice.

After making his call, Owen offered to help her up and she allowed him to draw her steadily to her feet. The pain in her ribs had subsided to a dull, red ache, and she was able to walk with him to the front door without undue discomfort.

'Which doctor did you see?' he asked unexpectedly.

'Someone at the hospital. I don't know his name.' She did not want the two men comparing notes.

'See you on Friday then.'

Zoe nodded.

'Call me earlier if anything urgent comes up,' Owen told her seriously. 'Remember what I said, Zoe.'

'I will.'

'Look after yourself.'

After he had driven away, Zoe shut the door and walked back into the sitting room in a daze. She had lied to him, of course – something which gave her no pleasure. She had no intention of abandoning Emmony and her life, or her attempts to save Ghyl – and Michael. But her one real ally was gone. Like it or not, she would have to go on alone.

# 28

Zoe spent only a short time at the hospital, telling Michael all that had happened, and asking for his renewed help. The optimism of the morning had been dulled by Owen's defection, but she was still able to sound positive and determined. Eventually, however, she ran out of things to say, and knew that it was time for action.

'Bye, sweetheart. I'm trying to do everything you told me,' she assured him finally. 'I love you.'

When Zoe returned home she was met on the doorstep by Stripe. The cat rubbed round her ankles and allowed herself to be tickled and then, unusually, decided to go inside when Zoe opened the door. This was not something Zoe usually encouraged, not wanting her neighbours to think that she was usurping their pet, but on this occasion she was glad. Some undemanding company would be comforting.

Stripe padded into the sitting room and Zoe followed, only to come to an abrupt halt in the doorway. The cat had also stopped, her back arched, hair standing on end as she hissed and spat. Zoe's blood seemed to freeze in her veins when she saw that *something* stood beside the telephone table. It was no more than an indistinct shape, a smoke-thin image, but it was undeniably *there*. And the cat saw it too! So much for this only being a figment of her imagination. With sheer willpower, Zoe managed to quell the terror that washed through her. Could this be the proof she needed to convince Owen? Stripe could hardly be asked to confirm her story. She suddenly remembered the old

Polaroid camera Michael kept in his workroom, and darted back across the hallway. Although the cupboard was full of clutter, she found the camera in a few moments, dragged it out and hurried back, hoping it was still loaded with film. But when she returned, the apparition had gone and Stripe was curled up on the sofa, preening herself with every sign of contentment.

Filled with a mixture of relief, frustration and anger – who *was* this creature who kept invading her home? – Zoe put the camera down and checked the answering machine. There were no messages, and it appeared to be undamaged. She sat down next to the cat, who soon lay purring in her lap. Stroking the animal helped soothe Zoe's nerves, but she knew she could not delay much longer.

'Sorry, puss,' she said as she tipped Stripe onto the floor. The cat gave her one resentful glance, then trotted to the front door. Zoe let her out and then made her preparations. Because she intended to use Owen's tape to induce hypnosis she would not be able to record the session, but she fully expected to remember everything this time. She turned the volume down on the telephone and answering machine, and fetched her alarm clock. How long should she allow herself? Whatever she chose, it was possible that the alarm bell would interrupt her at a vital time. But there was no help for that. Then something else occurred to her, and she was ashamed at not having thought of it before. What had happened to Emmony while Zoe took over her life? Was she aware at all? Would she 'remember' what Zoe had done in her place? There was no way to answer any of these questions. She would just have to do the best she could and try not to leave Emmony in any kind of danger. Of course, she could always try a regression while not wearing the ring. That way, Zoe presumed, she would return to the earlier 'sharing' of their body and would be able to talk with Emmony. Experimentally, she tried to ease the ring off but found – without any real surprise – that although it sat perfectly comfortably next to her wedding band, it would not go over her knuckle. The decision had been made for her. Perhaps

229

it was better like that. Emmony's memories were available to her, after all, and this way she was in control. It was her responsibility.

Her preparations complete, Zoe mentally recapped her objectives for this regression. She had thought about it a great deal during the afternoon – indeed, she had thought of almost nothing else – but her goals were obvious. First she had to retrieve the talisman, then escape from the warlock's prison, and finally get to Ghyl at the Sanctuary. This was all very well, of course, except that she did not know how she was going to *do* any of it.

Deciding that three hours was the longest time she dared risk, Zoe set the alarm clock, composed herself and turned on the tape. Owen's calm and confident voice soon had the desired effect, and she relaxed . . .

In the next instant, Zoe was in Emmony's body, sitting up in Emmony's bed. Ellissa was still at her post, looking thoroughly bored. There was a knock on the door and when the maid got up to open it, Mason came in carrying a tray. He was holding it very carefully, the tip of his tongue protruding from his lips in concentration as he walked to the bedside. Ellissa signalled to someone outside, then closed the door as Mason laid the tray down. Savoury smells wafted into the air from bowls of soup.

'B–broth . . .' Mason began, then looked at Zoe and stopped abruptly. His head was held crookedly and his large, pale eyes widened even further. 'You're not—'

'Shhh!' Zoe hissed urgently, realising that somehow he knew she was not Emmony.

Mason remained silent, but her exclamation had drawn the maid's attention.

'Are you still in pain?' Ellissa asked dispassionately. 'Do you need more cordial?' A phial sat next to a familiar goblet on the bedside table.

'No.' Zoe wanted no more drugs. Their use, she was sure, was partly responsible for the fact that she was still in bed. She preferred the pain.

Ellissa shrugged indifferently.

'You can go now, Mason,' she said. 'We'll ring for you to collect the tray.'

When the boy hesitated, as though he had not understood what had been said, Zoe wondered if he had another motive. Emmony had told her that he would be bringing word of Ghyl. Was he reluctant to leave because he had news to give her, but could not pass it on in Ellissa's presence? Zoe wished she could think of some way of helping him, but was given no time.

'Get out, imbecile!' Ellissa snapped impatiently.

Mason reacted violently, flinching away and raising his arms defensively, as if expecting to be beaten. His movements were so clumsy that he hit the tray, slopping soup everywhere and then, in his attempt to rectify matters, knocked over a goblet of wine.

'You moron!' Ellissa cried, scowling furiously. 'That was my wine.' She slapped his face hard.

'Leave him,' Zoe ordered.

The maid turned to look at the woman who was her nominal mistress, her expression filled with contempt. Mason took advantage of her distraction to try and make amends. He picked up the wine decanter and began to refill the goblet. Even in this he was clumsy and spilt more of the dark red liquid, whose scent now filled the room. Ellissa snatched both containers from him, and furiously ordered him out, before pouring herself more wine and drinking deeply.

It was only after nibbling at some bread, finding she had no stomach for food, that Zoe noticed that the phial of cordial had vanished. She thought Mason must have knocked it to the floor, its fate unnoticed in the general mess. But there was another possibility, one she hardly dared contemplate. She glanced over at Ellissa, who was finishing her wine, and saw her yawn. Zoe's hopes rose.

The maid yawned again, and seemed about to rise from her chair.

'Don't go,' Zoe said quickly. If Mason's clumsiness had, by some miracle, masked his real intent, then she needed to stop Ellissa from calling for a replacement. 'I need someone to talk to.'

Ellissa stayed where she was, her expression blank and her eyes glazed.

'When will my husband be back?' Zoe asked, saying the first thing that came into her head.

'Wouldn't you like t'know,' the maid replied with a mocking half smile, slurring her words a little. 'You'll be in for it then.'

'All because of the talisman?'

For a moment, Ellissa's dull eyes registered renewed interest.

'Tell me . . . where . . . is,' she said, every word an effort now.

Zoe was saved from the necessity of having to reply when the maid slowly keeled forward and fell in a heap on the rug.

'Wouldn't you like to know,' she said quietly as she got out of bed and went to examine her prostrate gaoler. Ellissa was unconscious, and looked as though she would remain so for some time. *Thank you, Mason*, Zoe thought gratefully. The boy was obviously far more resourceful than anyone gave him credit for. His bravery had achieved what Zoe had not even known how to attempt – and now the next move was up to her.

Her first objective was the talisman. She glanced down at her hand, but the ring had gone, of course. Emmony's fingers were unadorned.

Zoe went to the door, but though she listened intently, she could hear nothing outside. Then she crossed the room to the secret cupboard, her bare feet making no sound. The sequence of points among the delicately carved decorations were already clear in her mind, and she pushed them quickly and precisely. The inner panel sprang open and she glanced inside. At first, all she could see was the book she remembered so well, but then her exploring fingers found what she was looking for.

The small satin bag was long and thin, and contained

something hard and angular. Zoe fumbled with the draw-string, and tipped the contents out onto the bed. When she saw what it was, she could not help laughing – but with quiet hysteria, not humour. Although she had not known what to expect, it certainly wasn't this!

On the bed lay a plastic ballpoint pen, the name 'Brands of Norwich' printed on its side.

# 29

*I should have known.* The ring had been exchanged for a pen, and each talisman was, for some reason, now in the wrong lifetime. Emmony's 'hollow feather' had been an attempt to describe the – to her – inexplicable new form of quill pen.

*But this is ridiculous! Completely insane!* Zoe thought hopelessly. How could the ballpoint have gone back in time? It was impossible, surely – and yet no more impossible than her injury, or the other incredible things that had happened to her. But even if she accepted that this was indeed Emmony's talisman, what could she hope to do with it? The whole thing was absurd. How could such a mundane article – however anachronistic it may be in Emmony's time – be in any way magical?

*I want you to use the talisman,* Michael had said. *You know how, you have the talent.* And Zoe did indeed know how to use it. Her talent, as she had told Emmony, was as a writer, but . . . was she supposed to *write* her way out of prison? *With one bound our heroine was free.*

Never had the words *the pen is mightier than the sword* seemed more ludicrous.

*Think,* she instructed herself. She must use this time well.

Ellissa might not remain unconscious for very much longer – and there may never be another chance.

Zoe remembered the awe Emmony had shown on hearing of her writing skills. *You have such power?* she had asked, adding that such talent was 'formidable'. But how was Zoe to use it? She suddenly thought of Emmony's book. Perhaps there might be a clue there. She took it out quickly and skimmed through the pages, glancing every now and then at the maid, who still lay fast asleep. A random selection of the text revealed only more inarticulate poetry. Clearly, this was not the sort of reference Zoe needed. There might well be something relevant in Jevan's library, Zoe realised, but to get there she had to escape from the bedchamber. She sighed, knowing that she was going round in circles.

Then her eye was caught by a new verse. The title, as far as she could make out, meant something like 'The Loremaster's Lament'. Once again the language was sparse and rough-hewn, to be interpreted rather than read. In essence, it was a plea to the stars, revealing that the writer was willing to exchange all his skill with the runes for the love of a particular woman – the only thing his magic could not win for him. One couplet, roughly translated, read: 'What use my hands to draw a single symbol to curse or bind, when they can never touch what I most desire?'

*A single symbol to curse or bind.* That could also refer to the shield around the chamber – a spell preventing the transmission of messages and also acting as a physical barrier. Could a single sign also release such a spell? Could it really be that simple? Perhaps, but only if the creator of the new spell was more powerful than whoever had imposed it in the first place. Zoe thought of the warlock who was presumably still sitting outside in the hallway. She certainly did not feel very powerful right now and, even if her theory was correct, she knew no symbols from Emmony's world, no puissant runes. But weren't runes supposed to derive their power from the talent of those who made them? Zoe realised that she had only one option. It was time to test her so-called talent.

She looked round for something to write on, but the only thing she could find was the book, and she was appalled by the idea of defacing Emmony's treasure, of ripping out even a single page. However, in the end Zoe convinced herself that Emmony would forgive her. If she succeeded, the end would certainly justify the means. She leafed through the book and found that the last page was blank, except for a watermark stamped in the top corner. As carefully as she could, Zoe tore the page out and then, because she did not want to use it all at once, folded it into six squares of equal size and tore them apart neatly.

*Now what?* Keeping the piece with the watermark, she looked for a pocket to stow the others and realised that her nightdress had none – and also realised that it was hardly a suitable outfit for what she had in mind. A short search provided her with a choice of clothes, and she dressed quickly in the most practical garb available – thick leggings, a shirt, a padded jacket and long boots. Then Zoe went to check again on Ellissa. The maid was breathing heavily and did not stir.

Zoe shoved the spare pieces of paper into a pocket, then sat at the dressing table and stared at her chosen square, pen in hand. A few moments' thought brought no inspiration, and she realised helplessly that her time must surely be running out. *You can't get writer's block now! Relax. Calm and strong.* The three words had become a mantra. *Calm and strong.* But it was not enough.

Emmony came to her rescue. As she gradually managed to relax, Zoe became aware of a sort of internal 'opening up' in her mind. Emmony's subconscious, her instincts, beliefs and knowledge were filtering into Zoe's by a curious form of osmosis. She realised suddenly that she *did* know some symbols, hundreds of them. But one in particular rose to the surface of her thoughts, one which meant much in her own time – and surely in Emmony's too. What else was a pentangle, if not a star?

Zoe put pen to paper, but at first the ink refused to flow. She scribbled furiously, anxiously wondering how long the biro had gone unused, but at last the pen functioned and Zoe hurriedly began to draw. Her rendition of a pentangle was not symmetrical – geometry had never been her strong point – but it would have to do. That was not enough, though. It had to be invested with a purpose, a direction. It needed power and belief.

Zoe hesitated, then took a deep breath. *Just do it.* Emmony believed. Why shouldn't she?

236

Carefully inscribing the unfamiliar letters, she wrote, 'Whatever holds me here is dispelled', then sat back and admired her handiwork. She especially liked that last word. In her own alphabet, she added her name. 'Zoe March'. Now the alien letters looked even more like runes. All around her the air quivered, as if waiting.

Zoe stowed the pen in another pocket, picked up her 'spell' and stood up, trying hard to retain her self-belief but feeling utterly foolish. For safety's sake, she put the book away and closed the secret panel. Crossing to the door, she listened intently but could hear nothing outside. Slowly she turned the handle, then pulled the door open. The action met with some opposition, as if some invisible force was pulling the door from the other side, but she overcame it easily.

There was no reaction as she stepped over the threshold, no sign of the guards she had seen earlier, nor of Mason. The only person in view was the warlock, who still sat in his alcove beside the brazier. The little man stared at her, his eyes bugging out from his round, comical head. Zoe was obviously doing something right.

As confidently as she could, Zoe advanced upon her adversary, holding the piece of paper in front of her. The warlock still did not move, even when she came to a halt just in front of him. He was sweating profusely now, his face was chalk white and his gaze was transfixed by the slip of paper.

'I am stronger than you,' Zoe stated, sensing a sudden rush of power within her. 'With this I remove your shield. Do not think to reimpose it.' Deliberately, acting on instinct, she dropped the paper into the brazier.

The wretched warlock made an ineffectual grab for it but missed, and cried out inarticulately as it landed on the glowing coals. The parchment curled and darkened, flared briefly and then scattered as smoke and wisps of ash. The man froze, as if all his muscles had solidified in that instant, and a long, high, thin scream was expelled from between his clenched teeth. For all Zoe's doubts, he clearly recognised the potency of her offering – and he was petrified. She felt no sympathy. If he chose to use his talent for such corrupt purposes, then his distress was overdue.

Triumphantly, Zoe turned away. She was not sure what she had done, or how she had done it, but she had won her freedom – at least for the time being. The warlock stayed where he was, and made no move to try and stop her from leaving. There was still no one else in sight. Zoe ran down the stairs, Emmony providing her with the route once she was beyond the limits of her own conscious recall.

Having achieved her first two goals, she now only had one thought in her head – to get to Ghyl – and for that she needed a horse. Once out in the deserted yard – where *was* everybody? – she hurried straight for the stables, preferring speed to stealth.

She could only have a matter of seconds before the warlock recovered his wits and raised the alarm, or before somebody came into the yard and discovered her. As she ran, Zoe began to appreciate and feel comfortable with the capabilities of her new body, its greater strength and athleticism – but it was her own sense of purpose that lent the necessary determination. Even the jolting pain in her ribs was easy to ignore now.

The entrance to the stables loomed before her, dark and forbidding. Zoe slowed her pace and only then realised that the strange wavering light which illuminated the scene came not from the few visible lamps but from the sky.

Turning slowly and looking up to the north, she gasped in wonder. A quarter of the night sky was painted with swirls of green, a luminous arch of colour with bands of red glowing within its span. Rays converged to a seemingly infinitely distant point; screens and coronas glimmered into life, only to fade a moment later.

Zoe had only ever once seen the northern lights, the aurora borealis, soon after her arrival in Norfolk, and it had not been nearly as spectacular as this. The amazing spectacle made her feel tiny, like a child, and invoked in her feelings of awe and veneration. Part of that, she knew suddenly, came from Emmony. To a society that revered the sky as much as they did, such a display must be truly spellbinding.

Then something else caught her eye, and she glanced up at the roof of the main house. The observation platform was crowded with people, all staring at the celestial display, completely mesmerised. *So that's where everybody is,* Zoe realised, coming back to her own concerns with a rush. Only the warlock had not dared to leave his post. It was an unbelievable stroke of luck – and one she must take advantage of.

At the sound of hooves on the cobbles behind her she whirled round, her heart racing. Zoe saw a man emerge from the darkness, leading a familiar horse, and for an instant she stood, poised to flee or fight. Then she recognised Mason and breathed a sigh of relief. Was he to be her saviour once again?

'Wind–d–dancer,' the boy whispered, his gaze straying to the lights in the sky.

Zoe already knew the mare, and went to her eagerly. The beautiful animal had a strange, half mad glint in her eyes, but allowed herself to be stroked. Zoe had not ridden on her own for many years, and could only hope that her body retained Emmony's skill – and her innate empathy with animals. As Mason helped her up into the saddle, she took the reins and tried to relax, to open up to Emmony's subconscious and allow the other woman's instincts to rise naturally to the surface of her mind. Only by acting together could they hope to succeed.

The ground seemed a long way down, but Zoe felt comfortable, her legs adjusting to the horse's movements as Mason led her slowly to the gate. The horseshoes clicked on the stone, sounding very loud to Zoe, but no one paid them any attention. Once they were on the soft earth beyond the paved area, the footfalls were silent. Mason halted, closed the gate quietly and looked up at her.

'Thank you,' Zoe whispered, getting ready to ride.

The boy still gazed at her, his wide eyes sad.

'You want to come?' she guessed.

239

Mason nodded emphatically, and his arms twitched wildly. Zoe leant down and helped him up behind her, finding the manoeuvre oddly familiar and easy. He clung to her unselfconsciously, obviously happy now. And then, almost of her own accord, Winddancer set off.

# 30

The wild ride beneath that wondrous sky was exhilarating.
The wind was cold, but rushed like thin music in Zoe's
ears, and as the forests and fields sped by, she found
ways to breathe and move that minimised the pain in her
ribs – which nevertheless hurt more and more as the ride
progressed. She was very glad to recognise the approach
to Blue Tiles, but when no lights beckoned to her from the
Sanctuary, she suffered a moment's unease. What if Ghyl
were no longer there?

'G–Ghyl is there,' Mason said in her ear.

Zoe was so relieved that she did not even stop to think
how the boy had responded to her unspoken question.

'B–but the air is b–b–bent,' he added.

'What do you mean?'

'The shields m–make the air go round,' he replied. 'We
c–can't see inside.'

By now they were close enough to make his obscure
meaning obvious, and Zoe slowed the mare to a walk. The
northern lights had faded, leaving the sky to the lordship
of the stars and a three-quarter moon, but even in the half
light she could see that the farmhouse and its outbuildings
simply were not there. But then her dismay evaporated as a
new awareness was fed to her. There were false patterns in
what she could see, repeated shapes and outlines.

*It's an illusion*, she realised, and rode on.

Passing through the curved shields was a disorientating
experience, but neither her mount nor Mason seemed at all

241

perturbed as the scenery slipped and rearranged itself about them. Once inside the invisible screen, Blue Tiles appeared before them, as solid as ever – but unless an onlooker knew it was there, all but the most curious could have been forgiven for being unaware of its existence. The air had been 'bent' around the place, creating a gap in reality and filling it with mirror images of the surrounding fields and trees. It was the ultimate camouflage.

Zenna was waiting at the doorway to greet them, lamp in hand. Mason dismounted eagerly, half falling to the ground, then offering his hand to Zoe as the witch walked over to join them.

Zoe got down slowly and carefully, her side now very painful. *You need rest*, she heard Dr Black say, and grimaced ruefully. Zenna regarded her with concern as she straightened up and handed the reins to Mason.

'It's n–not m–my lady . . .' he began.

'I know,' Zenna reassured him. 'Her name is Zoe. You have done well to aid her cause, Mason.'

The boy's smile glowed at this praise, making Zoe's heart melt. His patent 'simplicity' hid a golden nature.

'Thank you again, Mason,' she said. 'You were wonderful. I would never have got away without your help.'

Mason looked down at the ground, filled with pleasure at Zoe's words.

'Take Winddancer to the stables now,' Zenna told him.

He went readily, still radiating childlike contentment, and the two women watched him fondly.

'He's a remarkable young man,' Zoe said.

'Yes. Sometimes those born under a dancing star are the best of us all,' the witch replied.

Zoe did not need a translation of the curious phrase. It was perfectly apt.

'I sensed you would come,' Zenna said.

'Can you always read the future?'

'Not always. But sometimes when there is need.'

'How do you do it?' Zoe asked, wanting to know more.

'By going outside.'

'Outside what?'

'Above. Like a kestrel looking down on a road,' the witch answered. 'He can see both back and forward along the way.'

'Time is like a road for you,' Zoe realised, remembering Emmony's anguished cry. *Even Zenna's eyes are blind. She sees only darkness on my road ahead.*

'Are there no people who can go outside in your world?'

'Not really . . .' Zoe replied, not sure how to explain her world's sceptical attitude to clairvoyance. 'Emmony said her road ahead was dark. Is it still?'

'Yes,' Zenna answered gravely. 'Prophecy is not a precise talent, and it fails many times.'

Zoe nodded resignedly. She was eager to go inside now, but Zenna put out a hand to stop her.

'You're hurt.' It was a statement, not a question.

'It's nothing.'

'Let me at least treat your injury,' the witch persisted. 'I have a salve—'

'How is Ghyl?' Zoe cut in. 'May I speak to him?'

'There is no change. He will not hear you.'

'Yes he will. He just can't respond yet,' Zoe told the other woman confidently.

'We've done all we can . . .' Zenna began, slightly defensive.

'I know, and I bless you for it,' Zoe said as she strode towards the house, her need urgent now.

However, before she was allowed access to Ghyl, Zenna insisted on looking at her bruises. She rubbed in a salve that smelt of herbs and stung Zoe's skin, but even though the gentle application hurt terribly, the underlying ache was eased a few moments later. Zoe was grateful, and Zenna's comment that Ghyl could wait a few moments longer for her benefit showed good sense. Even so, being held up in this manner made her anxious, and she had to remind herself to stay calm.

This time the sight of Ghyl, and his immediate identification with Michael, was not the awful shock it had been before, though it still made Zoe shiver. A nurse – a witch, Zoe corrected herself – sat at his bedside but she left at a nod from Zenna, and Zoe knelt down and took his hand in her own. It was cool and lifeless to the touch, and she felt dual emotions rise within her.

'I love you, Ghyl,' she whispered, meaning it with her whole heart. 'In all our lives.'

Behind her, Zenna was silent, watching and listening.

'I know you're in touch with another,' Zoe went on. 'One who shares your thoughts. You must help Michael tell me what to do. Will you do that? Please.'

Her gaze fell upon the locket around his neck, and she picked it up and opened it. Inside was a miniature portrait of Emmony. *Like my photo at the hospital.* Would Ghyl react to that as Michael had seemed to? Michael had responded by affecting the technology around him, randomly at first, but later with more purpose. Ghyl had no such technology available – *there are no machines here* – so his reaction, if there was one, must be expressed differently. And *magic* was the equivalent of science in this world.

'Show me, Ghyl,' Zoe breathed. Before Zenna could react, she pulled sharply at the pendant and the chain snapped as the wrench shifted Ghyl's unresponsive head. 'Show me!'

'What are you doing?' Zenna cried angrily, but broke off when the flame in the oil lamp, which hung on a wall bracket, flared brightly and then went out. From outside came the sound of a boy wailing and a horse snorting in terror.

'What did you do?' Zenna asked in the darkness.

'Nothing,' Zoe answered triumphantly. She had her proof. '*Ghyl* did it.'

Moments later Iven burst into the room.

'What's going on?' he gasped. 'Mason's gone mad and the horses are acting crazy.'

Zoe looked up at him fearfully. *What have I done?* She put the locket back on Ghyl's chest, and curled one of his hands around it. On the wall, the lamp flickered back to life and burnt serenely once more.

'You have much to explain.' The witch's anger was gone, replaced by amazement and curiosity.

'I'm not sure I can,' Zoe replied.

Just at that moment they were all distracted by the clatter of many horseshoes on cobbles and the sound of angry voices. Before they could react, heavy footsteps were heard in the corridor.

'Your witchery doesn't frighten me!' a man's voice shouted. 'Out of my way.'

He appeared in the doorway, his face red and sweating, his eyes wide. Then his expression changed to a gratified smile as he took in the scene before him.

'Well, *my lady*, this is an interesting sight,' Killian remarked, putting sarcastic emphasis on her title. 'My brother will be most interested to know how you spend your time during his absence.'

# 31

At first, Zoe was too horrified to respond. She glanced at Zenna, who made a gesture of apology. This was evidently one visitor she had not been able to deceive with her screening spell. Nor had she been able to foresee his arrival. Killian's dark, threatening presence dominated the room.

'Why should Jevan be interested in my visit to a sick friend?' Zoe asked eventually.

Killian laughed.

'A friend? No more? Rumour has it—'

'Rumour is no concern of mine,' Zoe told him, as defiantly as she could.

'Your husband may be a dullard, but I am not,' Killian snapped. 'I've seen the way you look at your *friend*. The Quarterman cannot choose to remain blind when I tell him of this cosy scene.'

'Tell him what you like,' she replied, forcing strength into her voice. 'I have nothing to hide.'

'Really?' His dark eyes widened in mock surprise. 'We'll see. Tell the witch and her cronies to leave us.'

Zenna and Iven hesitated, but Zoe nodded as Killian's fingers curled round the hilt of his sword. Their talents could not help her now, and she had no wish to see them hurt. *Our lives will all be forfeit*, Zenna had said on her earlier visit. It was up to Zoe to save her new-found friends. She had no idea what magical talents Killian had, if indeed he had any, but she knew that he would be capable of appalling violence. Her main concern now was to prevent him from harming the helpless Ghyl.

When they had been left alone, Killian seemed to relax a little – which was unnerving in itself – and began to speak in a quite different tone. If Zoe had not known better, she would almost have thought he was being friendly.

'The Quarterman is still at the Pyramid, of course, embroiling himself in court intrigues,' he began, 'so that gives us time to sort a few things out.'

'Why aren't you with him?' Zoe asked, cursing whatever circumstances had led him to his change of plans.

'You think my brother is the only one to employ long-hearers?' he replied. 'At least *my* servants keep me properly informed.'

*So that was it*, Zoe thought bitterly. Someone had passed on a message by telepathy, just as in her own time they would have picked up a telephone, and told him of her escape.

'I simply made my excuses,' Killian went on smugly, 'and returned to Ridge Hall.'

It was the first time Zoe had heard Emmony's home referred to by name.

'I underestimated you,' he admitted with a smile. 'Ellissa was still sleeping, and you reduced that pathetic little warlock to a gibbering idiot. I'd not like to be in either of their shoes when Jevan gets back and hears how you duped them. You were lucky that the skies provided you with a ready-made distraction, of course. But the surprise you left in the bedchamber was a very pretty joke. A lesser man might have been frightened.'

'What surprise?' Zoe asked, puzzled.

'How forgetful you are becoming,' Killian remarked sarcastically, and did not explain further except to say, 'The blindness only lasted a few moments. What did you hope to achieve?' He went on without waiting for an answer. 'Working out where you'd gone was not exactly hard. A child could have followed your trail.'

*What trail?* Zoe wondered. Surely the hoofprints would not have been obvious in the dark.

'Besides,' Killian added, 'I've had my eye on this place for a while. The stars know what these do-gooders are really up to.'

Zoe wanted to defend her friends, to protest that they were a genuine force for good, in spite of his derision, but decided that it would be safer not to interrupt.

'Now, before we return you to your home,' he went on, in business-like fashion, 'there are two things I require. I could take them by force, if necessary, but it would be so much more civilised if you were to yield them up willingly. I might even consider saving you from my brother's fully justified wrath. It should not be beyond your wit to invent a less damning version of today's events – and I'll back your story, *if* you make it worth my while.'

'What do you want?' she asked, her heart sinking.

'First, the talisman,' he replied evenly. 'And then you.'

As Zoe stared at him, she felt as though she were being embalmed in ice. The sight of his feral grin was more chilling than even Jevan's fury had been.

'I don't have the talisman,' she said eventually, ignoring the second part of his demand.

'Of course you don't,' he said, more sarcastic than ever. 'It just *happened* that one of your meagre talents was suddenly able to elude guards, break seals and set traps.' He paused. 'Just give it to me.'

'It's not here,' Zoe told him, desperately stalling for time. 'It's back at the house.'

'Why would you . . .?' he began, then broke off and fixed her with his hawk's gaze. 'If you're lying to me, you'll regret it, I promise you. Take off your clothes.'

Stricken with horror, Zoe did not move.

'I will never submit to you willingly,' she said, forcing courage into her voice. 'And violating me would be treachery beyond the scope of my innocent actions. Jevan is still Quarterman – and he would kill you.'

'He would kill you rather,' Killian replied, but Zoe could see that her words had struck a nerve. For the first time she could detect just a touch of uncertainty in those baleful black eyes.

'You are already an adulteress,' he accused, pointing at Ghyl.

'That's a lie! And I can prove it,' Zoe claimed.

'How?' he demanded.

'Women have their ways,' she told him, hoping that a bestial chauvinist like her adversary would know little of her sex beyond their obvious use to him. 'Jevan would see your treason for what it is and Chandos and the lawgivers would back their Quarterman.' Repeating this was the only way she could threaten him, her only hope, and she clung to it tenaciously. She would defend Emmony's body – her body – as best she could, though she knew that Killian would easily beat her in a contest of brute strength. And her words seemed to have distracted him at least.

'Their Quarterman!' Killian snarled, his sharp face contorted with disgust. 'It is *I* who should be Quarterman, but for an accident of birth when he breathed the air a few moments earlier than I. I am more worthy in every way – and Jevan knows it. If you were to bear a son, *my* son, it would be the final proof, his ultimate humiliation . . .'

'That will never happen,' Zoe stated firmly, seeing now that his lust was not entirely for herself, but for yet another possession that his brother had, by Killian's reckoning, stolen from him.

'How can you be so sure?' he asked menacingly, and advanced a single pace. 'I am twice the man Jevan is, and many times the worth of that insignificant cripple in the bed. Instead of fawning over him, wouldn't you like to know what a *real* lover feels like?'

Zoe forced herself to stand her ground.

'Lay one finger on me and you will live to regret it,' she informed him coldly.

Killian laughed, but uneasily.

'The Sanctuary is a place which allows no violence,' Zoe added, hoping that her words were true. 'If you violate its peace, my friends' talents will be turned against you. Witches make dangerous enemies.'

'Those worthless drudges?' he exclaimed in disbelief. 'One word to my men, and your *friends* would be a danger to no one.'

Confirmation that Killian had not come alone did not surprise Zoe, but it gave her even less scope for manoeuvre. However, she had given him pause for thought. He was quiet now, weighing the alternatives, and his devious nature evidently overcame his brutish desires as he reached his decision.

'Come,' he told her abruptly. 'We will ride for the Hall now – and you will give me the talisman. Then perhaps you will prove more amenable.'

It was more of a reprieve than Zoe had dared hope for, and she nodded in mute acquiescence. With one last despairing glance at Ghyl – whom Killian had evidently forgotten, or dismissed as unimportant – she walked from the room.

There were several men on horseback in the yard and she heard them calling to others as their commander emerged. There was no sign of Mason as she remounted, and Zoe hoped the boy would remain safely hidden. She doubted that he would ever be able to return to his master's house. Zenna appeared in the doorway as they were about to leave, but a warning glance from Killian kept her quiet. *I hope they have the sense to move Ghyl somewhere else, somewhere he'll be safe*, Zoe thought as she rode away, with Killian just behind her and his men all around.

From inside, the curved screen that hid Blue Tiles had no effect on their line of sight, but there was still a strange frisson in the night air as they passed through the invisible veil. Zoe noted that several of the horses became skittish for a moment, and some of the soldiers looked nervous.

The journey was no more than half completed when a distant ringing sound made Zoe aware of the inevitability of returning to her own world. She did not want to go, knowing that she would be leaving Emmony in an awkward predicament, and not sure whether the other woman would even be aware of what had happened. But she had no choice. The implanted command brought her out of her trance and she was once again sitting in the chair in her own home, feeling immensely weary, her ribs throbbing. She did not move for some time, her thoughts still in the other world.

She wondered whether to repeat the hypnosis immediately and return to face the consequences of her actions. But it was clearly impossible for her to spend *all* her time there, and she was sure that she had acted as Emmony would have done in the given circumstances. She would just have to hope that Emmony would be capable of dealing with her changed situation until Zoe was ready to return.

She got up slowly and headed for the door, when her attention was drawn to the Polaroid camera. One of the flash bulbs was burnt out, and a photograph had been ejected. Curiously, she picked it up and peeled back the protective layer. What she saw beneath made her skin crawl. The picture showed her sitting room, with her appearing to be asleep on the chair. But beside it was the figure of a man, his hands half raised as if in self-defence.

*The blindness only lasted a few moments . . .*

Zoe stared in disbelief as Killian's rat-like features glared back at her from the photograph.

# 32

Zoe found it hard to sleep that night. No matter how hard she tried to stop them, her thoughts kept spinning in ever-decreasing circles. She was worried about Emmony's predicament – and Ghyl's – but her speculation about recent developments only produced even more questions. Had the pen really gone back in time? And if so, how? Had the ring come forward to the future?

Then there was the photograph. She had brought it upstairs with her and now it lay, face down, on her bedside table. Had the camera gone off on its own, faithfully recording the bizarre scene? Or had some outside force – her own subconscious, perhaps – pushed it into action? Or was the picture entirely her own creation? She thought of the psychic photographs of Ted Serios, who could imprint images onto film without the need of a camera. And, regardless of the picture's origin, how was it that Killian had been in her sitting room? Was he the poltergeist? At least that would explain those earlier feelings of animosity. But how – even though she had been in a hypnotic trance – could she have remained unaware of his presence? In a way, that was the most frightening aspect of all, implying a horrifying vulnerability. Then again, she was assuming that the photograph was an accurate representation of what had been before the camera.

Zoe switched on the bedside light and picked up the print to study it for the umpteenth time. But now she concentrated not on her own image, nor on the figure of Killian, his hands half raised in a vain attempt to protect himself from the flash, but on the background, the room itself. Most of it was out of focus, but she could identify the far end of the sofa, the television and the telephone table. But there were other vague shapes there that did not fit, which she could not explain until she realised that a few details of Emmony's bedchamber had been superimposed on her own sitting room. The dark column was one of the bedposts, and those shadowed squares in the background looked like wood panelling. It was like a double exposure, and yet only one flashbulb had gone off, taking a photograph of two places at the same time.

Could she use this picture to convince Owen that he should continue the investigation? Zoe would have been willing to accept his anger at her breaking her promise if only she felt that it would change his mind. But it was a forlorn hope, and she knew it. Even though this was concrete evidence, proving the existence of Emmony's world, Zoe knew that Owen could easily explain it away. He would argue that it was just another facet of her self-delusion, like her bruised ribs and the messages from Michael. So she decided not to tell him. Of course, there was always the possibility that Owen was right, that she was going mad. But even if that were the case, she knew she still had to try to go on, to try and help Michael.

Zoe's thoughts returned to Emmony, left on that perilous ride. It was hard to believe that it had all happened long ago, that Emmony and Killian had arrived at Ridge Hall maybe centuries earlier, and that all the problems had been resolved – one way or another. But this did not diminish her sense of responsibility. Once again she was tempted to go back, to face the consequences herself, but she was desperately tired now and knew that she needed to sleep. She hesitated, though, half afraid of what her dreams might bring. In the end she took a sleeping pill, although she hated doing so, and surrendered to the darkness with Dr Black's words echoing again in her ears. *You need rest.*

She was woken by the arrival of the post, and staggered out of bed, feeling drowsy but glad that she could remember no dreams, and went downstairs. She found a pile of junk mail on the doormat, together with more of Michael's computer magazines and an envelope franked by her agent's office. Inside, with a brief note from Alex, was the list of questions from the journalist. Zoe had forgotten all about this, but dutifully skimmed through them as she pottered in the kitchen. The neatly typed list contained the usual stuff about her background and work, but then a question near the end caught her attention.

'I have read, in an earlier interview, that you call your novels your "other lands". Have you ever considered writing a novel set abroad, or even in an entirely imaginary world?'

Zoe stared at the last four words. Was that in effect what she was doing? Although she instinctively rejected the idea, she also challenged herself to prove it. But to do this she had to *be* there – no matter what Owen said. Adrenaline surged through her and she dashed back upstairs. After dressing quickly, she returned to the sitting room and picked up the phone to call Owen while her new-found determination lasted. After a few rings, Zoe found herself connected to his answering machine, and she smiled with relief. It was so much easier lying to an inanimate device.

'Owen, this is Zoe. I'm cancelling my appointment for tomorrow. I hope that isn't inconvenient. I'm going to take your advice and go away to a hotel for a few days. I haven't decided where yet. Thanks for all your help. I'll call you when I get back. Bye.'

With that out of the way, Zoe wondered whether to make the trip into Norwich to see Michael and tell him what she was planning. After brief consideration she decided not to. She was convinced that his interests would be best served by her other plans, and she was too anxious to learn of Emmony's fate. Killian would not have been an easy man to appease – or to fool for long. Unwanted images of violence filled her head, and she tried to push them aside before her fear grew too great. There would be no turning back now.

She made her preparations as before, hesitating only over how long she should allow herself in the other land. The old fashioned alarm clock would only give her up to twelve hours

– but was that too long? Did she dare remain in hypnosis for such a long time? Then again, if something bad was going to happen, did it matter whether she or Emmony suffered the consequences? If they were to save Ghyl – and thus Michael – they would *both* be needed.

The time was 10.15 a.m. Zoe set the alarm for 10 o'clock, giving herself the rest of the day and most of the evening, then tried to calm her nerves. As she began the induction process, she found herself rubbing the ring, her talisman, as if for luck.

She fell into absolute darkness. She could see nothing at all and, for a moment, she feared that Emmony had been blinded. But then the other details of her situation registered and that fear was replaced by another. She was crouched in a tightly enclosed space, like a cupboard. Reaching out with her hands revealed that she was surrounded only by bare stone and wood. There was no room for her to stand up or lie down, and she was forced to kneel or sit with her knees drawn up. She found cracks in the wood, which presumably framed a door, but no light came through, and the door itself would not budge. It was obviously barred from the other side.

Zoe began to panic. Twelve hours trapped here would be unbearable – and she would achieve nothing.

Was this Emmony's punishment for deceiving Killian? Had he taken the talisman? It was not in her pocket, although the squares of paper were. What else had happened? Her body was stiff and cramped but, apart from her still sore ribs, unharmed. Zoe took a deep breath to calm herself, then reached for the memories in the hidden part of her brain and called them forth.

When Emmony had taken control of her own body she had found herself riding back to Ridge Hall with Killian and his men. Her brief bewilderment had soon been replaced by understanding and then determination as the memories came back to her. She had found the talisman and resolved to keep it from Killian at all costs, aware now of its importance to her spirit counterpart. Zoe found it odd to be thinking of herself in the second person, but continued the recollection eagerly.

Emmony had sensed the nervousness of the horses around her. They were riding too fast over poorly lit terrain, and the fever induced by the lights in the sky earlier that evening had not entirely dissipated.

The party had reached the edge of the forest and begun to cross the fields which surrounded the house. When Emmony had seen a pair of barn owls, skimming through the night on silken wings, she had taken her chance. She called to them silently, and rejoiced as she saw them change direction and swoop towards the horses, their white, heart-shaped faces ghostly in the starlight. As they drew nearer, Emmony urged them on, until the two birds were whirling round in between the riders, frightening the men and alarming the horses – who started and whinnied nervously. Emmony's long association with Winddancer meant that her own mare was biddable. In answer to her rider's commands, she reared and skittered, spinning round, her hooves flying in every indication of panic. Her actions helped add to the confusion of the other mounts. When Emmony set her off at a wild gallop, the mare lived up to her name, and they raced across the open fields with Killian and some others in ragged pursuit, their shouts unheard in the wind. Emmony pretended to try to control her horse but in fact was urging her on, clinging to the reins and saddle for dear life.

They were headed for the ring of ash trees which could be seen from Emmony's bedroom window, and as they plunged inside branches whipped past her head. They came to a shuddering halt within the bower and Emmony half fell, half leapt down and quickly shoved the pen into a rotten, hollow tree stump. Then she threw herself onto the ground, as if she had fallen, just in time for Killian's less precipitate arrival, and prayed that he had not seen what she had done.

Killian's snarl of anger turned to laughter as he looked down at her.

'It's a good job the leaves make for a soft landing,' he commented. 'I'd hate to see you break your neck just yet.'

## 33

Watched by Killian and several of his guards – none of whom offered to help her – Emmony had got to her feet, dusted herself down, then remounted and completed the journey at a more leisurely pace.

'Well, where is it?' Killian demanded without preamble once they had dismounted.

Without hesitation, Emmony had led him to her bed-chamber, only to find a group of people gathered there. Lanier, the chamberlain, was evidently grilling both Ellissa and the warlock, whose name was Gouveia, watched by two worried-looking guards. They all turned as Emmony came in with Killian on her heels, and Gouveia cringed, his eyes wide. Ellissa watched dully, clearly resentful and angry, while the soldiers were rigid with fear.

'My lady . . .' Lanier began, then saw Killian and fell silent – but his relief was plain. The runaway had been recaptured.

The presence of these extra witnesses suited Emmony well. She marched over to her secret cupboard and opened it without hesitation – much to the others' amazement. Her precious book was removed and tossed onto the bed, and then she searched the empty space with increasing panic, proving herself to be a good actress.

'It's gone!' she exclaimed, feigning shock. 'Stolen!' The hysterical outburst that followed had been convincing, and she accused all of those present in turn of having taken her treasure. Each of them denied it, with varying degrees of vehemence and hostility until, eventually, Killian had had enough.

'You think I am fooled by this play-acting?' he snapped. 'Where is it?'

'It's gone, I tell you!' Emmony declared angrily. 'If I'm play-acting, then why would I have betrayed my secret, my book, if I knew the talisman wasn't there?' It was a persuasive argument. Everyone there knew that the book was forbidden property. Killian then began to suspect the others, but though he questioned them fiercely, he got little satisfaction. Ellissa was still half asleep, and Gouveia's stuttering attempts to describe the day's events were made all but incomprehensible by his terror. The guards were monosyllabic while Lanier replied carefully and coolly, appearing unruffled but perhaps hiding his own fear.

Killian's fury was rising again, and Emmony knew that it was only a matter of time before he returned his attention to her. She decided to take the initiative.

'When does my lord return?'

The sudden interruption took them all by surprise, but eventually the chamberlain answered.

'Tomorrow afternoon.'

'Protect me from Killian until then,' she demanded. 'He has tried to rape me.'

There was a deathly hush in the room, and no one dared answer her declaration. Emmony herself broke the silence.

'When Quarterman Jevan returns,' she told Killian, emphasising her husband's title, 'he will deal with you.'

Killian gave her a look that would have reduced lesser mortals to jelly, but Emmony stood her ground. Her enemy abruptly turned on his heel and stalked from the room, only to return moments later with four of his own soldiers. Emmony was terrified, wondering if she had gone too far, but still clung to the hope that he would not dare to attack her now. Jevan's servants made no attempt to stop him as he led her away to the disused storage cell which was her present prison. There she had remained all night, cold, cruelly constricted

258

and with no prospect of escape, nor any idea when she might be released.

In spite of her unpleasant predicament, Zoe was full of admiration for her counterpart's courage and ingenuity. Bluffing Killian had been a supreme act of bravery, and her sacrifice in giving up her most prized possession had been worthy of her fighting spirit. What was more, thanks to Emmony, Zoe was now the only one who knew where the talisman was. Her problem was that she had no means of escaping in order to reach it; all she could do was wait helplessly, perhaps until Jevan returned. What she was likely to face then hardly bore thinking about. She might have avoided Killian's carnal intentions for the moment, but the Grey Wolf would gain his revenge somehow – of that she was certain. Who could tell what he would have told Jevan and what *his* reaction would be? In any case, in the continued absence of the talisman and with the knowledge of her escape and defiance, Jevan was not likely to be well disposed towards his wife. Zoe could only hope to fuel the brothers' suspicions of each other. If they were constantly at odds, then perhaps they would pay less attention to her. But, of course, she could do nothing until . . .

Time passed agonisingly slowly in the unchanging darkness. Shifting position only seemed to intensify her discomfort and her occasional attempts to gain someone's attention by calling out or banging on the door brought absolutely no response.

Zoe was close to despair when at last she heard footsteps outside. She hammered on the door and pleaded, her voice hoarse, and was rewarded by the wonderful sound of heavy bolts being drawn back. The door creaked open reluctantly. Even though the light in the little-used corridor outside was dim, it seemed almost blinding to Zoe and she blinked furiously as tears formed. She crawled out on her hands and knees, then lay on her back on the floor, stretching her cramped limbs. It was some time before she could recognise her saviour. Lanier stood above her, a half smile on his narrow face, self-contained as always, saying nothing.

'Where's Killian?' she asked eventually.

'Gone,' the chamberlain replied. 'But he promised to be back soon.'

It was a double-edged reply that allowed Zoe only a small measure of relief.

'Jevan?' she asked.

'We expect the Quarterman back within a few hours.'

'Who told you to let me out?'

'Jevan sent instructions. He said that it would give you time to prepare for his arrival.'

That sounded ominous.

'Has the talisman been found?' Zoe asked, knowing that the question would be expected of her.

'No. The Quarterman was hoping you might be able to assist with its recovery,' Lanier answered evenly.

Zoe shook her head, doing her best to look both disgusted and bewildered, then held up her hand. With half concealed reluctance, the chamberlain helped her to her feet.

'You wish to retire to your bedchamber?'

'No.'

'Some sustenance?'

'No.' Why was he suddenly concerned for her welfare? 'You could bring my horse to the door,' she added, and grinned, her spirit still strong enough to risk teasing the chamberlain.

'Jevan has instructed that you are not to leave the house, my lady,' he replied with patently insincere regret.

The pins and needles in her legs were making it hard for Zoe to concentrate. Without the talisman, how could she escape again – in broad daylight this time, without the distraction of the northern lights? At the moment she hardly felt capable of walking.

'I will wait for my lord in his study,' she decided eventually. 'Bring some refreshment there.'

Lanier glanced at her in surprise but then nodded and left. Confused by her sudden freedom, Zoe stood still for a while, then tottered to the study. At least there she might have a chance to learn something and to think in peace.

The movement gradually allowed her legs to grow stronger, but she was still tired from lack of sleep and the long confinement, and was glad to reach her destination. Inside the study the air was cool and a maid was hastily laying a fire in the cold grate, but she scurried out as soon as Zoe arrived. Collapsing into one of the large chairs, she breathed deeply. Hunting trophies stared down at her balefully, glass-eyed. Even though she was apparently alone, she felt as if she was being watched.

Perhaps, she thought, they hoped that she would lead them to the talisman – hence her apparent freedom. They would be disappointed, of course. But what *was* she going to do?

Another maid came in, carrying a tray with a hot drink – some kind of herbal infusion – and some biscuits. She set this down, glanced about nervously but did not speak. After the servant had left again, Zoe sniffed, then sipped cautiously and felt better. Her eyes strayed to a row of books on a high shelf. Even from where she sat she could see that they were dusty and rarely used. Did she dare get them down? She got to her feet and began to cross the room when her gaze fell upon a map spread out on the desktop. Curiously she bent to study it, wishing the lamplight were brighter. The chart clearly showed the extent of the lands which belonged to the Quarterman, with Ridge Hall at the centre of the estates. It covered a large area, but without knowing the scale Zoe could not tell just how big.

Another map lay beneath. She removed the top one, then gasped, staring in disbelief. For all the unfamiliarity of the setting and its details, she was undoubtedly looking at a map of East Anglia. It showed the familiar bulbous outline of the coast of Norfolk and Suffolk, with the angular indentation of The Wash to the northwest. There were the wriggling shapes of the rivers – the Yare, Waveney, Wensum, Bure and Ant – but there almost all the similarities vanished. None of the names of her time existed. Several sites of towns were the same – King's Lynn, Wells and Great Yarmouth – but the names given to the settlements were quite different here, and one, where Norwich should be, had no name at all. Instead, it bore the unmistakable sign of a pyramid.

The more Zoe studied the map, the more she found that was unfamiliar. Only the shape and character of the land itself remained unchanged – and even then there were some subtle differences: The Wash was bigger than she remembered, and there were some strange indentations in the northern coastline. Everything else was new. A few names – Gosheen, to the northeast, and Flagg, an island near the mouth of the Yare – seemed vaguely familiar, but the others meant nothing at all.

This then was the Eastern Dominions, Chandos's domain. Emmony, like Zoe, lived in Norfolk – but a Norfolk changed beyond all recognition.

# 34

Still in a state of shock, Zoe pored over the map, trying to work out its true significance. At one point she noticed a strange symbol shaped like an antler, and there, just to the northwest of where Thetford would be in her own time, was something marked 'old flint mines'. This was in the exact spot – if Zoe remembered correctly – where Grime's Graves lay, flint mines dating from the New Stone Age. They had remained in use until the Bronze Age, the prehistoric miners hacking out the black rock with picks made from deer antlers. Zoe had visited the site, been down into one of the four-thousand-year-old shafts, and seen the pagan shrine to the Earth Goddess – an eerie but very rewarding experience. Was there any hidden meaning to the fact that the only similarity between Emmony's world and her own seemed to be one established in ancient times?

There were no further revelations, just a few half connections with her own time: the flat lands to the west were obviously the forerunners of the Fens, and some of the marked highways seemed to follow routes known to her. Much else that was depicted, however, appeared impossible for *any* period of history. Zoe's mind balked at the idea of a gigantic, translucent blue pyramid covering Norwich. And the Norfolk Broads, that interconnected series of lakes so well known to present-day yachtsmen, anglers and holiday-makers, seemed to have disappeared altogether, replaced by an area marked simply 'marshland' and crisscrossed by lines which could represent anything – roads, canals or boundaries.

What did it all mean? This crazy, inexplicable discovery, like so much that had gone before, seemed designed only to lead Zoe deeper into confusion. She felt like crying. So much of what she had seen simply could not come from an earlier period in Norfolk's history – and yet here she was.

Ridge Hall was real, as were the inhabitants of this strange world, of that she was certain. It was inconceivable that they could exist only in her deluded imagination. But where – and when – *had* they existed?

The map had prompted a mass of questions without Zoe being overtly aware of them, and Emmony's subconscious was gradually able to increase her knowledge. She learnt that she was indeed in part of the island which in her own day comprised England, Scotland and Wales – Great Britain – but, for Emmony, this was not a unified country in any sense. Instead it was divided into numerous small princedoms – Chandos's was one of the largest in area – ruled by despotic lords of varying degrees of competence and cruelty. It corresponded to no period of history Zoe was aware of – unless the archaeologists had got it drastically wrong and she was now in some unimaginably distant past, a magical civilisation, all traces of which had vanished into the mists of prehistory. It did not seem at all likely. And yet what was the alternative?

Only that it was her own creation, formed out of her own obsession.

Chilled by the thought and drained of energy, Zoe sat down again. Helplessly, she reviewed what she knew of Emmony's world, trying to fit it into a pattern; trying to make some sense of it all.

It was not just the political geography that was different. Socially and technologically, her own time and Emmony's were like chalk and cheese. This world had no machines; magic took the place of science, with witches, warlocks and sorcerers the equivalent of technicians and engineers. It was magic that built pyramids and sea walls, protected the health of humans, animals and crops and provided means of long-distance communication – and who knew what else? It

264

was a world of wonders and yet in other ways was harsh and limited. Its feudal system seemed barbaric to Zoe, its written language was crude and little used, and the people themselves were religiously obsessed by the movements of the heavens. In short, it was a fantasy world.

But whose fantasy? The very fact that it centred on Zoe – judging from the map, Emmony's home seemed to be at the same location as Thornmere – made it all too apparent, yet she fought shy of the obvious conclusion. Didn't the fact that she could still question her sanity mean that she was sane?

'It doesn't matter,' she told herself aloud. 'Whatever – and wherever – this is, I still have to save Ghyl.' It was the only way she could help Michael, she was convinced of that, and the only reason she was determined to go on. It was why she had begun in the first place.

'I've started so I'll finish,' she said, mimicking the often used words of a well-known TV quizmaster, and almost laughed.

But her quick burst of humour did not last long. What was she supposed to *do*? There was the conundrum again: was she changing history or replaying it? She could only proceed on instinct – which said that she was acting of her own free will. She was there for a purpose.

'I'm *here*,' she claimed aloud. 'In Norfolk. I'm *here*.'

And then something else occurred to her. *What if I'm here now? What if this alternative Norfolk is a parallel world, just as real as the 'real world'?* This was the stuff of science fiction, but then so was much of what had happened to her recently. And the idea felt right. The more she thought about it, the more it seemed to fit.

If she and Emmony existed in separate streams of time, the only things that would remain constant would be those relating to the land itself, as the map appeared to confirm. But because their worlds operated in parallel streams, the regression had not moved her back in time, but *sideways*. This would explain why she was not able to move within her so-called 'past life', and why Emmony's future was as uncertain as her own. It hadn't happened yet! It also explained why the points at which she entered Emmony's life were chosen for her – it was the *present*. And that explained the feeling of synchronicity she had experienced earlier. The same amount of time always seemed to have passed for Emmony between regressions as it had for Zoe. On each occasion she had joined her counterpart at the same time of day as in her own world and, as far as she could recall, at the same point in the lunar cycle. The celestial chronometers operated simultaneously for both worlds.

Zoe made herself stop and think things over cautiously. Even if her outrageous theory seemed to fit the facts available to her, it was clear that there were still inexplicable 'gaps' in reality, in the borders between the separate streams. That sounded like a recipe for chaos. Having accepted the premise, however, it was much easier to believe that the ring and pen had been swapped sideways than to accept their physical translation back and forth in time. The same gaps that allowed her to go from one world to the other could surely also be utilised by others. Her poltergeist could be a ghost not from the past but from a parallel existence, a world where magic was commonplace and science virtually unknown. And Michael had made the same trip in the opposite direction, the accident-induced coma propelling him across the invisible border.

*Is this just desperate rationalisation?* Zoe wondered. *Covering up the fact that I've gone completely loopy?*

By its very nature the question was unanswerable, but her emotional response was to say no. This was real, and her natural inclination was to believe that she was there for a reason. That could only be to save Ghyl, to help Ghyl and Emmony find their destiny together, and return to a reunion with Michael in her own world. All of which sounded very simplistic and naive, but what was the alternative? To believe that the whole thing was an elaborate, meaningless charade? A creation of her writer's over-fertile imagination, born of her desperate need to help Michael?

'So what do I do?' she asked aloud, returning to the obvious question. If she was right, then Ghyl had still to be saved, his recovery was still in the future, and Zoe's task was even more important.

As before, all she could do was set the self-evident objectives: to escape from her confinement, retrieve the talisman, use her talent, be with Ghyl . . . Only this time she had even less idea about how she was to achieve her goals. But nothing would get done if she continued to sit there feeling sorry for herself. She got up, tested her legs – which felt normal again now – and stretched. Even the ache in her ribs had lessened noticeably. Zenna's salve was obviously working. It was time to test the limits of her freedom.

For a while she roamed aimlessly around the warren of the vast house. While no one barred her progress, Zoe was aware that she was being watched all the time, often surreptitiously, sometimes openly, by members of the household. They were presumably still hoping that she would lead them to the talisman. However, whenever she approached any of the doors leading outside, she found them either locked or guarded inside and out. Lanier was taking no chances.

In frustration, Zoe returned to the study, wondering if she could use any of the weapons which hung over the fireplace. A single glance told her that they were all fixed firmly in place and, in any case, they were too big and heavy even for Emmony's strength. What could she hope to achieve anyway, one against many? Some other method was necessary.

Magic.

Did she need the talisman? Would *any* writing instrument be as effective if she believed in it? She began to search the desk for any quills, chalk or charcoal, but could find nothing. The papers she found were all written in stilted but neat and formal lettering and she knew, on quizzing Emmony's memory, that they had been produced by specialist scribes. Jevan himself would not use such tools.

It was no wonder that books were so rare and, in some quarters, highly prized. Zoe looked up again at the high shelf, trying to read the titles. She was about to move a chair and climb up to reach them when she heard familiar voices in the corridor outside. She groaned, and glanced automatically at her watch – only to find, of course, that it was not there – thinking that surely it could not be time for Jevan's return yet.

The sound of heavy boots approaching told otherwise and, transfixed, Zoe listened to the conversation as the two men came closer. They were talking loudly, jovially.

'Dead?' Killian asked in amazement.

'Yes. Poison, they say,' Jevan replied. 'The fool had no tame witch on hand to find the antidote, and he choked to death on his own tongue.'

The brothers laughed heartily.

'Good riddance,' Killian concluded. 'Urbani deserved no better, foreign scum worming his way into court.'

'The wonder of it is,' Jevan added, 'that Chandos learnt the principles Urbani taught him so quickly – and put them into practice. The tin-trader ordered his own execution, and now we all have one less enemy in the Pyramid.'

There was more laughter at this, and Zoe realised with a sinking heart that the twins seemed to be on uncommonly good terms. What would that mean for her? She was about to find out.

The door was thrown open and the Quarterman swaggered in. His brother was close behind him, wearing a thin smile as his dark eyes met hers.

# 35

'Well, wife, it seems you've become quite the adventuress while I've been away.' Jevan stood foresquare, his feet planted wide, staring at Zoe with an expression of apparent good humour.

Zoe said nothing, unable to gauge his mood. She could not resist glancing at Killian, wondering what he had reported to his brother.

'Killian told me of your escape,' Jevan went on, noting the look. 'I did not think you had such spirit in you.' When Zoe still did not respond, he added, 'I am disappointed in Ellissa. You duped her easily, and I had thought her more intelligent. She made the mistake – of which it seems we've all been guilty to some extent – of underestimating you. Still, she will not disappoint me again.'

Killian snorted with laughter. He had helped himself to wine, then slumped in a chair and was watching the confrontation with barely concealed glee. Zoe wondered, with a sick feeling in her stomach, what revenge had been inflicted upon the maid. Jevan's next words confirmed her fears.

'Since she can no longer be trusted to watch anything for me, she no longer needs her eyes.'

'She won't need them in the darkness of the bedchamber,' Killian added, grinning. 'That's about the only place she'll be of any use now.'

Jevan shook his head.

'She is no loss there,' he said dismissively. 'I have had many better.'

Nauseated as she was, this statement had no effect on Zoe, despite Jevan's blatant attempt to hurt her with a further admission of his infidelity. Cruelty like this no longer had the power to touch her – nor Emmony. But Ellissa's fate was a terrible responsibility – whatever her faults, the maid had not deserved that – and also a possible indication of the horrors which might await Zoe herself.

'Of course, you may have had help in drugging her,' Jevan went on. 'Where is Mason now?'

'I have no idea,' Zoe said quietly, hoping the boy was far, far away.

'I don't suppose his addled wits will take him any distance,' Jevan decided. 'When we find him, I shall have to devise a punishment even he will understand.' He sounded as if the prospect pleased him.

Zoe shuddered inside. This man was truly a monster.

'I've already taken care of the guards who were foolish enough to desert their posts,' the Quarterman stated, matter-of-fact. 'They have been whipped until they lost consciousness. I'm probably being too lenient, but we all have to make some sacrifices. I'll have need of every sword arm before long – and I doubt they'll disobey orders again.' He paused, watching her calmly. 'Which only leaves me to decide what to do with that incompetent warlock . . . and with you, of course.'

'I have done nothing wrong,' Zoe said, fighting to keep from showing her growing fear.

For a moment, Jevan's features contorted with fury, but he controlled his temper in an instant, and the smile returned.

'Really?' he said, in mock surprise. 'Leaving aside the simple fact that you disobeyed my wishes when you left your chambers – something for which I could have you publicly flogged – there is your theft of the talisman.'

'It was stolen *from* me,' Zoe protested. Then – too late – she saw the trap into which she had fallen.

'But how did you come to have it in the first place?' Jevan enquired, his smile widening.

She said nothing.

270

'Yet that is not the worst of your crimes,' he went on remorselessly. 'Whether you used the talisman or not, your display of talent was a double treachery. First, that you should use it to directly counteract my desires and, secondly, that you concealed your abilities from me, as you did that degraded, blasphemous book. Such talent could have been of use to me in earlier years. Why did you hide it?'

'You have always known what little talent I possess,' Zoe replied. 'I've hidden nothing.'

'Then how did you escape?' he asked simply.

'I just walked out. No one tried to stop me.'

'You didn't use forbidden runes, a direct counterspell?'

'No.' Zoe thought of the paper in her pocket and was filled with relief that no one had thought to search her. She made up her mind to dispose of the incriminating evidence as soon as she could.

'Gouveia says otherwise,' Jevan remarked.

'Then he's lying, to save his own skin.'

Jevan and Killian both laughed at this.

'He'll have to come up with a better story if he wants to do that,' Killian commented.

'Let's see if he's changed his mind, shall we?' Jevan said. He went to the door, opened it and yelled instructions. Moments later, the warlock was led in between two soldiers. They held him by each arm, supporting him as though he did not have the strength to stand upright.

Gouveia looked at Zoe, terror filling his bulbous eyes. His absurd clothes were stained with sweat, and he was rank with the smell of fear. He no longer appeared a comical figure, only pathetic and disgusting. When the guards were dismissed, he remained on his feet but shivered and swayed, his gaze unsteady.

As Zoe watched him, she felt the first stirrings of pity, though she could not understand how she had managed to reduce him to such misery. However, her earlier contempt returned when she remembered to what use he had chosen to put his precious talent. To imprison an innocent, helpless woman was corruption beyond forgiveness – and now it was

271

his word against hers. One or other of them would certainly be destroyed.

'Tell us what happened, Gouveia.'

For a moment, the warlock stared stupidly at his master, as if he did not understand what was required of him. When he did speak, the words rushed out, half garbled.

'Yes, m'lord. Guards'd gone t'see th' sky-gods at play. Left me alone. I knew my duty but nothing I could do.' His self-righteous whining turned to abject fear, and his eyes flickered back and forth between Jevan and Zoe. 'Two women, two, walked through th' door as if not there, like ghosts. Ghosts. Stars all round them. One her, but someone else too . . . and there were devices . . . metal, with power of th' lightning in them, voices without tongues, echoing, echoing all around. My power not match them all.' He began to cry softly, his wild eyes blurring. 'Seal already weakened. But she . . .' He paused and, as he raised a shaking finger in accusation, his voice grew a little stronger. 'She broke it. Counterspell . . . runes. Sacred. Couldn't believe my eyes. Alien, alien . . . but such talent. Glowed in the air, then dropped runes into my brazier, *my* brazier. Everything turned to fire, everything.'

'How much more of this nonsense do we have to listen to?' Zoe demanded, trying to make her disdain apparent, although, inside, she was shaking with fear. How had Gouveia seen so much, including things she had not been aware of herself? Had she really carried parts of her own world with her? How had the warlock perceived electrical machinery? And much of what he said made no sense even to her. *Stars all round them?*

'It's true, I swear,' Gouveia said weakly. 'I lost everything.'

'This man is mad,' Zoe declared. 'You said yourself he was incompetent. All that happened was that his protection failed. He was asleep when I came out.'

'No!' Gouveia protested, horrified.

'When I opened the door and walked out,' Zoe went on relentlessly, 'I had no need of sorcery, even if I had been

272

capable of any. Have you ever seen me walk *through* a door, like a ghost?' She was still speaking directly to Jevan. 'I came through that door like anyone else. And I was alone.'

'So you didn't use the talisman then?' he asked mildly.

'Yes, yes,' Gouveia put in eagerly. 'Must have.'

'No, I did not,' Zoe stated firmly. 'This is a poor excuse for a warlock. His head is full of delusions, not talent.'

'There at least we can agree on something,' Jevan remarked. 'Whatever your part in the process, it's clear he believes that his brazier is corrupted – which means that it is. He's worse than useless without it.' Turning to the door, he yelled for the guards. 'Take this piece of offal away and put it out of its misery.'

Fear flared briefly in Gouveia's eyes, only to be replaced by a dreadful acceptance. He shot one last baleful glance at Zoe, then allowed himself to be led away. She watched him go, horrified by the fact that she had had to sacrifice him in order to save herself – and knowing that she was still far from safe.

'Not the most reliable of witnesses perhaps, brother,' Killian commented jovially. He was evidently enjoying the show.

'Shut up!' Jevan snapped, then turned to Zoe. 'We keep coming back to the talisman, don't we? It's hard to believe you achieved so much without some help.'

'I don't know what the talisman is or how to use it, any more than you do,' she claimed. 'I did take it from you.' There was no point in denying that. 'But it's gone now.'

'Do you really expect us to believe that?' Killian asked sarcastically.

Ignoring him, Zoe continued to address Jevan.

'If I'm lying, if I'd known where it was, why would I have revealed my secret place?' She had no need to mention the book.

It was a powerful argument and Jevan, like Killian before him, had no answer. Instead, he chose to reveal another piece of malice.

'Ah, your precious book,' he said. 'You'll be relieved to

know that you're no longer in danger of being tainted by its foul corruption. It has been torn apart and burnt.'

Zoe shared Emmony's instinctive dismay at this not unexpected news, but Jevan did not allow her to dwell on it.

'Even Chandos is aware of the talisman's existence now,' he told her. 'He's sending one of his court sorcerers, one whose unique talent is to sniff out such things. He'll find it soon enough – and if we trace it to you, then your life will not be worth living. You would be much better off telling me where it is now. Do I make myself clear?'

Zoe nodded grimly.

'If I knew where it was, I'd tell you.'

'Would you?' Killian asked carelessly.

'I am beholden to my husband, not you!' she said sharply. Killian merely smiled sweetly, not reacting to her angry words. His complacency was making Zoe nervous.

'We'll know soon enough,' Jevan concluded ominously. 'But your treachery did not end at your escape. There is also the question of your later actions.' His expression was stony now, as if the game no longer amused him.

'I rode to see a friend in distress,' Zoe said, pre-empting the obvious accusation. 'There is no wrong in that.'

'No wrong?' Jevan was obviously fighting to control his temper. 'You cannot be unaware of the rumours of an illicit liaison between you and this man? You leave your home, against my express wishes, and use the time to visit this *friend*? And you see no wrong?'

'The rumours lie,' she said hopelessly, but Jevan only snorted.

'How am I to believe that?' he asked. 'How could anyone? Your actions speak otherwise.'

'Is common pity a crime? He lies unconscious—'

'I know,' Jevan cut in. 'It was my horse's hoof that left him so.'

Zoe heard Michael's recorded voice again, and another piece of the puzzle fell into place. *I couldn't see the horse, Zoe. It was too dark. I could hear it but I couldn't . . .*

'Even then there was sorcery in the air,' Jevan added, 'or I should have finished the job. As it was, the blow would have been enough had it not been for those blasted witches.' Then, with an apparent return to his earlier good humour, he added, 'Still, your friend can do no more harm now.'

Judging from the way he spoke, he was referring to more than Ghyl's comatose condition, and Zoe was assailed with sudden terror. Had Ghyl already been murdered? Or taken prisoner? Either way, the task of saving him seemed all but impossible now.

'And here I owe my brother a debt of gratitude,' Jevan acknowledged. 'For finding you and bringing you back.'

'Killian is the would-be adulterer, not Ghyl,' Zoe claimed abruptly. 'Your beloved brother threatened to take me by force.'

'Killian has already told me of your absurd charges,' he replied evenly. 'He may be headstrong and occasionally ruled by his lust, but even he would not dare attempt what you suggest.'

'I can have all the women I want,' Killian said smugly. 'Why would I risk my brother's anger for a barren old sow like you?'

Jevan's face twitched at his twin's choice of words, but otherwise he did not react.

'And he wanted the talisman for himself,' Zoe added, though she knew it was hopeless. Jevan would never believe her.

Killian, with uncharacteristic restraint, merely shook his head and shrugged as if in disbelief.

'You cannot help yourself by trying to shift the blame to others,' Jevan told her.

'You won't be so sure of your precious brother when they pull his knife from your back,' she replied venomously, anger finally getting the better of her fear.

With an inarticulate cry of rage, Killian leapt to his feet, but a gesture from Jevan kept him at a distance.

'After I took you from your lover's arms, I brought you straight back here, you bitch!' Killian snarled. 'I have already told Jevan so. Don't compound your sins by falsehood against me.'

Zoe watched his performance with disgust, but felt a glimmer of hope. It seemed that he had not told Jevan about the owls and the fact that her horse had broken away, perhaps fearing that this would be perceived as a failing of his own. Which meant she still had a chance of retrieving the talisman for herself – and, if the worst came to the worst, of convincing Jevan that there was no connection with her if and when it was located by Chandos's sorcerer.

'The Sanctuary is guarded on all sides now,' Jevan said, 'by men as well as by concealment. No one will go in or out without my knowledge and permission. That too is thanks to Killian's percipience and watchfulness.'

Killian smiled. He had evidently heard all he needed.

'I have duties elsewhere,' he said. 'I will leave it to Jevan to tell you of our plans.' He graced Zoe with one last malignant grin, then turned and left.

'What plans?' she asked, new anxieties rising within her.

'War grows nearer,' Jevan answered with satisfaction. 'Chandos is aware of treachery beyond his borders – and within – and we are making preparations. One of the tasks he had entrusted to me has afforded me the perfect punishment for your *friend*.'

Zoe's heart was in her mouth. She could not speak.

'A new stone bridge is to be built across the Brown River, so that our armies will have an easy passage when they march west. Ordinarily, as you know, the foundations of such a bridge would be sanctified by the offering of a bull or ram from one of the nearby villages. But for this construction a stronger protection will be needed.' He smiled malevolently, knowing that she had already guessed what was coming next. 'We shall be returning to the old ways. Ghyl is already as good as dead. He will make the perfect burial sacrifice.'

# 36

'That's murder!' Zoe cried, aghast. The reasons for the twins' good humour had become obvious; the imminence of war – and now this.

'Hardly,' Jevan replied, enjoying her distress. 'I am told he shows few signs of life. In the past it was considered a privilege to be offered to the sky-gods, for your spirit to guard an important place.'

'That's barbaric,' she exclaimed. 'And it's still murder. You're doing this purely for revenge – revenge for a crime Ghyl has not committed.'

'And never will, now,' he told her with satisfaction. 'You see where your treachery leads?'

'There has been none,' she claimed desperately. 'This is not justice.'

'In my Quarter, my word is justice,' he told her. 'And tomorrow I will announce my decision to the stonemasons and builders. With war coming, the local people will be glad of such secure protection – and glad that none of them will have to give up any of their prize beasts. It's perfect.'

'No, please . . .'

'Quiet!' Jevan roared, finally allowing his anger full rein. 'If you so much as whisper that man's name ever again, you'll suffer for it, I promise you.'

Zoe fell silent, but in the privacy of her mind she had made a dreadful decision. It had not been reached by a process of rational thought but had arrived fully fledged – and now could not be dislodged. She had never seriously contemplated murder before but, one way or another, she knew she would have to kill Jevan.

One murder to prevent another? Could that ever be justified? But Zoe already had her answer: Jevan was irretrievably evil. In her mind, he deserved to die. And if that might save Ghyl, then the argument was unanswerable. Would she have killed Thomas rather than see him murder Michael? Yes, she would, though the idea was chilling. Was murder morally worse in her own world than here, where life seemed so cheap?

Her thoughts were interrupted when she realised belatedly that Jevan was speaking again, his voice stern but calm.

'. . . to your bedchamber. I'll provide an escort, in case you should forget the way. Remain there until this evening. Then you will change into attire fitting for a Quarterman's wife. We have guests to entertain. Until then – unless you change your mind about the whereabouts of the talisman – you will go nowhere, do nothing, speak to no one. Do you understand?'

Zoe nodded meekly. It seemed that Jevan was still intent on keeping up appearances, at least for the time being. This would make it easier to keep herself – and Emmony – relatively safe. She had dreaded some vile punishment, but realised now that Jevan was intent on the vilest punishment of all. He would force his wife to go on living as if nothing had happened, trapped by hatred and lies. The prospect left her chilled, and strengthened her resolve for drastic measures – though she had no idea yet how to achieve any of her goals.

'Guards!' Jevan shouted.

Armed men came and led Zoe away. When she reached her bedchamber, she was ushered inside unceremoniously and the door slammed and locked behind her. Zoe stood still, looking about her. The room had obviously been searched and, although a half-hearted attempt had been made to clear up some of the mess, it was still in a terrible state. Most of the movable furniture had been shifted. Even the rugs had been thrown about. Wardrobe doors were open, with some of her clothes strewn on the floor. Drawers had been ransacked, their contents in disarray. The bedclothes were piled in a tangled heap on the mattress, which lay askew, leaking feathers. Worst of all, the formerly secret cupboard door hung open, its hinges broken, and there were gouges in several wooden panels. Zoe knew Emmony had had no other hiding places, but that had not stopped them looking.

She quickly hid the pieces of paper in one of the drawers then, picking her way through the debris to the window, Zoe looked out longingly. Ghyl was somewhere out there, needing her as much as she needed him. But how was she to get to him? Jevan had made sure that his security arrangements would not fail as they had done before – and she did not even have the talisman to give her some hope.

*A fat lot of use you are*, she told herself bitterly. What was the point of her extended twelve-hour visit if she accomplished nothing? But what was she to do? She had to get out somehow – and quickly. Who were the guests Jevan was expecting? Would they include the sorcerer who was supposed to find the talisman? If so, her need was even more urgent.

Zoe consulted Emmony's memory about previous evenings of entertainment, in the hope that it might provide her with some mode of escape – or some way to destroy Jevan. The vivid scenes that came to her held several surprises, but the only promising note was Jevan's habit of becoming very drunk. Perhaps in such a state he would be more vulnerable, or at least less watchful. It was small consolation, and by the evening her time would be running out. *Think*, she told herself. At least this time she had been left alone and so should be able to concentrate.

However, even that minute advantage was soon taken away. The door was unlocked and another maid, Oliva, came to join her mistress. She was very young, no more than eighteen, and – not surprisingly, given the fate of her predecessor – seemed very nervous. She curtseyed awkwardly, then went to sit in a corner without a word. Zoe noticed that the girl was clutching something metal in her hands. Her knuckles were white.

'What are you holding?'

Oliva looked startled, obviously not expecting to be spoken to, and did not reply for a few moments.

'A beacon,' she answered eventually. 'If I let go of it, they'll know, and the guards will come.'

Jevan evidently was not taking any chances. The two women stared at each other until the maid dropped her gaze. Then, obviously remembering that she was there to observe the prisoner, she raised it again.

'Are you happy here, Oliva?'

'Yes,' she replied, though she did not sound very sure.

'Your family?' Zoe knew the answer before the maid spoke, courtesy of Emmony's subconscious.

'Still on the farm,' Oliva said, sounding surprised. 'Quarterman Jevan is a good landlord.'

*Provided you give good service*, Zoe thought. There was no hope of suborning Oliva as an ally. The girl had too much to lose.

'And is Jevan good to *you*?'

Oliva nodded uncertainly.

'Do you sleep with him?'

Colour flooded the maid's young face, and her fists clenched even tighter.

'Do you?' Zoe repeated, although she already knew the answer.

'Don't be angry with me, my lady,' Oliva begged at last. 'He comes to me on occasion. He has the right. It's not by my choice.'

Zoe found herself hating Jevan even more, something she would not have believed possible. She wanted to shout at the girl, to make her see the folly of her meek acceptance of such repugnant tyranny. But she could not. Oliva's subservience had been ingrained from birth, enforced by circumstances and made bearable by its necessity. It should not be so, but it was. Besides, the girl would mistake her motives.

Zoe retreated into silence – which could also be misconstrued, but there was no help for that – and her own thoughts. The situation seemed more hopeless than ever. Sooner or later she would have to do something reckless, putting herself and Emmony in danger. But before too long she *would* have to do something, no matter how perilous. Better to die in the attempt . . .

Time passed in a mental fog of frustration and helplessness. To cover her preoccupation, Zoe made a few listless attempts at tidying her bed and finding suitable clothes for the evening. Several times she saw Oliva half rise, obviously wanting to help, but then sink down again, her captive hands clasped as tight as ever round the beacon. The maid watched her mistress's every move like a nervous hawk, but said nothing.

Both women turned sharply when there was a knock at the door.

'Come in.'

Lanier entered, his expression as always one of carefully concealed insolence. He left the door open.

'Leave us for a few moments,' he told Oliva. The maid rose obediently and left, closing the door behind her, while Zoe wondered what the chamberlain wanted. Then, to her surprise, he raised a finger to his lips for silence. As Zoe stared at him in amazement the features of his narrow face seemed to melt, blurring in a way which made her gasp, not able to trust her own eyes. Once the rearrangement was completed, Zoe found herself looking at Iven, the warlock from the Sanctuary. Her heart leapt in astonishment. Was this to be her chance?

'Can anyone overhear us?' Iven whispered, coming closer.

'I don't think so. Can you get me out of here?'

'No, but . . .' A hand drew forth the talisman from his pocket and held it out to her. Zoe took the pen, hardly daring to believe her luck.

'How did you find it?'

'I have the far-sight. Zenna told me to follow your progress as far as I could. You were at the limit of my range, but when Winddancer bolted towards the ash ring, I knew it was for a reason. Once I got there, the talisman was easy enough to find.'

Zoe nodded, gratefully accepting another miracle.

'How did you change yourself into Lanier?'

'It's a very rare talent – not mine, but others at Blue Tiles. Although I don't change physically, the way others see me is altered.'

'An illusion.'

'Yes, but it can only be kept up for a few moments at a time. I can't stay long, in any case. The real Lanier is alone in his room now but could come out at any time.'

'How's Ghyl?' Zoe asked quickly.

'The same. He needs you – but getting in and out of the Sanctuary is more difficult now.'

'But obviously not impossible.'

'No,' Iven confirmed without elaborating. 'Ghyl needs you,' he repeated. 'Em–, Zoe. You know that, don't you?'

Zoe nodded.

'How can I escape?'

'Use the talisman?' he suggested blithely. It seemed that he had put all his faith in that, and had not thought beyond its safe delivery. Still, it was more than Zoe could have hoped for.

'There's something else,' she said hurriedly, and told the warlock of Jevan's plan to sacrifice Ghyl. Iven was horrified.

'Mason tried to get us to move him as soon as you'd left,' he said, and Zoe wondered if the boy had somehow picked up on her parting thought. 'We should have listened to him, but it's too late now. A single person can slip in and out, but in his condition . . . We'll do what we can to protect him, though. We're not friendless.'

'Thank you.'

'Anything else?' He seemed anxious now, and obviously wanted to go.

'Could you get me some poison, by tonight?' Zoe explained that she wanted to kill Jevan before he made public his plan for the bridge.

Iven was plainly terrified by the idea.

'Jevan is protected in many ways,' he told her. 'His own

talent and that of many others are at work. Such curses as we are capable of would have no effect on him. Violence would have to be on an overpowering scale to succeed. Poison might work if he remained unaware of it for long enough, and if his own warlocks were distracted. I wouldn't count on it, though. Are you sure you want to do this? Do you know what you are risking?'

'I've got to try.'

'I'll see what we can do.'

'Thank you again.' His visit had restored the beginnings of hope.

'I must go.' Iven closed his eyes for a moment and Zoe watched, feeling slightly queasy, as his face rearranged itself once more.

'Fare you well,' the false Lanier said. He knocked on the door to be let out, and Zoe quickly hid the talisman before Oliva came back into the room.

## 37

Oliva returned with the message, delivered nervously, that Emmony would shortly be expected in the Quarterman's Hall. Zoe consulted Emmony's memory to see what would be considered suitable attire, then dressed herself slowly, being very careful not to show the maid that she had something to hide. By the time she had finished, the pen was concealed inside the lining of her dress. Emmony's clothes felt bulky and awkward, but that was the least of her concerns.

Her main worry was that Iven's subterfuge would be discovered. It would only need Oliva and Lanier to compare notes . . . How had Iven known that the chamberlain was in his room? Were there unsuspected allies within the household? And if so, would that be how the poison was passed to her? Zoe's stomach clenched at the thought. To deliberately murder another human being, no matter how evil he was . . .

Then her thoughts returned to the talisman. She still had the pieces of paper – somewhat crumpled now – having transferred them surreptitiously from her riding clothes. But whenever she considered using them, she was frozen by indecision. She could hardly just whip out the pen and start scribbling away in front of Jevan's spy. Zoe told herself that she had to be patient, to wait for the right moment – because she might never get a second chance. In any case, she still did not know the scope – and the limitations – of what she could do. Her only effort so far had been to counteract an already existing spell. It was obviously possible for her to react, but could she *act*? Could she use the talisman to kill Jevan? It seemed unlikely, given what Iven had told her. *Such curses as we are capable of would have no effect on him.* Or could she revive Ghyl? That was a wonderful thought, but was surely too good to be true. If only she knew what the talisman was capable of. If she wasted the opportunity, she would never be able to forgive herself.

Before she knew it, Zoe had been summoned by guards and, under their discreet but watchful supervision, escorted down to the hall. From her earlier probings of Emmony's subconscious, she knew roughly what to expect of the evening, but the sight of the banquet still surprised her. The hall had been completely transformed. Torches burnt brightly in the braziers, casting a warm, uneven glow over the scene, and large tables had been laid out round three sides of the upper end of the room, leaving a space for the entertainers to use as a stage. Plates piled high with food and pitchers of wine and mead added their heavy scents to the smoky atmosphere, and silk drapes and banners added colour to the previously bare walls at the far end of the hall.

As Zoe entered she caught sight of Lanier, and her heart raced, but he ignored her, concentrating instead on the actions of his staff. Jevan and several other men rose as Zoe approached.

'Gentlemen, this is my wife, Emmony. You look beautiful, my dear.' The smooth words and his smile of welcome were convincing to all but Zoe. Once again she was reminded of Thomas, and of the difference between his private and public personae.

She was introduced to the principal guests, minor noblemen from the surrounding districts in the western borders of Chandos's Domains, and accepted several compliments from them as graciously as she could. These men were obviously eager to ingratiate themselves with their host. Zoe spoke as little as possible, to Jevan's approval, and soon they were all seated again and roast meats were served.

Although she had eaten very little for some time now, Zoe found she had no appetite, but the others ate with much enthusiasm. While Jevan held court, dominating the conversation, she looked around hoping, in vain, for some sign, some indication from an unknown friend about where the hoped-for poison might appear. Eventually she gave up and listened to the men's discussion, which revolved around a single topic – the coming war with Prince Oroc. All the guests seemed to share their host's enthusiasm for this prospect, although in some cases, Zoe judged, this was only for Jevan's benefit. The talk was all of mustering men and supplies, of logistics and possible routes across the wetlands of the lowland fens, of seaborne diversions – and of ensuring that the army had enough talents to overmatch the enemy's and would thus gain every advantage.

To Zoe it sounded much as a similar discussion of a medieval plan of conquest might have done – except for the presence of the talents. *A war waged by magic?* Why should it not be so? In her own world, humanity had been stupid enough to harness the extraordinary powers of technology to feed an apparently insatiable appetite for violence. The same had evidently happened here, except that bombs, tanks, aircraft and early warning systems had been replaced by sorcery beyond her imagination. It was a cheerless thought. Was the human race inherently belligerent, destined to turn the greatest achievements of their civilisations into the accoutrements of war? Zoe stopped listening to the depressing conversation and returned to her own preoccupations.

All the time, almost unnoticed in the general clamour, there had been music playing, though Zoe could see no musicians. Then she noticed a small man, sitting in a corner, who to judge by his attire was obviously a warlock. He was hunched over, head lowered, with his hands wrapped around an unseen object. It was from there that the gentle, sweet sounds were coming. Although it had none of the demonic overtones of the music Jevan had produced on an earlier occasion, Zoe knew that it was the 'chanters stone. Was the nature of the music created by the stone determined by the nature of the player? Or was the range of melodies, rhythms and instrumentation available so vast that it could produce compositions suitable

286

for any occasion, any need? However, she was soon to discover that this was only the most basic aspect of the evening's entertainment.

As the diners' attentions began to switch from food to drink and some of the debris was cleared away, Lanier gave a signal, the 'chanters stone gave forth a brief fanfare, and a man appeared in the relative gloom of the far end of the hall. His feet made no sound as he walked over the bare stone floor, and he seemed to carry his own light with him, like a spotlight. He bowed low, and the music stopped.

'Quarterman, my lords and ladies, my name is Fader. Together with my partner, Oblong, it is my privilege tonight to provide entertainment for this august gathering.' In a lighter tone he added, 'Fader and Oblong are our stage names, of course.'

For some reason the audience found this amusing.

'Some of you may think you know us by other, more prosaic names,' he went on, 'but we beg your indulgence. For tonight we are Fader and Oblong, artists of wonder! And we will be ably assisted by our fool.'

A large man, in a baggy yellow and orange striped costume, stumbled out of the shadows, almost tripping over his own bare feet. His face was blank and unintelligent.

'Our assistant is called Brickhead, though this is *not* a stage name,' Fader explained with a smile. 'He comes from a long and venerable line of Brickheads.' This announcement provoked more laughter, which the big man ignored stolidly.

'Let the entertainment begin!' Fader exclaimed, and clapped his hands. As he lived up to his name by gradually becoming invisible, several of the audience gasped – but others had evidently expected no less, and smiled and nodded at each other. Zoe had been fooled completely; to her the image of Fader had appeared quite solid and to discover that it had been an illusion came as quite a shock. Able to forget her own troubles for a few moments, she watched in amazement, waiting to see what would happen next.

The 'chanters stone then played a boisterous country dance and Brickhead, left alone on the stage, began to stomp bow-legged across the floor. His huge feet battered out the simple rhythm on the stone, his hands slapping his thighs, chest and even the sides of his head. His expression was one of intense concentration, and this made his appearance all the more comical. Zoe, like the rest of the audience, watched entranced – although in her case the laughter was uneasy. Was Brickhead really as stupid as he seemed, performing like a circus animal? She hoped not.

Faster and faster the music played; faster and faster Brickhead whirled, his movements becoming a manic blur. Only gradually did it dawn on the onlookers that there was more to this dance than met the eye. At first the adjustment was only tiny, but it was soon obvious to everyone. Fingers pointed and the audience gasped, laughing now in amazement. Brickhead's stamping feet were no longer touching the floor! Higher and higher he rose, still performing his grotesque masque. His eyes were closed, and he seemed to be in a rapturous trance.

The music stopped abruptly, then changed to a single swirling note, in complete contrast to the driving beat of the dance. Brickhead froze in midair, opened his eyes, then struck a ridiculous, dainty pose and gently floated down to the floor. When he landed, he held the pose for a few moments, smiling idiotically as the applause and laughter rang out. Then he curtseyed – an action unsuited to his vast, inelegant frame – and left the stage.

Zoe stole a glance at Jevan, who muttered something inaudible and then pointedly turned away to speak to a guest on his other side. He had been drinking steadily the whole time, but as yet showed no signs of drunkenness. There were knives on the table, and for a moment Zoe considered picking one up and driving it into his ribs. She doubted whether she possessed the speed or strength to kill him outright – even discounting the protection Iven had told her of – and the consequences of failure were unthinkable. The moment passed.

Next to appear before them was a man whom Zoe took to be Oblong. He began by juggling three brightly coloured spheres, the size of tennis balls, but shiny and hard. After a few seconds he added a fourth ball, then a fifth, taking them from voluminous pockets. When the sixth and seventh joined the ever-spinning set, his deft hands were moving so fast that they were difficult to follow, and the audience clapped and commented approvingly.

But that was just the beginning. When an eighth ball was introduced, one of the original three simply stopped moving, hanging in midair at the top of its arc. Once Oblong was sure that most of the audience had noticed, he began to bounce some of the others off the stationary red ball, making the coordination required to keep all the moving spheres in the air even more exacting. Then others came to rest above the juggler, and he began ever more elaborate ricochets and cannons.

What was more, some of the balls now appeared to have mouths painted on them – mouths that moved and spoke. Childish voices could be heard, squealing and laughing as they collided with each other, and giggling with glee as they rose and fell. This went on for some time until, with the onlookers either convulsed with laughter or holding their breath, all eight spheres grew still. Oblong took a bow beneath the gravity defying tableau, then walked off, leaving them in midair. Brickhead then appeared and stood beneath the balls, looking up at them with a puzzled expression. He made a pantomime out of trying to reclaim them, jumping up and pawing ineffectually at the air, but they were out of reach even for one of his great height. He scratched his head in obvious bafflement as the audience laughed. The balls laughed too.

Fader and Oblong came on stage and watched for a moment or two.

'He can't reach,' Fader decided. 'Give him a hand, will you.'

'Of course,' Oblong replied. He snapped his fingers and the balls instantly rained down on the fool, bouncing off his head, shoulders and flailing arms, and knocking him to the floor amid further waves of laughter.

While he slowly dusted himself off, the other two quickly

collected the spheres and began a two-man juggling act over their prostrate assistant's head. Every time Brickhead tried to rise, one of the flying balls hit him and he fell back, much to the delight of the audience. The juggling became more and more elaborate, with balls curving and swerving sideways, rising or falling unnaturally and even halting and reversing course – all these actions matched by animated cries from the balls themselves. Every time Brickhead thought he had managed to work out the patterns of their flight, they altered and he was knocked down again. It *was* funny, but the relentless cruelty began to wear on Zoe. If the blows the fool was taking were as real as they sounded, he would truly have to be accurately named not to feel any pain. Eventually, much to her relief, they relented and Fader was left alone on stage.

The music resumed, this time a graceful, balletic piece. Fader began to move, slowly at first, then more energetically, until his leaps and twists were more acrobatic than any gymnast or dancer Zoe had ever seen. Was this performance magically enhanced? It didn't seem like it . . . but then she saw that it had become so. Rolling away from a spectacular backflip, there were suddenly two Faders on the floor, jumping, somersaulting and seeming almost to fly, all in perfect synchronisation. Which was real and which the doppelganger? It was impossible to tell, even when the two came into contact, linking hands and arms, whirling around each other like the most perfect pair of ice-dancers. Finally the two identical Faders came to a halt, turned to face each other and bowed ceremoniously, then jumped full tilt at their opposite number. There was a blur of colour and movement, and once again only the real Fader was left, accepting his well-earned acclaim with a broad smile.

Zoe was enchanted. Magic, it seemed, like the technology of her own world, could be harnessed for acts of creative beauty as well as for the brutality and ugliness of war. Beside her Jevan led the applause, his voice now slightly slurred with wine. The hall had become very warm and her enemy was perspiring freely, obviously enjoying the impression the entertainers were making on his guests. *Enjoy it while you can*, Zoe thought venomously.

The applause had not yet died down when both Oblong and Brickhead rejoined their leader. Each of the trio now held an unidentifiable metal object. All three stood very still, and the audience grew quiet in anticipation. Suddenly, there was a flare of light from the metal – and then such a rush of imagery and illumination that it was impossible to follow it all. To Zoe's amazed eyes, it was like an improbable combination of a marvellous firework display and holographic laser technology – except that this was all magic, not science. It was literally brilliant, mind-boggling and emotive. It was mesmerising. And it was over all too soon.

'Thank you, Quarterman, my lords and ladies,' Fader said when the rapturous applause finally began to die down. 'We have just one more entertainment for your delectation tonight – and for this we require a volunteer.' He was looking straight at Zoe, and she shrank back. The last thing she wanted was to be the centre of attention.

'Quarterman Jevan,' Fader went on grandly, 'would you do us the inestimable honour of allowing your beautiful wife to join us? It is traditional that the lady of the house should take centre stage now.'

There were cries of encouragement and agreement from many of the guests and, after a moment's hesitation, Jevan nodded his assent. He stood and, amid a chorus of approval, helped Zoe to her feet with every appearance of courtesy. Fader made his way round the tables to meet her, took her hand lightly and led her to where his companions waited. Zoe went reluctantly, her nerves almost at breaking point, but knowing that she had no choice. Fader quietly told her to stand next to Brickhead, then he and Oblong took up their positions to either side.

'There is a secret hiding place within this house,' Fader announced dramatically.

'Within this very room,' Oblong added.

'Allow us to demonstrate,' his partner concluded.

Both men raised their arms then, and made strange circling

motions, their forefingers pointing to the floor as though they were stirring invisible potions in the air. As they did so, a thin veil of mist appeared around Brickhead and Zoe, enclosing them in a circular curtain which spun around, growing thicker and more opaque with every instant. Then Fader and Oblong abruptly spread their hands and a fanfare played.

The column of mist had vanished. And so had Zoe and the fool.

# 38

Jevan jumped to his feet in anger and confusion. Others gasped and began to applaud, but stopped quickly when they saw their host's expression. The guards by the door stiffened, suddenly alert.

Fader smiled broadly.

'Fear not, Quarterman. No harm has come to your wife,' he said. 'This is our regular finale. It ensures that our fee is paid in full . . . for otherwise . . .' and he winked theatrically at the breathless audience, '. . . otherwise we may not return what our host prizes the most.'

For a moment Jevan eyed the entertainer darkly, then he laughed and the tension in the atmosphere dissolved.

'You will be paid in full – when my wife is returned,' he stated, evidently determined to be a good sport – and to keep up the pretence that he did indeed prize his wife above all else.

Fader waited for the applause and laughter to die down.

'That is good to hear,' he said pompously. 'You'd not believe the lengths some lesser men would go to to avoid spending a few coins. Why, I could tell you stories . . . but I see I'd better not. Have we been worthy of fair reward?' he asked the audience.

There was a roar of agreement, which he milked for all it was worth.

'Then perhaps we should keep the Quarterman's wife as payment,' Fader suggested innocently. 'She is fair indeed. What do you think, Oblong?'

His partner stroked his chin, as if thinking hard.

'Well . . . she *is* very fair,' he concluded, 'but I like cash myself.'

They were playing with fire, and the onlookers knew it. Jevan's temper was legendary – as was his jealousy.

'Return her then, and you will have gold,' the Quarterman said good-humouredly. Only the coldness in his eyes betrayed his real feelings.

Fader paused for as long as he dared, then glanced at Oblong and shrugged.

'A Quarterman's word is his bond. Let us release the captives from the secret chamber.'

Once again they raised their arms, stirring now in the opposite direction. The opaque column of mist reappeared and gradually grew thinner. Shapes appeared, which could soon be recognised as Brickhead and Emmony. The sharper-eyed among the onlookers saw that the pair were talking until the big man shook his head and they waited for release. The process took longer this time, but eventually the mist became still and Brickhead handed his companion out. He was grinning idiotically, while Zoe looked dazed and confused – almost stupefied – but managed to smile weakly as the entire gathering rose to its feet in acclamation.

Zoe walked slowly back to her seat while the entertainers took their final bows and departed. She was indeed in a daze. What had just happened to her was incredible, and yet it had all happened so fast that she had hardly taken it in. As Jevan muttered something and everyone sat down to continue the revels, the murmur of conversation growing louder all around her, Zoe sat back quietly and went over it in her head.

She had not known what was happening while the mist whirled and thickened about them, but Brickhead had whispered to her.

'No one can hear us. When the mist vanishes they won't be able to see us either.'

Abruptly, plunging them into total silence, the mist was gone – though Zoe and Brickhead were still standing there in the middle of the floor. The onlookers appeared animated, but none of the sounds of the gathering could be heard.

'We are friends, my lady,' the big man told her hurriedly. 'Of you and Ghyl.'

Zoe gasped at the sound of the name. She was unable to believe that they could not be seen – they appeared to be in full view of everyone, including Jevan who was now standing, staring straight at them. And she hardly dared to believe in the audacity of the contact. Right under Jevan's nose! Sensing the urgency, she looked at the fool and, for the first time, his face did not appear at all unintelligent – just anxious. Was he really an ally – or was this some kind of trap?

'We have very little time,' Brickhead told her. 'I must speak quickly. There are those of us in the Eastern Dominions who wish to overthrow Chandos and his lackeys. He is a cruel man, and we have suffered his tyranny for too long. Ghyl is one of us, and has a vital role to play. There are secret envoys from other lands coming here soon, and Ghyl is their contact. He failed to meet them last time they came, through no fault of his own, but unless he is present this time, years of planning will be lost. We need Ghyl – and he needs you.'

Zoe was struck dumb. She could see everything that was going on around her, as Fader shamelessly played to the audience, but could hear nothing. How could she be invisible? And yet Brickhead's words overrode her doubts. She had to trust him.

'I know,' she whispered. 'I need him too.' The confirmation of Ghyl's hidden importance did not surprise her, but the realisation that she was not alone in the fight was a great comfort.

'We are gathering friends, doing what we can to protect him,' the fool, who was no fool, went on urgently, 'but the only way for him to be really safe is for him to recover. Zenna is convinced you're the only one who can help him do that. Jevan's plan must be stopped.'

'I'll do what I can,' Zoe promised. 'Ghyl and I have been in contact . . . in a way . . .'

'We thought as much. We've talents of our own trying to help now. You have hidden talents too. No one knew.'

'I . . .' Zoe began, then decided not to try to explain. Zenna had obviously not told them everything. 'How can I help Ghyl?'

'Do you have the talisman?'

'Yes. Do you know what it can and can't do?'

'You know that better than all of us,' he replied, looking surprised.

'Can you get me poison? Did Iven tell you about that?'

'We've been working on something special,' he said, producing a tiny phial and handing it to her. 'It needs to mature, though. Don't use it for at least an hour, longer if possible. Even then we can't be sure it'll be effective. Jevan is well protected . . .'

'I know,' Zoe told him, quickly secreting the poison in the pocket of her dress. Her companion was growing agitated now. They were obviously running out of time. 'Whether it works or not, can you help me escape?' she asked, hoping to cover as many options as possible.

Brickhead shook his head.

'We've no more time,' he said. 'Good luck.'

The mist was swirling around them again now, and moments later Zoe stepped out into the maelstrom of sound. Brickhead smiled and capered, a buffoon once more.

Now, only a few minutes later, it seemed as though it had been a dream, another illusion. Had it really happened? She clung to the hope. *We are gathering friends.* She was not alone.

The music had risen again, summoning the next entertainment – a young woman whose sultry appearance and exotic dance made her blatantly attractive to all the men present. Jevan, who had drunk a great deal by now, was clearly eyeing her lasciviously. It did not take much imagination to see where the night would end for the dancer.

*But where will it end for me?* Zoe wondered.

She was still wondering this when, sooner than expected, the gathering began to break up. Zoe almost panicked. Had she lost her chance? Although she did not understand why the poison had to mature, she knew she had to trust Brickhead. The hour must nearly be up. She slipped her hand into her pocket and held the phial tightly, but Jevan had stopped drinking now, and no opportunity presented itself. He seemed to have lost all interest in his wife, something Zoe would have been glad of earlier.

She railed against fate as she was escorted back to her chamber and her frustration increased when it became clear that even there she would not be alone, even for a moment. Two maids came inside with her, one of them holding a beacon. Cursing herself for her inaction, Zoe was about to retrieve the talisman and do *something* – however foolish or irrevocable – when a faraway ringing demanded her attention. The real world had been entirely forgotten but, like it or not, her regression was ending. What happened next would be up to Emmony.

Back in her own world, Zoe's first instinct was to return immediately, but she was inordinately tired and the temporary delegation of responsibility was something of a relief. She could rest for a few minutes, have a drink and then go back. Emmony had demonstrated her resourcefulness and resilience before, and Zoe had no doubt that she would cope this time.

She got up stiffly, flexing long dormant muscles and then, in a reflex action, glanced at the answering machine. The indicator showed five.

Zoe had been through this many times now, and surprised herself by remaining relatively calm. If the messages were from Michael – as she hoped they were – then panicking would not make the tape rewind any faster. She wondered if he would give her the advice she so badly needed.

The first voice on the tape, disappointingly, was that of her hypnotherapist.

'Zoe, it's Owen. Thanks for your message. I'm glad you're taking a break, but I'd still like you to keep in touch. Phone me when you get back – or before, if you pick up this message. All the best.'

The second voice was the one she was longing to hear, and her heart leapt with excitement.

'Zoe? You can hear me, can't you?' Doubt was then replaced by determination. 'This must be hard for you – I know what you're like with machines. But I'm using technology because it's the only means available to me. It was so hit and miss to start with, I was just flailing about in the dark, and most of it didn't work. But some of it must have got through. That was why your coming to see me was so important. I *knew* then, and it gave me the strength to keep trying.' There was a pause and, when he began again, Michael sounded much more optimistic. 'I'm being protected now – and helped. I never knew . . . They've told me so much, Zoe. It's so different to our world. We split everything up; dreams and reality, intuition and logic, knowledge and imagination, left and right, conscious and subconscious. They use it all *together*. Imagine using all your brain at once, Zoe. It's possible, here. I've only seen glimpses so far, and I'm learning slowly, like a child, but . . . it's wonderful. We've eliminated mysteries; here they embrace them.' His voice was filled with excitement, but then became more sober as his immediate concerns returned. 'I need to hear you, Zoe. You always came before. Where were you today? Come and see me. I love you.'

Zoe knew the message would end there, and it did. She was stunned by what she had heard. The vagaries of his earlier communications were explained now, but his description of the other land needed some thinking about. And the last part of his message had been both encouraging and devastating. It was the final proof that he had heard her all along – as Zoe had hoped and believed – but it also left her feeling wretched and guilty about not having gone to see him that day.

The next message began then, leaving Zoe no more time to think.

'Zoe . . . er . . . it's Nick, Nick Black from the hospital. I'm told you didn't come in today . . . Um . . . There's no change in Michael's condition but I . . . just wanted to check you're OK.' He sounded slightly embarrassed and the call ended there.

The next was even more brief.

'Hi, Zoe, it's Alex. Just calling to see how you are. Ring me when you have a moment. Bye.'

Zoe hoped that the last message would be from Michael again, but when it came she could only stare at the machine in horror. It was a voice she had hoped never to hear again.

'Hello, Zoe,' Thomas said. 'I've been thinking about you a lot recently. Can't think why.' Her ex-husband gave a short, bitter laugh. 'How's Michael? Not too well, I hope. Sometimes, when I think of him . . .' He broke off angrily, but a moment later sounded falsely convivial again. 'Sooner or later you'll realise what a mistake you made leaving me. I never thought you were that much of an adventuress.' Zoe's skin crawled at the echo of Jevan's words. 'How did you escape?' Thomas asked, redoubling the sinister echo. 'Not that I miss you, you understand,' he went on. 'I can have all the women I want.'

The repetition of Jevan's words was becoming horribly unnerving. Zoe felt herself trembling, wanting to stop the tape, but she could not bring herself to touch the machine. It was only then that she realised where she had heard that last sentence before. It had been said by Killian, not Jevan.

However, the message ended on an even more ominous note.

'I don't think you've seen the last of me, Zoe.'

She felt sick. How had Thomas got their number? Was it ridiculous to have expected it to remain secret for ever? And why had he phoned now? Was he somehow being sucked into the other land too?

A small movement caught her eye. It was dark outside but the sitting room curtains were not drawn, and there were faint reflections in the panes of the bay window. Zoe screamed and the three figures vanished, but not before she had had time to see who they were, to know instinctively that together they were responsible for the malevolent presence in her home. During their brief spectral appearance, both Jevan and Killian had worn feral grins. Only Thomas had remained stony-faced.

# 39

The 'ghosts' had gone – but the horror of the apparition remained. And Zoe was caught in a dilemma. Should she respond to Michael's plea and go to the hospital now? Or return to Emmony's world, where she still had work to do? In the end, the fact that she needed Michael's help, and the emotional tug of her love for him, made her decide to go to Norwich. She told herself that Emmony would come to no harm in the next few hours. And to her somewhat guilty relief, the decision also meant she did not have to stay in a house which now felt haunted, no longer a safe haven.

Before she left, Zoe reset the answering machine, not caring if the latest messages were recorded over. She knew she would remember every word of Michael's, hoped fervently that she would be able to forget Thomas's, and the other three were more or less irrelevant. She turned the central heating on to constant and switched several lights on, then went out to brave the bitterly cold night.

Although the journey passed quickly, with very little traffic on the roads, Zoe still found herself with time to think. She was becoming more and more convinced that Emmony's world was parallel to and concurrent with her own. But if that *was* the case, if there were two worlds, why not more? Perhaps there were an infinite number. And if that was true, why was the link between just these two? Had anyone else found the 'gaps'? In the end she gave up her hopeless quest for answers, and just drove. In a sense none of these things mattered; it was the events that were still to come – in both realms – that were important.

Though far from still – work went on there around the clock – the hospital was naturally much quieter than usual when Zoe arrived. The reception staff were surprised to see her in the middle of the night, and were a little hesitant about letting her in to see Michael until she explained that circumstances had prevented her coming during the day. One of the nurses recognised Zoe and knew that she was familiar with hospital routines. As Michael was in a private room, she saw no reason why Zoe should not visit him.

Michael seemed very peaceful when Zoe let herself into his room, the crisp white sheets tucked neatly over his chest. His breathing appeared even slower than usual, and she wondered briefly whether his body still reacted to the cycles of day and night, light and dark. Leaning over, she kissed his cheek. He smelt clean, antiseptic. *Oh, Michael, you've been gone so long you don't even smell like you any more.*

'Hello, my love. I'm here,' she said aloud. 'I've got a lot to tell you, but I can't stay too long so listen carefully.'

As succinctly as she could, she described everything that had happened since her last visit. There was so much to tell, so many details that suddenly seemed important, that she found herself backtracking occasionally, getting muddled and fretful. In the end, though, she managed to cover everything she could remember.

'I'm sorry, Michael. I have to go now.' She was very tired, and her voice was hoarse. 'I don't think I missed anything important.' She looked at his still face, hoping she had told him enough, praying that he had been listening and would now respond in the only way he could. 'Please help me, sweetheart. I can't do it without you.' She kissed him, and whispered, 'I love you too,' and then went out to the car.

On the way home she almost fell asleep at the wheel, jerking awake to find herself on the wrong side of the road. The shock made her angry with herself. What use would she be to Michael, or anyone else, if she ended up in a ditch? She opened the window, letting in the freezing air, put the radio on and concentrated fiercely as the headlights snaked their way back through the undulating lanes.

Ash Ring was warm and bright, and the first thing she did when she got home – once she had reassured herself that the house was free from the alien presence – was to check the answering machine. Her hopes leapt when she saw that there were two messages waiting, but fell again when the first was from someone whose voice she did not immediately recognise.

'Hi, Mikey. It's not that late is it? Get outta bed, you lazy saddo. Where've you been anyway? We don't normally get to scroll with your new mega-creations for this long. I thought you were going soft until this afternoon.'

Zoe had it now. It was one of the Terrible Triplets, the one who called himself Billy Virus. Why did he have to pick this night to phone? And what did he mean about 'this afternoon'?

'Just to let you know,' the voice went on, '*Otherlands* went in the post today, with the usual six-handed paint job. Actually, we thought it was pretty neat, although you kept the best bits for yourself didn't you? Can't hide anything from the Virus. And don't hack into my stuff at work again, you sod. That could've got me into trouble. Still haven't figured out how you did it – but we could make some money, eh?'

The message ended there, and Zoe was left pondering the fact that Michael had apparently broken into Billy's computer *that afternoon*. And it was no wonder it could have got him into trouble. Billy, to his eternal shame, worked in a bank.

But then all such considerations flew out of her mind as Michael's voice sounded from the machine.

'Turn them all on, Zoe. Turn everything on!' He was talking fast, excited and afraid at the same time. 'It's very important. They can be my eyes and ears. When you see it all . . . it's like one vast network. Interconnected. That way . . .' He broke off, giving the impression that he was listening to someone else. 'Come back at sunrise, Zoe,' he resumed. 'The poison will still work, and she'll be asleep till then anyway. You *are* coming back, aren't you?' His momentary doubt was soon banished.

'Don't forget to switch everything on when you do. That's *our* magic . . . I'm so proud of you, my love.'

Zoe looked at her watch through eyes clouded with tears. It was 2.30 a.m. When was sunrise? Did she really dare wait until then? She was so tired she could hardly think, and the prospect of a few hours sleep was immensely attractive. If it would do no harm . . . It made sense. If Emmony was indeed asleep – and who else could Michael be referring to? – then presumably the rest of the household would be too. Including Jevan. There would be a much better chance of using the poison effectively in the morning.

So Zoe crawled up to bed, marvelling at the proof that her husband had been listening to her rambling monologue at the hospital. He even knew about the poison. She set the alarm for six o'clock and immediately fell into a deep, empty sleep.

Waking up was hard, like climbing out of a bottomless well, but she managed it. To her relief it was still dark outside and, by the time she had dressed and had a coffee, she was feeling refreshed and wide-awake – and nervous. As the eastern sky lightened, she made her preparations. Well before the sluggish winter sun rose, everything was ready. The television was turned on, with the sound muted; there were tapes in the VCR and the stereo cassette deck ready to record; all Michael's computers were switched on, although they were not operating; and, of course, the answering machine was already operational with the volume set to zero.

Zoe decided on a two-hour regression because that was the maximum length of running time for the audio cassette. After that she would check to see whether Michael had sent her any further instructions, and then return immediately to the other world. Part of her decision was also based on the surmise that unless she took some action against Jevan during that time then she would be too late. Setting the alarm accordingly, she initiated the recordings, then went to her chair and tried to relax.

Zoe was confident in her ability to induce self-hypnosis without the use of Owen's tape by now. She was well practised and the process came easily as the relaxation techniques

303

overcame the distractions – the faint hiss of tapes and the silent flicker of the television behind her.

She arrived in the other world just as Emmony was being shaken awake, and immediately sensed her body's tiredness. That her counterpart had slept so soundly was hardly remarkable. She had had no rest at all the previous night.

'My lady, wake up,' Oliva said, shaking her again. 'The Quarterman wants to see you. Now.'

Another maid stood in the background, clutching a beacon. They were still taking no chances.

For the second time that day, Zoe dragged herself out of bed, immediately reviewing Emmony's memory of what had happened the night before. The talisman and the phial of poison were still concealed in her clothes. Zoe was able to insist on a degree of privacy while she dressed herself, and thus reclaimed her two prized possessions. Then, feeling anxious and cold in the grey early morning light, she allowed herself to be led downstairs.

Jevan was in his study. He looked ravaged, and had not even changed his clothes. The room stank of sweat and stale alcohol. He had evidently had even less sleep than his wife. He was not alone, and Zoe was able to identify the warlock attending him as Pinot, the household physician. Jevan barely glanced at Zoe as she came in. His face was set in an ugly scowl.

'That's what I pay you for,' he told the physician irritably. 'To stop me from getting ill.'

'I cannot prevent self-inflicted maladies,' Pinot replied truculently. 'If you will insist on drinking so much . . .'

'Strengthen my protection,' Jevan said shortly, rubbing his eyes and temples.

'I'm already doing all I can. There are limits to—'

'Then I shall have to get a new chief protector,' the Quarterman threatened. 'Get out. And tell Lanier to bring me some brandy.'

'You should not . . .' Pinot began, then saw the look on his master's face and retreated quickly.

Zoe had watched the exchange with interest. Jevan was

clearly not at his most alert, and the mention of brandy had raised her hopes. If she had anything to do with it, the hair of this particular dog would be rather more than Jevan had bargained for.

He turned baleful, red-rimmed eyes on his wife. He was suffering, and Zoe knew that made him dangerous, like a wounded animal. Neither of them moved or said anything for several heartbeats.

Lanier knocked and entered without waiting for permission, carrying a tray with a decanter and a large round glass. He had obviously anticipated his master's request. He left again without a word, his expression carefully neutral, as Jevan poured himself a sizeable measure, gulped it down and poured another.

'This is your last chance, Emmony,' he said, quietly menacing. 'You've tried my patience for too long. Where is the talisman?' Zoe said nothing.

'The locators from the Pyramid will be here soon,' he told her. 'You won't be able to hide it then. I am prepared to be lenient if you tell me willingly. It would be much better for you.'

Zoe realised suddenly that he was lying. There were no such experts. It was a bluff! The intuition gave her strength, but she knew better than to reveal her knowledge. Jevan's own warlocks must have tried and failed to find the pen, and he was getting desperate. Perhaps, if Chandos really *had* heard of the talisman, he might indeed be sending someone to inspect it – and Jevan's failure to produce it would be counted as a sign of weakness and shame. However, if that was the case, her situation was made all the more perilous. As Jevan still believed – or hoped – that she knew where it was, he might well resort to other, more unpleasant methods of persuasion.

'The talisman was stolen,' she said eventually, when he began to show signs of impatience. 'Why not ask those who had the opportunity to take it?'

'You think I haven't, you stupid slut? None of them are capable of hiding such a thing from me. Until now I did not think you were either.' His face was quivering with anger, and he took another swallow of brandy.

'I'd tell you where it is if I knew,' Zoe lied. 'What have I to gain from denying you in this?'

'Oh, the so dutiful wife!' he exclaimed sarcastically. 'One that runs off to her sickly lover as soon as my back is turned.'

'He is no more my lover than Killian is,' she retorted.

'Leave my brother out of this!' he snapped. 'For all your lies, you would like to save Ghyl's life, wouldn't you? Admit that at least.'

Zoe hesitated, then did as she was told. As she spoke, she was wondering how to get close to the decanter.

'I would save a friend from unjust execution, yes.'

Jevan spluttered at her choice of words, his face redder than ever.

'If you tell me where the talisman is, I might consider a reprieve,' he said tightly, every word costing him pain.

Zoe rejoiced inwardly at this tiny victory. She had been right. Even though she knew that his offer was false, the very fact that he had made it at all was a measure of his desperation.

'I don't know where it is,' she repeated. 'And bargaining with justice ill becomes a Quarterman.'

For a moment, she thought he was going to explode, and she recalled Thomas's red-faced bouts of rage. Her small triumph was forgotten now. The silence stretched agonisingly as they both stood quite still. Then Jevan moved so fast – impossibly fast – that he was just a blur. As his glass shattered in the fireplace, the spirit flaring briefly, he loomed over her, his movements having taken less than an instant. The tip of the short-bladed dagger in his hand was held no more than two inches from her right eye.

# 40

'There are ways of cutting women so it won't show in public,' Jevan spat malevolently. 'I can make your life a permanent torture.'

Zoe was shaking with fear now, but was otherwise unable to move. She did not understand how he had been able to get so close to her so fast.

Jevan slipped the knife into her bodice and sliced off the top button. The thread parted as if it were made of water, and a flap of material fell down.

'You understand?' he demanded.

Zoe nodded, not able to speak.

He laughed. Now that his wife was clearly terrified, her brief defiance ended, the balance of power was back as it should be. He turned away and sat in a chair.

'Get me another glass,' he ordered.

Zoe's heart started hammering. Though she was still shaking from Jevan's terrible threat, she knew this was her chance. For a moment she stood petrified, trying to remember where to find a glass. Then, as she forced her trembling legs to move, her hand sought out and found the phial, her fingers clasping it tightly. The only glass available was a plain beaker normally used for water. As she brought it over to the decanter, the phial was now in her other hand, the stopper already loosened while her back had been turned. She was certain that her movements must have betrayed her, but Jevan seemed to be paying her little attention.

'Come on, come on. My head . . .' He broke off, unwilling to admit any weakness to her.

Zoe's hands shook as she picked up the decanter, but she steeled herself to calm and poured a sizeable measure. At the same time, she tipped the entire contents of the phial into the glass and hurriedly returned the empty tube to her pocket. She gave the drink to Jevan, who took it without a word. Trying hard not to stare at the glass, Zoe retreated. The Quarterman raised it to his lips, but then lowered it again and looked up. Zoe almost cried out in exasperation. *Drink!* she pleaded silently, wondering whether he could detect the poison by its scent. The tincture should have matured to a deadly potency by now, but would the brandy be enough to mask its presence?

'You know, I shall enjoy this afternoon,' Jevan remarked conversationally. 'And I'll make sure you have a good view when the foundation stones crush the first of Ghyl's bones.'

Zoe did not react, still mentally imploring him to drink. But the glass remained in his hand, resting on the arm of his chair as if to spite her.

'Lost your tongue?' he enquired nastily.

A knock at the door made Zoe jump. To her immense frustration, Jevan put his glass down and stood up.

'What is it?' he shouted angrily.

'The masons are here, Quarterman,' Lanier replied. 'As you requested.'

'They're early,' Jevan muttered. 'Tell them to wait,' he added more loudly.

He was advancing on Zoe again, the knife in his hand once more. She began to back away.

'Stand still!' he roared. 'I have enough time left to loosen your tongue.'

Zoe flung herself backwards, colliding with the desk, and her disobedience infuriated him further. He mouthed obscenities as he came on. As Zoe's hands searched frantically for a weapon, one of them closed upon a hard sphere – the 'chanters stone. Snatching it up, she flung it at him as hard as she could. Her aim was poor and it flew wide, but the effect upon Jevan was electric. He turned in disbelief to see it crash onto the floor and bounce under a chair, then spun around to glare at Zoe again, his face now suffused with hatred.

'How dare you!' he shouted, cursing vilely again. 'How *dare* you!'

Zoe was now at the end of her tether, her hopes dashed at every turn. She had nothing left to lose and, without thinking, played her last card. Taking the pen from its hiding place, she held it up, one end in each hand.

'One step closer and I'll break the talisman.'

As Jevan froze, staring in horror, his mouth moved wordlessly. Then all colour suddenly drained from his face and sweat shone on his forehead. The dagger fell from nerveless fingers and he clutched at his chest as his breath came in rattling gasps. With one last incoherent croak of pain, Jevan collapsed heavily to the floor and lay there, twitching.

Zoe stared, transfixed, unable to believe what had happened. The door burst open then, and the physician rushed in, closely followed by Lanier and another servant. Zoe hid the pen again, but they paid her no attention. The warlock and his assistant went immediately to the stricken Quarterman, while Lanier only glanced at her, his expression unreadable.

'His protection is holding for now,' Pinot reported, his face almost as white as his master's, 'but this is serious. I don't know how—'

'Save your excuses,' Lanier told him coolly. 'Just keep him alive.'

Zoe slumped down in a chair beside the desk, her legs no longer able to support her. The chamberlain left the room, ignoring her, while Pinot called for assistance. The study was filled with bustle as servants came and went.

Zoe watched blindly, wondering what could have happened. He certainly hadn't drunk any of the poison, so what was wrong with him? A heart attack? *His protection is holding for now*. Slowly she turned around so that her back was to the room. She found a piece of paper which was blank on one side, took the pen out and quickly drew a rough pentangle. Then she wrote 'Jevan's protection is dispelled' and added her own name as before. *Believe it*, she told herself. *Make it true*. She hid the pen again. There was no brazier available here so she did the next best thing, tearing the paper into as many tiny pieces as she could manage, then screwing them up and dropping them into a dark corner beneath the desk. Her actions were lost in the frenetic activity behind her, and she was unobserved as she turned round to inspect the results of her handiwork.

Pinot and Jevan were at the centre of a group of people, the physician's hands cradling his master's head, while others rubbed his hands and feet. The other onlookers did not appear to be doing anything, but their faces were also filmed with sweat, and several looked worried or in pain. Jevan's breathing was still weak and fast, and Pinot was perspiring freely. His concentration was fierce, while his own agony was not in doubt.

'It's failing. Something's changed!' the physician cried, looking up at the other warlocks gathered round him. 'What are you doing, you fools?' He was desperate now.

Shortly afterwards, Jevan stopped breathing. After a few moments of profound and ominous silence, Pinot spoke.

'He's dead,' he said quietly, his voice filled with weariness and despair.

Zoe felt numb. She was both relieved and shocked beyond measure. Her purpose had been achieved, however fortuitously. She was not even sure if she was a murderess or not.

Pinot looked up at Zoe for the first time, his expression distraught, as the others drifted away.

'I'm sorry, my lady.'

Lanier returned to the room and, to Zoe's dismay, Killian followed hard on his heels. The younger twin knelt beside his brother, then glanced up at her.

'What happened?'

'I don't know,' she whispered, having to make no effort to sound distressed. 'We were arguing and he just collapsed.'

Killian stared at her for a few moments in open disbelief, then looked around the room. His eyes fell immediately on the glass of brandy. He went to pick it up, and sniffed suspiciously before handing it to Pinot. The physician held it to his nose and recoiled violently.

'Poison!' he exclaimed. 'Augmented and distilled. Whoever prepared this is a powerful warlock indeed.'

'Or witch,' Killian amended, looking at Zoe.

'Lanier brought the brandy in, not me,' she said despairingly. 'I know nothing about poison.' This was too cruelly ironic for words. The poison had not even been put to use, and yet it was still the measure of her guilt.

'You should know, Quarterman,' the chamberlain said to Killian, who seemed to swell with pride at the use of his new title, 'that I am incapable of such treachery. She was alone in here with Jevan.'

'It seems that our grieving widow is a murderess,' Killian stated with a degree of satisfaction. 'Guards!' When the soldiers appeared, he ordered them to take the Lady Emmony to the cellar and bind her in irons. 'I will visit her shortly. I have to meet with the bridge masons and confirm our plans for the foundation sacrifice.' He smiled to see Zoe's look of horror. 'Did you think to win a reprieve for your friend so easily?'

Zoe could not think at all as she was led away. She was physically manhandled down to the cellar – which might as well have been called a dungeon – by two burly soldiers, with others in close attendance, their weapons drawn. In the rank-smelling, torchlit room, she was shoved roughly against a dank wall and iron manacles were clamped around her wrists and neck. The height of the neck iron was such that she could neither stand straight, nor sit or kneel, but had to half crouch, her legs bent at the knees. Her arms were less restricted, as the wristlets were on the end of thick chains, but all of the iron hurt terribly. It was as if it burned her skin like acid – and some remote part of Emmony's brain supplied the unwanted information that the metal had been cursed for that very purpose – to inflict pain.

But it was the terrible constriction that made Zoe want to scream. Her phobia had always made it unbearable for her to wear even soft material round her neck or wrists if it was tight, but these cold and sorcerous restraints were beyond her worst imaginings, her worst nightmare. All she could think of and pray for was for the two hours to be over, so that she could escape from this intolerable torment. Everything else fled from her mind, until she felt she must go mad.

# 41

In his luxurious London flat, Thomas Forbes lay in bed, listening to the erratic beating of his heart, and wondered if he was going to die. The pain had come on suddenly, waking him from a dream which he had now forgotten – but which he knew had made him very angry. The mind-numbing agony had begun in the centre of his chest, then radiated outwards rapidly – down his arms, to his abdomen and neck. He felt nauseous and cold, but he was sweating. Even breathing was difficult.

His heart seemed to have gone mad; his pulse was rapid and weak, fluttering as if a frightened bird were trapped inside his ribcage – and then thumping alarmingly for a few seconds as though trying to shift an obstruction. Thomas knew that he should call for help, but he was too frightened even to reach out for the telephone. He lay very still, telling himself fearfully that it would go away, that he would be all right.

There was a small, sleepy movement next to him in the bed, and he remembered that he had not come home alone the night before. She was a young journalist, a book reviewer for some magazine or other but, for the life of him, he could not remember her name. They had met at a launch party where, as usual, Thomas had made a striking impression, his suave wit and knowledgeable small talk made even more entertaining by the endless flow of wine. There had been a late night supper in Soho, more wine and brandies, and then they had come back to his flat. She had seemed beautiful then, desirable and willing. But the ease of his latest conquest gave him no pleasure now. The pain in his chest dominated him completely.

He had had a lot to eat and drink the night before, and although he normally boasted an iron-clad constitution, this was perhaps just a bad attack of heartburn. He prayed to a God he did not believe in for that to be true, to *make* it true. There was a bitter taste in his mouth, and the thought of alcohol made him want to gag.

After a while, the pain eased slightly and his hopes rose. Another memory nagged at him, something he had done last night that had seemed a good idea at the time but which would probably appear foolish now – if he could only remember what it was. The pain really was lessening, and he glanced across at the still sleeping face of the girl, at her smooth skin and light brown curls. She reminded him of someone, someone he had known a long time ago. And then he remembered what he had done.

He had phoned Zoe, something he had vowed never to do even after he had discovered her number, and had talked to her answering machine. At first the memory made him feel stupid, and he thought that he must have been very drunk to even consider such a thing. But then he felt a spurt of anger. She deserved to hear a piece of his mind, the bitch. Thomas could not remember what he had said but, he told himself, it did not really matter. It would teach her to think she could just walk out on him and get away with it.

He was almost without pain now, the searing anguish of the first attack just a fading memory, and the relief was so great that he almost felt like laughing. But that changed abruptly as soon as he glanced at the bedside clock. He had less than an hour to get to the office in time for Friday's regular review meeting. For the first time in years he had forgotten to set the alarm.

Zoe returned to her own sitting room in a state of near collapse, both physically and mentally. She ached every-where, there were raw marks circling her wrists and neck, and her whole body was clammy with perspiration. For a

314

time the relief at her escape was so great that it swamped all thought, but eventually she forced herself to breathe slowly and fought for a return to calm. Was it only an unfortunate coincidence that Emmony's punishment had matched Zoe's phobia so exactly? Or was there more to it than that? Could she somehow have had foreknowledge of her incarceration, and could that have been enough to *cause* the phobia in the first place? Either way, the experience had been a nightmare – and the whole situation now was equally appalling. Jevan was dead, but that seemed to have achieved nothing. Ghyl was still under sentence of death and now Emmony, after whatever horrors Killian chose to inflict upon her, seemed certain to die as well, condemned as a murderess.

Zoe shuddered as she recalled, through the red haze of her fear, the visit Killian had made to the dungeon. She had expected violence from him, but what had happened was, in a way, even more chilling. The new Quarterman had told her, quite calmly and with a malign smugness, that her fate was to be decided with all due solemnity by the legal authorities of the land. He would be leaving soon to bring back one of the Prince's judges who, after the trial, would give his blessing to her prolonged and public torture. Killian informed her, smiling, that he would preside over this personally, and that she would beg to die long before the end. Only when he was satisfied that she had fully paid the price of her crimes would her wish be granted.

The outcome of the trial was obviously a foregone conclusion. Whatever the rights or wrongs of what had actually happened, she would be pronounced guilty, and both Killian and Zoe knew it.

Emmony was now imprisoned, shackled and guarded, and so everything depended on Zoe. She was the only one left with the freedom to act, and the responsibility lay heavily. If she failed . . .

In principle, her task was simple. She must return to Emmony's body, escape from the prison, prove her innocence if possible, but – above all – get to Ghyl and use whatever was needed to revive him and help him to escape. All their lives

315

– and the destiny of an entire princedom – depended on her success. Yet, in practice, it seemed impossible. As soon as she returned, she would be trapped by iron manacles, helpless to do anything but wait for appalling pain and death. The very thought of submitting voluntarily to that cruel constriction made Zoe tremble and doubt her ability to do it. She could take nothing with her from her own world. All her clothes and jewellery were replaced by Emmony's, otherwise she might have been able to transfer something – tools? – to help her escape. Zoe felt like crying with sheer frustration. It was hopeless.

Behind her, the cassette player clicked to a halt and it was only then that she remembered the machines – and the one ally who might still be able to help her. She quickly went to inspect everything. Automatically, as she had done after every regression, she turned the volume up on both the telephone and the answering machine. Although there were no messages showing, she played a bit of the tape anyway, just to make sure. But nothing new had been recorded.

*Did you hear, Michael?* she asked silently. *Please talk to me, tell me that you heard. I need your help more than ever now.*

The television was playing an old movie, though without the soundtrack. The VCR was still recording and Zoe stopped the machine and set it to rewind, then turned to the audio cassette deck. After winding it back a bit, she pressed 'Play', but there was nothing on the tape except background hiss. She tried again after further rewinding, with the same result. Reversing the direction of playback meant that she was near the beginning of the two-hour tape, and this produced the first results. Zoe heard her own voice say, '. . . if I knew. What have I to gain from denying you in this?' Then there was a pause before she spoke again. 'He is no more my lover than Killian is.' Further investigation confirmed that this was simply a recording of her side of the conversation with Jevan – which she could remember easily anyway. It was no use to her.

The videotape had rewound by now, and she set it to play. At first the TV screen was blank, filled with the fuzzy black and white pattern of a blank tape, with only a hiss on the soundtrack. But after a few seconds Zoe thought she began to see outlines, vague shapes in the shifting dots – and whisperings from the speaker, unintelligible but variable noises which could not be explained as mere static.

*Talk to me, Michael.*

Feeling more hopeful now, she fast forwarded the playback – so that the dots leapt and danced more quickly, the familiar lines streaking across the screen – stopping every so often and returning it to normal speed. At last the shape took on a recognisable form, a human head that looked like an electric ghost, colourless, almost featureless, but undeniably there. At the same time, a voice could be heard, barely more than a whisper, and almost lost in the hissing of the tape.

'It's too hard like this, but we have the power . . . all of us. The link is there . . . we can use it together . . .'

There was a loud crack, and then the screen went blank. For a few moments Zoe stared in incomprehension. The VCR had gone dead, the tape had stopped moving, and all the lights and indicators had gone out. It could not be a power cut because everything else was still working. The voice had seemed like Michael's, though she could not be certain. What was she supposed to do now? What was the link she was supposed to use? There was only one thing left she could try.

Zoe got up, her muscles protesting, and went out into the hall, heading for Michael's workroom. There was a package lying on the mat together with some letters, and as she stooped to pick them up she was thinking furiously. The first inklings of an idea had begun to form. If Michael had been able to get a message onto Billy's computer at the bank, then surely he would be able to communicate with his own.

Putting the post down on one of Michael's tables, Zoe sat down in front of one of the screens. She wondered how to start. Around her the complex technology hummed quietly, waiting. *Write!* she told herself. *That's your talent.* Looking at the keyboard, she pushed several letters experimentally. Nothing happened. *Come on*, she urged the inanimate circuitry. *Help me, Michael.*

She pressed other buttons, whose signs she did not understand, and at last one of her random choices produced a sharp
bleep and a white colon appeared on the blue screen. Zoe took
her chance, and began to type rapidly.

: MICHAEL, IT'S ZOE. CAN YOU HEAR ME?

She pressed the key marked 'Enter'. The computer responded
with the discouraging message 'UNKNOWN COMMAND'
and gave her another colon prompt.

: ISN'T THIS EASIER, MICHAEL? I NEED YOUR HELP.

The response was the same and Zoe was just about to give
up when the whole screen flickered, changing colour several
times then returning to blue. At the top of the display now
was a simple message.

I'M HERE.

Her pulse racing, Zoe quickly pressed 'Enter' again, and
typed.

: MICHAEL?

YES.

Zoe stared at the three precious letters, almost overwhelmed
by emotion. At last they could respond to each other directly –
for the first time in so long. There was so much that she wanted
to say, to see him say, but there was no time. Blithely assuming
that Michael knew about the latest situation in the other land,
she outlined the beginnings of her plan. Half an hour later,
they had done all they could to prepare themselves.

: GOODBYE MICHAEL. FOR NOW. I LOVE YOU.

I LOVE YOU TOO, ZOE.

Zoe left the workroom and went in search of a pair of
scissors.


Thomas had returned to his own office once the meeting was
over. It had been a boring, routine affair, and he had found it
hard to concentrate. He felt very strange. The pain had gone
but he was still weak, and his thoughts kept wandering. He
was just trying to make himself read the draft of the latest
sales team note when Roger Gilchrist, the international sales
director, put his head round the door.

'Got a moment?'

'Sure. Come in.' Thomas and Roger were old friends, having shared several legendary drinking marathons at the Frankfurt Book Fair in their younger days.

'You look a bit rough. Are you OK?' Roger asked as he shut the door behind him.

'I'm fine,' Thomas began automatically, then thought better of it. He needed to talk. 'No, I'm not really. I felt a bit rough this morning. It was just heartburn, but it scared the shit out of me at the time.'

'Too much booze,' his friend concluded sagely. 'Or perhaps the lovely Joanna gave you indigestion. She's a bit young for you, after all.'

'You're just jealous,' Thomas said, grinning, then grew serious again. 'The truth is, I've not been sleeping well these last few weeks. I keep having really weird dreams. God knows what a psychologist would make of them. And bimbos like Joanna don't seem to help. I just end up wanting to hit them.'

'Take it easy, old man,' Roger advised, sounding worried now. 'Your little temper tantrums at work haven't gone unnoticed either.'

'Oh, God,' Thomas moaned. In the past, he had always managed to keep his personal problems from affecting his work.

'You need a holiday.'

'When do I get the chance?'

'You are, of course, indispensable. We couldn't do without you even for a day,' Roger told him, mocking gently.

'Piss off.'

'Lunch?'

'I can't,' Thomas said regretfully, returning his colleague's amiable grin. 'I've got to meet the new buyer from Brinkleys.'

'Should be exciting,' Roger commented, meaning the exact opposite. 'Try to take it easy, OK?'

Thomas was left alone with his thoughts. He had not revealed the most disturbing facet of his recent malaise – which was that he couldn't keep Zoe out of his mind. He was over her, of course, but she would not leave him alone. He thought of her constantly, in dreams and while he was awake.

319

And the overriding emotion he felt was one of pent-up anger. That was why he had tried to phone her last night, to release some of the pressure. But it had not been enough. Thomas slammed his fist down on the desk, making his pens rattle and spilling his coffee.

Not nearly enough.

# 42

Zoe had moved her usual chair from the sitting room into Michael's workroom. That was where the important things were going to happen now, even though she would not be able to control anything directly once her regression had begun. She knew that she had prepared as much as she could. Now she just had to trust Michael, and the others.

Zoe was guiltily aware that she had left Emmony to suffer the incarceration for much longer than she would have wished, but even so, the thought of returning to those spiteful iron manacles did not make her eager to start. Giving the ring one last rub for good luck, she tried to relax. The process took longer than normal and she became anxious, which slowed it even more. But eventually Owen's training began to exert its influence and she felt herself falling, sliding through the gap between the worlds.

The iron chafed and burned her skin, and Zoe had to fight with inner demons to stop the irrational terror rising up and engulfing her. She was going to need all her wits about her. Slowly, one small step at a time, she was able to calm her nerves, trying to convince herself that her heart was still beating, that she was not suffocating, that she was not going to die.

At last she opened her eyes and looked about. There was no one else in the dungeon. She carefully lifted one of her hands, trying to ignore the pull of the chain, and felt along the lining of her blouse. The pen was still there, and she breathed a long sigh of relief. No one had found the talisman. Together with her ring, also in the 'wrong' world, it was acting as one of their own beacons, signalling the way for the necessary links – the links between magic and machine, between imagination and reality.

Zoe took a deep breath, filling her lungs.

'Guards!' she yelled. 'Guards!'

There was no reaction at first, but after repeated shouts she heard movement outside the heavy door at the top of the stone stairs.

'What do you want?' an unknown voice called. He was obviously nervous and did not open the door.

'Come in here and I'll show you.'

After a whispered exchange, the key was turned and bolts drawn, and a soldier appeared at the top of the stairs. He advanced cautiously down the first few steps, his sword drawn and his colleague just behind him. Zoe had no time to wonder about their timidity. *Now, Michael,* she begged silently. *Help me now.*

'What do you want?' the first man repeated suspiciously.

Zoe felt rather than saw the first glimmer in the air, and rejoiced.

'It's not what I want. It's what *he* wants,' she told them, pointing awkwardly.

The two soldiers stared, open-mouthed in amazement, as a shimmering image of Killian appeared at the foot of the staircase. They had not known that their new master was such a powerful warlock; projecting one's double-image over such a distance was something only sorcerers could do.

At first Killian's duplicate stood still, then he looked up stiffly and raised an arm to point across the cellar. When he spoke, his voice sounded oddly metallic, but the words had the stamp of authority – and there was no doubt that it was him. The grey clothes, sharp face and black hair were unmistakable.

'You will release the Lady Emmony immediately,' he told the soldiers. 'Get the keys.'

'But . . .'

'Do it!' he ordered harshly.

The second guard spoke up.

'My lord, you told us yourself to hold the witch here until your return . . . in person . . . this afternoon.'

Listening and praying, Zoe's anxiety increased. She had not known that Killian would be back so soon.

'Your zeal is commendable,' the double said with realistic sarcasm, 'but you seem to forget who you're talking to. May I not countermand my own orders?'

'Yes, but . . .'

'Release her now. Or, as sure as I am the new Quarterman, it will be the worse for you!' Killian roared.

The second guard pushed his colleague forward, urging him to act. Although the first man was still suspicious, he went carefully down the stairs, selecting keys from the large bunch tied to his belt. He glanced nervously at the doppelganger as he stepped past, then stopped in front of Zoe, only to turn away again. *What now?* Zoe wondered, her nerves close to breaking point.

'Is she free to go, my lord?' the gaoler asked.

'Of course not. She is to accompany me to where I wait with the judge – and the executioner.'

The guard frowned, then nodded, apparently satisfied. Zoe watched breathlessly as the key unlocked the first manacle. As her hand came free she almost cried out with the pain. Her second hand followed and then – the greatest relief of all – the cruel iron necklace was removed. The soldier backed away quickly as Zoe slowly straightened up, fighting an almost uncontrollable desire to cry – or to laugh hysterically.

'Come,' Killian said shortly.

Somehow, Zoe forced her maltreated legs into action and walked over to the stairs. Killian made his way up behind her, and the guard followed at a distance. The second man stood aside, and as they continued along the passages, making their way towards the courtyard, they were watched disbelievingly by several guards and members of the household staff.

'Bring her horse,' Killian ordered, and one of the servants hurried to obey.

Zoe stood in the open air, the image of Killian still sparkling beside her, and waited as confidently as she could –
though her heart was pounding. Success was almost within
their grasp.

The captain of the guards approached.

'Do you wish us to escort her, Quarterman?'

'Do you think me incapable of the task myself?' Killian
snapped.

'No, my lord, but . . .'

'But what?' he demanded irritably.

'Surely your image has no power to hold her,' the captain
said hesitantly. 'What if she should try to escape?'

'Fool! No woman escapes me, image or not. Watch.'

Killian's arm snaked out, his fingers seemed to clasp Zoe's
wrist and he jerked her towards him. She played her part
beautifully, crying out in pain and staggering as if she
could really feel his grip. The onlookers gaped. This was
talent beyond imagining – even the warlocks had never seen
anything like it. The new Quarterman rose hugely in their
collective estimation. Under such a master, each of them was
sure to benefit.

Winddancer, already saddled, was brought to them. Zoe
mounted, pulling her skirts up around her, and then Killian,
with a spectacular backflip – which made her hope that
Michael was not going too far – leapt up behind her. Moments
later the beautiful horse carried them both out of the yard and
across the fields at a gallop.

Alone now, with the cold wind of freedom blowing in her
face, Zoe laughed and yelled in triumph. It had worked –
like a charm. *We did it!* Back in her own world she had
trimmed the photograph of Killian so that only his likeness
remained. Then she had fed it into Michael's machine and
placed the computerised image into the program of *Otherlands*
– just as she had done with her own portrait three weeks
earlier. After that, Michael – and perhaps Ghyl too – had
used the links to run the program and project the facsimile
into Emmony's world. Zoe had not known who the voice
belonged to, but she was sure most of the actions had

come from Michael. That backflip was one of his trademark moves.

'Time to go,' said a voice behind her.

'Thank you.' She glanced round in time to see the image flicker out of existence.

It was up to her now, and she was determined to make the most of the chance she had been given. But as she rode on, her earlier exhilaration began to fade. There was still so much to do, and she had no way yet of knowing how she was to do it. She must save Ghyl before the real Killian returned – and there was very little time left.

The pre-lunch drinks had passed in general trade chat, and Thomas had begun to feel much better. Even his usually excellent appetite had returned. After he and his guest had eaten their *escargots* and tested the wine, they turned to more serious business, feeling each other out on the subject of incentive discounts. All was going smoothly until the waiter brought their main courses.

Thomas looked at his *canard à l'orange* and saw only crude, roast meat. Ignoring the cutlery, he picked up the joint in his hands, disregarding the hot sauce as it dribbled through his fingers, and tore off a leg. As he began to gnaw at it ravenously, the buyer from Brinkley Wholesalers stared at him in horror, wondering if this was some sort of bizarre joke. Thomas paid him no attention, tearing at the succulent meat with his teeth and letting the juices run down his chin. Other people were watching now, and the waiter was hovering. When the slurping noises became unbearable, the buyer leant forward.

'Please!' he hissed.

Thomas looked up, his eyes entirely devoid of understanding, tossed some of the savaged bones onto the floor and grabbed his wine. He took a deep noisy draught as the maître d' made his way quickly through the crowded tables.

'Monsieur, please.'

Five minutes later, Thomas stared at himself in the mirror of the restaurant's washroom. His eyes were wild, and he was sweating. For a few moments he had actually believed himself to be sitting beside a soldier's campfire. He had no idea what had come over him – but he was frightened, and angry. Somehow he knew who was responsible for this mess, for his pain that morning, for all the stupid things that were happening to him. If pressed, he would not have been able to give a rational answer as to *how* he knew – but he was certain of one thing. It had to stop. Images of violence filled his mind.

He closed his eyes and tried to calm himself but the visions would not go away.

When Zoe crested the ridge that brought her within sight of Blue Tiles, she was amazed and worried to see the building surrounded by a huge crowd of people. She slowed Winddancer to a trot, then a walk as she drew closer. The gathering was mostly made up of ordinary men and women, though there were a fair number of uniformed soldiers mixed in with them. Angry voices carried to her over the cold air. Some sort of confrontation was taking place, but it was a confused affair, subject to no control, no organisation.

A young lad ran past her, heading for a better vantage point, and Zoe called out to him. He hesitated, noting her fine clothes but evidently not recognising her.

'What's going on here?'

'They're tryin' to get the sleeper out, for the sacrifice,' he replied breathlessly, belatedly adding, 'm'lady.'

'Who are?'

'The bridge builders – and the villagers from hereabouts,' he told her. 'There's others tryin' to keep 'em back, sayin' it's murder, 'cause he ain't properly dead yet. But what's really keepin' 'em back is the witches. They don't trust 'em.'

'Witches make bad enemies,' Zoe said.

'That's true enough. Better to watch from 'ere,' he said excitedly, anticipating some entertainment.

'I can't do that,' Zoe told him soberly and rode forward again, glad that Ghyl had some friends here at least. Zenna would not give up her charge lightly, and if Brickhead had

326

been true to his word, then he would have armed protection as well. As she rode on, she could see that some guards had indeed been posted in the outbuildings.

As she drew closer still she could see that several of the crowd were brandishing weapons, and it was clear their mood was getting uglier by the minute. Zoe began to hear individual voices, raised above the general angry murmur of the mob.

'Bring him out or we'll set the whole place afire!'

'We've the Quarterman's authority.'

'You defy him at your peril.'

'Blasphemers! It's the sky-gods you defy by denying their offering. You are cursed.'

None of the defenders seemed willing to be drawn into the argument, and Zoe saw that several of them had scarves or kerchiefs tied over their lower faces, concealing their identities. She wondered if the three entertainers were among their number. There was no sign of Zenna or any of her fellow witches.

Inevitably, someone soon caught sight of Zoe and pointed, yelling. As several people in the crowd recognised Emmony, there was a hubbub of speculation. Gossip and rumour had already spread the news of her arrest and to see her here now, alone and free, was quite astonishing.

Zoe kept Winddancer walking forward steadily, ready to urge her forward or wheel about and try another approach. However, the crowd shrank back before her, opening a passage to the entrance to the Sanctuary. The shouting subsided to a mutter and then to comparative silence as she rode along the human aisle. Zoe saw several people making signs meant to ward off the power of witches' spells. Her reputation had obviously preceded her – murderess and now witch, a witch moreover who was capable of escaping from the Quarterman's dungeons. It was little wonder that no one tried to halt her progress. No one, that is, until Killian arrived.

'Stop where you are!' His voice rolled across the field like thunder. 'Any further and my archers will skewer you like a stuck pig.'

Zoe froze, and Winddancer reacted to her rider's tension

by halting immediately. The mare was nervous now, but still obedient. The crowd fell even further back, leaving Zoe exposed. She turned slowly, with dread in her heart, to see her nemesis astride his own sweating mount, flanked by archers, their arrows already nocked. There was a sizeable number of guards coming up behind him.

*But I'm so close!*

'This is becoming a habit, my lady!' Killian called with mock civility as he came nearer. 'I would have thought you'd learnt your lesson by now. But this time there will be no escape. We will be joined shortly by Judge Conal. He will pass sentence and I will carry it out.'

With his last words he drew out a long, jagged-edged dagger and held it up for all to see.

# 43

'What do you think, Thomas?'

He had been called into a meeting with a few senior colleagues to discuss the possible acquisition of a major new novel, but he had not been able to concentrate, his mind still dwelling on the hideous implications of his disastrous lunch. Because it had taken place in that particular restaurant, there was little chance of it not becoming general knowledge in the trade. Worse still, his mind was still overflowing with images of violence, the rending and tearing of flesh.

'Thomas?'

'What? I'm sorry.' He looked around the room, then without a single word of explanation, stood up, left the room, went down to the car park and drove out into the London traffic.

Emmony's trial took place outside the Sanctuary, with the three principal characters in this deadly courtroom drama only a few paces apart at the centre of a wide circle formed by the crowd. A makeshift wooden bench had been set up for Conal, the judge, whose face remained professionally impassive but whose shrewd eyes took in everything. Zoe and Killian remained standing, their mounts having been led away.

Conal was an old man, who had clearly not been able to match the pace of Killian and his guards. He had arrived some time after the new Quarterman, and by then the stage was set. Killian's men, some of them still mounted, stood at strategic points all around, guarding against any attempt at escape, or any assistance from Zoe's friends inside the Sanctuary. Zoe had watched the arrival of the judge's party, wondering what sort of man now held her fate in his hands. She had been interested to see that Lanier and Pinot were among those who escorted the old man. Presumably they had been brought by Killian to present their evidence directly to the judge.

When Conal was settled and ready, he looked at Killian.

'Begin,' he said shortly. His bones were aching from the hard riding and the gathering cold, and he did not understand why they could not conduct their business inside.

'Lord Justice, good people of my Quarter,' Killian began, his voice carrying to everyone present, 'these proceedings take place at my request. I need not have been so fair-minded, for the Lady Emmony's guilt is self-evident. I could have cut her down where she stood, exacting revenge for the murder of my brother, with no one to gainsay me or to breathe a word that she got anything other than her just reward.'

The onlookers listened quietly, knowing that he spoke the truth. They did not understand why he was bothering with this trial, but Killian was about to let them know.

'But I want you – all of you – to see that your new Quarterman is a man of enlightenment, who obeys the Prince's laws for the benefit of all.' He was speaking pompously now, like a politician, revelling in the fact that he was at last the centre of attention. 'Jevan will be avenged, but only after all points of the law have been satisfied. Then my knife will do its work, and you will all have seen justice done. After that we will assist the bridge builders to take possession of their rightful sacrifice.'

Killian smiled as a ragged cheer went up from his audience. His condescending speech had not been greeted well by everyone, but this last promise was of immediate popular appeal.

'What is more,' he went on, 'the man who is to be sacrificed deserves to die, even if he had not been honoured so, for he is further proof of Emmony's iniquity. Before she murdered my brother, she was an adulteress. You have all heard the whispers. Her presence here – the second time I have

330

discovered her so – gives truth to those rumours. And then there are her crimes against me. Today, in order to escape from rightful custody, she created a false image of me!'

The crowd gasped. This was going to be more of a show than they had expected. Many eyes turned to look at Zoe, eyes full of mistrust and resentment – but also full of awe.

'Before that,' Killian went on, 'she had falsely accused me before my brother and imposed upon me vile visions and dreams, creations of a diseased talent.'

This last was news to Zoe but, when she thought about it, it was logical enough. If Killian were appearing in her world as a ghost, then the gap in time must surely leak the other way. He must have had glimpses of her seemingly incomprehensible, mechanistic world.

'But all of this is secondary to the main charge,' Killian concluded. 'Murder. And the proof of that is incontrovertible, as you shall now hear.'

'Good,' Conal muttered. He for one had grown tired of Killian's rhetoric.

'My brother died this morning, in his own study. That is something even the Lady Emmony cannot deny.'

'Do you accept this as fact?' the judge asked Zoe.

'I do.'

'Lanier, step forward,' Killian commanded.

The chamberlain did so.

'Tell us what happened.'

Lanier described how his master had seen his physician in the early morning and then sent for his wife. When the physician left, Jevan had sent a message calling for some brandy.

'You took the brandy yourself?'

'Yes.'

'No one could have tampered with it?'

'No.'

'And you are a loyal servant of Jevan.'

'I am . . . I was. I served him for twenty years.'

'Was anyone else in the room when you left the brandy?'

'Lady Emmony,' Lanier replied, pointing a delicate finger at Zoe.

'And was she the only person in the room with Jevan from then until the time he fell ill?'

'She was.'

'What were the two of them doing?'

'I don't know for certain, but she said later that they had been arguing.'

'What about?'

'The talisman, I presume. The Quarterman was convinced she was hiding it from him.'

'Thank you, Lanier. Come forward, Pinot.'

The physician shuffled into the ring, looking about him nervously. His reputation was at stake here. He had failed to keep his master alive, and he had yet to gauge the new Quarterman's attitude to him.

'Tell us what happened after you were recalled to the study later this morning,' Killian instructed him.

Pinot told how he had found Jevan prostrate, obviously in serious distress, how he had tried to protect him but eventually failed. He described Killian's arrival, the discovery of the poison in the brandy and the arrest of Emmony. At the end of his statement, Killian took over, turning to speak directly to Conal, and recapped the evidence.

'As you have heard, Lord Justice, only Emmony had the motive and the opportunity for killing her husband. Her guilt and treachery are amply proven. I ask now for you to declare it so, and to allow her punishment to begin.'

Conal gazed solemnly at Zoe.

'Do you dispute the facts given by these witnesses?' he asked.

Zoe had been listening carefully, with outward calm but a sinking heart. Her only hope was in Conal and his integrity. If he failed her, all was lost. Everyone else was already convinced of her guilt. She was even unsure of it herself.

'I do not dispute the facts,' she replied, surprised to find that her voice was steady. Then she had to override the buzz of speculation in order to complete her answer. 'Only the conclusions drawn from them.'

'What other conclusions could there be?' Killian demanded

332

incredulously, looking at the judge. 'Are you going to waste our time—?'

'If this is to be a fair trial,' Conal interjected sternly, 'Emmony must have the opportunity to speak, to defend herself, if she can.'

Zoe's tattered hopes rose a fraction while Killian tried hard not to look aggrieved.

'May I question the witnesses, Lord Justice?'

Conal nodded, and Zoe turned first to Pinot. The physician looked anxious. He had not expected this.

'Why did you first come to see Jevan this morning?'

'He sent for me, complaining of headaches and fever.'

'What cause did you ascribe these to?'

'How is this relevant?' Killian cut in angrily. 'It was not then that he died.'

'I only wish to ascertain all the facts,' Zoe said coolly. If nothing else, delaying the end of the trial might give her friends inside the Sanctuary the chance to plan her rescue. 'Their relevance will become clear later.'

Killian snorted derisively but was overruled.

'Continue,' Conal ordered, thinking that this woman had some spirit at least. 'Answer the question, Pinot.'

'The Quarterman had been drinking heavily the previous night,' the warlock replied obediently. 'I'd often told him it'd be . . .' He stopped himself in time, but most of the audience guessed that he had been about to say 'the death of him'.

'So Jevan's health was not good?' Zoe persisted.

'Good enough. He had the best protection,' Pinot said defensively.

Zoe accepted this half answer without demur.

'When you returned to him, what were the symptoms of his illness?' she asked.

As she had hoped he would, Pinot went into detail about Jevan's obvious pain, his breathing difficulties and his sweating. Then he described how he – and his assistants – had tried to revive their master. He was beginning to ramble, his hands twitching with nerves, when Zoe cut short his self-justifying monologue.

333

'What type of poison was it?' she asked sharply.

'Eh? . . . Augmented and distilled.' He sounded almost reverent.

'Please explain what that means so that everyone can understand.'

'The essence is distilled from several different sources so that an antidote is hard to find,' the physician replied, feeling on safer ground now. 'It is prepared by a powerful warlock – or witch – and then allowed to mature while curses augment its venom, its potency. This particular poison was the work of a master of this evil craft.'

'So the poison could explain why Jevan's protection failed?' Zoe asked. 'It was potent enough for that?'

'Of course. Yes, indeed,' Pinot answered confidently. 'It would have acted instantly.'

'Instantly?' she repeated, raising her eyebrows. 'Yet you were able to keep Jevan alive for some time – and it was only later, *when you were with him*, that his protection finally failed.'

The physician began to look very uncomfortable, glancing nervously at Killian for guidance. But he was given no respite. Zoe was getting into her stride now.

'And,' she went on energetically, 'you would have us believe that you treated him and sensed no poison in him, and only when the poison was discovered in the glass did you jump to the conclusion that he had been killed that way.'

Pinot said nothing. His embarrassment was plain.

'Are you really that incompetent a physician?' Zoe's voice lashed out like a whip.

'No!' he protested. 'I—'

'What else could have caused Jevan's death?' Killian interjected angrily, feeling control of the situation slipping away from him.

'What about a seizure of the heart?' Zoe suggested quickly. 'Would that produce symptoms like those you described?'

'Well, yes,' Pinot admitted, 'but . . .'

'But what?'

'Jevan's protection would have prevented any such thing.'

'In the same way that it prevented his hangover?' she asked sarcastically.

'That's not the same,' the physician exclaimed, but he was floundering now.

'When a life is due to end of natural causes, is it not possible for the protection to fail, however professionally it is formed?'

Killian interrupted again before Pinot had a chance to answer.

'Are you saying my brother died of natural causes?' he demanded in open disbelief.

'Yes,' Zoe responded calmly, 'for I *know* he was not poisoned.'

Killian opened his mouth to speak again but was beaten to it by Conal.

'Can you prove this?' the judge enquired.

'I believe so,' she replied. 'We've already seen that Pinot could not detect any poison in Jevan's body. That speaks for itself, but there is more.'

'Then proceed,' the old man decided firmly, overriding Killian's indignant objection.

Zoe turned back to Pinot.

'Was there any poison in the decanter?'

'No. Only in the glass.'

'When you examined the glass, had it been drunk from?'

'What do you mean?' The physician was confused again.

'Was there any sign that the glass had been used?' Zoe explained patiently. 'Was it full? Half empty? Were there any marks on the rim?'

'I . . . I don't know.' Again he glanced at Killian and then at Conal, who was watching him carefully. 'It was quite full. I didn't see any marks, but that doesn't mean—'

'So it's possible that Jevan may not have drunk from it at all?' Zoe persisted.

'He must have done,' Pinot said weakly.

'What do you base that opinion on?' she asked. 'You have no evidence for it, by your own admission.' Without waiting for an answer, she turned to Lanier. 'When you brought the brandy in, how many glasses were there?'

'One.'

'Was it the one in which the poison was found?'

'No,' the chamberlain answered, frowning. 'The Quarterman's usual glass – the one I brought in – was found smashed in the fireplace. The poisoned brandy was in a water beaker.'

'If there had been poison in the smashed glass, would you have been able to detect it in the fumes from the fire, Pinot?' Zoe asked.

The physician started at the sound of his name. He had thought that his ordeal was over.

'What? Oh, yes,' he gabbled. 'It would've been unmistakable.'

'So there was no poison in the decanter, nor in Jevan's original glass,' she concluded.

By now many of the onlookers were muttering curiously and glancing at each other. There was obviously more to this than met the eye. Several among them had begun to feel some sympathy and admiration for the woman who was standing up to the arrogant new Quarterman.

'May I now speak as a witness, Lord Justice?' Zoe continued. 'I was the only one who was there the whole time.'

'By her own words she condemns herself!' Killian crowed triumphantly. 'You cannot accept the testimony of a murderess. It is worthless!'

'How am I to judge its worth unless I hear it first?' Conal asked mildly, refusing to be browbeaten. He was curious to see where all this was leading. 'Continue, my lady.'

'I freely admit that Jevan and I were arguing this morning,' Zoe said, 'but he drank no poison. His death was no murder.'

'If you had no thoughts of murder,' Killian broke in loudly, 'what was the poison doing there at all?'

It was the question Zoe had been waiting for, and in the stillness that followed Killian's words, she steeled herself to play her final, decisive card.

'The glass was mine. The poison was for me,' she stated

calmly. 'I am innocent of murder, as I am of adultery, but guilty of love. It was Ghyl's fate we were arguing about. If Jevan had not agreed to a reprieve, my life would not have been worth living. I would have ended it.'

Having said all she could, Zoe did her best to ignore Killian's enraged bluster and the sudden tumult of noise from the crowd, and turned to face Conal, awaiting his verdict.

# 44

Thomas accelerated past two lorries, then cut across three lanes of the M25 motorway, ignoring the angry horn blasts from other drivers. Speeding into the slip road for the M11, he headed north.

Zoe's apparent sincerity and her strength of character had had a profound effect on all around her, particularly the elderly judge. The only exception was Killian, who knew that he had been outwitted, but who was determined not to be denied his prey. However, his arguments grew more and more incoherent, especially when he included new accusations about the theft of the talisman – and in the end Conal lost patience.

'Be quiet!' the judge roared with astonishing ferocity for such an apparently frail old man. Killian, looking both shocked and murderously angry, subsided resentfully.

'In my estimation, Lady Emmony is innocent of murder,' Conal stated firmly, and the crowd gasped.

Zoe shut her eyes and let out a long sigh of relief. Now if only she could be allowed to go to Ghyl, to complete her mission. But Conal was determined to have his say, addressing himself directly to Killian.

'As for your charges of adultery, I find it hard to imagine how such a crime could be committed with a man who lies unconscious.'

To Killian's fury, the crowd burst out laughing at the judge's remark.

'What may or may not have occurred before Ghyl was struck down is not for me to say,' Conal went on, 'but I will not judge anyone on common rumour. The Lady Emmony's only offence – and for that we have only her own word as proof – is that she loves unwisely. If that is a crime, then half the population should hang.' There was more laughter, which Conal seemed to enjoy. 'And this offence was against one who is now dead.' The old man held up a wrinkled hand to forestall any comment from Killian, then continued. 'Her recent feats have been ingenious, and tell of unsuspected talent, but that is no crime. Indeed, removing yourself from imprisonment when you have been placed there for something of which you are innocent is legally permitted. To be encouraged, in fact. You have offered no proof of her alleged intrigues against you, Quarterman, and, furthermore, if in any of her deeds Lady Emmony used the power of the supposed talisman, I have yet to hear any evidence that she was not as entitled to this object as anyone else.'

Killian was left speechless, while silently cursing the senile old fool.

'My lady, you are a free woman,' Conal said.

'Thank you, Lord Justice,' Zoe replied with a blazing smile.

'Wait! I am still Quarterman in this district.' Killian spoke up again, trying to retrieve something from this shameful and embarrassing situation.

'That no one can deny,' Conal said with barely concealed contempt.

'Then my decree concerning the bridge sacrifice still stands,' Killian declared.

'No!' Zoe cried instantly. 'This is not justice!' Turning to Conal, she asked, 'Would you legalise the murder of an innocent man?'

The judge remained silent for a time, obviously deep in thought, while Zoe waited impatiently. This could not be happening. After all she and Emmony had been through . . . They could not fail now.

'The Quarterman has spoken,' Conal said eventually, 'and

he has the right to do so. To deprive a man who has no life, of his life, cannot be murder.' Zoe was plunged into despair, and Killian glowed at the thought of his belated revenge. 'However, natural justice decrees that the Lady Emmony be given the chance to avert such a fate,' the judge added. 'If she or anyone else can rouse Ghyl from his stupor before sunset today, then – on my authority as the Prince's judge – he will not be sacrificed. You will instead use a bull, to be provided from one of Prince Chandos's own herds.'

The crowds muttered their approval. Whatever happened now they could not lose. Killian, certain of his vengeance upon Ghyl at least, did not object – although he was galled by the delay. Only Zoe was horrified. One glance at the sky was enough to tell her that sunset was only about two hours away. What could she hope to achieve in such a short time? The coma had already lasted for three weeks. And yet the opportunity was more than she could have hoped for only an hour ago. *You have your chance. Take it!*

With a nod to Conal, Zoe turned on her heels and walked towards the Sanctuary, feeling as though she had been reprieved from the gallows only to be condemned to be burnt to death over a slow fire.

Thomas left the motorway at Junction 9, then took the A11, heading towards Norfolk. He was still driving very fast, his mind filled with images of blood and the thought of revenge.

Before Zoe reached the gate, it opened and another woman came out. The crowd drew back as the two walked towards each other, but Zenna did not slow her pace.

'Go inside,' the witch told her quietly. 'I'll be with you in a moment.'

Zoe hurried on, but glanced back in time to see Zenna talking to Conal. At her words the old man smiled and got to his feet. Killian looked on silently, his fury evident in his dark face.

Once inside the compound, Zoe was joined by two men

340

who fell into step and pulled off their masks as she crossed the yard. One was the unmistakable figure of Brickhead, the other his supposed master, Fader.

'I'm glad you talked your way out of that one,' Fader commented wryly. 'We would have tried to rescue you by force, but we're badly outnumbered and the chances of getting you out alive weren't good. Even with help from the talents around us.'

'I've only got two hours,' Zoe told them, grateful for their assistance but desperate to get to Ghyl.

'We know about the deadline,' Brickhead said. 'We'd hoped for more, but it's a chance, at least. If it's not enough, we can still fight, give you a bit longer. We've a deadline of our own to meet. The envoys from the west are due tomorrow. Ghyl must be there.'

'I'm sorry we couldn't let you – I mean Emmony – know about his involvement earlier,' Fader added. 'He felt badly about it, but it was safer for you not to know, you understand.'

Zoe nodded as they reached the door to the main house.

'I need Zenna,' she said, looking round. 'Where's she gone?'

'To invite Conal inside,' Brickhead replied. 'An old man like that'll appreciate the hospitality, especially as the afternoon gets colder . . .'

'And Killian isn't likely to forget himself and attack before the time is up if Chandos's judge is inside,' Fader completed for him.

'As if our beloved Quarterman would do such a thing,' Brickhead added sarcastically.

'Good luck,' Fader said, with a sympathetic smile. 'Our thoughts are with you.' They parted then, the men remaining outside.

Mason was waiting in the hall, and his eyes lit up at the sight of her. Zoe could not help but be touched by his ready smile. For a moment she was reminded of Owen, another person on whose help she had relied for so much. She wished that he could be there to guide her through this now, but it seemed that it was all up to her.

'G—Ghyl's waiting for you . . . Zoe,' Mason said. 'Iven's with him n–now.'

'Thank you, Mason.'

She clasped his hand firmly for a moment, then set off along the dark passageways as fast as she could. But by the time she reached Ghyl's room she still had no idea about what she was going to do. Zenna caught up with her as she was about to go inside.

'How is he?'

'No change at all,' the witch replied. 'We've tried to be positive when we're near him – after what you showed us – but there've been no more signs. Our healers see no hope of an early recovery. But at least his condition hasn't got any worse.'

It was a familiar conversation, and when Zoe opened the door she was almost surprised to see no charts at the foot of the bed, recording the patient's vital signs.

Iven nodded to her as she went in and knelt by the bed, taking Ghyl's hand in hers. The locket chain had been repaired, and was back round his neck. Zoe felt a flood of almost incapacitating emotion; longing and need, love and pity, helplessness and rage. *And hope*, she told herself. *There's always hope. I've opened Pandora's box, and that's the only thing I have left now.*

'Do you have the talisman?' Zenna asked.

'Yes.'

'Do you know how to use it?'

'Not really, but I'm going to try.' Zoe knew in her heart that whatever she wrote would be irrelevant now. What she really needed was something much more fundamental. This was not just a matter of removing a spell with her naive tricks . . . Or was it? Perhaps that would at least give her a starting point.

'Is there anything you need?' Iven asked.

'No. Leave me alone with him, will you? I'll call if I need your help.'

Zenna nodded, though the warlock looked doubtful, and the two left the room.

Although Zoe was still not sure what she was going to do,

342

her instincts told her that the responsibility was now hers, and hers alone.

The phone was ringing as Owen got home, and he reached it just before the answering machine picked up.

'Owen Pemberton.'

'Thank God you're there,' said an unknown voice. 'I didn't know who else to call. I've had quite a job finding your number.'

'What can I do for you?' Owen asked. He was used to getting strange phone calls in his line of work, but this woman sounded unusually distressed.

'I'm sorry. This is Alex Henderson. I'm Zoe March's agent.'

'I see,' he said, though he was puzzled. Why would Zoe's agent phone him?

'Have you seen her recently?'

'On Wednesday morning,' Owen replied. 'I was due to meet her this afternoon, but she cancelled. That's the only reason you caught me at home. I'd've been on my way there now. Is something wrong?'

'I don't know, but I'm worried,' Alex told him. 'Did she tell you why she'd cancelled the appointment?'

'She was going to a hotel, for a rest. You must know she's been under a lot of strain recently.'

'Of course, but she usually lets me know when she's going to be away from home.'

'Why are you worried?'

'Well, I've been trying to phone her all afternoon, but her number's either been engaged or unobtainable the whole time,' Alex said. 'Eventually British Telecom admitted that the entire exchange is out of order, though they don't know why yet.'

'If the whole exchange has malfunctioned, why should that make you worry about Zoe?' he persisted.

'This is going to sound silly.'

'Try me.' Owen had an awful feeling in the pit of his stomach now. Had Zoe lied to him? Had she put herself in danger again?

'I got a fax from Zoe about an hour ago,' Alex told him, 'from her home number.'

'I thought it was out of order.'

'Exactly. But that's not all. It's what the fax said.'

Owen's heart sank.

'Read it to me,' he said.

'The first bit is just garbled, complete nonsense,' Alex reported, 'but then it says "G–Ghyl is waiting for you. Wish he was here to help me." Then there's a gap, before it goes on: "The curses that b–bind him are d–dispelled". It's signed "Zoe March".'

'I'll go over there now,' Owen said, his fears confirmed by the mention of Ghyl's name.

'Would you?' Alex was obviously relieved. 'I'd be very grateful. It might be nothing, but . . .'

'I'll be glad to,' he told her. 'Those stutters – were they you or the fax?'

'It's written like that,' she replied. 'But that's not the strangest part.'

'You mean there's more?'

'Yes,' Alex said. 'Zoe and Michael don't even *have* a fax machine.'

Thomas braked hard, and screeched to a halt at the side of one of the narrow Norfolk lanes – which to his fevered brain all seemed to look exactly alike. Impatiently he studied a large-scale map of the area, eventually pinpointing his location, and grinned when he found that he was only a few miles from Thornmere, the village where Zoe lived.

He crunched the gears and drove on, his hands gripping the steering wheel convulsively. *It would be soon now.*

# 45

After a few minutes quietly seeking inspiration, Zoe decided that she had to act. All she could think of was that she needed an immediate purpose – any purpose. Opening the door, she called for Iven and asked for some paper. He returned quickly with a small, battered piece, apologising that this was all he could find. Zoe reassured him that it was enough, and closed the door again. Retrieving the pen, she wrote 'The curses that bind him are dispelled' under a pentangle, and then printed her name. As she wrote she heard another voice speaking the words softly – inside her head – and knew who it was, even though she did not know why he was doing it. She had felt a faint telepathic link with Mason on previous occasions, and was not disconcerted by his insubstantial presence. If anything, it was reassuring. Perhaps, in his apparently naive way, he was helping her to do the right thing.

When she finished writing, Zoe took the paper over to the brazier, whose glowing coals were keeping the chill from the room, and dropped it in. She felt she should say something, but the words would not come. She only hoped that it would do some good.

Turning back to the bedside, she found that her spirits had lifted slightly, as though some malign weight had indeed been removed from her shoulders, but Ghyl was as unresponsive as ever. If Zoe's words had opened the door to the dark cell in which he slept, it was obviously going to take more than that to bring him out into the daylight.

'It's just us now, Ghyl she told him gently. 'I know you

can hear me. Why don't you wake up? There's nothing to stop you now.'

After that, time seemed to slip by, sliding like water between her fingers. She kept talking to him, imploring and prompting with memories given to her by Emmony – anything to try and stimulate his dormant consciousness – but nothing happened. Just talking to Michael had not worked either, but in this case Zoe did not know what else to do.

She held Ghyl's hands, gently stroking his palms and fingers, and then his arms, but soon that contact was not enough. Deciding that she should take her need to touch him to its logical extreme, Zoe stripped naked, removed Ghyl's nightshirt and climbed into bed beside him. Pulling up the covers, she slid one arm under his neck and put the other over his chest, hugging him to her. As she brought their physical bodies together, she wished with all her heart that she could be next to Michael.

It was a strange sensation to be in bed with the man who was her husband in all but name, yet feel no answering pressure from his limbs. His skin was cool and soft, perfectly relaxed. Her longing for Michael was mixed with an almost overwhelming sadness, which she did her best to push aside. She had to be positive – to believe – though that was easier said than done.

All the time she whispered in his ear, promising her love forever, desperately hoping that he could hear, that he would eventually respond. Although their bodies were together now, growing in shared warmth, his mind still remained aloof, stubbornly fixed in whatever remote plane it now inhabited.

'We're all here, Ghyl,' she told him. 'You and Michael, me and Emmony. We can do this together. All the links are there. I know you need her. I know you want to wake up . . .'

She suddenly remembered a dream she had had the previous weekend. In it she had been driven to Michael's peculiar hospital by Woody Allen. In that dream, her husband had been awake when she arrived, and the memory of the joy she had felt on their reunion, his eyes alive and his kisses warm and passionate, filled Zoe with a bright glow of pleasure.

346

She told Ghyl about it, hoping it might revitalise him in the same way, and then realised that the filmmaker had provided her with more than just dream images. He had also pointed to the way in which she could *use* them. When Michael had drawn her attention to *The Purple Rose of Cairo*, it had been a clue to finding the ring, but was it also a signpost to her actions now? She had to make her dream 'real', in the same way that Gil Shepherd had made Tom Baxter real – enabling the fictional character to leave the screen and enter the living world.

'That's it, isn't it!' she exclaimed. 'Michael told me as much in his message.' She began to quote from memory. '"We split everything up; dreams and reality, intuition and logic, knowledge and imagination . . . They use it all together." That's what *we* have to do. Use it all together.'

A small bubble of excitement welled up inside her; a drop of undiluted happiness slipped into her sea of worry and made the whole ocean shine like gold. All at once her instincts and emotions were heightened, and she felt as though she was flying far above the road of fate. Every sound, every vision, every scent, was magnified, enhanced.

Their skin contact grew warmer, almost electric in its intensity, and her hopes rose.

But as time fled past and Ghyl still did not respond, Zoe began to doubt her intuition, began to lose her faith. She wanted to cry, felt like screaming and wailing like a bereft child, but instead she just kept talking, repeating her now less than heartfelt encouragement over and over and over again. She massaged Ghyl's inert body, kissed his unmoving lips, and prayed.

Outside, the sun sank towards the horizon.

Thomas was still driving fast, hurtling round the country lanes, compelled to go on by forces he did not understand. In his mind's eye he kept seeing a knife, a jagged-edged blade which could rip and gouge. It was clean now, ready for use, but he knew that it would soon run red.

On another road, Owen was travelling almost as fast, worried about what he might find at Ash Ring.

347

As sunset approached, both cars were only a short distance from Thornmere.

Outside the Sanctuary, Killian waited with the throng of people whose allegiance was wavering back and forth. Many were now hoping that Emmony would succeed, that she would restore her lover to life, but they kept these thoughts to themselves when they were within the hearing of the Quarterman or any of his men. Killian himself was overcome with anger, so impatient that he could not keep still. In order to gain a better view of the entire scene, he had remounted his horse, and as he paced the charger back and forth he kept drawing and inspecting his knife, anticipating its use, then replacing it in its scabbard. On the other side of his belt hung the dark-jewelled sword he had inherited from his brother. He was watching the downward progress of the sun eagerly, planning Ghyl's death – and looking ahead to his revenge upon Emmony. One way or another, he vowed, that would come soon.

Inside, knowing that their time was running out, Zoe made one last effort of will. She spoke aloud, telling herself – and Ghyl – that in this world she was a witch, a miracle worker. And suddenly the idea was taken up and broadcast throughout the networks of magic and technology, two realms with one voice. Belief came in a flood, and the insane fountain of happiness flowed once more in Zoe's head and heart. Her whole world seemed to be on fire, and she fed the heat to Ghyl. She begged him to accept it, to talk to her, just to open his eyes and *look* at her.

It was as if her consciousness had somehow exploded in slow motion, allowing her mind to spread beyond the confines of normal thought, of the rational world. She saw, heard, smelt, tasted and felt everything she had ever known, good and bad, beautiful and ugly, joyful and sad. It was overwhelming, but it was truly wonderful. And she was not alone.

*Imagine using all your brain at once, Zoe.*

For one endless, perfect moment, all the worlds lay under

the dancing stars. Zoe had no need of a pen to write of her desires, to record her love. Without effort, she emblazoned it across the heavens. She launched it across the world in golden waves of light and laughter.

*Dreams and reality . . . left and right . . . conscious and subconscious.*

She need only take what she wished. And the whole world knew what she wished.

*Now, Emmony. Now, Michael!*

Zoe pushed herself up on an elbow and stared down at Ghyl's face, silent music thundering in her ears amid the many voices of her friends. The scent of every spring filled her nostrils, and her desire burnt more fiercely than any fire. It had all come together, in *all* her worlds.

*Now, Ghyl. Now!*

As his eyes fluttered open and slowly focused on her face, Zoe's heart turned somersaults. The whole universe swept inwards to this one moment, this one most precious point in space and time. *Here and now.*

The momentary wonder on Ghyl's face, as he realised where he was and who was with him, vanished abruptly as he looked into her eyes.

'You . . . you're not Emmony,' he whispered fearfully, his voice hoarse from long disuse. 'Who has possessed her?'

'I am Emmony – and more,' she replied, her smile radiant as she kissed him for sheer joy.

Her familiar voice reassured him a little, though he was still very confused. But Zoe knew they had no time to waste in explanations.

'Come on,' she said firmly. 'We have work to do.'

The sun was now half hidden below the horizon. Ghyl recognised her urgency, even though he did not understand what was happening, and they dressed quickly. Emerging from the room, Ghyl moved slowly, as if still in a dream. He seemed to be walking through deep water as Zoe dragged him along, intent on proving to both Conal and Killian that she had succeeded in time.

The first to greet them were Zenna and Iven, their joy and

349

astonishment plain, but Zoe only wanted to see the judge. When she burst in, the old man was sitting beside a roaring fire, cup in hand, talking to another of the witches.

'This is Ghyl!' she cried, pulling him in behind her. 'He's awake!'

Ghyl blinked and swayed, holding Zoe's hand tightly.

'I can see that for myself, my lady,' Conal replied, with a smile. 'I did not think you would succeed, but I'm glad you did.'

'Quickly!' she went on. 'We must tell Killian. The sun is almost set.'

'You need have no fear on that score,' the judge informed her. 'My word is final here. But you are right. We should end this matter.'

By now all the household was astir with the news, and everyone was waiting to catch a glimpse of the man who had risen from the dead – and of his saviour.

With Conal leading the way, progress was painfully slow, at least as far as Zoe was concerned, but it gave Ghyl a chance to catch his breath. Someone had draped a blanket over his shoulders – his nightshirt would provide little protection against the chill evening. He still did not know where he was or what was happening, but he was with Emmony, and they were among friends. Someone would surely explain it to him soon.

When the party emerged from the house into the gloom of the approaching dusk, the Sanctuary's defenders strained to see what all the excitement was about and then some, Brickhead and Fader among them, recognised the bemused figure of Ghyl, and let out a great cry of gladness.

When they saw what was happening, the crowd's reaction was a mixture of joy, terror and astonishment. Was there to be no end to the wonders they would witness this day? Killian, however, knew only one emotion. His rage overpowered everything else and, intent on murder, he drew his sword and spurred his mount towards his enemies.

Conal raised ineffectual hands in warning and some of the defenders tried to react, but they were too slow. Ghyl was

350

still too dazed to do anything, and it was left to Zoe, acting purely on instinct, to respond. She screamed, throwing all her fear and protectiveness into the shrieking sound, using Emmony's latent empathy with the minds of animals to imbue it with a fearsome potency. To Killian's horse, it was the howl of demons.

The charger, already made nervous by the noise of the crowds and his master's distraction, could take no more. It panicked and, in madness, reared up violently. Killian was taken unprepared and was flung from the saddle, flying in a spreadeagled arc to crash heavily onto the hard-packed earth, his sword clattering in his wake. He landed only a few paces in front of Zoe and Ghyl, and lay still, while his terror-stricken horse fled.

In the deep hush that followed, Zenna stepped forward to examine the fallen Quarterman. She stood up and turned to look at Conal and Zoe before confirming what everybody already knew.

'He's dead. His neck is broken.'

Zoe could not speak. She could hardly think. *It's over*. She turned to Ghyl, and, though still bewildered, he returned her embrace fervently. Meanwhile, Conal told the crowd to disperse, promising that the sacrificial bull would be sent in a day or so.

It was only when Zoe drew back to look at Ghyl's face, vaguely aware that his friends were gathering round them, that she realised it was not all over. Her joy shattered into a thousand pieces.

Her body, her *own* body, sat in a chair in Michael's workroom. The alarm clock remained in the sitting room and, in her haste, she had not remembered to set it. Without the hypnosis-ending bell, her mind might never be able to return to her own world – and to Michael.

## 46

The roads along which Owen and Thomas were driving joined together at a fork just before a narrow hump-backed bridge, on the outskirts of Thornmere. As Owen approached the junction in the fading light, he saw a horse and rider on the bridge, outlined against the sky, and braked hard, skidding to a halt. An instant later, he saw another car flash past from the other road. It ignored the Give Way sign, and flew over the bridge.

If Thomas had seen the horse, he gave no sign of it, because he did not slow down at all. He realised his peril too late, as all four wheels left the surface of the road. When he landed, with an appalling crash and grinding of metal, there was no way he could bring the car under control. Still travelling very fast, the front of the car smashed into the sturdy trunk of an ancient oak tree. Metal buckled and glass shattered. And then all was still, except for the gurgle of escaping liquid.

Owen sat in his stationary car for a few moments, shocked into immobility by what he had seen and heard. He had only narrowly escaped an accident himself. Although the other car had disappeared from view as soon as it had crested the bridge, he was in no doubt as to the severity of the subsequent crash.

Getting out of his car, Owen ran across the bridge, and his heart sank when he saw the wreckage. He approached gingerly, expecting to see blood and mangled remains, but when he got close enough to see inside, he was surprised. The driver was still in one piece, an air bag having saved him from the worst of the impact. However, his head lay at an impossible angle and Owen was sure that his neck was broken. Reaching through the smashed window, he felt for a pulse. There was none.

As the therapist took a deep breath, steadying his nerves, he thought that the expression on the dead man's face was strangely peaceful for one who had died so suddenly. Then he set off for the nearest house, in search of a phone to report the accident to the authorities.

It was only then that he remembered the horse. There was no sign of it – or of its rider – anywhere.

In Zoe's sitting room, the telephone began to ring. Its insistent, alarm-like tone only sounded four times before the answering machine went into action, but it was enough. Zoe bid her final goodbye to Emmony, and returned to her own life.

Still dazed from her experiences, she stumbled from Michael's workroom to hear the end of her own pre-recorded message.

'. . . Please speak clearly after the tone.'

'Zoe? It's me . . .'

'Michael!' she yelled, her voice cracking. Almost falling over herself in her haste, Zoe rushed to pick up the phone, knowing that this time it really was him.

# Epilogue

Michael had been home for four months now, and the memory of their dreadful separation was beginning – like so much of that time – to seem like the slippery remnants of a bad dream. They were together again, and life had resumed its normal pattern – something Zoe would never take for granted again.

She often thought of Emmony, and knew that she would do so for the rest of her life. She was still not resigned to the fact that she would never know what happened to Emmony in the rest of *her* life, and could not help speculating. The assumption that she and Ghyl were together came naturally, but what else was happening? Had the revolution succeeded in ousting Chandos? If so, would Oroc prove a more enlightened ruler? Would life be better for the people of the Eastern Dominions? While admitting her own bias, Zoe could only think that because Ghyl had been involved, the last two questions must surely be answered in the affirmative. But beyond those issues, there was an endless list of things Zoe wanted to know, ranging from the trivial to the profound. Had Emmony been able to replace her book, the loss of which still bothered Zoe? Would books eventually become more readily available in the other land? Perhaps Emmony, inspired by her counterpart's example, might even attempt to write her own. And what was going to happen to all the other people Zoe had come to care about; Zenna, Mason, Brickhead and Conal? Had the gap between the worlds allowed any glimpses of her *own* world's technology to be seen by a people who relied on magic? And, if so, how would they have been affected? Were there people there, like the psychics in Zoe's own world, who could see a little of what might be possible?

The list of questions had grown to such an extent that eventually Zoe had decided, almost against her better judgement, to try another regression, just to get some answers. Michael had not been altogether happy with the idea, but had recognised her need to make the attempt, and Owen had been willing enough. He had known that, this time at least, he would be there to help. However, the experiment had failed; Emmony was no longer within reach of Zoe's mind. The gap between their worlds was closed, and the other land was gone forever.

Owen was the only person, other than Michael, to whom Zoe had told the whole story. He had been horrified and fascinated by turns – and had naturally been delighted by the eventual outcome, in spite of his obvious disapproval of the risks she had taken. Although Zoe was never quite sure whether he actually believed all her tale, that had not stopped the three of them from becoming firm friends. Even so, Zoe never found herself able to tell Owen about one aspect of the other land – the fact that he too had a counterpart there. Somehow, he was the equivalent of Mason, whom Zoe remembered fondly and whose long-term happiness she hoped for fervently. On the surface, the two were so different – the dapper, articulate hypnotherapist and the wild, seemingly witless boy – but Zoe knew there was a link between them, not least in their desire and ability to help people in general and herself in particular.

It was from Owen that Zoe had learnt of the impossible fax which Alex had received, the mysterious failure of their local telephone exchange, which had started working again of its own accord around the time Michael woke up – and of the exact circumstances of Thomas's death. Owen had not been aware, of course, that the man in the other car had been her ex-husband, but when that macabre fact had come to light, he had told her the entire story. They had all been shocked by the circumstances of Thomas's death, and Zoe had seized

355

upon Owen's vision of a non-existent horse as final proof of the coexistence of the two worlds. The fact that Thomas and Killian had died in such a similar way could not just be a coincidence. But no one could explain what Thomas had been doing there in the first place. This was something Zoe did not like to dwell upon, especially when she remembered his last phone call. She was confused for a time about the fact that her ex-husband had apparently been two people in the other land, but eventually convinced herself that, because Jevan and Killian had been twins, they were really like two halves of the same being. Alex had told her some of the gossip concerning Thomas's behaviour before his last fateful journey, and this only confirmed Zoe's belief that he must have been affected, one way or another, by the gap between the worlds. She could not pretend to be sorry that he had gone, but she could have wished that his final removal from her life had been in other, less distressing circumstances.

Zoe had already left the house, on her way to the hospital, when Owen had finally arrived at Ash Ring. He and Alex had been left to worry until they discovered the truth – and had then shared Zoe's happiness.

As far as Michael himself was concerned, he was back to his old self almost immediately. His awakening had been sudden, and the first the hospital staff had known of it was when he was spotted limping down the corridor, dressed only in a gown, in search of a telephone. By the time Zoe arrived he had already been thoroughly examined and tested and, beyond the obvious effects of his enforced lack of exercise, pronounced remarkably fit.

When Zoe had entered the reception area at a run, Dr Black had seen her but had wisely not tried to stop her headlong rush to Michael's room. He had just grinned widely, and waved her on her way, sharing in her joy at the news. It was only afterwards that Zoe realised that she had seen in that smile an echo of Zenna's delight – and wondered if Nick would mind being compared to a witch.

Michael had been leaning on the edge of the bed, talking to Amy, when Zoe burst in and threw herself into his arms.

356

The nurse quickly left the room, a broad smile on her face, while Zoe cried and laughed and looked and held him tight, revelling in the touch of her skin on his, in the renewed living scent of his body close to hers, in his eyes focused and watching her. He cried too as the reality of what had happened to him – and what it had meant to her – slowly began to sink in, but for Michael the whole three weeks or so had passed in an instant, and his happiness was mixed with some bewilderment. He could remember nothing of the other land, nothing of Ghyl, nor of his strange contacts with Zoe.

Since he had returned home, Michael and Zoe had naturally talked a great deal about her experiences, but he had not been able to shed light on any of them. Zoe showed him all the evidence she had gathered – the photograph of Killian, the interruption to the video of *The Purple Rose of Cairo*, the fax that Alex had posted to her – which reminded her of Mason again – and played him the tapes of her regressions and of his own messages. Although he admitted that these last certainly sounded like him, they prompted no revelations. He simply could not remember sending them. Zoe suggested that he might be able to remember under hypnosis, but Michael had refused point blank to do this, and Owen agreed with his decision. He said that if Michael had forgotten, then there was a reason for that. While initially disappointed, Zoe had finally accepted her husband's decision. It did not really matter now anyway.

However, in her own mind, she kept searching for explanations, and eventually produced a theory she believed in, even if she could never prove it. In much of her reading into esoteric subjects she had come across the fascinating subject of split-brain research, and also the supposition that the European mind and brain had undergone fundamental changes around 1200 BC. Before that time there was evidence to suggest that men's minds had been bicameral, with both left and right halves of the brain fully aware of each other and cooperating, which meant that people were intuitive, working together with and in touch with the forces of nature – and thus able to produce what, in Zoe's own world, would be called magic or miracles. However, modern man was decisively non-bicameral, with the split between the conscious, logical left half and the mute, dreamy but vastly more knowledgeable right brain being quite marked. Zoe's theory was that time itself had split into two streams at the same time as these changes had occurred, and that the ancient, 'magical' mankind had survived and evolved in Emmony's parallel world. For them, as for earlier man, religion and science were the same thing; to Zoe's world they were irreconcilable opposites. There, magic had done everything for which Zoe's world needed technology.

One of Michael's messages from the other land had included words which were etched in her memory.

*It's so different to our world. We split everything up; dreams and reality, intuition and logic, knowledge and imagination, left and right, conscious and subconscious. They use it all together.*

Even Michael had to admit that this fitted very neatly with Zoe's theory, even though – frustratingly for her – this was the only one of the later messages she no longer had on tape.

The other point she seized upon to back up her argument was the map she had seen in Jevan's study. The only man-made site it had in common with her own Norfolk was Grime's Graves, the prehistoric flint mines which would have predated the supposed split in time. The evidence was by no means conclusive, but it was the best she could come up with – or was ever likely to.

That a parallel world existed was something Zoe no longer doubted. She had been there, she had seen it. If other people chose to believe that the whole thing had all been in her mind, that was no concern of hers. Owen was noncommittal, but Michael professed to believe her, although she knew the ideas sat awkwardly with him. He cheerfully admitted to being dominated by his logical left brain, but knew better than to suppose that everyone else was the same.

The days and months passed. Zoe finished *Fields of Plenty* and Michael's *Otherlands*, suitably revised and retitled, was set for production, and they celebrated their dual achievements with an expensive meal at their favourite restaurant. It was on that occasion that Zoe surprised her husband by wearing the necklace he had made for her. She had removed it on impulse from the frame in her study, and found that even though it sat high on her neck and was as tight as ever, this no longer caused her any discomfort or anxiety. The dreadful iron manacles that had been responsible for her phobia were now safely in her – and Emmony's – past, and so could no longer affect her. Michael had been astonished and delighted, told her that she looked even more beautiful than ever, and kissed her in such a way that they nearly never made it to the restaurant at all.

Just when it seemed that Emmony's world could no longer impinge upon their lives, Ash Ring received an unexpected visitor. Zoe and Michael both went to answer the doorbell, arriving there together. Michael opened the door, then suddenly grew very still. Looking past him, Zoe saw why.

A ragged, unshaven tramp stood on the doorstep. In one gnarled and dirty hand, he was holding up a ballpoint pen with the words 'Brands of Norwich' engraved upon its side. For a few moments no one moved or spoke, their communication and understanding needing no words. Then Zoe could not help herself.

'Can you tell me . . .?' she began, but faltered at a look from the derelict's rheumy eyes.

The tramp shook his head, straggly grey hair swinging.

'Go and get the ring, Zoe,' Michael said quietly.

She turned reluctantly and went upstairs. Having found after her final regression that she could take the ring off quite easily, Zoe now kept it with her other jewellery on her dressing table. She came down again to find Michael and the visitor still standing in silence, both apparently quite at ease. They were even smiling, perhaps remembering their earlier encounter, twenty years before.

There were a thousand questions Zoe wanted to ask, but she knew she could not. Instead she reached out, took the pen and dropped the ring into the tramp's grimy hand. He gave it a quick glance, then shoved it into his coat pocket, nodded and, still smiling, turned and went on his way.

'Did he say anything?' Zoe whispered.

'No. He didn't need to,' Michael replied.

Zoe watched the old man go, knowing that her last ephemeral contact with Emmony was gone now, and feeling a pang of loss. Michael, sensing her mood, slid his arm around her and pulled her to him. Zoe nestled close to his warmth and love, and knew that this was right. This was where she was meant to be.

*Oh, Emmony,* she thought, her whole being filled with a bittersweet frustration as she realised that she would never know the answer. *I wonder what you're doing now?*